Ace Books by Richard Paul Russo

DESTROYING ANGEL
CARLUCCI'S EDGE
CARLUCCI'S HEART

RICHARD PAUL RUSSO

CARLUCCI'S HEART

ACE BOOKS, NEW YORK

This is an Ace original edition,
and has never been previously published.

CARLUCCI'S HEART

An Ace Book/published by arrangement with
the author

PRINTING HISTORY
Ace Edition/November 1997

The Putnam Berkley World Web site address is
http://www.berkley.com

Make sure to check out *PB Plug,*
the science fiction/fantasy newsletter, at
http://www.pbplug.com

ISBN: 0-441-00485-7

ACE®
Ace Books are published by the Berkley Publishing Group,

a member of Penguin Putnam Inc.,

200 Madison Avenue, New York, New York 10016,
ACE and the "A" design are trademarks
belonging to Charter Communications, Inc.

PRINTED IN THE UNITED STATES OF AMERICA

10 9 8 7 6 5 4 3 2 1

Again, this is for Dianne
with love

And for my sisters, Janiece and Ronna—
my two biggest fans

ISABEL

Her keepers had called her Isabel, but she had not heard that name in a long time. She missed the sound of it, the warmth she felt inside whenever Donya, one of her keepers, had said it. *Isabel.*

She rarely got close to people anymore, though she often saw men and women here, watched as they moved past her hiding places. Strangers, all of them. But it was even more rare that anyone saw her.

Isabel was a long-tailed macaque, and she now lived in the Core, deep in the heart of the Tenderloin, wandering along its dark, subterranean passageways, squeezing through old ventilation shafts and rusted, twisted metal ductwork, climbing shadowy stairways through ruined buildings. Her fur was a rich brown and gray that almost shined on the rare occasions she stood in full sunlight, the sun beaming down on her through some jagged opening in the brick, stone, metal, or concrete. Her eyes were rimmed with soft brows. Her right index finger had been cut off at the first knuckle, but she did not remember how that had happened. She ate insects, and food scraps stolen from the people who lived in these old and crumbling ruins, and she drank water from pools that formed after the rains. She thought she had seen other monkeys in here, but she could not be sure.

Life was different for her now. She did not really know where she was, but most of the time it was darker and damper than it had been where she had lived before. She also felt heavier, and it had taken a while for her muscles to adapt to the extra weight. Here, no one came to feed and water her, no one came to talk to her. But here there was no cage. Here she was free.

Isabel had been quite sick just before she'd been released into the Core, and she had almost died. She couldn't be sure, but she thought her keepers had done something to make her sick. And when she had recovered, they had done something else, this time to make her sleep, and when she had awakened, she had been here, in the Core. Alone, and free.

She was a quiet, careful monkey now.

Isabel dozed, warm and comfortable. Dream images flickered through her thoughts. She sat on a flat stone, bathed in the light from the sun shining down on her through an uneven opening in the brick wall.

Sounds alerted her—scrape and click.

Isabel's eyes opened, her head jerked, and she whirled around, blinking in the light. A shadow moved toward her, a man holding up some kind of netting.

Isabel didn't hesitate. She attacked.

She lunged at the man's face, sharp incisors bared, clawing at him with her hands.

The man cried out, threw his arms across his face. Isabel's teeth slashed skin and muscle of an arm, a shoulder, her fingers clawed at air, then found hair and clothing, dug into something. The man jerked back, Isabel continued slashing and biting. Then the man fell backward, twisted around, and landed on top of Isabel, crushing away her breath. He kept rolling, and she let go.

She lay with eyes wide, gasping for breath that wouldn't come. Sharp pain sliced her chest. The man, howling now, scrambled away from her.

Breath returned with more sharp pain, and she bounded to her feet, dizzy but prepared to defend herself. But the man was gone, leaving behind a pile of netting. She could hear his screams fading into the darkness.

Isabel tasted blood, and knew it wasn't hers.

PART ONE

EXPOSURE

Caroline entered the DMZ at dusk. Not a great time of day, but better than it would be in an hour or so when darkness fell. She didn't want to be here at all, but this was where Tito lived. Tito didn't want to be here either, but he was broke and dying and he had no real choice.

Walking the streets of the DMZ—the narrow strip that ran along the north and west outer walled edges of the Tenderloin—was all right during the day if you really watched yourself; but at night the place turned into a free fire zone. After dark, the Tenderloin itself was a lot safer; even the cops avoided the DMZ once night fell.

Street traffic was practically at a standstill, cars and trucks and pedalcarts and bikes and jits creeping forward in jerking fits and starts amid shouts and curses and blasting horns—the final rush while light remained. The sidewalks were just as crowded, and Caroline had to shove her way along, pressed in by bodies on all sides.

She wore blue jeans and an old gray sweatshirt. Her sidepurse was wrapped tight against her ribs under the sweatshirt. In her back pocket was a canister of Ass-Gass.

A man wearing a wire head-cage blocked her way and screamed something at her, but his handler banged a shock stick against the head-cage, sparks flying and shutting him up. Caroline pushed her way around the man, who was now whimpering and shaking his head and blinking spasmodically. A shiver of pity rolled through her. The handler, a short squat woman in boojee overalls, snarled at Caroline as if she had been responsible for the man's outburst, and Caroline hurried away.

She worked her way along the block, fighting her own edgy claustrophobia and generalized anxiety. Across the way, the outer walls of the Tenderloin rose above the street like dark, inanimate guardians, buildings attached to one another, all gaps, streets, and alleys filled in, barricaded to keep the DMZ from leaking into the Tenderloin. In the dimming light, street lamps cast vague, amorphous shadows cut through with the glare and flash of shop signs, the syncopated flicker of slithering neon. The air was heavy with the stench of sweat, bubbling grease, and a sweetish, drifty burnt odor.

Just past Turtle Joe's she ducked into an alcove unmarked except for a crude skull-and-crossbones spray-painted in red on the crumbling brick arch. The grille-covered door was unlocked, as always, and she pushed it open. When she closed the door behind her, she cut off the noise and stink of the street.

The dimly lit entry was small, with a close, musty smell. Stairs were on the left, and directly in front of her was the hallway leading to the ground-floor rooms. On the right wall was a bank of mailboxes, but it had been years since any mail had actually been delivered to this building. The place was quiet. The Sisters of the Forgotten had already been through, delivering meals and comfort. The death house was settling down for the night.

A pale, thin girl about nine or ten stepped out of the hall and stared at Caroline. The girl was dressed in ragged, faded red overalls and black tennis shoes, and the right side of her face and neck was streaked with welts. She opened her mouth wide, hacked once, then ran back into the hall. A man yelled from far down the hallway, and a door slammed. Caroline turned away and started up the concrete stairs.

The stairwell was lit by bare bulbs screwed into ceramic sockets set in the cracked plaster ceiling. The walls were smeared with green and blue paint, streaked with soot. Graffiti was surprisingly sparse, and she didn't bother to read what was there. She was already familiar with most of it, and all of it was depressing.

Everyone in the building was dying. Some would die soon; others would be able to stretch out the pain and misery for a year or two. A few would die of newer, exotic diseases such as Chingala Fever or Pilate's Chorea or Passion, but most were sick with more mundane terminal diseases. Like Tito, who had AIDS. Caroline was grateful for the knowledge that, no matter how bad she got in the next few years, she would never end up in a death house like this.

She stopped on the third-floor landing and leaned against the wall, trying to catch her breath. She tired easily, so far the only manifestation of the Gould's Syndrome that would almost certainly kill her within the next several years. But she no longer felt sorry for herself. She would probably die before she was thirty, but it would be with less pain and suffering than most of those who lived here; it would be a hell of a lot less than what Tito was going through right now.

Tito was being ravaged by spiking fevers and monstrous headaches and a severe, recurring ear infection; some sort of neuropathy made his hands ache constantly; and right now he had a good strong case of thrush going so he could hardly swallow a thing. But he'd called her this morning from Mama Chan's where he'd actually eaten some breakfast, and said he was feeling better, so maybe some of the meds were finally working and he was through the worst of this phase. They were going to watch a couple of movies, and then she'd spend the night on the sofa, keeping him company.

She pushed away from the wall and walked toward Tito's room. The hallway was carpeted with a thin, stained brown runner worn through in spots and dotted with dozens of cigarette burns. The air smelled of sickness—a thick, warm, cloying stench. Muted sounds of televisions and radios leaked through the walls, interrupted by the occasional fit of coughing or other, unidentifiable noises.

She knocked on Tito's door. She thought she heard

movement from inside, but there was no answer. She knocked again. "Tito, it's me. Caroline." More scrabbling sounds.

She tried the door, found it unlocked. She pushed it open and looked inside.

Mouse crouched in the rear corner, stuffing Tito's coin box into an already overloaded duffel bag. He looked at her and grinned, metal teeth flashing. Mouse was just under five feet tall and skinny, with short, spiky blond hair he never combed, and a neuro-collar grafted onto his neck. He wore a Mutant Alligators T-shirt, faded green jeans, and black Stasi boots. The neuro-collar flashed a patterned series of red lights, and Caroline wondered what that meant.

"Where's Tito?" she asked.

"Gone," Mouse said. He finished stuffing the coin box into the duffel bag and squatted on the floor with his back against the wall, blinking at her. He had tiny pink mouse eyes, and she never trusted them.

"Gone where?"

Mouse shrugged. "Mens came and took him."

"Who?"

"Two mens."

Tito's room was about fifteen feet square, and sparsely furnished—a foam rubber mattress, an old sagging camel-back sofa, a small metal desk and chair, a couple of short, rickety bookcases; a half-size refrigerator and a double-burner hot plate on top of some cheap plywood cabinets. There was a toilet stuck back in a tiny alcove; no bath or shower. Tito didn't own much, but as Caroline looked around the room, all the surfaces and shelves were pretty much bare. She stared hard at Mouse, at the huge, bulging duffel bag at his feet. Only the TV remained, still on its stand by the window. Maybe Mouse was going to come back for it on his next trip. Some friend he was.

"What the hell are you doing?" she asked him.

Mouse grinned and snapped his metal teeth. "Tito's not coming back. He don't need this stuff."

"How do you know he's not coming back?"

Mouse just shook his head.

"How do you know, Mouse?"

"Those mens. They take you away, take you to the Core, you never comin' back. I know."

Caroline shut the door, leaned back against it. She was starting to get pissed. "When were they here?"

"Half hour ago."

"Where were *you*, Mouse?"

"Hiding?" Then he tipped his head back and hacked out a laugh.

"Mouse. What did they want with him?"

"Don't know," he answered, with another shrug. "Don't want to know."

"Didn't you hear anything? They must have said things to Tito, asked him questions."

"Try not to listen. Hear no evil." Grinning again.

"Mouse. You heard something, didn't you."

"Maybe."

"Maybe what?"

That damn shrug again. Then, with a heavy sigh he said, "Maybe something about Cancer Cell." Mouse closed his eyes for a moment, grimacing.

"Cancer Cell?" The name was only vaguely familiar. "What the hell's that?"

"Ask you daddy," Mouse said. "You daddy's cop man, yes?"

"My father's a cop, yes."

Mouse got to his feet, grabbed the duffel bag, and hefted it. The weight gave him a definite list.

"Leave that here," Caroline said. "Tito might be back."

"No," Mouse said. "He's not coming back. You don't coming back from the Core."

"Leave it, Mouse."

"No." He crouched, then with his free hand pulled a gravity knife from his boot, chunked the blade into place. A nasty blade, gleaming. "No." He flashed his metal teeth at her one more time. The neuro-collar was now blinking a deep blue.

All right, Caroline thought. Everything Mouse was taking could be replaced when Tito came back. *If* Tito came back. She didn't think Mouse would actually hurt her, but it was always a possibility. So she moved away from the door, gave him a clear, wide path to it.

"Go, then," she said. "Now."

Mouse nodded. He closed up the blade, tucked the knife back into his boot, then staggered to the door, half-carrying, half-dragging the duffel bag. "You keep the TV," he said, grinning at her one final time. "Piece of shit, anyway." Then he opened the door, lurched through it, and headed down the hall.

Caroline slammed the door shut and threw the two dead bolts. She was suddenly very afraid for Tito. What the hell was Cancer Cell? She'd heard the name before, but she couldn't remember anything about it. She couldn't imagine Tito involved in anything that could get him kidnapped or killed. Or had he gone with them voluntarily? She wasn't sure she could trust Mouse's version of what had happened. Maybe no one had come for Tito. Maybe he'd just gone out for a while, and Mouse had decided to ransack the place. Mouse and Tito had been something like friends, but that might not mean that much to Mouse.

She crossed the room to the sink and opened the cabinet above it. It looked like all of Tito's meds were still there, forty or fifty little plastic bottles. She picked one up, shook it. Maybe half full. Same thing with two others she checked. If Tito had gone somewhere on his own, he would have taken some of them with him. But why hadn't Mouse taken them? Probably because they were all half-ass meds, the only things Tito could get from the free clinics—cheap antibiotics, weak painkillers, ineffective antidepressants, and unproven immune system boosters. Mouse probably couldn't get shit for them on the street.

Caroline took a quick tour of the room, but except for what was missing nothing seemed out of place. No signs of struggle. She went to the window, pulled it open, and looked out into the air well between the buildings. Night was falling quickly, and she could barely see the weeds and garbage at the bottom of the air well. She wasn't sure she'd be able to see a body if one was lying there. Then she

craned her neck around, looking up. Brick walls rose to a
rectangle of darkening sky three more floors above her.
Boarded windows, screened vents, cracks of light, the
rusted remains of what had once been a fire escape.

She pulled her head back inside, but remained at the
window, her gaze unfocused. She would wait for Tito. Yes.
She would wait through the night and see if he came back;
she was better off not going out into the DMZ now anyway.
And if Tito wasn't back by morning? Maybe wait some
more; she'd worry about it then. She turned away from the
window, walked over to the hot plate, and put on water for
tea.

Caroline woke in the middle of the night, sitting up
abruptly. She listened intently, unable to see a thing. Something had awakened her, some sound. Street noise filtered
in through the window, the DMZ night—some kind of irregular banging, a motor revving, muted popping sounds,
someone screaming in a strange, deep monotone—but she
was sure that wasn't it. Something else. Something inside
the building.

Heartbeat loud and fast, she sat without moving, eyes
gradually adjusting to the darkness. The room was empty,
no strange shadows or movements, and she didn't hear anything unusual—faint snoring from the room next door;
tinny, Spanish music from somewhere below her; a creaking floorboard above.

There. Something. A hum she felt more than heard.

She eased the blanket aside and stood, then padded barefoot across the room to the door and put her eye to the
peephole. The hall lights were out, but there was a faint,
shifting blue glow. Her view was distorted by the peephole,
and the glow was dark and dim and shadowy, but she could
make out hooded figures moving past the door, steps slow,
bodies swaying in unison to a slow, unheard rhythm.

What was this? Who were they?

Phantoms. She could almost see through them; inside the
hoods, where their faces should be, she saw only darker
shadows and a deeper blue glow. She shivered, feeling and

hearing the deep, penetrating hum, feeling suddenly cold. She wanted to back away from the door, retreat into a far corner of the room, but she remained where she was, transfixed, hardly breathing, hardly moving. The ghostlike figures moved past the door and progressed slowly along the hall, humming and swaying, the glow fading until it was out of the peephole's range, and only complete darkness remained.

She returned to the sofa and sat, knees pulled up to her chin, and wrapped herself in the blanket. Where are you, Tito? What happened to you?

She remained on the sofa, watching the dark and listening to the night. She did not sleep.

CHAPTER 2

Ryland Cage crouched on the Tenderloin rooftop just before dawn, gazing out across the street at the dark, crumbling ruins of the Core. The Core was four square blocks of Hell in the black heart of the Tenderloin. Or four square blocks of Chaos, if you were a different kind of believer. Maybe it was a little of both. Walled off by street barricades and crash nets from the rest of the Tenderloin, the Core was a bleak pocket of ruined buildings, unnatural darkness and eerie quiet, and rubble-strewn streets deserted except for the shadowy movement of animals or ghosts. Strange lights did break through the darkness on occasion: flickering candles or fires visible through windows or shattered walls, pulsing glows of shimmering blue, pale drifting clouds of phosphorescence. Some people thought there was something supernatural about the Core, that it was inhabited by spirits, demons, banshees. Cage suspected the truth was far more horrible—that only human beings lived inside the Core.

Cage wore faded denims, a charcoal gray long-sleeved shirt, and black leather boots. His dark brown hair was long and straight and, though he was only thirty-nine, heavily streaked with gray. He wasn't tall, just five-foot-nine, but he was strong and quick. Sometimes not quick enough, though. A long thin scar ran along his jaw—a souvenir from a reluctant patient whose life Cage had been trying to save. And there were other scars, too, that weren't visible. A muted flapping sound came from somewhere within the Core, and Cage searched the shadowy ruins for its source. He didn't see anything at first, only heard a faint, high whistle added to the flapping. Then a dark, shivering form rose from one of the taller buildings near the center. A strange glow came to life within the thing, giving it shape. It appeared to be an enormous dove, frantically flapping its wings and craning its neck as it climbed in an ever widening spiral. But the motion of its wings was wrong, stilted and far too regular, and Cage knew it wasn't alive. When its spiraling route brought it closer to him, he could see pale white jets of propellant streaming from it.

The mechanical dove rose high above the Core, circling and climbing, becoming smaller and dimmer. The flapping sounds faded, and only the dim glow of its internal light was visible, a pale and shrinking blotch against the sky.

Suddenly the dove exploded with a brilliant burst of light followed by faint popping sounds. Hundreds of glittering message streamers fell through the darkness, like skyrocket flares that didn't burn out. The streamers drifted and fell with the air currents, spreading out over the Core and the Tenderloin.

One of the streamers drifted near Cage, and he stepped to the edge of the roof, steadied himself, then reached out over nine stories of empty air. He caught the message streamer and stepped back from the edge. The streamer glowed and tingled in his fingers, like electrified tinsel. He stretched out the streamer and read its message:

YOU ARE BECOMING.
NOTHING CAN STOP YOU NOW.

Fortunes from the Core, but without the cookie. He smiled, wadded the streamer into a tiny ball, and tossed it over the edge of the roof.

He stood gazing at the Core for a long time. Almost certainly he was going to end up in that godforsaken place before this business was over. He didn't much like the idea, but it was going to happen. He knew it.

Gravel crunched behind him, and he turned to see Nikki cross the roof toward him. She was a couple of inches taller

than he was, and probably just as strong. Dreadlocks, gold
cheek inlays, and a smile to die for. Black shock suit that
hid her weapons and med-kit better than it did her figure.
Cage loved her.

Nikki stopped about a foot away from him and frowned.

"These people are bloody assholes," she said. "Haven't
even met them, but just talking to them, I already know
they're assholes."

"I know," Cage said. "But we need them for this."

Nikki closed her eyes for a moment and shrugged. "Angel says they've arrived."

"Good. Let's go."

"Afterward, you want to go dancing?"

Cage nodded. "Maybe." Then, "Sure, we'll go dancing." And he got just what he was hoping for—Nikki's
smile. "But first, let's see what we can do with the assholes."

They were to meet Stinger and his jackals in Binky's Arcade down on the second floor of the building. *Stinger.*
Everyone's got to have a fucking moniker, Cage thought.
It was absurd.

He and Nikki walked into crashing waves of sound and
shifting colored lights. The place was crowded, the music
and voices loud. The front section of Binky's was a series
of stunner booths, and Cage watched the jerking forms visible through the opaque glass, the jerking almost in sync
with the thumping sounds coming from within the booths—
he'd probably end up treating some of these people over
the next few days.

He moved past the stunner booths and onto the dance
floor, Nikki right behind him. They pushed their way
through the gyrating dancers, bumping and shoving and
fending off flailing limbs. The air was stifling, heavy with
perfume and smoke and sweat. His eyes burned.

The rear section of Binky's was a restaurant and bar.
Cage and Nikki stepped through the array of acoustic baffles, and the sound cut back by more than half. It was still

fairly noisy, but now the music was relatively muted. Conversation was possible.

Cage stopped and looked out over the tables and booths. He spotted Angel at the bar, who cut his glance toward a booth near the back. A tall, thin man in the booth caught Cage's eye. The man was older and better dressed than Cage had expected—he wore a dark suit and tie, and his short, thick, styled hair was more than half gone to gray. Mid to late forties, maybe even a little older. Cage had expected a young techno-punk or street medico. Three people sat in the booth opposite the man, but Cage could only see the top of the back of their heads.

"That Stinger?" Nikki said.

"I think so." Cage turned to her and smiled. "Maybe it won't be so bad."

"Hah."

Cage and Nikki made their way through the tables, and as they approached the rear booth the thin man nodded at those seated across from him. The three jackals slid out of the booth, walked to the rear, and stood side by side against the back wall of the restaurant, keeping their attention on Cage. All three were heavily muscled and wore cheap black suits over black T-shirts; all three looked ramped up to their eyeballs.

Up close, Cage could see that the thin man's suit was probably silk, and the dark green tie was made from reptile skin. The man sat with both arms on the table, hands relaxed. His jacket and shirtsleeves were too short, exposing his wrists. Or maybe this was the current fashion.

"You Stinger?" Cage said.

The man nodded. "You must be Cage."

"Yeah, I must be." He slid into the booth, and Nikki slid in next to him.

"Who's the nigger bitch with you?" Stinger asked. His voice was calm, his tone matter-of-fact.

Cage hesitated a few moments, eyes going hard, then said, "That's not helpful."

Stinger smiled. The index finger of his right hand rubbed

at the pitted surface of the table, but he made no other response.

Nikki's hand lashed out across the table and latched into Stinger's wrist with her barbed finger hooks. She smiled back at him.

"Just try pulling away," she said. "We'll see what I rip out from under your skin."

Stinger didn't move, just looked down at the blood leaking from the tiny holes in his skin. Cage kept an eye on the jackals, who were leaning forward, tense, eyes wide, but waiting for a signal from their master.

"The nigger bitch's name is Nikki," Cage said.

Stinger looked at her, tipped his head slightly. "My apologies, Nikki."

The barbs retracted with faint clicks, and Nikki released his hand. Stinger brought his wrist to his mouth, then gently licked and sucked at the blood until his skin was clean and white again. He laid his arm back on the table and sighed. "Business, then?" he said.

Cage nodded. "Business."

A waitress approached the booth, but a look from Stinger warded her off. Cage stared at the man, assessing him. Stinger was twisted up way too tight, despite his outward appearance of calm; too slick and hard and mean. But there was something else, something he couldn't quite identify. Something *wrong* with Stinger.

Without shifting his gaze, Cage took a folded piece of paper from his back pocket and slid it across the table. "That's a list of the drugs we need, and the quantities."

Stinger took the paper, unfolded it, and read. His mouth twitched into a slight smile. "Don't want much, do you?" His voice was overly sarcastic; there wasn't much subtle about Stinger.

"That's what we need," Cage replied. There was something about Stinger's eyes. They were red, but in a strange way—not bloodshot, exactly. Injected. And the way his lips and tongue worked at themselves . . .

"You used to be a doctor," Stinger said to him, shaking his head. "What a fucking waste."

"I'm still a doctor," Cage replied.

Stinger continued to shake his head. "Slaving your ass off in street clinics and death houses. You used to have a hell of a practice doing image enhancements, making a goddamn fortune. A lot safer, too. And you slammed it all to do this? What happen, you get a dose of brain fever from one of your patients?"

Now Cage caught a whiff of something masked by Stinger's Body-Scent—like sweat gone sour. And a foul stench to his breath. Christ, Cage thought, the man is sick. Not with the flu or a cold, nothing simple like that. Drug-induced? Maybe. Some other toxin? Something bacterial? Viral? Something. Something bad.

"Well? Why'd you give it all up?" Stinger asked. He frowned, apparently waiting for a response.

But Cage wasn't going to give him one. He wasn't going to talk to this stranger about his life, the decisions he'd made. The only person he talked to about things like that was Nikki, and not always with her.

Nikki. Cage glanced at her hand, the one that had grabbed Stinger and finger-hooked him, drawing blood. His hand out of sight under the table, Cage reached into the med-kit belted around his waist and removed two disinfectant wipes, pressed them into Nikki's hand. He rubbed her fingers with them until she got the message and began to work them herself.

Stinger sighed heavily, finally giving up on an answer. He tapped at the list. "You can't afford to buy all this," he said.

"No," Cage replied, working hard to keep his concentration on the business. He glanced at Stinger's wrist, at the tiny fresh droplets of blood that had formed on the surfaces of the finger-hook punctures.

"But you're willing to trade your services."

"Up to a point, yes."

"One day a week of image enhancements at the clinics of our choosing. Or perhaps other surgeries or treatments, depending on our needs. For one year."

Cage hesitated, still having difficulty concentrating. He

was worried about Nikki, though he knew there was probably no reason to be. But he'd seen too much weird shit in the past few years. "One day a *month*, for a year," he finally said. "*If* we get monthly shipments of that size." He gestured at the piece of paper still laid out on the table under Stinger's hand.

Stinger laughed. "Too much, Cage. You overvalue your services." He paused, shrugging. "One day a month, fine. But only four shipments, one every three months. Not negotiable."

It probably wasn't. Besides, Cage didn't have the stomach for hard-edged negotiating with this man right now. Stinger was ill, and Cage wanted to get away from him; the man probably didn't even know he was sick. Cage hoped whatever it was wasn't an airborne transmitter, or that his nose filters could do the job; or the I.S. boosters he'd taken last week.

"All right," Cage said. "One year, four shipments. First delivery before I make a single cut."

"Good enough, Cage. We'll be in touch with delivery place and time, and with your first assignment."

Stinger put out his hand, but Cage didn't move. He stared at Stinger's hand, then up into Stinger's red-rimmed eyes. He nudged Nikki, and she slid out of the booth.

"I want to see you at the delivery," Cage said.

Stinger smiled. "What, is this some kind of setup? Entrapment?"

Cage didn't answer. Stinger and his people knew him better than that. But he very much wanted to see Stinger again, see if the guy got any sicker, see if he could figure out what Stinger had.

"We'll see," Stinger said, still smiling.

Cage and Nikki stood on the sidewalk, the signs for Binky's Arcade pulsing directly above them. The air out here was cool and fresh, and Cage breathed deeply.

"What the hell was all that in aid of?" Nikki asked him. "With the wipes? What was that about?"

He shrugged. He didn't want to worry her about what

was probably nothing. "Stinger's sick," he answered.

"With what?"

"No idea. Just didn't want to take any chances."

"Great." Nikki dug into her shock suit with her left hand, brought out a wipe, and gave her right hand another thorough scrub, including the finger hooks. She walked over to a burn canister and tossed in the wipe.

"So what do you think about these people?" she asked when she rejoined him.

"Just what you said," Cage replied. "Assholes. And Stinger, in spite of his silk suit, the biggest asshole of all. But we'll do business. These guys have pharmaceutical resources no one else has, and at costs that beat the hell out of the streets."

"So you're pretty sure he's linked up to Cancer Cell?"

"Oh yeah. No one else could provide this shit, outside of New Hong Kong."

Nikki didn't seem convinced, but she half-nodded. "Let's go dancing, then."

Cage nodded back, and smiled. "Sure, Nikki. Let's go dancing."

CHAPTER 3

Carlucci felt like shit. He threw off the covers and sat up in bed, slightly dizzy. A sheen of sweat coated his skin; his throat hurt, and his eyes ached. He looked at the clock. Almost noon. Christ.

He pushed himself up and onto his feet and staggered into the bathroom, where he threw cold water on his face, then drank deeply, wincing with pain each time he swallowed. Then he raised the toilet seat and pissed, one hand on the tank to hold himself up. He flushed, lowered the seat and lid, and sat down, resting up before getting into the shower.

Goddamn spring vaccination; every time it hit him like this. The semiannual vaccination cocktails—five or six vaccines mixed together—didn't bother Andrea much, and Caroline and Christina, his two daughters, hardly felt any effects at all from them, but Carlucci got sick every damn time. He'd be all right by the end of the day, or maybe the next morning, but right now he wanted to drop into a coma for a few hours.

He popped some aspirins, took a shower, and by the time he got dressed and moved around a bit, he was feeling better. Andrea had set up the coffee maker before going to work, so all he had to do was start it. He ate two pieces of toast while waiting for it to finish, then took his coffee out onto the deck in the backyard.

The temperature was mild, and the sky almost clear, the blurred sun shining down through a pinkish-brown haze.

Early spring after another mild winter, and there had been no heat waves yet. A pleasant time of the year in San Francisco. In fact, it was Carlucci's favorite time of year—the weather was usually good, and the homicide rate almost always took a dip.

Frank Carlucci was half an inch over six feet, and half a dozen pounds short of two hundred—a bit stocky, and constantly struggling to keep from changing from stocky to fat. He was closing in on fifty-six, and he needed more exercise than he got, but right now he felt like he could hardly walk.

He sat in one of the cushioned chairs, set his coffee on the small square table beside him, and looked out over the garden. The garden was lush and colorful and overgrown and streaked with rot and burn. It needed a lot of work. Neither he nor Andrea had managed to put any time into it yet, no weeding or pruning or thinning; nothing, really, since the fall. The big camellia in the back corner had already bloomed and dropped, the crocuses had come and gone, and half of the other plants in the yard were already beginning to flower. But there was too much brown streaking the leaves—it looked like rust—and there would be other problems less visible, all consequences of the crap in the air and the rain. He and Andrea needed to get out and do the special fertilizing, get some clean soil, and give the plants more filtered water.

At times like this, Carlucci thought seriously about retiring. He could sure spend more time out here, sitting in the sun and drinking coffee, puttering around in the garden; and more time sitting down in the basement and playing his trumpet. He'd like to build a greenhouse and grow vegetables. He'd like to read more. He was only fifty-five, but there were times when he felt older, and he was sick of that. A lot of it, he knew, was the job.

He had spent more than half his career in Homicide, and maybe that was too long. Carlucci was very good at his job, and he took satisfaction from that, from the cases he was able to solve, from the stimulation and rush he sometimes got from the work, and from the conviction that he in fact did some good.

But since his promotion to lieutenant, which pretty much took him off the streets, he had become less and less satisfied. The position was primarily administrative, supervising teams of detectives, assigning cases, overseeing his part of the division, and he didn't care that much for the job. He felt too distanced from the cases, almost uninvolved. He tried to make the job work better for him by stretching things—with a few of the Homicide teams, like Hong and LaPlace, or Santos and Weathers, he would attach himself as a kind of informal extra detective, working directly but unofficially on an occasional homicide. He also tried to get out on the streets with some regularity, maintaining his contacts and informants, his leeches and weasels. His superiors knew what he was doing, but they let it go because he was good, and because he never got too far out of line, and because they knew he was never going any farther up the ladder in the department.

But there were limits to what he could do, and those limits were getting to him. He wasn't sure how much longer he could put up with the situation. Recently he had been thinking he might have to do something drastic—either resign the commission and go back to the streets (which almost nobody ever did voluntarily); or retire. Vaughn, the Chief of Police, might not let him do the former, while he would happily encourage Carlucci to do the latter.

He got up and went back inside for a fresh cup of coffee. The house was quiet and peaceful; yet it also felt empty to him. Caroline had moved out several years earlier, soon after the Gould's Syndrome had been diagnosed, but it had only been a month now since Christina had done the same and moved into an apartment with her best friend, Paula Ng. He felt he should appreciate the quiet, the time alone with Andrea, but without the presence of his daughters he brooded even more than usual. He wished he saw them more often; Caroline, especially.

When he returned to the deck, he left the main door open, closing the screen. Let some fresh air into the house. He

sat again, and looked up to see Farley, the gray kitten from
next door, standing atop the fence, big eyes staring at him.
A year earlier Frances and Harry's old cat Tuff had died,
and six months later they had come home with Farley, who
was tiny and skinny, but almost exactly the same shade of
gray as Tuff had been, with the same gold eyes. Harry said
it almost made him believe in reincarnation.

Farley scrambled down the fence, jumping the last three
feet, and dashed up onto the deck. He pranced toward Carlucci, made a sound in his throat that was pretty damn close
to a growl, then flopped onto the deck, purring and playing
with Carlucci's shoelaces.

Carlucci sipped his coffee and closed his eyes, leaning
his head back against the top of the chair. He *was* feeling
better now, with the aspirin, the shower, the coffee, and the
warmth of the sun. Still exhausted, but no longer feeling
awful, and that was worth a lot.

He thought he heard the front door close, which surprised
him, and he opened his eyes. Why would Andrea be home
so early? He sat up, the movement startling Farley; the gray
kitten jumped a few feet away, golden eyes wide, his attention on the screen door. Carlucci turned, but didn't see
anyone.

"Andrea," he called. "I'm out here."

A few moments later someone appeared behind the
screen, then the door squealed open. But it wasn't Andrea.
It was Caroline, and she looked awful. Christ, had the
Gould's gone active already? He stood up, too quickly, and
nearly lost his balance. He reached out, got a hand on the
chair arm, and steadied himself as Caroline hurried to him.

"Papa," she said, putting her arm around him to hold
him up.

"I'm okay," he said. And then he put his arms around
her, hugging her tightly. "Caroline." He didn't want to let
her go. Her face was drawn, and she smelled funny. He
held her slightly away from him, gazing into her face.
"What's wrong? Are you sick?"

"I'm fine, Papa." She gave him a tired smile. "Better

than you, I think. You look terrible. Your spring cocktail, yeah?''

Carlucci nodded. He sat back down, still holding Caroline's hand, and she sat beside him. ''Are you sure you're okay?''

''I'm sure,'' she answered. ''I'm just beat, and I'm really worried about a friend of mine.''

He released her hand. ''You want some coffee? There's still some in the pot.''

''No.'' She turned away from him, her gaze toward Farley, who had settled at the far end of the deck, watching them, but Carlucci was pretty sure she wasn't even seeing the gray kitten.

''So what is it?'' he asked.

Caroline rubbed her eyes with her palms, made a heavy sighing sound, then finally turned back to him. ''It's my friend Tito.'' She left it there for a moment, then went on. ''He's got AIDS, and he's living in a death house in the DMZ. Two days ago I went to visit him. He'd called me in the morning, he'd been pretty sick, but he was feeling a little better, and I was going to go see him. We were going to watch some television, nothing much, and then I was going to sack out on the sofa, keep him company.'' She frowned. ''He was expecting me,'' she said. ''That's the thing.

''When I got there, he was gone. A guy we know, Mouse, was cleaning out the place. Stealing everything he could jam into this big duffel bag he had. Mouse said two men had come and taken Tito away, and that Tito was never coming back. He said the men had something to do with Cancer Cell, and they'd taken Tito to the Core. And he said no one ever comes back.'' She shook her head. ''I think I may have heard of them before. Cancer Cell. But I don't know who they are. I don't know anything about them.''

Carlucci did. Not much, really, and most of that was gossip and rumor, tasteless jokes and unreliable speculation by other cops. But none of it was good.

''I waited for him,'' Caroline went on. ''All through the

night, then all day yesterday, and again last night. He never showed up, he never called. I finally gave up this morning and called your office, but Morelli said you were at home recovering from the vaccinations. I didn't want to call, in case you were sleeping, so I just came by." Her mouth turned into a bitter smile. "What was I going to do? Go to the police and file a missing persons? For a gay Mexican dying of AIDS and living in a death house in the DMZ?"

She was right, he thought. It would have been a waste of time. The report would have been tanked before she got out of the building.

"I asked Mouse what Cancer Cell was, and he told me to ask you." She rubbed at her right temple, grimacing. "Is there anything you can do, Papa?"

Carlucci shrugged. "Something, maybe. I've heard of Cancer Cell, but I don't really know anything either. A real low-profile group of people. Unlike most wackos, they don't like publicity. So maybe they aren't wackos. I don't know what they've done, or what their cause is, if they have one. Something medical, but Christ, these days that could mean anything, good *or* bad." He paused, thinking. "I'll ask around some, do some checking on Tito. I go back into work tomorrow, but I can make a couple of phone calls today, get something started."

Caroline reached across the chairs and squeezed his hand. "Thanks, Papa."

"Anything else? You want some lunch or something?"

She shook her head. "No. But I could really use a shower. Haven't had one in two days. I didn't really want to use the communal at the death house."

She stood, leaned over and kissed him on the cheek, then turned and went into the house. He watched her closely, the way each step seemed slow and deliberate. Maybe it was just what she'd said, exhausted from too much worry and not enough sleep. It was crazy, he knew it, he knew he couldn't change anything, but he could not stop himself from intently observing her every time he saw her, watching her closely and searching for some sign that the Gould's had gone active; some sign that her death was approaching. It was tearing him apart.

He sat back in the sun, drinking his coffee, listening to the faint sounds of the shower, and thought about what he could do for her, and for Tito.

CHAPTER 4

Late the next morning, Carlucci sat at his desk, still feeling crappy, but with a lot of the backed-up scutwork done—the stuff he just could not put off another day. He figured he could give himself an hour or so to see what he could do for Caroline and her friend Tito.

He had called in the day before and asked Lacey to put in a system tracer on Tito. If anything came in on Tito Moraleja—arrest, detention, parking citation, credit chip violation, warrants search, *anything*—Carlucci would be notified immediately. He didn't hold out much hope for that, but it was something. Then he'd talked to Diane Wanamaker in Info-Services and asked for a complete records search, see if Tito's name would come up anywhere. He hadn't held out much hope for that either, which turned out to be an accurate assessment. Diane's report was waiting for him first thing this morning. There were blood and print records available from an emergency admission at S. F. General two years earlier; an ID chip had been implanted at the same time. And there was a routine vice pickup from several years earlier that had been dropped. No criminal record, no association hits, nothing that would give a clue to what had happened.

Which left only one thing—Cancer Cell.

Carlucci activated the phone, called up the directory, then punched in Martin Kelly's number. Kelly worked in Counter-Intelligence. Not the top guy in CID, but probably the best. If anyone knew something about Cancer Cell, it would be Martin Kelly.

"Kelly here."

"It's Frank Carlucci."

"Hey, Carlucci. *Come estai?*" Sometimes Kelly talked and acted like he wished he was Italian.

"Bene. Grazie." Carlucci smiled to himself, shaking his head. "It's almost noon. Can I buy you lunch?"

"Christ, no. I'm swamped here. You need to talk to me about something?"

"Yeah."

"You can buy me coffee, then. I can get away for a few minutes."

"Okay. You want me to come up there?" Carlucci asked.

"No. I'll meet you in Narcotics. They've got better coffee."

And a couple of private interview rooms, Carlucci thought. "Meet you there in ten minutes?" he asked.

"Ten minutes."

Carlucci did have to buy their coffees. Narcotics brewed the best coffee in the building, and they sold it to their fellow officers at a buck a cup. The proceeds paid for their annual forty-eight-hour-long New Year's bash out on Alcatraz.

Kelly and Carlucci took the coffee into a free interview room, which was small but quiet. They sat across from each other at the table, and Carlucci glanced around the room, noting the video cameras that should be off line, thinking about the hidden cameras and mikes. Narcotics guaranteed their interview rooms to be secure, but Carlucci never completely trusted them.

Kelly was dressed, as always, in a flashy, expensive suit, dark blue with glowing silver pinstripes and a tie with a wave pattern that continually washed across the fabric. Carlucci had known him for more than ten years, but they had never become friends. They got on each other's nerves when they spent too much time together, but Carlucci thought there was always something like mutual respect between them.

"So what's up?" Kelly asked.

"What do you know about Cancer Cell?"

"Jesus Christ, Carlucci. That's about the last thing I expected you to ask me." He leaned back in his chair. "What the hell case have you got going, and why haven't I heard anything about it before?"

Carlucci shook his head. "There is no case. Not exactly. Someone my daughter knows has disappeared and I told her I'd look into it. There's a chance it has something to do with Cancer Cell. That's all."

Kelly didn't say anything. He moved the paper coffee cup around and around in small circles on the table, staring at him.

"What is it?" Carlucci asked.

"You trying to run something on me?"

"Of course not. It's just what I said. Why? What's going on?"

Kelly frowned. "I wish I knew." He continued to stare at Carlucci, as if trying to decide something. "I've never liked this Cancer Cell business," he eventually said. "It always bothers me when you hear about something, or somebody, but you can never find out anything about them. The name pops up, but no one knows anything. You dig and you dig, and then dig even deeper, and all you come up with is a lot of what you know is horseshit." He sipped at his coffee, started to put it down, then drank again. He stared into his cup for a minute, then finally set it down and resumed making circles with it. "Cancer Cell is like that. I've been digging around at it for, I don't know, four or five years now, and I don't know much more now than I did before."

He paused again, looked around the room, then back at Carlucci. "Then a few weeks ago, I get a query on Cancer Cell from one of the slugs." He left it there, giving Carlucci a twisted smile.

The slugs were technically still human beings, though they didn't look much like it anymore. They lived in individual quarters on the top floor of the building, surrounded by all the computers and information access networks they wanted, and they pumped themselves full of intelligence boosters and metabolic enhancers until they became bloated, barely mobile creatures encased in form-fitting, shiny black environment suits. Their job was to help the police solve difficult cases, but Carlucci didn't know a single cop who wanted to have anything to do with the slugs. Even his old friend Brendan, who had worked a lot with the slugs, had eventually resigned and was now trying very hard to drink himself to death.

"I didn't think much of it," Kelly resumed. "I didn't have anything to give the fucker anyway. But then you show up and ask me about the same thing just a few weeks later. Makes me very suspicious."

"Which slug made the query?"

"Does it matter?"

Carlucci shrugged.

"Monk. You know him?"

Monk. That made *Carlucci* suspicious. "Yeah, I know him. I had a session with him a few years ago." He pictured Monk the slug, a goggled, bloated thing enclosed in slick black, hardly able to walk, hardly human. "But I haven't had anything to do with him since." He shrugged again. "Didn't like the bastard much."

Neither of them spoke for a couple of minutes. Carlucci wanted to reassure Kelly and get some information out of him. At the same time, he was trying to imagine what Monk's interest in Cancer Cell was all about.

"Carlucci, tell me. No bullshit. What's this with your daughter's friend?"

Carlucci related everything Caroline had told him. It really *wasn't* much—a strange deal, but with the added factor of Cancer Cell.

"You're being straight with me?" Kelly asked.

"Absolutely," Carlucci replied. "So what's bothering you so much?"

"I don't know," Kelly answered, shaking his head. "I've just got a bad feeling."

"What *can* you tell me about Cancer Cell?"

"Ah, hell, I don't know. It's one of those things. I'll be working on something else, maybe trying to track down the pipeline for black market pharmaceuticals coming down from New Hong Kong, and I'll be going through files on different people, this case or that, and the name comes up. Maybe someone mentions Cancer Cell in a recorded conversation, or an arrest interview. A couple of years ago someone, I don't remember who now, referred to them as 'medico-terrorists.' But what the hell does that mean? Do they try to block medical research, or are they running around performing experimental operations on people who don't want them?" He shook his head again. "Everything I ran across went nowhere."

"That's it?" Carlucci said. "That's all you can tell me?"

Kelly hesitated a long time before answering. Carlucci had the feeling the CID man was still trying to make some decision about him.

"I'm not the one to talk to," Kelly finally said.

"Who, then?"

Kelly looked down into his coffee cup, then pushed it away and leaned back in his chair. "Maybe two, three months ago, I ran across someone who seems to know something about Cancer Cell. She wouldn't tell me anything, but it was clear she had some hard data. She told me that if the time came that I really needed to know more, an important case, something like that, then maybe she'd be willing to talk to me some more. But maybe not even then."

"And what about when Monk sent that query? You tell him about her?"

"No, I didn't give him shit. Fuck the slugs."

"Who is she?"

Kelly hesitated one final time, then frowned and took one of his cards and a pen from his coat, jotted something on the back of the card, then slid the card across the table. Carlucci picked up the card and put it inside his shirt pocket without looking at it.

"Thanks, Kelly."

"Keep me hip on this thing, will you?"

Carlucci had to smile at that word. What decade did Kelly live in? What *century*? "I will," he promised.

He left the building to make the phone call. He walked several blocks, then stopped at a phone booth and looked at the back of Martin Kelly's card. Scribbled on it was the name Naomi Katsuda, and under that, Mishima Investments. He knew that name from somewhere. A Financial District company, he was sure of that, but why else was it familiar?

He used his dead-account card to activate the phone, called up the city directory, then clicked and scrolled through it until he found the number. He selected it, and someone answered immediately.

"Mishima Investments." A disembodied, sexless voice.

"Naomi Katsuda, please."

"One moment, sir."

The line went silently dead, then came back alive with a gentle, muted ring.

"Naomi Katsuda's office." A real person's voice this time, definitely male.

"I'd like to speak to Naomi Katsuda, please." With a place like Mishima, it was best to be as polite as possible.

"And who is calling, please?"

"Frank Carlucci."

"Ms. Katsuda is occupied at the moment, Mr. Carlucci. If you could leave me your number and the nature of your business, Ms. Katsuda will get back to you when she can."

Carlucci looked at the phone. It wouldn't take incoming calls, but that didn't really matter. What was he going to do, hang out here all afternoon waiting for a call that might not come?

"Sorry, I won't be reachable. I'll try back later."

"As you wish, sir."

Carlucci hung up, then crossed the street and went into Bongo's Heaven. All the tables were occupied, but he found a stool at the counter. He was beat, still recovering from the damn vaccination, and wasn't too sure about stomaching a Bongo Burger. So he ordered a bowl of the split pea, which was always good, and iced tea.

As he ate, he thought about Caroline, and Tito Moraleja, and his conversation with Martin Kelly, and Mishima Investments. He tried to remember where he knew that company from. Something from years before, maybe. But what? Then it finally snapped into focus, and he knew. Mishima Investments was one of New Hong Kong's two official Earth-based financial arms. The other was China Moon Ltd., which was headquartered directly across the street from Mishima in the heart of the Financial District. One Japanese arm, and one Chinese.

New Hong Kong. Carlucci had pissed off the orbital three years earlier, and he was sure they hadn't forgotten. He had been partially responsible for the public revelation that the medical research teams up in New Hong Kong were working on serious long-term life extension and that their research involved, among other things, abductions of people from Earth, forced experimentation, vivisection, political bribery, corruption, and murder. In the long run, there had been no serious consequences for New Hong Kong, more annoyance for them than anything else, but he suspected they still didn't care much for him.

When he was done with lunch, Carlucci went back to the phone across the street and called Mishima Investments. He got the same man, and the same noise about Naomi Katsuda's unavailability.

"All right," Carlucci said. "When will Ms. Katsuda be available? It's important I talk to her."

"If you could leave a number . . ."

"I told you before, that's not possible. When should I call back?"

"I'm sorry, Mr. Carlucci." A slightly condescending tone had worked its way into the man's voice. "Ms. Katsuda says she does not know you. If you would leave a number *and* tell me the nature of your business with her, perhaps Ms. Katsuda would be willing to return your call. Otherwise we cannot help you."

"I am *Lieutenant* Frank Carlucci, with the San Francisco Police Department, and I would appreciate your cooperation. I will not be available at my office, and I need to talk to Ms. Katsuda. So if you could please give me a specific time when I can call back and talk to her . . ." He left it at that.

There was a long pause, then the man said, "If you would hold just a moment, Lieutenant Carlucci."

"Sure."

Dead air, then the man's voice returned. "I'm putting you through to Ms. Katsuda."

"Thanks." But the man was already gone.

"Lieutenant Carlucci. Naomi Katsuda here. What can I do for you?"

"I'd like to talk to you."

"Talk away, Lieutenant."

"In person, I think."

She laughed softly. "That's dramatic. What about?"

"Martin Kelly gave me your name."

There was a slight pause, then she said, "Martin Kelly."

"Yes."

There was a longer pause. "I'm not sure I can help you," she said.

"I'm not sure, either, but I'd like to find out."

"I don't think you understand me," Naomi Katsuda said. "I'm not sure I *want* to help you, even if I can."

"I understood you," Carlucci said.

He waited through a long silence, trying to hear her breathing, some sign of life.

"Would tomorrow afternoon be all right?" she finally asked.

"Sure. Whatever works."

"Call tomorrow morning, then, and Tim will tell you where and when."

"Your secretary?"

"My assistant. I'll see you tomorrow, Lieutenant."

The line went dead again. Permanently, this time. Carlucci hung up the receiver and stood there beside the phone for a while, gazing at the street around him.

He should just let this Cancer Cell stuff go. It felt like trouble. But he couldn't, not yet anyway. His daughter had asked for his help, and he couldn't refuse.

CHAPTER 5

Wednesday evening, when Caroline arrived at home after work, her sister Tina was waiting for her. She was sitting on the porch steps of the apartment building, a large paper bag beside her; she was wearing a short, dark blue shimmer skirt over a white body stocking. No bra, but then she didn't really need one—small breasts ran in the family. Tina looked just great, Caroline thought, smiling to herself.

"Hey, sis," she said.

"Hi, Cari." Tina was the only one who called her that anymore. She stood up and they hugged each other.

"What's up?" Caroline asked.

Tina shrugged, smiling. "I just decided I wanted to see you. I thought maybe we could spend the evening together, sit around and talk and like that." She bent over, picked up the bag, then straightened, smile broadening into a grin. "I brought rum and Coke."

"Oh, no," Caroline said.

"Oh, yes. You're off work tomorrow, aren't you?"

"I'm afraid so." She could not keep from smiling at her younger sister.

"Then let's get shitfaced."

Caroline was fairly drunk, but was trying to pace herself. Tina wasn't trying to pace herself, and she'd also smoked half a joint; now she had the giggles. Caroline had made a pot of tea, which they drank between glasses of rum and Coke. They were both going to pay for this the next morn-

ing, but Caroline didn't really care; she was relaxed and
content and she hadn't had a good time like this in a long
while.

"Have you seen Mom and Dad recently?" Tina asked.
She was sitting on Caroline's bed, leaning back into a pile
of cushions and pillows propped against the wall, holding
her rum and Coke in her lap with both hands. On the nightstand beside her was a mug filled with tea and an ashtray
with the remaining half joint.

Caroline was settled into her old overstuffed chair, feet
propped on a cushioned ottoman that leaked bits of foam
on all sides. She felt incredibly comfortable, her muscles
slack. She had no desire to move. She managed to sip at
her drink and nod at her sister.

"Saw Papa a couple days ago. At the house. He looked
like crap." She smiled. "He'd just had his spring vaccination cocktail."

Tina picked up the joint, stuck it in her mouth, but didn't
light up. She spoke with her lips pressed together, the joint
wiggling up and down. "He'd better not make a surprise
visit," she said, "or he'll have to bust our asses for pos-
session." She giggled and the joint spit out of her mouth,
slid off her body stocking and onto the bedspread. She
picked it up and put it back in the ashtray.

Caroline's apartment was a large, spacious studio—one
large room with a small kitchen separated from it by a
counter and ceiling cabinets. She really couldn't afford it
here in the Noe Valley Corridor, but her parents kicked in
some money each month so she could live in a relatively
safe part of the city. It made them a little crazy that Tina
lived on the fringes of the Mission.

There was a scratching at the back door, in the kitchen
alcove. Caroline tried to ignore it, but when it sounded
again, more insistent this time, Tina sat forward, looking
toward the kitchen.

"What's that?" she asked.

"That's just Lucas," Caroline said. "Ignore him. He'll
go away."

"Who's Lucas?"

"Stray cat. He was hanging out a lot on the back stairs, and I made the mistake of feeding him a few times." She shook her head. "He was so skinny, all beat up and scrawny. I felt sorry for him. Now he's in better shape, all fattened up, and he won't go away. I try to discourage him."

"Why?" Tina asked. "You like cats. You should take him in."

Caroline shook her head again. "No. I don't want anything to be dependent on me." She paused, then looked away from Tina. "I mean, what would happen to him when I die?"

The room got very quiet. She hadn't meant to be that direct with Tina. Or maybe she had. She turned back to her younger sister, who looked like she was about to cry. Caroline smiled and shrugged.

"Is that why you stopped seeing Bryan?" Tina eventually asked.

Caroline gave a short laugh. "No. I slammed Bryan because he was a jerk." Lucas scratched at the back door again and Caroline grinned. "He was just like that damn cat, always scratching to get in."

Tina laughed, rocking forward and almost spilling her drink. She took a long, deep swallow and giggled.

"I need another drink." A glance up at Caroline, a sloppy grin. "You?"

"Not yet." Pacing, Caroline thought. One of us has to stay conscious.

She'd been feeling lonely again lately, and tried not to think about it too much. She almost missed Bryan. But she knew it wasn't Bryan she missed; she missed the company, affection, having someone to talk to; she missed the presence of another person, someone she cared for, and who cared for her. She'd never really had that with Bryan, but she felt as if she'd sensed hints of what that would be like. At times it depressed her that she probably would never know what love truly was. Tina, at least, would have years to find it.

She finished off her rum and Coke, but wasn't sure about

another one, and she set her glass on the coffee table. She was already feeling a little bit out of control, and now her left eye was acting up again. It felt as if a kind of film had formed over it, not quite blurring her vision. She blinked several times, trying to clear it.

"What's wrong with your eyes?" Tina asked.

"Nothing. Just a twitch." Caroline kept blinking, but couldn't get rid of the strange sensation.

"How come you didn't see Mom the other day?" Tina's eyes were almost completely closed now, and her head and shoulders were swaying, as if she were listening to some music that Caroline couldn't hear.

"She was at work," Caroline said. "It was Papa I wanted to see, anyway. I wanted to ask him for a favor."

Tina opened her eyes, interested. "What kind of favor?"

"I've got a friend who has AIDS, and he's living in a death house in the DMZ. He's disappeared, and it looks like someone may have kidnapped him. I was just asking Papa if he could check into it, maybe help find out what happened."

"Why would anyone want to kidnap someone who's dying?" Tina asked.

"I have no idea."

"Did Dad find out anything?"

"I haven't heard from him, so I guess not yet."

Tina made a face. "Are the death houses as bad as I hear?"

Caroline nodded. She hoped Tina wouldn't ask for details; she didn't want to talk about it.

Tina didn't say anything for a long time, just sipped steadily at her drink, staring at Caroline, her mouth beginning to tremble.

"What is it, Tina?"

"You're not going to end up in one of those places, are you?"

Caroline tried to brush it off, smiling and shaking her head. "Of course not."

Tina took another long drink from her glass, put it down

on the nightstand, hiccupped, then covered her face with her hands and started crying.

Caroline shut down. She couldn't take this, and so she cut off all feeling. It was something she had learned to do during the past couple of years, a kind of emotional survival strategy. *Bang, bang, bang, bang* went the barriers, and she simply stopped feeling anything at all.

She stood and deliberately walked over to the bed. Her left eye still threatened to blur out on her. She stopped beside the bed for a minute, watching Tina cry, then sat beside her younger sister.

Tina twisted around and reached out for Caroline, hugged her, and cried even harder. "I don't want you to die," she managed to get out between sobs.

"I'm not even close to being dead," Caroline whispered. She brushed at Tina's hair with her fingers, over and over, sensing vaguely that she was trying to comfort her little sister, but not really feeling it. "I've got a few years at least," she said. It might even be true.

They sat together on the bed for a long time, holding each other, Tina crying and Caroline running her hand along Tina's hair. The smell of bitter incense wafted in through the open window, followed by someone's laughter out on the street. Caroline wanted to go out on the street right now, walk up and down the corridor, the night sky above her, colored light all around. Move in and out of the crowds, look at people sitting inside cafés and bars or touring through entertainment arcades. She did not want to be in this room thinking about her own death.

"I'm sorry," Tina finally said. She'd pretty much stopped crying, though she still held tightly onto Caroline.

Jesus, Caroline thought, maybe I do need another drink. "You don't have to be sorry," she said. She eased her sister away so Tina would look at her. Caroline smiled. "Why don't you smoke the rest of that joint and I'll have another drink. All right? We're supposed to be having fun."

Tina nodded, trying to smile back. But her hands shook as she picked up the joint.

Caroline got up from the bed and started across the room. She'd only taken a few steps when the vision in her left eye darkened, like a hand cupping her eye. She froze, afraid to move, but a few moments later her vision cleared. Even the filmy sensation was gone. She continued forward, slowly now; she picked up her glass from the coffee table and headed for the kitchen counter.

Halfway to the kitchen, she lost control of her left leg. It buckled under her, and she stumbled, pitched forward, and sprawled across the floor. Somehow she managed to hang onto the glass, though the ice cubes scattered across the rug.

"Cari, are you okay?"

Caroline nodded quickly. "Yeah, I'm fine. I just tripped."

"Maybe you don't need another drink," Tina said, giggling.

"Yeah." But she knew it wasn't the alcohol. Elbows burning, she slowly, carefully got to her feet, using her right leg for support. Her left leg seemed okay now, and she took a tentative step forward on it. Fine. Then another. Still fine. She turned back, knelt on the floor, and scooped the ice cubes into her glass. Every motion was slow and deliberate. She stood, skirted the counter, dumped the ice cubes into the sink, and rinsed out the glass.

Back at the counter, she put fresh ice in her glass and mixed another drink. Heavy on the rum. She stood at the counter, hand around her drink, and watched Tina smoke the joint. Tina seemed to be relaxing again.

But Caroline wasn't. Her heart was beating hard and fast, and she tried to breathe slowly and deeply. She didn't want to be afraid. Her left eye felt funny again, that damn filmy sensation, but she could still see with it. And her leg seemed fine. She took a long swallow of her drink and almost coughed from the extra rum.

Everything's fine, she told herself. Just fine. But she didn't believe it.

She walked carefully over to her chair and sat, holding her drink with both hands. Tina dropped the last bit of the joint into the ashtray and lay back against the pillows, closing her eyes.

"That's better," Tina said.

But it wasn't, Caroline thought. It wasn't better at all.

CHAPTER 6

Early the next morning, Carlucci went out to the DMZ death house with Binh Tran. Tran's partner, Mahmoud Jefferson, was home with some nasty flu that was running through the department, a flu the vaccination cocktails apparently weren't targeted for, so Tran was solo for the day. Carlucci did not really want to go into the DMZ on his own, so he took Tran with him.

They drove a department car, parked a few blocks from the DMZ, then walked in. Early morning was the quietest part of the day in the DMZ, just like in the Tenderloin. Street traffic was steady, but the sidewalks were practically empty except for a few Dead Princes wrapped in their metallic shrouds and crouched against a building, and the occasional scrounger half lying on the ground with plastic begging jugs held out.

Carlucci and Tran were only a block into the DMZ when the clouds came in and the rain began. The rain was warm and light, little more than a drizzle. Looking around the DMZ, Carlucci realized the rain would never be strong and heavy enough to wash all this away. Which was a shame.

Caroline had given him directions and the keys to Tito's room, and he had no trouble finding the entrance to the death house with its red skull-and-crossbones painted across the bricks. Before entering, he and Tran put on surgical gloves and masks. A woman across the street screamed at them, and a guy hanging out in front of the shock shop next door told them to get themselves fucked.

Tran shrugged, opened the death house door, and they stepped inside.

An old man lay on the lobby floor, just a few feet inside. His eyes were open and he looked dead. Carlucci watched him closely, but saw no signs of movement, no rise or fall of the chest, not a twitch in the mouth or eyes. Tran knelt beside the old man and put a gloved finger against the man's neck. He kept it there for a minute or two, shifting it from one spot to another, then shook his head and stood.

"What do we do?" he asked. His eyes seemed calm. "Is there someone we should call?"

Carlucci shook his head. "They take care of their own in here." He breathed deeply once, the mask only partially blocking the stink of death. "Let's go."

He led the way up the stairs to the third floor, reading some of the graffiti on the way: WAITING FOR DEATH/ WITH BAITED BREATH. GOD MUST BE ONE MEAN SON OF A BITCH. GET ME OUT OF HERE NOW!!! DON'T FUCKING BOTHER—WITH *ANYTHING*. The stairwell didn't smell much better than the lobby.

When they emerged from the stairwell on the third floor, someone was walking down the hall toward them—a bald, gaunt man in jeans, no shirt covering a hairless chest that starkly revealed each rib. When the man saw Carlucci and Tran, he abruptly turned around and headed back the way he'd come, almost hopping, like some gangling, storklike bird, slapping his thigh with each step. He grabbed a doorknob, threw the door open, then hopped inside, slamming the door shut behind him.

Carlucci walked down the hall to the door Caroline said was Tito's, Tran just behind him. Mounted on the door was a printed notice, a white sheet of plastic with bold black letters:

ALL CONTRACTS WILL BE ENFORCED

He looked at Tran, who shrugged and shook his head. Carlucci didn't have any idea what it meant, either, nor who it was intended for. He'd have to ask Caroline if the notice had been posted the last time she was here.

He used the keys to unlock the dead bolts, slowly pushed open the door, but remained out in the hall. The door swung all the way open until the knob cracked against the wall. The room was quiet and empty.

Carlucci took a step inside. Suddenly there was a screech and a flash of movement and he dropped to a crouch, instinctively reaching under his arm for a gun that wasn't there. He threw himself back through and around the doorway and into the hall, hearing a click as Tran chambered a round into his Beretta and dropped into a crouch, ready to fire. There was another screech, and flapping sounds. Tran's head jerked, then he broke into a grin barely visible under the mask, sagged slightly, and lowered the gun. The flapping sounds continued for a few seconds, then stopped.

"What?" Carlucci asked.

"Parrot," Tran answered, still grinning. He straightened, gun in hand, and leaned carefully through the doorway. He took two more steps inside, then holstered the Beretta and looked back at Carlucci. "Just a parrot."

Carlucci followed Tran into the room. Sliding back and forth on the edge of a two-burner hot plate was a large blue parrot with just a few traces of yellow on its face. The parrot bobbed up and down, then cocked its head and squawked out something like, "I bow to you, o master."

There was no way this parrot had been here when Caroline had locked up the room. She would not have forgotten to mention it; more than that, she would never have left the parrot in the first place; she would have taken the bird with her, made sure it would be cared for.

Carlucci looked at the window. Closed. What other way could the parrot have used to get in? No fireplace, no open vents. Nothing that he could see. The parrot must have been deliberately placed in this room. But why? Then, looking back at the window, he noticed a rectangular piece of cardboard taped to the bottom of the glass. He crossed the room, inspected it more closely. Handwritten in blue marker were the words *ALL* CONTRACTS.

"What's it say?" Tran asked.

" 'All Contracts.' 'All' is underlined."

"Somebody's sending a message. With the parrot, too."

Carlucci nodded, then said, "Any ideas?"

"This Cancer Cell?" Tran turned back to the parrot, observing it without getting close enough for the parrot to lean forward and take a bite. The parrot weaved from side to side, never taking its eyes off Tran. "Maybe the parrot has the message," Tran said. "Maybe the parrot says something."

" 'I bow to you, o master'?"

Tran made a sound that might have been a laugh. "No. Something else." He straightened, took a few steps back from the parrot.

The two men spent ten or fifteen minutes going through the room, searching the cabinets and shelves, under the sofa, the blankets and sheets, the refrigerator. Carlucci opened a cabinet above the sink and saw dozens of pill bottles. He picked up a few, but they all seemed to be empty. Other than that, neither of them found anything of real interest.

Tran stood in front of the parrot again, watching it bob and weave, shifting back and forth with tiny clicks of its claws.

"What do we have?" Tran said. "No crime, right? Just a missing persons?"

"That's right."

"Give it to CID." He turned to Carlucci. "The room, the two notices, the parrot. Have them come in, do the room, take the parrot in. There's something funny here. That Cancer Cell business. They can put someone on the bird, or have recorders going, see if it says anything. If it does, they let you know."

It wasn't a bad idea. Normally CID would have to be talked into it, be convinced there was something of real interest and substance here, the work of some group or gang or organization they might have to deal with; under normal circumstances, they probably wouldn't go for it. But he could call Martin Kelly in on it, and because it might have something to do with Cancer Cell, he would want it. He'd want it bad.

The parrot took off from the hot plate, flew around the room twice, then landed on top of the television set by the window. It rocked from side to side, then screeched out, "Asshole! Asshole!"

Carlucci sat on the arm of the sofa, half watching the parrot and half gazing out the window at the bricks and boarded windows of the next building just a few feet away. His nose itched and he raised a gloved hand toward his face, stopped, then scratched his nose with the cuff of his jacket sleeve.

There was something more going on here than just a missing persons case. He could feel it, deep in his gut. He peeled off his surgical gloves, tossed them onto the sofa, then took his phone out of his jacket pocket. "Yes," he said. "We'll call in CID."

Six hours later, Carlucci was processing himself through one of the Financial District checkpoints, on his way to meeting Naomi Katsuda. Even though he was a cop, he had to put up with the processing since he wasn't chipped for the Financial District, and he had to submit to a body search before going through an array of detectors.

He hated the Financial District. Gleaming metal and smooth concrete and polished stone and glass, shining towers rising from more concrete and asphalt—the Financial District was like an island in time. It was just about the only part of San Francisco that looked as if it existed in the twenty-first century, that seemed to belong in its own time. Walled off from the rest of the city, surrounded by huge subterranean vehicle parks for the tens of thousands of daily commuters, its own streets were relatively traffic-free, served by frequent clean-shuttles, bicycles, and pedalcarts. All freight deliveries were made between midnight and 5:00 A.M., and all the cleaning crews, inside and out, worked the same shift.

Clean and sterile and morally dead—that was the only way Carlucci could see it anymore. Money and data producing only more money and data, while the rest of the city went to shit.

Once through the checkpoint, he looked back across the barriers to the buildings of the Chinatown Corridor, which ran smack up against the Financial District border. The buildings were older, darker, dirtier, but that was real life out there; in here was something else altogether.

He walked the several blocks to the Embarcadero Centers, thirty- and forty-story office buildings perched atop three floors of interconnected retail space—shops and restaurants that only those who worked inside the district could afford. The morning's rain had stopped several hours earlier, but dark clouds overhead threatened new showers. The air had a warm and damp and electric feel to it.

Carlucci had liked the Financial District when he was in his late teens, early twenties, more than thirty years ago. It hadn't been cordoned off from the rest of the city then, there had been no checkpoints, no body searches, no arrays of detectors to pass through before entering. It wasn't his favorite part of the city—the goals of the businesses and law firms weren't any more high-minded back then—but he had liked the sense of motion and purpose that filled the streets.

He would take a bus downtown from the Richmond and wander the streets, walking in and out of the shadows of buildings anywhere from five or six stories high to more than fifty. Normal people worked here, coming in by car, bus, and streetcar from all parts of the city. Men and women who stank of weeks-old body odor and stale booze sat on benches and barked incoherently at passersby, or hunkered against stone steps, sticking their hands or cups out toward men and women in business suits. It wasn't always pleasant, but it was real.

He would buy a Polish sausage from a cart vendor for a couple of bucks, including all the onions he could scoop onto the thing. Now there were no street vendors of any kind. And there certainly weren't any stinking men or women asleep on the benches—they'd all been moved out.

At Embarcadero 2, he took the escalator to the second level, then wandered about until he found the open-air café where he was supposed to meet Naomi Katsuda. He stood

by a mortared stone planter near the outer ring and looked
out over the tables, all of which were sheltered by white
umbrellas in case it rained; he had no idea what she looked
like, but he assumed she was Japanese, and he assumed she
would be alone. Fewer than half the tables were occupied—
it was well past lunchtime and well before the dinner
hour—and most of them by two or more people.

His gaze stopped on an attractive, dark-haired woman in
her thirties who looked only vaguely Asian. But she stared
back at him, nodded once, then looked away and casually
lit a cigarette.

Carlucci worked his way through the tables and stopped
by the woman. She looked up at him with dark brown eyes.
She smoked with her left hand, and kept her other hand on
her lap. Her fingernails were painted a pale pink and her
lips were silver.

"Naomi Katsuda?"

She gave him another crisp nod, then put out her right
hand. "Lieutenant."

He took her hand, which was warm and dry, like the
smoothest sandpaper.

"Please, Lieutenant, have a seat." She took one more
quick, deep drag on the cigarette, then delicately crushed it
out in the crystal ashtray that held two other butts. She'd
either been here a while, or she was quite a smoker. Or
maybe just nervous. But she didn't appear to be nervous,
not in the least.

He sat down in the lightly cushioned plastic chair, which
was surprisingly comfortable. Naomi Katsuda leaned forward and pressed a button on the umbrella pole.

"It will be just a moment," she said, settling back in her
chair.

She didn't say anything more, and it was clear she wasn't
going to right away. Carlucci studied her, and changed his
guess about her age, raising it by a decade—forties, yes,
not thirties. She probably colored her hair, but it looked
quite natural, long and dark and straight. She wore a white
linen jacket over a light blue blouse; he could no longer

see her skirt or legs, but he remembered the skirt being short, the legs long and slim, like her arms.

A woman rolled a cart up to the edge of the table, the cart loaded with steaming coffee, teas, and trays of pastries.

"Tea," Naomi Katsuda said. "Darjeeling. And . . ." She pointed at a long, thin pastry traced with delicate lines of chocolate.

The waitress poured hot water into a small ceramic pot, added a tea bag to it, then set it along with a cup and saucer in front of Naomi. Then she used tongs to move the pastry onto a small plate, and set that beside the cup and saucer. She looked at Carlucci, waiting.

"Just coffee," he said. All of the pastries looked far too rich, and he really had no idea what most of them would taste like. "Black," he added.

The woman poured coffee into a cup, set it in front of him on a saucer, then said, "Will there be anything else?"

Naomi Katsuda shook her head, a short, quick gesture. "We will not want to be disturbed."

The waitress nodded, and rolled the cart away.

A flicker of light flashed through the dark clouds above them, and several seconds later came a dull rumbling. The air felt even heavier now, but there was still no rain.

"I'm only half Japanese," Naomi Katsuda said. "You *were* wondering, weren't you?"

"Something."

She smiled, started to light another cigarette, then stopped and looked at Carlucci. "Do you mind?"

"No."

"Do you smoke? No? I thought all policemen smoked." She smiled in a way that seemed both self-amused and condescending at the same time.

He was going to tell her that he'd quit a few years earlier, but suddenly he realized he did not want to tell her even the smallest personal detail about himself. Already he didn't like her. "No," was all he eventually said. "I don't smoke."

Neither spoke for a couple of minutes. Carlucci sipped at his coffee, and when Naomi finished her cigarette, she poured herself a cup of tea. She took a sip, then looked at him and said, "All right."

"Cancer Cell," he said. "Martin Kelly says you know something about them."

"Why are you interested?"

"My daughter has a friend who's been abducted by two men. A witness seemed to think the two men were involved with Cancer Cell. I'm trying to find out what happened to my daughter's friend."

Naomi Katsuda smiled, and raised one eyebrow. "That's it? That's what all this is about?" As if she couldn't quite believe it.

"Yes."

She shook her head, laughing quietly. "I'm sorry, Lieutenant. I'm sorry about your daughter's friend. But I can't help you."

"You know something about Cancer Cell, though, don't you?"

Her smile shifted into a frown. "I would rather you didn't mention that name again," she said. "It's not a good idea."

"What the hell is all the goddamn mystery about these people?"

"If you knew anything about them, Lieutenant, you would not ask that question."

"That's just the point, isn't it? I don't know anything about them. That's why I'm here. I've known Martin Kelly a long time, and if he says you know something substantial, then I'm sure you do."

"I'm not denying anything, Lieutenant." She paused. "There's an old expression, I'm not sure I have it precisely, but it's something like, 'A little knowledge is a dangerous thing.'"

"I'm familiar with the expression," Carlucci said. "I'm a cop, my job involves dealing with both knowledge and danger. I've been doing it a long time."

Naomi shook her head. "I'm not concerned about you, Lieutenant. I'm concerned about my own safety. Revealing knowledge to others can be even more dangerous than just having it.''

''Kelly said you told him that if he needed to know more, for a case, you would help him.''

Her expression had grown hard and unyielding. ''I made no promises to him. But I agreed to meet you. And when I asked you what this was all about, you told me it's about some unimportant abduction. I am not about to take any risks for that.''

''What if it had been my daughter who had been abducted, and not her friend?''

''I would have expressed greater sympathy for your loss, but my answer would have been the same. I would tell you nothing.''

''And if my daughter's friend turns up dead, and abduction becomes murder, will you help then?''

She sighed with exasperation, smiling faintly. ''There's something fundamental about this you just don't understand, Lieutenant. One insignificant murder would change nothing.''

''Then what the hell would it take to get you to talk to me about these people?''

''Much more, Lieutenant.'' All traces of the smile hardened away. ''You can come back to me when people are dying. Maybe I'll talk to you then.''

''What the hell is that supposed to mean?'' Carlucci asked, angry now. ''People are dying all the time. People are dying right now while we're sitting here talking about bullshit.''

''You'll know what I mean when it happens, Lieutenant. You'll know exactly what I mean.'' She shifted her gaze away from him, brought her teacup to her mouth, and drank. ''We're done talking, Lieutenant. You can go now.'' She glanced back at him, the corner of her silver-painted lips turning up into a kind of smile. ''I'll cover the check. I doubt you can afford it.''

Coffee, tea, a pastry, how much could that be? But she was probably right, in here it would cost a fortune. Everything here was out of reach, including Naomi Katsuda.

He got up from the table, started to thank her, then thought, screw it, why should he? "Good-bye, Ms. Katsuda." She didn't reply, and she didn't look at him. Fuck you, too, he thought. He pushed the chair back in against the table and walked away from her.

ISABEL

There was blood everywhere. Monkey blood.

Isabel watched from the shadows of an old heat duct high above the floor, the grating long gone, her view unobstructed. A woman was skinning a dead monkey, and making a terrible mess of it.

The room was small, with plaster walls and a wood floor partially covered by cracked, stained linoleum and scraps of thin carpeting. The windows were boarded and papered over, and the door was barred shut; light came from a lamp on a wooden crate. Isabel could smell the blood and the stench of fuel from the makeshift stove against the far wall, burners lit beneath an enormous pot filled with water.

The lamp cast jerking, distorted shadows across the floor as the woman moved, but it brightly illuminated the monkey's face, which was as yet untouched.

Henry. Isabel thought it was Henry, who had been in a cage across the aisle from her in her old home; she thought she recognized the odd tuft of gray above his right eyebrow. She had a vague memory of Henry being sick, too, at the same time she was; a memory of Henry lying on the floor of his cage and looking at her, eyes blinking slowly. Now his eyes weren't blinking at all.

Isabel closed her own eyes, feeling sick, down inside her belly. She wanted to stop the smells, the images. But she couldn't, and she opened her eyes again and stared at the scene beneath her.

The woman was awash in blood, and she was breathing

hard, swearing as she worked at the dead monkey. Blood covered her hands, streaked her arms, soaked into her clothes; some had splashed across her face. She rested a moment, wiped her face with the back of her hand, and smeared more blood across her cheek and eye. She swore again, blinking crazily. Then she breathed in deeply, dropped the knife to the ground and picked up a larger one, gripped it tightly. Staring into the dead monkey's face, she began sawing at the neck, trying to cut off its head.

Henry, Isabel thought.

She couldn't look anymore. She was feeling sicker, her throat burning now, something coming up from her stomach.

Isabel closed her eyes, then inched her way slowly and silently back along the heat duct, getting away from the room, away from the images and smells, just getting away. . . .

PART TWO

INFECTION

Nikki guided the pedalcart around the corner and into the alley; Cage sat beside her, pumping his foot pedals, providing half the power. The gray early morning light darkened as they moved deeper into the alley, blocked by the buildings rising high on either side, the fire escapes, and the shaky planked walkways that crisscrossed the alley several floors above them. Cage was exhausted, working on two hours of sleep and half a pot of coffee; Nikki didn't look much better.

There was a lot of activity in the alley—people loading and unloading merchandise into and from carts and pinkyvans and scat trucks, other people standing around talking and drinking coffee, or walking across the creaking, sagging wooden planks, people and vehicles squeezing past each other in both directions—but it all was relatively lowkey this time of day, not like the amphetamine buzz of the Tenderloin at night. The smell of bacon and frying butter was strong, filling the alley, and Cage's stomach burned with acids of morning hunger and coffee. Maybe he'd take Nikki out for breakfast when they were done here.

They let the cart roll to a stop on the right-hand side of the alley, ten feet short of a wide blue metal door set in the brick wall. The first- and second-floor windows of the building were painted over in dark brown and covered by rusting spiked metal grilles.

"This it?" Nikki asked.

"I think so. I'll see."

Nikki set the wheel brakes and Cage climbed down from the cart. The ground was uneven beneath his feet, the asphalt cracked and fissured, scattered with loose gravel and rock. He approached the dark blue door, each step a crunching sound, and banged on it. Almost immediately the door cracked inward, an inch or two at first, then a few more. There was only darkness behind the door, and he couldn't see anything more than shadows and the faint reflection of light from someone's eyes.

"Cage," a voice said from the darkness. Recognition rather than a question. But it wasn't Stinger's voice.

The door swung open another foot, letting in more light and illuminating the man inside. He was dark, thin, and young, in his twenties, dressed in pale khakis, his right arm meshed in silver and wired for body jolts.

"Come on in," the man said, stepping back. "I'm Tiger."

Another fucking moniker. And not very imaginative at that. Cage looked back at Nikki, gestured for her to stay with the pedalcart, and when she nodded he stepped through the doorway. Tiger closed the door, complete darkness returning for a moment, then dim lights came up.

They were in a narrow, empty corridor running the length of the building. Tiger led the way past several interior doors, then stopped in front of the last one at the end of the corridor. He pulled the door open, nodded for Cage to go in. The door automatically swung shut behind them, hydraulics hissing.

The room was small, maybe fifteen feet square, with dark gray painted cinderblock walls. No windows, but there was another door in the back corner, and beside the door, sitting on an overturned plastic crate, with her back against the wall, was a large, beefy woman dressed in pale khakis like Tiger's. Her hair was short and stiff, and she wore a dead neutral expression on her face. She gazed steadily at Cage, almost unblinking, but didn't say a word.

In the middle of the room, open for inspection with their foam-pack lids stacked to the side, were ten or twelve cartons of pharmaceuticals. Cage glanced at them, then looked at Tiger.

"Where's Stinger?"

"He couldn't make it," Tiger answered.

"He was supposed to be here."

Tiger shrugged, glanced at the woman sitting on the crate, but didn't say anything.

"Why isn't he here?"

Tiger hesitated, then finally said, "He's sick."

"Sick with what?"

Tiger cut his glance at the woman again, and shrugged once more. He wouldn't look directly at Cage. "The flu or something." He sniffed once, then pulled sheets of paper from his back pocket and handed them to Cage. "Here's the inventory list, you can check it against the merch. When you're done, we seal up the cartons and load you up."

Cage looked over at the woman, but her expression hadn't changed. There was clearly something about Stinger that made Tiger nervous. More than nervous—Tiger was scared. But it was obvious he wasn't going to talk about it here, not with this woman around. Cage decided to let it go for now.

He didn't spend more than fifteen minutes checking the contents of the cartons against the inventory sheets; he was more concerned with Stinger's health right now than he was with the pharmaceuticals. Besides, he and Madelaine would do a more complete inspection back at the clinic, and he knew it would all check out; these people weren't going to try to rip him off yet, not before they got any work out of him.

When he was done, Tiger helped him put the foam-pack lids back on the cartons, sealing each one with strip tape. The woman didn't make a move to help.

"Let's go get Nikki," Cage said, "and we can load up and get out of your way."

Another glance at the woman from Tiger. Cage didn't have any doubts about who was in charge.

"I think I'd better wait here," Tiger said.

"Thanks a lot." Don't push it, Cage told himself. He

left the room, walked down the corridor to the big metal door, but didn't open it. He returned to the room, pulled the door open, and stuck his head inside.

"Hey, Tiger. The door's locked."

Tiger seemed confused for a moment, then nodded once and said, "Okay, I'll get it."

Halfway along the corridor, when the door to the room had swung completely shut, Cage stopped and faced Tiger, bringing the young man to an abrupt halt.

"All right," Cage whispered. "What the hell is wrong with Stinger?"

"I told you," Tiger answered without conviction. "He's got the flu or something."

"Bullshit. I saw him two weeks ago, and he was starting to get sick then, and it wasn't the goddamn flu. So what the fuck is it?"

Tiger tried to step back, but Cage grabbed his left arm to keep him close. He didn't think Tiger would use the body jolts on him.

"I'm not supposed to say anything," Tiger tried, a whine sliding in his voice.

"I don't care. I spent half an hour sitting across a table from the bastard, and I want to know what the hell it is I've been exposed to. I want to know what the hell it is that's got you so scared."

Tiger didn't say anything for a minute, but he was starting to sweat, and the sweat stank of fear.

"What is it?" Cage asked once more, his voice slow and quiet and firm.

"I don't know," Tiger finally said. "He's real sick. I think he's dying. But *nobody* knows what's wrong with him."

"Or nobody's saying."

Tiger shook his head. "I don't think they know."

"All right." Cage let him go. "What are the symptoms? Tell me what's happening to him."

"I don't really know that much. They're keeping him isolated. But he was getting really bad headaches, and his eyes were completely bloodshot, almost solid red, and he had red patches all over his skin, and he was starting to act real crazy. But I haven't seen him for a couple three days.''

"Are you sure he's still alive?"

"I guess. They'd tell us if he died.''

Cage gave him a wry smile. "Would they." Then he sighed, and asked, "Who is this 'they' you keep talking about?''

"The people I work for.''

"Who are they?''

Tiger shook his head. "You know I can't tell you that. Don't even ask.''

"Maybe you should bring me to him," Cage said. "I'm a doctor, maybe I can help.''

"We've got doctors," Tiger said.

"Yeah, I'll bet. Lots of doctors, don't you?'' He was tempted to come right out and ask Tiger if it *was* Cancer Cell he worked for, but there was no point. Tiger might not actually know it was Cancer Cell, and Cage was pretty damn sure he knew the answer, anyway.

"So what's got you so scared, Tiger?''

Tiger breathed deeply once and licked his lips. "I was helping carry him to see the docs, and he had some kind of seizure, whacking out all over, and he then he puked up blood all over the place . . . all over *me*." Tiger shuddered. "I got his blood all over me.''

And Nikki had put her finger hooks into him. Nikki had drawn blood.

"How long ago was this, Tiger?''

Tiger blinked a couple of times, wiped sweat from his lip. "T-two days ago? Maybe three.''

"And how are you feeling? Besides scared?''

"Okay. I think.''

"I'm sure you'll be fine," Cage lied. He couldn't be sure at all. "You look fine." He nodded down the corridor. "Go on back to your baby sitter.''

"What about the door?''

"Christ, Tiger. The door's not locked." Cage turned and headed down the corridor, leaving Tiger to figure it out for himself.

When Cage opened the door, he found that Nikki had
backed the pedalcart to the door, ready for him. She was
sitting on the hold, smoking a cigarette. He hadn't seen her
smoke in three or four weeks; she'd tried to quit several
times in the past year, and this last time had gone the longest. But he didn't mention the cigarette. Nikki smoking was
the least of his worries right now.

"We ready to go?" Nikki asked.

Cage nodded. Nikki slid off the end of the cart, dropped
the cigarette butt, and ground it out with her boot. How
long had it been since the meeting with Stinger? Cage
worked it out. Fifteen days. Nikki didn't seem to be sick
at all, and she hadn't complained about anything, not even
a headache. She was tired, but so was he. Fifteen days. It
didn't mean shit.

They propped open the door with two wooden wedges,
then Cage led the way down the corridor to the room where
Tiger and the woman waited.

Cage made the introductions. "Nikki. Tiger." Then, with
a gesture at the woman still sitting on the crate, he said, "I
have no idea who she is. She doesn't talk." He looked at
Tiger, who seemed uncomfortable again. "You going to
help us load up?"

Tiger shook his head. "I can't."

Cage smiled, looked back at the woman. "How about
you?"

The woman didn't reply, didn't move except to blink and
breathe.

"That's not her job," Tiger said.

Cage laughed. "I know, Tiger. I know what her job is."
He and Nikki each picked up a carton, and he raised an
eyebrow at Tiger. "Are you allowed to get the door?"

Tiger hurried to the door, pushed it open, and held it for
them. Cage and Nikki carried the cartons through, along
the corridor, then out into the alley. Nikki opened the hold
of the pedal cart, and they carefully placed the cartons inside.

"I'll get the next one," Cage said. They couldn't leave
the cart alone now, so they would alternate trips.

She nodded. "Fine. And I'll have another smoke." Almost daring him to say something. When he didn't, she said, "No Stinger?"

"Nope. Didn't show."

"Why not?"

Cage shrugged and shook his head.

"Why not, Cage?"

"Tiger said he was sick. The flu."

"The flu."

"That's what he said."

Nikki took a cigarette from the pack in her top shock suit pocket, lit it with a stone-lighter. Neither of them said anything for a minute.

"I wouldn't worry about it," Cage eventually said.

"Yeah." Nikki dragged in deep on the cigarette, held it, then blew a long, steady stream of smoke into Cage's face. "Go get another carton," she said.

Cage nodded and headed back inside.

As he was leaving the room, carton in his arms, Tiger out in the hall holding the door open, Cage paused, seeing that Tiger was out of the woman's line of sight. He leaned toward Tiger and whispered rapidly. "Listen, Tiger. You'll probably be fine. But if you start to get sick, get the hell out of wherever you are. Come find me at the RadioLand Street Clinic, we'll take care of you. Got that?"

Tiger's eyes were wide, scared again, but he nodded. "RadioLand."

"You'll be fine." Then Cage headed along the corridor.

Twenty minutes later, he and Nikki had all the cartons packed and the hold locked up; they closed the blue metal door and climbed up onto the cart. Cage worked his feet into the pedals, but Nikki remained motionless, her arms lying across the wheel and her gaze unfocused.

"How sick is he?" she asked.

"Stinger?"

She nodded.

Cage shrugged. "Tiger didn't know."

Nikki turned to stare hard at him. "How sick?"

"Tiger didn't know," Cage insisted. "Besides, what are

the odds? You used the antiseptic wipes. This is all a lot
of worry about nothing.''

Nikki stared at him a few moments longer, then turned
to face forward. She gripped the steering wheel, dug her
feet into the pedals, and started pumping.

CHAPTER 8

Wet and uncomfortable, Carlucci stood at the edge of the cliff and gazed down through the sagging chain-link fence at the ruins of the old Sutro Baths sixty or seventy feet below him. The heavier morning rain had eased, but still came down as a warm, dense mist, graying out the ocean and almost completely obscuring Seal Rocks out on the water. The drizzle masked all sound, and the air was unnaturally quiet around him; it was thick with the smell of salt. He could just make out the moving figures in the ruins below, perhaps half a dozen at the moment—two uniformed cops and several detectives. Soon there would be more. The two uniforms were erecting a protective tarp, sheltering the others and, presumably, the body.

Carlucci disliked this place intensely. Being here made him feel awful—as if he'd just awakened from some profoundly disturbing dream he could not remember. Disoriented, vaguely afraid, and depressed. Melancholy and bad memories.

There was, to him, something incredibly sad about the ruins, which had been here for more than fifty years; maybe a lot longer than that. He wasn't sure of the dates. But what he did know was that the Sutro Baths had been built at the very end of the nineteenth century—the largest public bathhouse in the world. He had seen pictures of the huge, glass-enclosed natatorium at the edge of the sea, interior photos of the half dozen saltwater swimming pools heated by enormous furnaces, the promenades and spectator galleries, hundreds, even thousands of people swimming, diving, shooting down water slides, socializing. But sometime in the second half of the twentieth century the baths had burned to the ground. The ruins—broken sections of concrete walkways, roofless remnants of small concrete or cinder block buildings scattered around the perimeter, and the old foundations, which filled with water like outdoor versions of the old swimming pools—had remained ever since, untouched except by vandals and the elements.

Carlucci turned to his left and gazed at the ugly rectangular buildings of the modern Cliff House, the source of his bad memories. Eight or nine years ago, out here to investigate the drowning death of a twelve-year-old girl, he had seen Andrea coming out of the Cliff House restaurant, hand-in-hand with a man he had never seen before. He had watched them kiss, then part, the man to a car and Andrea across the street to the bus stop. He had stood, not far from where he was right now, and watched her waiting, saw her smile and wave at the man as he drove past her, and Carlucci had wondered why the hell the man didn't give Andrea a ride, why he made her take the bus back into town. He had remained there unmoving, numb and disoriented, until the bus arrived; Andrea climbed aboard, and then the bus pulled away.

That night, as they lay in bed with the lights off and bright moonlight streaming in through the window, he had come right out and asked her about the man. After a long silence, Andrea had told him she'd been having an affair with the man for nearly a year. She'd also told him that, now that he knew, she would bring it to an end; she didn't want it to threaten their marriage. He had expected her to tell him who the man was, something about him, how the affair had started, things like that. But she didn't. He had wanted to know *why,* but she wouldn't talk about that, either. She said it didn't matter, that it had nothing to do with him, or the family, or their marriage, that it was something to do with her alone. Although he couldn't believe that entirely, Carlucci had sensed that in some important ways it was true. They hadn't talked about it again. As far as he knew, there had been no other affairs, before or since. But the memories of that day still hurt, even after all these years.

"Lieutenant?"

Carlucci turned to see Jefferson and Tran walking downhill along the cracked sidewalk toward him. Jefferson looked like he was still sick with the flu that had kept him home for more than two weeks—he was gaunt, his eyes were heavy, and he seemed out of breath.

"You all right?" Carlucci asked him.

Jefferson shrugged. "Better. The old boneman says I shouldn't be contagious anymore, and that maybe it would be good to get out a little." He smiled. "Don't know that this was what he had in mind, checking out a murder in the rain, but what the fuck."

They stood in the mist, which was getting heavier, and looked down at the cops standing under the protective tarp down near the edge of the ruins.

"Who was first on scene?" Tran asked.

"Santos and Weathers," Carlucci answered. "They'll be in charge of the case."

Tran nodded, said, "Ruben and Toni, good. We can do that."

Jefferson coughed several times, shook himself, then said, "Let's get down there."

Carlucci frowned at him. "You want to stay up here? Have Binh fill you in later?"

Jefferson was looking down through the drizzle at the muddy slope, the makeshift trails that twisted down and through the rubble. He nodded. "Yeah, maybe I'd better."

"Go on back to the car," Carlucci told him. "Get out of the rain."

Jefferson nodded again, said, "Thanks, Lieutenant," and started back up the hill. Carlucci and Tran walked in the opposite direction, along the sidewalk to an opening that had been cut in the chain-link fence and flagged. The opening was at the head of what appeared to be the best path down to the ruins. The slope wasn't as steep here, almost terraced. They worked their way slowly down the hillside, past crumbling walls half buried, past the remains of floors and pipes and an occasional piece of roofing. They used chunks of concrete or rock or tufts of grass for footing whenever possible. The drizzle had become so heavy now that he could barely see the vague outlines of the Cliff House, could barely see the ocean.

"Anything on that parrot, yet?" Tran asked.

"No. It swears a lot, but they haven't picked up much more than that. The CID people are starting to think we're crazy. Maybe we are. Maybe it's all a goddamn waste of time." Carlucci smiled. "Kelly's growing fond of the parrot, though. Says he might take it home when they're done with it." He stopped, trying to find a way past a steep, slick streak of mud. "How *is* Jefferson?"

"He'll be fine," Tran said. Carlucci looked at him, and Tran repeated himself. "He'll be fine."

Carlucci backtracked a couple of steps, worked uphill, then out along a strip of crumbling brickwork, dropping a couple of feet to a thick patch of sea grass. Tran dropped down beside him.

"Do you know why we've got extra teams called in on this one?" Tran asked. "It's only one victim, isn't it?"

Carlucci shook his head. "Ruben just said it was a hot one, and to get two extra teams down here as soon as possible. He wouldn't say why. I think Hong and LaPlace are already here. Yeah, there's Hong." The tall, thin detective was apart from the others, crouched at the edge of the old foundation, gazing into the leaf-covered water. His glasses were misted over, and Carlucci wondered how he could see anything.

The ground leveled out as they neared the old foundations, covered by large patches of ocean grasses and succulents, and walking became easier. A narrow path had been marked out along the beds of ice plant and concrete slabs, a futile attempt to preserve the integrity of the crime scene. They stayed on the path and made their way to the group of cops huddled under the tarp. There were two uniforms, who kept back, only partly out of the rain, and three detectives—Santos, Weathers, and LaPlace. Several feet away, still crouched by the water, Hong looked up and nodded at Carlucci. At the feet of the cops was a covered form laid out along the edge of the concrete foundation.

"I'm sure as hell glad you're here," Santos said as Carlucci and Tran squeezed in under the tarp. "I was afraid you'd be too late."

"Too late for what?" Carlucci asked.

"Someone's going to try to take this case away from us." He stared hard at Carlucci. "I don't want that to happen. You might be able to hold on to it for us."

"Who's going to try to take it?"

Santos shrugged. "Someone." He shifted to the side and looked up the slope to the road and fence at the edge of the cliff. Carlucci followed his gaze, but didn't see anything. Tran lit a cigarette, and almost immediately Toni Weathers and one of the uniforms followed suit. The falling drizzle on all sides kept the smoke contained, and it built up under the tarp, hovered around them.

"Morgan," Santos finally said.

Morgan was homicide lieutenant for the Financial District, which had its own separate department within the force. But the ruins of the Sutro Baths weren't anywhere near the Financial District.

"Do we have an ID?" Carlucci asked. That had to be what had Santos spooked.

"Oh yeah," Santos said. "She was chipped, and we got an instant hit, complete with goddamn flares and alarms."

"Who is she?"

"It's not who she is. It's who her father is."

"Who is she, Ruben?"

Santos shrugged again. "Naomi Katsuda."

Carlucci didn't say anything, just looked down at the covered form at their feet.

"You know her?" LaPlace asked.

Carlucci stepped toward the head, the other cops making room for him. He knelt beside the body and pulled the dark nylon cloth away from the face. Her skin was gray and cold and lifeless, the lips a smeared silver now, the eyes closed and bruised, but he recognized her. The initials

"CC" had been neatly carved into her forehead. He stared at her for a minute, feeling almost dizzy. Then he covered her face and stood. A cold tremor of fear rattled through him, settling in his stomach where it continued to tremble.

"I met her once," he finally said.

"Cancer Cell," said Tran. When the others looked at him, he pointed at the body. "The letters carved in her forehead. Cancer Cell."

Only Carlucci knew why it had occurred to Tran, but he didn't want to explain now. He turned to Santos. "Why all the flares and alarms? And why are you worried about Morgan?"

"Her father, Yoshi Katsuda, is the CEO of Mishima Investments. And Mishima Investments is New Hong Kong."

Carlucci nodded, trying to work things out. Martin Kelly had never mentioned Naomi's father. Didn't he know? She hadn't mentioned it either. But Santos was right. Morgan would try to suck this case in, take it for his own, into Financial District jurisdiction where it would be investigated in complete secrecy, investigated in whatever way Mishima Investments and Yoshi Katsuda, and maybe even New Hong Kong, wanted it investigated.

"I won't let him take this case," Carlucci said. He looked up the slope, understanding now why Santos had been looking up there earlier. When Santos and Weathers had locked onto the identity chip in Naomi Katsuda's shoulder, and her identity had been confirmed, a bolt would have been transmitted directly to Morgan. It was surprising he wasn't here yet.

"Coroner's crew and crime scene techs should be here any minute," said Weathers. She looked at her cigarette, which was almost gone, then flicked the butt away, toward the ocean. Tran did the same. It probably didn't matter much, Carlucci thought. With all this rain and mud the crime scene was a mess anyway.

"Any idea how she was killed?" Carlucci asked.

Santos and Weathers both shook their heads. "You could almost wonder if it was accidental, except for the letters carved into her forehead. I'm pretty sure the carving was postmortem.''

"She wasn't in the water, was she?" What he'd seen of Naomi Katsuda's face hadn't looked like a floater, unless she'd been in the water a very short time.

Santos shook his head again. "We found her just where she is now."

Carlucci glanced at the two uniforms, but they both shook their heads as well. The older of the two, a woman in her forties, said, "We didn't touch her, Lieutenant. We were just a few blocks away when the call came through, we flashed over here and marked off the path, then waited for the detectives."

"Who called it in?"

"Manager of the Cliff House restaurant," Weathers said. "A customer spotted it." She smiled. "I guess it spoiled their lunch."

Hong joined them under the tarp, his hair soaked, water dripping down his face. He wiped his glasses with a hand-kerchief.

"You find something over there?" Carlucci asked.

"No. I was primarily thinking about the job the crime scene techs are going to have." His mouth worked into the faintest of smiles. "They're going to have to drag all that, aren't they? Can you imagine the crap they're going to find in there? And probably none of it will have any connection to this."

"Oh, fuck," LaPlace said. "They're here."

They all looked up at the road that curved its way along the edge of the cliff. Two cars were just coming to a stop, pulling up over the curb and onto the sidewalk—a gray BMW, which was probably Morgan's, and behind it a black, medium-sized limousine. Two men got out of the BMW, Blaise Morgan and Alex Warsinske, Morgan's flunky. They approached the chain-link fence and looked down through the misting rain at the group of men looking back up at them. They wore slickcoats over their suits, but no hats, and they didn't look too happy to be standing out in the rain.

No one emerged from the limousine.

"Is Morgan waiting for us to come up there after him?" Santos wondered aloud.

"You don't want him to get his shoes muddy, do you?" LaPlace said. "Fucking thousand-dollar Italian shoes."

"Watch it," Carlucci said. "Italians make the best shoes."

LaPlace snorted. "Yeah, but who can afford them? Where the fuck were *your* shoes made?"

"Probably Guatemala," Carlucci said, smiling. The other cops laughed.

"Fuck him," LaPlace said. "He wants this case, let him climb on down here."

"Yeah," Weathers added, "and maybe that ferret Warsinske will end up on his ass."

Two more vehicles pulled up behind the limousine—the coroner's van and an old department junker with crime scene techs. Men and women climbed out of the two vehicles and, loaded with equipment and cases and a jacked-up stretcher, headed toward the break in the fencing. Morgan and Warsinske remained where they were, looking down at the ruins.

Carlucci turned back to Santos and Weathers. "All right, Ruben, Toni. This is your case. You've got Hong and LaPlace, and Tran and Jefferson. You need more help, just ask. You get any flak from Morgan or anyone else, send them to me. I'll run interference." He glanced at Tran. "Binh might be right about Cancer Cell. I'll let him explain. I don't know what the hell is going on here, but there's more involved than just Naomi Katsuda's death. We're keeping this goddamn case."

"Here he comes." LaPlace pointed up the slope.

Carlucci turned around and saw Morgan and Warsinske taking the first cautious steps through the break in the fence. The coroner's assistants and the techs were about halfway down the slope. Carlucci breathed in deeply once, let it out. "All right."

He stepped out from the shelter of the tarp; the drizzle was even heavier now, though he still wouldn't call it rain, exactly, and it was still fairly warm. The salt smell had grown stronger. He worked his way along the marked pathway, eyes to the ground.

Just before he reached the foot of the slope, he met the crews coming down and stepped to the side to let them pass. Most of the men and women nodded to him as they went by, and he nodded in return. When they were by him, he took a few more steps, then sat on the remains of a cinderblock wall, his slickcoat protecting his ass from the wet, and waited for Morgan and Warsinske. They were still only halfway down the slope, struggling with their footing, slipping on the mud, and Carlucci could hear Morgan swearing.

He looked back at the raised tarp. The body was no longer even partially visible, surrounded now by close to a dozen people. It was going to be a long and miserable afternoon for everyone. Maybe he *didn't* want to go back onto the streets. Maybe it *was* time for him to get out.

Morgan and Warsinske finally reached the bottom of the slope and approached. Warsinske hung back, as though trying to hide behind his boss.

"I want this fucking case," Morgan said.

Blaise Morgan was a handsome man, an inch or two taller than Carlucci, but probably five or ten pounds lighter. Even with his dark hair soaked by the drizzle, he looked slick and polished—he was the perfect man to run Homicide in the Financial District. He was also a good cop, though Carlucci thought that politics held way too high a priority for him. He looked down at Morgan's shoes; they probably *were* expensive Italian leather, but it was hard to tell with all the mud smeared over them.

"What are you looking at, Frank?"

Carlucci looked up. "Your shoes."

Morgan made a snorting sound. "They're probably ruined." Then, voice hard, "I want this case, Frank."

Carlucci shook his head firmly. "It's not your jurisdiction, B.J. It's not even close."

"You know who the victim is?"

"Yes."

"Her father is head of Mishima Investments, for Christ's sake. She worked for them, too. Mishima is my jurisdiction."

"If she'd been killed in the Mishima building, I'd agree completely. But she wasn't. We're miles from the Financial District, B.J."

"Maybe she *was* killed in the district, and her body dumped here."

Carlucci just shook his head, not bothering to respond.

Morgan pointed back up the slope at the limousine parked above them. "You know who's in that limo?"

"Yoshi Katsuda, would be my guess."

"Damn fucking right, Frank. He's her father, and he wants me to run the investigation. He knows me, he knows the teams that work in the Financial District, he knows we'll be discreet."

"I don't care," Carlucci said. "And I won't even be insulted by that. It's not your jurisdiction."

"You afraid I'll ghost the case? Find out who did it and let Katsuda work his own family justice?"

"It's not yours to ghost, B.J., so I don't think anything."

"You want to tell that to Yoshi Katsuda? Tell him you're ignoring his wishes?"

"If I have to."

"He's a powerful man, Frank, you know that. He could make your job a misery."

"I just don't give a shit."

Morgan didn't say anything for a minute, staring hard at Carlucci. Warsinske had come out from behind Morgan, but still hung back, waiting to see how all this was going to play out.

"And what if I go to Vaughn?" Morgan asked.

"He might give you the case. And he might not. Either way I'll raise a big fucking stink about it, and what will Yoshi Katsuda think about that?"

Morgan went silent again. He looked away from Carlucci, gazed at the people clustered around the body, then slowly turned to look up the hill at the limousine. Still no one had emerged from the limo, and Carlucci wondered if

Yoshi Katsuda was staring down at them right now through the smoked windows. Or was he sitting calmly in the rear seat, eyes straight ahead, not really seeing anything, just waiting for Morgan to come and talk to him? Carlucci almost felt sorry for Morgan.

"We can work out some kind of cooperative arrangement," Carlucci finally said. He could play some politics, too, when he had to. He was probably going to need Morgan's help with this.

Morgan turned back to him. "In what sense?"

"Santos and Weather have caught this one. They'll need to do interviews with people at Mishima, maybe other people in the Financial District. If you help slick the way for them, I'll keep you regularly informed of the progress on the case. And then if you want, you can keep Katsuda up to date."

Morgan hesitated for a few moments, then sighed. "Sure, that could work. And you won't hold anything back from me?"

"Of course I will," Carlucci replied. "If I think it's necessary. But I'll give you enough."

Morgan smiled, shaking his head. "You know, Frank, it's a fucking miracle they made you lieutenant. I wish I knew what you had on the bastards."

"It's not like that, B.J."

"Yeah, yeah, yeah." He sighed again. "Okay, I guess that's about as good as it's going to get, isn't it?"

"Yes." Carlucci tipped his head toward the limousine. "You want me to talk to Katsuda?"

"No. I'll explain our 'cooperative arrangement.' I'll be able to do a better job of selling it to him than you would." They shook hands. "I'll be in touch, Frank. You too, all right?"

"I will, B.J."

Morgan turned and started up the hill, Warsinske just a few steps behind, scrambling after his boss like a sycophant. Warsinske would get his one day, Carlucci thought. Karma would catch up to the little ferret and bury him.

Carlucci turned and headed back toward the body.

•   •   •

That night, after dinner, Andrea made a pot of decaf and poured cups for both of them. Carlucci took his to the stove, opened the upper cabinet, and took out a bottle of Irish whiskey. He poured a good slug into his coffee, trying not to look at Andrea, who was almost certainly watching him. He sipped at the coffee, savoring both kinds of heat as they slid down his throat and into his stomach, like soothing liquid fire. He took one more long swallow, and finally turned around. Andrea was already gone from the kitchen; he followed her into the front room.

She was sitting in her chair, table lamp on beside her, a book open in her lap, reading glasses perched on the end of her nose. Carlucci crossed the room to his ancient recliner, set his cup on the book stand beside the chair, and sat. The chair had been his father's, and the leather was as dark and worn as his father's face had been the last years of his life. Sitting in the chair always made him think of his father, and gave him a sense of comfort and security.

"Rough day?" Andrea was looking at him over the top of her glasses.

"Yeah. I'm beat." He took another sip of the coffee. "I was out at the Sutro Baths this afternoon. There was a dead woman down in the ruins." He paused, revisualizing the scene, the heavy drizzle and gray skies and the cops working around the body. Andrea didn't say anything; she'd been through this so many times, and years ago she had stopped saying things like, "How awful." Now she just listened and waited, let him talk about what he needed to get out. It was something he greatly appreciated.

"I've got a real bad feeling about this one," he continued. "I had just talked to the woman a couple of weeks ago." He decided not to mention Caroline's part in the story. "I had asked her about a group of people I was looking into for a small thing at work, a missing persons I was checking out for a friend. But she wouldn't tell me anything, though it was obvious she knew something about this group." He paused, thinking back to the conversation, trying to remember her words. "She told me to come back and talk to her when people started dying."

Andrea took off her glasses and laid them on her book. "What did she mean by that?"

"I have no idea. She said I'd know what she was talking about when it happened. But I don't think she meant this. I can't exactly talk to her again now, can I?"

Neither of them spoke for a while. He took another long drink, but the whiskey didn't really seem to be helping much.

"While I was out there," he resumed, "I was standing up on the road, and I looked over at the Cliff House, and I couldn't help thinking about that day."

Andrea didn't reply immediately. She seemed almost frozen, staring at him, not even blinking. She closed her eyes for a moment, then looked at him again. "Frank, that was nine years ago."

"I know. But do you think I'll ever forget?" She didn't answer, and he shook his head. "I'm sorry, I'm giving you the wrong idea. It was a bad day. I mean, today was a bad day, and I want you to know I'd have a harder time getting through days like this without you. I'm doing a lousy job of it, but what I'm trying to tell you is, I love you, Andrea, and I'm glad you're here with me."

She sighed and gave him a soft, warm smile. But she didn't say anything. She didn't need to. Neither of them did.

CHAPTER 9

This night, Caroline entered the DMZ well after dark. Not a smart thing to do, but she didn't care. Let the street scavengers swoop down on her and pick her clean. What the hell did it matter?

Two days of rain had given way to a mild heat wave. The temperature climbed into the eighties during the day, and didn't cool off much at night. It was still spring, so the heat wasn't too bad, but right now it was probably still above seventy, and humidity was fairly high. She liked this kind of weather.

The street was a mindless swarm of people and vehicles, flashing colored lights and barking voices, competing blasts of alarms and pounding music, all infused with the stench of weed smoke, spilled alcohol, rotting plants, and burning oil. She heard glass break nearby, an explosion of some kind, a hammering sound, then a loud braying laugh. Someone pawed at her face, and she knocked the hand away.

She wanted a drink. She wanted several drinks, but she didn't want to sweat and fight in the bars, so she went without.

Traffic was stopped at the intersection ahead, and a crowd had formed in the middle of the street. Feeling reckless, she climbed on the back of a bus stop bench to see what was happening, using a power pole for support. There was a large open space in the middle of the crowd, roughly circular, and inside it were three men in wire head-cages, bare from the waist up and all three lightning-leashed to their handlers. Caroline thought she recognized the stocky woman handler on the far side of the circle, the one she'd run into two weeks ago on her way to see Tito. The handler was shouting through the head-cage at her charge, presumably giving him instructions.

The crowd around the three men and their handlers was growing, and people were climbing onto stalled and parked vehicles, sidewalk stands, balconies, anything that afforded a better view. Before long, Caroline's own view would be completely blocked. Just as well, she thought, she didn't really want to see this. She knew what was coming—she could already hear the betting begin.

The three men were roped together in a kind of circle, or rough triangle, fewer than ten feet of rope between each of them; each man remained leashed to his handler, and the collars around their necks shimmered with electricity.

A man in body armor went to each of the head-caged men and slapped dermal patches onto their necks, half a dozen to each—probably crashers, deadeners, and skyrockets. Within minutes, the three men in head-cages would be completely wired and crazed. Finally, a set of metal hand-claws was strapped onto the right arm and hand of each man. They would tear each other apart.

That was enough for Caroline. She climbed down from the bench and pushed into the crowd, working her way toward the buildings until she could get past the intersection. A frenzied roar swelled from the crowd, and she knew it had begun.

Once past the intersection, the crowds thinned, but the sidewalk was still full and hectic. A man bleeding profusely from a head wound staggered toward her, hissing at her as he went by. Two teenaged tattoo-girls shuffled along a few feet in front of her, arms wrapped around one another, their ponytails laced together with wire webbing. A rat pack ten or twelve strong marched steadfastly along the sidewalk, forcing people to move out of its way. Caroline got jammed up against a pokey booth; the gooner inside grinned and breathed a foul, warm stench into her face, nauseating her.

Finally the rat pack swept past, the pressure eased, and she pushed away from the booth.

She walked along in a kind of daze, hardly paying attention to her surroundings, almost unconsciously fending off the hasslers and pervs. She just didn't feel much of anything.

She had been in this numb and dazed state of mind almost constantly since the night Tina had come by. She couldn't shake it, and most of the time she didn't even *want* to shake it. Most of the time she just didn't care.

In the years since the Gould's Syndrome had been diagnosed, Caroline had thought she'd come to terms with the disease. She knew its activation was inevitable, she knew it was ultimately terminal, and she had thought she had come to terms with the fear and the dread, and the self-pity.

Clearly she hadn't.

She'd been fooled, it seemed, because in all these years, other than developing a tendency to tire easily, the Gould's had not gone active. The markers had been picked up in a routine screening, and she'd been informed of what they meant. She had been given all the details of the disease, including the possible and probable ways it would progress once it had gone active, and she'd been told what the ultimate prognosis was. She'd known she would have several years before it went fully active, before the myelin sheathing of her central nervous system would begin to degenerate in earnest, but she'd also known that it was unlikely she would live to see thirty, and that no one with Gould's had ever lived past thirty-two. And she'd known there was no treatment for it, no cure. She'd known all that.

But apparently, in some deep and real way, she hadn't.

When the vision in her eye had gone funny and she'd lost control of her leg and sprawled to the floor, *then* she had known.

She was scared now, and she didn't want to be scared. And she was afraid she would never be able to get away from that fear.

She had stopped walking, and now stood at the inner

edge of the sidewalk, leaning against a building wall. How long had she been standing here, people moving past her? She looked up, saw the sign for Turtle Joe's just above her head, and nodded to herself; probably this was where she'd been headed all along.

She walked past Turtle Joe's and turned into the alcove entrance to the death house. Everything looked the same: the crude red skull-and-crossbones, the grille over the heavy wooden door, the cracked brick and crumbling mortar of the arch and walls, the chipped and cracked and stained marble flagstones under her feet. Caroline pushed the door open, stepped inside, and closed the door behind her.

Quiet and dim light. Familiar smell of damp and sickness, and something acrid, almost burning her nose. The lobby was empty.

She took the stairs slowly, one deliberate step at a time, keeping her attention on her feet. Since that night with Tina her vision had been fine, and she hadn't lost control of her leg again, but she knew it could happen at any time, and she spent much of her time *waiting* for it to happen again. She couldn't help herself.

When she reached the third-floor landing, she didn't need to rest; instead, she kept right on walking down the hall toward Tito's old room. The black door looked just the same. But everything was so quiet she imagined that if she unlocked the door and found Tito inside, it would only be if he were already dead, lying on the floor, eyes open, waiting for someone to come and take him away.

She unlocked the dead bolt, then put her key in the knob, turned it, and pushed the door inward. There were lights on inside the room, and she froze, the door only half open. She remained motionless, listening, but didn't hear anything. Her heart was beating fast and hard, and her mouth went dry.

"Tito?" she ventured. She slid the key out of the knob, gripped it tightly in her right hand.

There was a slight rustle, then a soft, timid voice. "Who is it?" A woman's voice.

Caroline stepped carefully around the door. Huddled against the far wall, on the mattress that had served as Tito's bed, were a woman and a young girl. The woman appeared to be in her thirties, and the girl about nine or ten. Both had straight, dirty blond hair and dark blue eyes, both were dressed in T-shirts and jeans. Both of them looked scared.

"It's all right," Caroline said. "I'm sorry, I didn't mean to . . ."

"Do you live here?" the woman asked. "We were told the room was empty."

"No. I had a friend who lived here. He's been gone for a while."

"Is he coming back?" The woman coughed, glanced at the girl, then turned back to Caroline. "We don't have anywhere else to go."

Caroline breathed in very deeply, held it for a few moments, then slowly let it out, shaking her head. "No." The truth of that sank into her completely for the first time. "No, he won't be back. You can stay here." Exhaustion washed over her, combining with the earlier numbness, and she wanted to lie down on Tito's old sofa, go to sleep, and not wake up for days. "I'm sorry I bothered you," she said to the woman and the girl. "I'll just go."

"Wait," the woman said. "Can we . . . can we have your key?" She pointed at the key in Caroline's hand. "We can lock the door when we're inside, but we can't lock it when we leave. No one had a key."

Caroline nodded. She crossed the room and handed the key to the woman, wondering if the woman was contagious, wondering why she cared. The woman thanked her. Then, feeling awkward, Caroline asked, "Why are you here?"

"We don't have anyplace else to go," the woman said. "We haven't got much money."

"No, I meant . . ." She shook her head. "I'm sorry, just . . ." She tried to wave it off. What was she thinking? What was wrong with her? Leave these poor people alone. She started to turn away, but the woman reached out and touched her arm.

"My daughter's dying," the woman said.

Caroline looked at the young girl. She didn't look sick. Tired, maybe, and hungry, but not sick. But then I don't look sick either, she thought.

"I'm sorry," she said again. "Do you have any money?" A stupid question, she realized as soon as she asked. If the woman had any money she wouldn't be here with her daughter in this godforsaken death house.

"A little," the woman said. Probably a lie.

"Food?"

"The Sisters bring us meals."

They had nothing. Caroline looked around the room, saw an open suitcase with a few clothes, a few children's books on the sofa, but nothing else that hadn't been left behind by Mouse.

"Is there something I can do to help?" Caroline asked.

The woman didn't answer. Caroline knew she was not doing this very well. She looked back and forth between the woman and the girl, feeling cold and afraid again. "I'm dying too," she finally said.

No one said anything for a long time. Eventually the girl said, "Can you help us?"

Caroline looked at the woman. "Something," she said. "If you want me to."

The girl nodded. Her mother just said, "There's some tea here. Would you like some?"

Tito's herb teas. Nobody thought they were worth stealing. "Sure," she said, smiling. "That would be nice."

The little girl smiled back.

CHAPTER 10

"I feel like shit," Nikki said.

She was sitting in a black plastic chair by an open window in her apartment, her head resting against the wooden frame, eyes closed. Cage stood just inside the front door, watching her. The air was warm and stuffy, and stank of burned food.

"Why aren't you in bed?" he asked.

She gave him a tired smile and opened one eye. "I'm not that sick. I just feel crappy." She closed her eye. "I was heating up some soup and nodded off. I burned it."

The apartment was a fairly large one-room studio, with a separate kitchen alcove, and a full bath off the back corner. There wasn't much furniture. Nikki slept in a sleeping bag on an old cot, and she ate on a sheet of plywood laid across stacks of plastic crates. There was a single stuffed chair beside a floor lamp, where she read at night, and several black plastic chairs she used when working at her tapestry looms. All three of the vertical looms were set up now, two with tapestries just begun, the other with one nearing completion. She'd been working on this last one for well over a year, and like most of her tapestries it incorporated both Native American and Native African motifs, heavily abstracted; hundreds of colored threads dangled from the back of the loom.

"Have you eaten anything today?" Cage asked.

Nikki shook her head, dreadlock beads clicking against the window frame with each movement.

"Want me to cook you something?"

"Soup?" Nikki said, smiling again.

"Sure. Soup."

He crossed the room to the kitchen alcove, glanced at the pot of burned soup soaking in the sink, then opened the cupboard under the counter and dug around for another pot.

"Soup's above the stove," she said.

The upper cupboard was pretty well stocked with canned goods, though about half of it was cat food. Nikki fed the neighborhood strays down in the alley. She was allergic to cat dander, so she couldn't keep any cats in the apartment for herself.

Cage took down a can of chicken soup with rice and vegetables. "Chicken soup," he said. "Best thing for you."

"Yeah, yeah."

He opened the can, poured the contents into the pot, then turned on the burner and set the flame low. He stirred the soup a few times, then left it and walked back across the room, sitting in one of the plastic chairs a few feet from Nikki.

"Do you have a fever?"

She nodded, the sun flashing off her cheek inlays. "Not bad, though. Just over a hundred."

"You take anything for it?"

"Of course."

"What else? Sore throat, muscle aches?"

"Sore throat and a nasty goddamn headache." She grimaced. "That's all."

"Bad cold," Cage said. "Maybe some kind of flu."

"Yeah, probably." She opened both eyes, raised her head a bit, and looked at him. "You hear anything about Stinger?"

Cage shook his head. He wished he could say something to make her forget about Stinger, but he knew it wasn't possible. He couldn't forget about it himself—he kept seeing those injected eyes and the blood on Nikki's finger hooks, kept smelling that awful breath. And he kept hearing the fear in Tiger's voice. At least Nikki hadn't heard Tiger's story.

He scooted the chair right up to her, reached out and raised her chin, then felt her neck with his fingers. "Lymph nodes a bit swollen, but not too bad."

"Of course they're swollen."

He tipped her head so the sunlight fell directly on her face. He looked into her eyes and felt relieved; they were bright and clear, with no signs of hemorrhage. "Open your mouth and try to work your tongue down." She did; he made a slight adjustment of the angle and got a fairly good look at her throat. A little red, but it looked okay. He nodded and let her go. "You look all right. You might feel lousy for a week or two, but you know what to do." He smiled. "And I'll stop by regularly to see how you're doing, give you a hand."

"Thanks, Mom."

Cage got up, went into the bathroom, and washed his hands thoroughly with cidal soap. She was going to be fine. He returned to the stove and checked on the soup; steam was rising from the pot.

"Soup's ready," he said. "Come on over to the table."

"I think I'll just eat here," Nikki said.

Cage poured soup into a bowl, got a spoon and napkin, took it over to her. He set the bowl on the windowsill, spoon and napkin beside it.

"Thanks," Nikki said.

"Anything else I can get you? Something to drink?"

"No, that's all right. I'll make tea later."

"You want me to bring you something from the clinic? I'm going there now."

"This is supposed to be your day off, Cage."

"Madelaine's shorthanded today."

"You're always shorthanded at the clinic. Seven days a week."

He shrugged. "I'm just going by to check in, see how things are. I won't stay long."

Nikki snorted. She spooned some soup into her mouth. "Thanks again. It's good."

"So. Anything from the clinic?"

"No, Cage. I'm not dying. I'll be fine."

"I'll see you later, then."

She nodded and waved her spoon at him. He turned and left.

The RadioLand Street Clinic was on the ground floor of an old brick apartment building, half a block from the Core and in the vague and blurred border between the Latin and Euro quarters of the Tenderloin. The clinic was flanked by a Nightgames arcade on one side, and a head juicer shop on the other. Above it were three floors of hooker suites, and above that six floors of overcrowded apartments. Cage's own apartment was on the fourth floor, with the hookers—he got free rent and irregular meals in exchange for providing the women with free medical care.

Madelaine and the crew were holding their own. She looked tired, but she smiled when she saw Cage come in through the clinic door, and shook her head.

"Get out of here," she told him. "This is your day off."

There were maybe fifteen people waiting, sitting on the chairs, benches, and old collapsing sofas scattered through the room. About half of them looked quite ill; all of them looked dead poor. Only five or six children, though. Often there were twice this many people waiting for medical attention, so this was a pretty quiet day.

Franzee, a short, chunky, and very pretty redhead, kept the clinic running, working as nurse, clerk, and office manager; she was kneeling in front of an old man, talking to him and making notes. Buck, the clinic errand boy, was moving a gurney down the left hallway. And Madelaine stood behind the main counter, one hand resting on a stack of folders, the other holding a ceramic cup with bright red letters on the side saying, "DOCTORS AREN'T GODS. NOT EVEN CLOSE." The cup would be full of god-awful herb tea that smelled nearly as bad as it tasted. Madelaine was tall and thin, closing in on fifty, her hair almost completely white. She'd been working street clinics for more than thirteen years, and it never seemed to get her down, which amazed Cage. The clinic work got *him* down all the time.

A young woman came out of one of the examination rooms and gazed hollowly at him. Her face was drawn, her eyes dark and sunken. A gauze bandage was taped to her inner arm, probably over an IV shunt. The young woman approached the counter, gaze shifting from Cage to Madelaine.

"Vashti, remember," Madelaine said, her voice soft but firm. "Try to drink a lot of fluids. Water, herb teas, soup, juices, whatever. But more important . . . we'll send Buck over later today with a case of IV fluids. Do a bag every hour, like I showed you, all right? And if you start to feel worse, come back in. Call us if you have to, okay? If you can't get here one of us will come see you."

Vashti nodded, then turned and walked slowly out of the clinic.

Madelaine sighed. "Third probable cholera case today," she told Cage. "We'll know for sure later this afternoon, but I wouldn't bet against it. We may be in for another epidemic this summer."

"Christ," Cage said. "Sometimes I think we're living in a goddamn Third World country."

Madelaine smiled. "Face it, Ry, most of the U.S. *is* a Third World country these days." She shook her head. "Come on, get out of here. Paul's coming by to help for a few hours, we'll be falling over each other."

"When's he coming in?"

"About an hour."

"Maybe I'll just stay until he gets here, help you get through these people." Franzee was leading the old man into the examination room from which Vashti had just emerged.

"Ry, we don't need you. It's a beautiful day, go somewhere and relax. Get the hell out of the Tenderloin, go have a good time."

Cage smiled and nodded, giving in. "Yeah, I guess I will. All right, I'll . . ." He stopped, seeing Madelaine's eyes widen and her face tense.

"What the hell . . . ?" Her voice trailed off.

Cage turned around. Just inside the clinic doors was a man who could barely stand. He was Hispanic, Cage guessed, but it was hard to know for sure with all the large, bright red patches blazing across his skin. The man groaned, staggered a few steps, his movements palsied and unsure, eyes blinking frantically.

Before Cage could moved toward him, the man dropped to his knees, then lunged forward and vomited blood across the waiting-room floor. Someone screamed and people scattered, trying to get as far from the man as possible. Cage couldn't tell if any of them had been splashed. Then the man vomited again, pitched forward, and collapsed in his own blood.

Cage ran behind the counter, where Madelaine was already pulling out gloves, masks, and oversuits. They both suited up, pulled on gloves and masks and booties—they were going to have to walk through the blood just to get to the man.

"Franzee!" Madelaine shouted. "Get the KillSpray! Now!"

Cage and Madelaine hurried to the man and knelt beside him. They turned him over and checked his air passage; it seemed to be clear, and the man was breathing almost normally. They rolled him onto his side so he wouldn't choke to death if he vomited again, and Madelaine checked his eyes while Cage checked the pulse. The man's heartbeat was strong, but fast, maybe a little irregular; nothing too serious yet. He glanced up at the man's face as Madelaine was shining a penlight into the man's left eye. The eye was severely injected, the vessels gorged and broken. Like Stinger?

"He needs to be in a freaking hospital," Madelaine said. She was just talking. They both knew no hospital would take him now; most would have dragged him out onto the street even if he'd collapsed inside their emergency rooms. No hospital would take him in, and no ambulance would pick him up unless he had a wad of cash or a nice fat insurance chip on him, and Cage was pretty damn sure the

man didn't have either; that meant "no" for any of the
private clinics. Only the organ scavengers would be willing
to take him.

"The iso rooms?" Cage asked.

"Both empty. Let's go."

They picked the man up between them, Cage under the
man's arms, Madelaine under the knees. The man was out.
Franzee had suited up and started spraying down the bloody
floor with the KillSpray, filling the room with the smell of
bleach and sour lemon. Buck was suited up right behind
her, dragging in the cleaners. Half of the people who had
been waiting were gone; those who remained huddled in
one corner of the room, watching with fear or exhausted
complacence.

Cage and Madelaine carried the man through the waiting
room, along the right corridor, and into the first isolation
room. They laid him out on the bed and pulled his shirt
off. Cage slapped vitals strips across the man's chest and
arm and connected them to the wall-mounted monitors,
which would give them heart rate, O_2 and CO_2 levels, and
a running blood pressure. He grabbed a b.p. cuff to get the
man's pressure; Madelaine started on a temp and went to
work with a stethoscope on the man's chest.

"One-oh-five over fifty-five," Cage said. "No problem
there."

Madelaine frowned. "Pulse is okay, but his temp's a
hundred and six. Shit." Then she squeezed the tip of his
finger, and they watched. Cap fill time was almost five seconds. Frown deepening, she said, "Let's get him on oxygen. His blood volume's crap right now."

Cage reached around the bed rail and pulled out a non-
rebreather mask, stretched the line, then worked the mask
over the man's face and turned on the oxygen.

They stood back a moment and looked at the man. His
skin was almost completely covered with red rashes, the
kind that were bleeding into the skin, and was peeling off
around the nails. Almost all the lymph nodes were noticeably swollen, even those by his elbows.

"I want to get some blood work done on him immediately," Madelaine said. "I know, we can't do shit here, but we have Patricia do what she can. CBC and diff, general tox screen, whatever. And I want to get a drip going, normal saline, and run some Chill and mycosatrine into it. And get some hemo going into him. Who knows how much blood he's lost." She looked at Cage. "What do you think?"

He nodded. "Sounds good. The mycosatrine can't hurt, but I wouldn't count on it helping any."

Madelaine nodded. "But it *could* be bacterial."

Cage shrugged. "It's *something* infectious. Something nasty." He shook his head. "Maybe viral."

"What? Some hemorrhagic fever?"

"Christ, I hope not. But I've heard about another similar case right here in the Tenderloin, a lot of the same symptoms. I don't know." He kept seeing Stinger's injected eyes, kept thinking about Tiger's story and his description of Stinger, the red patches all over his skin, vomiting blood. Stinger's symptoms seemed awfully close to those of the man lying on the bed in front of him, and they were only half a block from the Core. And Cage could not get Nikki out of his mind. A bad cold or flu, he told himself again.

"Okay, let's see if he's chipped." Madelaine pulled the scanner from the portable diagnostics, got on-line, then pressed the scanner to the man's shoulder and shifted it around. The scanner beeped, and Madelaine said, "I'll be damned." She turned to the monitor as the info came up on the screen. "Tito Moraleja," she read. "Mexican national, expired residency permit. Great. He's got AIDS. No known medical allergies."

Cage shook his head and waved at the rashed and fevered body in front of him. "It isn't the AIDS that's doing this to him."

"No," Madelaine said. "But it's not going to help him fight this, whatever the hell it is."

Cage stared down at the man, then looked up at Madelaine. "He's going to die."

Madelaine nodded without looking at him. "Okay, Ry. Let's draw some blood, get the drip going, the hemo. But don't use too much of anything that might be crucial to someone else." She sighed heavily. "Then let's get cleaned up and out of here. I've got other people to take care of."

An hour later, the clinic was almost back to normal. Paul Cardenas, the third regular clinic doctor, had arrived, and Patricia, the med tech, was in the tiny makeshift lab in back, running Tito Moraleja's blood work. The waiting room still smelled of bleach, but it was clean. Madelaine had tried to get Cage to leave, but he wanted to stick around and see if anything turned up with Tito's blood.

He was sitting in one of the waiting-room chairs, drinking coffee and listening to a middle-aged woman mumble incoherently at him, when the phone rang. Franzee answered it, talked to someone for a minute, looked up the corridors at the closed examination-room doors, then over at Cage.

"You want to talk to this guy?" she asked. "He's a cop. He wants to talk to someone who's in charge here."

"*You* talk to him, Franzee, you're always in charge. You run this place."

Franzee scowled. "Very funny, Dr. Cage." She held up the receiver. "Now, you want to talk to him, or you want me to go bust in on Dr. Samione or Dr. Cardenas?"

Cage got up from the chair; the woman didn't stop mumbling. "I'll talk to him." He put his coffee cup on the counter and took the phone from Franzee. "This is Dr. Cage."

"Dr. Cage, this is Lieutenant Carlucci, with the San Francisco Police Department."

"Yeah? Is there a problem?"

"About an hour ago you ran an ID scan on someone. Tito Moraleja."

"That's right."

"Was he a patient?"

Cage hesitated, wondering what this was about. He'd never been a big fan of cops. But he went ahead and answered. "Yes, a patient."

"I don't suppose there's any chance he's still there?" The man didn't sound hopeful.

Cage hesitated again, even considered lying. But he just didn't have the strength for it right now. "Yes, he's still here."

"He is?"

"That's what I said."

"Would you be able to keep him there for a while? Not by force . . . uh, you could tell him Caroline's looking for him, that her father . . ."

"He's not going anywhere, Lieutenant. He's critically ill, and we've got him in an isolation room."

"I'll be there as soon as I can."

"What's this all about?" Cage asked. But the lieutenant had already chopped the connection. Cage handed the receiver back to Franzee. "I guess he's coming here to see our mystery patient."

"Maybe he'll get the guy into a hospital," Franzee said.

Cage snorted. "Not fuckin' likely. Probably a jail cell."

A patient alarm went off behind the counter, a high-pitched squeal. Cage bent over the counter, but couldn't see the panel. "Who is it?" he shouted at Franzee, already knowing.

"The mystery man!"

"Goddamnit." And he was at it again, hurrying around the counter and grabbing the suit Franzee handed him, ignoring the booties, jamming hands into gloves as Franzee tied the mask behind his head. Then he was running to the isolation room and crashing through the door.

The mystery man, Tito Moraleja, was convulsing violently. Tonic clonic, rocking the bed. The IVs had been ripped out of the shunts, and his eyes were half open, eyeballs completely red now and rolled up under the lids. Cage moved to the man's side and grabbed his upper arms, holding him down so he wouldn't take a flier off the bed. Hold on and wait, he told himself.

Madelaine came through the door, hurried around to the other side of the bed. Franzee and Paul rushed in behind her.

"Let's get him intubated," Cage said. "We still got some paralytics?"

Franzee nodded. "Pavulon. I'll get it." She shook her head. "But we don't have anything else for a rapid sequence. Maybe a sedative." Then she was gone

Cage grabbed Tito's left arm, got an IV back into the shunt, which had, amazingly, stayed in the guy's arm. Franzee came back, and Madelaine first gave Tito a sedative, then injected the Pavulon. Almost immediately he stopped moving, though Cage knew that the poor bastard's brain was probably still seizing like mad; now they just weren't seeing it.

They got Tito intubated, then tried Ativan to stop the seizure. But the guy's vitals were bad—the fever was spiking, blood pressure was dropping. Then *bam,* he went into cardiac arrest before they could do a damn thing.

They worked hard on him. CPR, several shocks with the paddles, epinephrine and atropine; they did everything but crack him open. Cage even considered doing that, for about five seconds; here, that was an absurdity. But nothing worked, and fifteen minutes later it was over. Tito Moraleja was dead.

Madelaine looked up from the body, glanced at Cage, then turned to Franzee. "Get a blood tray over here now. Let's get some more blood out of him while we can, see if we can't find out what the hell it was that killed him."

"What we really need," Cage said, "is an autopsy."

"I know," Madelaine replied. "You're not suggesting we do it ourselves, are you? Here?" She cocked her head at him. "You're not *that* whacked, are you?"

Cage shook his head. "No. I know we can't do it. I just wish we knew someone who could. Or at least somewhere we could store the body."

Franzee came in with the blood tray. Madelaine took the syringe, lined it up just under and to the left of Tito's sternum, then plunged it in and up at an angle and right into the left ventricle of the heart. She got eight vials of blood out before it started clotting.

After the blood came nose, throat, and rectal swabs, and

finally a sample of the vitreous humor from the left eye for toxicology. Franzee and Paul left to label and store all the specimens.

Cage and Madelaine stood on either side of the bed, gazing down at the body.

"Any more ideas?" Madelaine asked.

Cage just shook his head. "Who do we know who can test for weird bugs and viruses?"

"Why the hell are you hung up on this thing?"

"Gut feeling. Some things I've seen recently. So, who do we know who could do it?"

"Unless Tito turns out to be someone rich and famous, no one. You still have connections to the CDC?"

"Yeah."

"Think you could get any of them to do something?"

"On the blood of a dead Mexican who had AIDS? Not a chance."

"That's what I thought."

Cage stepped back from the body. "But we keep the blood and the other stuff, even if we lose the body. I've got a bad feeling Tito isn't going to be the only one to die this way."

Franzee stuck her head into the room. "Dr. Cage? Lieutenant Carlucci is here to see you. And to see him." She pointed at Tito Moraleja's body.

Cage nodded. "Tell him I'll be right out."

Franzee let the door close. Cage looked at Madelaine. "Let's go tell the lieutenant the wonderful news."

CHAPTER 11

The RadioLand Street Clinic smelled of bleach, sour lemon, unwashed bodies, and the faint, cutting aroma of incense. A weird mix, Carlucci thought, but strangely not unpleasant. He stood at the counter, sweating, waiting for the doctors, hip and elbow against the rough plastic. A dozen people sat around the stifling waiting room, and most of them looked pretty sick. None of them looked at him; they probably didn't like cops. He imagined they had good reason for the sentiment.

Carlucci was damn glad he didn't have to come to a place like this for his own health care. The Police Department had its own fully staffed, fully equipped clinic and hospital, which made being a cop a highly desirable job, despite the risks and the bad hours and the low pay. Most of these people, on the other hand, were probably happy to have *any* kind of place to come to.

A man and a woman emerged from a doorway along the right hall and proceeded to strip off gloves and suits, tossing them into a molded plastic container built into the wall. The woman was older, her hair almost completely white, and her thin face was striking—still quite handsome. The man was probably in his thirties, though his hair had some pretty good streaks of gray. Carlucci could buy the woman as a doctor, but this other guy, with his faded black denims and boots and color-slashed T-shirt and neck tattoo—even if the tattoo *was* a caduceus—couldn't be. A street medico, maybe. The two of them approached the counter, and the man put out his hand.

"Lieutenant? I'm Dr. Cage, I talked to you on the phone. This is Dr. Samione."

Dr. Cage. Carlucci shook hands with each of them. Then the man said, "Madelaine, I'll talk to him about all this."

The woman smiled and nodded. "He's all yours, Ry."

Dr. Cage turned to Carlucci and raised an eyebrow. "You want to see him?"

Carlucci nodded. "Sure."

"Follow me." The young man led the way back along the corridor, then stopped in front of a large glass observation window.

Carlucci looked inside the room. A figure lay on the bed, sheets and blankets thrown back and bunched across his legs, his upper body and face exposed. The man's eyes were closed, but his mouth was open, rigid in a silent scream; his dark skin was covered with enormous red patches and blistered welts, spotted with blood.

"Dead?"

"Dead," the young man replied.

"He had AIDS," Carlucci said.

"It wasn't AIDS that killed him."

Carlucci nodded, but didn't say anything. He had a feeling there was more to come, and that he wasn't going to like it.

"So, is that Tito Moraleja?"

Carlucci shrugged. "I suppose. I've never seen him before. He was a friend of my daughter's."

Dr. Cage breathed in deeply, then slowly and loudly let it back out. "So you weren't planning on throwing him into a cell."

"No."

"I think we need to talk about this."

"All right, Dr. Cage."

"Just call me Cage. And let's go on back to the staff lounge." Cage smiled to himself. He continued along the corridor, and Carlucci followed after taking one more long look at the body of Tito Moraleja.

The "staff lounge" was a small, cramped room with a
table and chairs, cheap plywood cabinets, a countertop
stove, three or four cots stacked on top of each other with
pillows and blankets, and two large refrigerators. A couple
of Vornado fans circulated the hot, stuffy air, providing at
least the illusion of relief.

"Have a seat," Cage said. He went to the larger refrigerator, which was covered with black and white photos cut
from newspapers, magazines, or books. All of the pictures
showed people with the weirdest expressions on their faces,
all of them with food or drink in their hands. "You want
something to drink? A beer, Coke, or something?"

Carlucci sat in one of the hard, wooden chairs. "A beer
would be great," he said.

Cage opened the refrigerator. Inside, the shelves were
packed with labeled vials and jars and tubes and plastic
bags, blood and fluids and drugs. On the bottom shelf were
bottles of beer and soft drinks. Cage pulled out two bottles
of Black Orbit, closed the refrigerator, and brought the beer
to the table, handing a bottle to Carlucci. The cap was a
twist-off; the beer was cold and very bitter.

"It's not that good," Cage said, grinning, "but it's
cheap."

Carlucci sipped at the beer, watching the young man
across the table from him. Dr. Cage. Cage. He wasn't sure
why it surprised him. Appearances had never meant that
much to him. Cage was probably a good doctor; his heart
was in the right place if he worked here, and the people
who came to this clinic were probably damn lucky to have
him.

"Why did he die?" Carlucci finally asked.

Cage shrugged. "No idea. But I'd sure like to know. It
worries me. I was hoping you knew him. I don't suppose
you have any idea where he's been the past couple of
weeks, do you?"

Carlucci shook his head. "I've been looking for him all
that time."

"Why?"

"I told you. He was a friend of my daughter's. He was

living in a death house in the DMZ. She went to see him one day, and he was gone. There were indications he'd been abducted.''

Cage sat back in his chair, staring at him. ''By whom?''

Carlucci hesitated, then said, ''No one knows.''

''So your daughter doesn't know where he's been, either.''

''No.''

Cage shook his head. ''Shit,'' he said, so quietly Carlucci barely heard him. ''I'd like to find out what killed him, and where the hell he picked it up.''

''Can't you do tests?'' Carlucci asked. ''An autopsy.''

Cage snorted. ''Look at this place. We've got a half-assed lab in back where we can do simple blood work, and simple almost certainly isn't going to tell us what killed Tito. We could send the work out to a real lab, but we don't have the money for that, and even that might not do shit anyway—it's all a goddamn shot in the dark. We've got *no* facilities to do an autopsy, there's absolutely *no* way we could get anyone else to do it, and we've got no way to keep the body here. Unless we find some relative or friend willing to foot the bill in the next few hours, we'll have to haul him to one of the crematoriums.'' He took a long drink from his beer, shaking his head; as he swallowed, the tattooed snakes seemed to writhe around the staff. ''We *will* keep the blood and other samples in case anyone else turns up dead like him, but that's all we can do for now.''

Carlucci felt like he was being invited to ask the question, and so he did. ''You think someone else will die like Tito?''

''Oh, sure, somewhere, someday. I've heard something about a similar case around here a while ago. But *I* probably won't see another one. It'll probably remain a mystery, like a lot of other deaths. People die all the time in this city from unknown causes, just like they die all the time from conditions or diseases we can prevent or easily treat. It's a disgrace, but that's the reality.''

Carlucci nodded, more to himself than to Cage. There

was something disingenuous about what Cage had just said,
about the way he'd said it. And Carlucci thought about
what he would tell Caroline. She would want to know
more. She would want to know who had taken Tito, and
why, and she would want to know what it was that had
killed him.

He looked across the table at Cage. The man was a doctor working in a street clinic in the heart of the Tenderloin,
close to the streets. No, a *part* of the streets, out on the
edges. And Carlucci was certain Cage was holding something back from him. He wondered if this was a kind of
game they were playing, sending out feelers, testing for
responses. He hesitated, reluctant to take the next step, but
wondered what the hell he had to lose.

"You ever hear of Cancer Cell?" he finally asked.

Cage didn't move, but Carlucci saw something in the
man's eyes, a brief widening of the pupils, a slight tensing
of muscles, and he felt a shiver of satisfaction, knowing
he'd been right.

Cage's mouth worked into just a touch of a smile. "Now
why the *hell* do you ask me that?"

"You *have* heard of them."

"Let's say I have. Why are you asking?"

Carlucci hesitated again, then almost laughed at himself,
at the absurdity. "Caroline, my daughter, said there was
someone who saw Tito's abduction, and this guy thought
Cancer Cell had something to do with it. That's all I know.
I've heard of Cancer Cell, but I don't really know anything
about them."

This time it was Cage who seemed to be evaluating Carlucci, trying to make a judgment. He pushed back from the
table, stood, and grabbed his bottle of Black Orbit, then
walked over to the counter and leaned against it, looking
at him. Carlucci returned the gaze, waiting for the man to
speak. Suddenly his stomach churned, and he knew Cage
was going to say something that would change how he saw
Tito's death, something that would change the coming
weeks of his life. He wanted to stand up right now and

walk out of the room and leave all this behind him. But he stayed.

Cage brought the bottle to his mouth, tipped it back, and drained the rest of the beer. He set the bottle on the counter and wiped his mouth with the back of his hand.

"I saw a guy two and half weeks ago," he said. "He looked and smelled sick. I haven't seen him since, but I just talked to someone who said this guy was in real bad shape, probably dying. Symptoms sounded a lot like Tito here." He paused, almost smiling, though Carlucci was sure it wasn't from amusement. "Thing is this," Cage continued. "This guy who's dying, who's probably dead by now, this guy worked for Cancer Cell."

Neither of them spoke for a while. The connection was obvious, but what did it really mean? Anything? Even if Tito and this other guy died from the same thing, did Carlucci have any business pursuing it? Tito was dead, and Carlucci's search for him was over. There was no evidence of a crime other than the original abduction, and even that was pretty shaky. Besides, it was just a dead Mexican who'd been living in a death house and would have died of AIDS pretty soon anyway, right? Who gave a shit?

Carlucci gave a shit, that was who, and so did Caroline. And then there was Naomi Katsuda, who definitely *had* been murdered and had the initials "CC" carved into her forehead, who had been a potential source of information about Cancer Cell and had told him to come back to her when people started dying.

It was all too much to walk away from. Carlucci felt a great weariness wash over him, settling in his bones. Whatever this all was, it was going to be a long, long haul, and none of it was going to be easy.

It was Cage, though, who broke the silence.

"I watch for disease," he said. "We've got so much of it these days. I look for patterns and strange occurrences and the signs of something deadly about to break out into the population." He shrugged. "I'm a doctor. It's not such a great time being a doctor. Or maybe the best time of all, there's so much work to do, so many people sick and dying

with so many things, and getting worse all the time. I've
given up much hope for reasonable large-scale prevention
in this city, this country—no one in power is willing to
spend the money. The wealthy, of course, are okay, but
they've always been good at taking care of themselves. But
for the rest of us, prevention's becoming a lost cause, with
water and air quality steadily deteriorating, increasing mal-
nutrition, decreasing health care resources . . . shit, I could
go on and on. Treatment's not a hell of a lot better anymore, with the same caveat for the rich. Though even if
you're rich and you get Chingala Fever or X-TB or Lassa
3 or half a dozen others, you're just as dead as the poor.
But the rich have a lot less exposure, and they're generally
healthier to begin with, and . . . and *blah blah blah.*'' Cage
laughed. ''Yeah, I know, I'm getting dangerously close to
making a speech here. The point is, I watch and worry
about shit like this, about two people dying from the same
awful disease I've never seen before, especially when
there's a connection to an outfit that does medical experimentation. And I worry that two is going to turn into a
much bigger number and it'll get out of control and there
will be dead people everywhere.''

You can come back to me when people are dying, Naomi
Katsuda had said.

''It's happened before in other countries,'' Cage went on,
''and it's come close to happening here a few times. It is
going to happen in this country someday, and it will probably come out of an area like this, like the Tenderloin, or
the DMZ, or the Mission, where there are so many poor
people crammed together with lousy health and lousy san-
itation. And so I worry when something like this happens.
It'll probably be nothing this time, but . . .'' He left it there
with a shrug.

''All right,'' Carlucci said. ''Then tell me about Cancer
Cell. Who the hell they are and why they worry you.''

Cage shook his head. ''*They* don't worry me, not exactly.
It's the connection to them that worries me, and that's not
quite the same thing.'' He looked at the empty Black Orbit
bottle, then at Carlucci. ''You want another?''

Carlucci thought about it for a minute. It was stifling in here, and the fans didn't seem to be helping much anymore, and his day hadn't gone well at all. He could do with *several* beers. "Sure," he said, unbuttoning the top two buttons of his shirt and pulling the knot of his tie halfway down his chest.

Cage walked over to the refrigerator for two more bottles. Carlucci had already revised his opinion of Cage a couple of times since he'd first seen him, and wondered if he would have to revise it again. Probably. Cage handed him a bottle, but didn't sit down again. He returned to his previous spot, leaning against the counter.

"First," Cage began, "I've got to say I don't know that I'd call Cancer Cell good or bad. I don't know enough about them, and I don't think even if I did that I'd make that kind of judgment. They're probably some of both, like most of us. I try not to make too many judgments about anyone." Then Cage laughed. "Well, I *try*." He drank deeply from the bottle, then stared at the label as if he was trying to decipher something. Finally he looked back at Carlucci.

"We get a lot of high-grade black-market pharmaceuticals from Cancer Cell. For the clinic. Now, no one we deal with ever actually says the words 'Cancer Cell,' but we know that's where it's all coming from. It *has* to be. Typical street stuff is just shit, and getting lab quality out of the domestic companies is just about impossible—the profits on it are so good they've got the best inventory control around. You *can* get the same stuff black-marketed down from New Hong Kong itself, but that's a lot more expensive, more than we can handle."

Carlucci knew. A friend of his, Louis Tanner, an ex-cop, used to barter black-market pharmaceuticals from New Hong Kong a few years ago. Some of it he sold, and some of it he gave away to clinics like this one.

"Most of what I know about Cancer Cell is distillation of rumors," Cage continued. "Working the essence of probable truth out of a mass of stories, guesses, wild speculation, street gossip, and wish fulfillment. What I do know is this: They do cutting-edge medical research. That's their main purpose. Everything else is in aid of that. And they do their research without any restrictions imposed by laws or regulations.''

"Or ethics," Carlucci put in.

Cage shrugged. "I wouldn't know."

"Like New Hong Kong."

Cage shrugged again. "I don't even know what their end purpose is. New Hong Kong's goal is profit, but I don't think that's true for Cancer Cell. I do know that if you have an incurable disease, or an irreversible, debilitating condition, you can volunteer for experimental treatments from them. It's a risk some people are more than willing to take."

"You make it sound like they have signs up somewhere. VOLUNTEERS NEEDED. EXPERIMENTAL SUBJECTS. INCURABLE DISEASE? CALL THIS NUMBER TO APPLY."

Cage laughed. "No, that's New Hong Kong's style, not Cancer Cell's. Cancer Cell is discreet. But you work street medicine long enough, you hear things, and the picture comes together. Besides, just like they're a source for us, we're a source for them."

"A source of experimental subjects, you mean."

"Something like that."

"Have you ever sent anyone to them?"

Cage sighed. "It's not that simple. I have mentioned them to some of my patients over the years. Not by name, more the idea. Let the patient know the option was available."

"Any of them exercise that option?"

"I don't know. Probably. If any did, I never heard from them."

Of course not, Carlucci thought, because they're dead. He drank from his beer, which was no longer very cold. In the peak of summer, this room must be a goddamn hotbox. He watched Cage, the hip young clinic doctor, medic of the streets. He felt certain Cage wasn't telling him everything he knew about Cancer Cell. But that was okay. He sure as hell wasn't going to tell Cage everything he knew about Naomi Katsuda and her New Hong Kong connections. But he was probably going to have to tell Cage *something*. Cage was the only solid potential source of information about Cancer Cell he had, and he was going to need Cage's help.

"So all this worries me," Cage said. "I wonder what Cancer Cell is doing. Some kind of viral or bacterial research that's gone out of control? Or something worse, like deliberately infecting people? No idea why they would do that, but then I don't know them very well, do I? Most of all I worry about how contagious this crap is." Cage rubbed at his nose, then pinched the bridge, as if he were trying to massage away a growing headache. "Probably it all ends right here," he finished up. "With Tito. Just a fluke, a couple of dead people, nothing further. Unsolved mystery." He smiled.

"Maybe not," Carlucci said with a heavy sigh.

"What do you mean by that?" Cage asked, suddenly wary.

Carlucci was still trying to decide how much to tell Cage. He'd spent his career developing a deep reluctance to divulge more information than was absolutely necessary, except with other cops, and even then he had to be careful. But you couldn't always hold back everything; keeping other people too much in the dark could sometimes have all kinds of unintended consequences, a lot of them bad.

"Another case I have," he finally replied. "A woman was killed a few days ago. She had the initials 'CC' carved into her head."

"Could stand for a lot of things," Cage said. "Christian Coalition. I hear they're back in business, ranting and raving and preaching and putting on mass self-flagellations. Or Canadian Club. Maybe whoever killed her had way too much to drink. Blamed the booze."

This was a game Carlucci didn't feel like playing. Not in this stifling room with two dead people to think about, one of them definitely murdered.

"I had talked with her about two weeks before she was

killed," he said, leaning forward in his chair. "I was trying to find out something about Tito, and her name was given to me as a possible source of information about Cancer Cell." He paused, staring at Cage, wanting to make damn sure the man was listening to him, paying close attention. "She wouldn't tell me anything. She told me Tito's abduction wasn't even close to being important enough for her to take any risks." One more pause, deliberately for effect. "She told me to come back and talk to her when people started dying."

Cage was silent for a few moments. Then, quietly, he said, "Shit."

Carlucci nodded. "Yeah, shit is right. I want your help, Cage."

"How?"

"I don't know yet. Not exactly. I'd like to talk to someone who's a part of Cancer Cell. Could you arrange that?"

Cage's mouth twisted into a kind of frown. "It *might* be possible. It would take time, and it would be risky. They don't like anyone weaseling around in their business. And a cop? Jesus. But maybe I can find out something."

"I'll arrange for Tito Moraleja to be taken to one of the police morgues, maybe even get an autopsy done. I'll call it a connection to this other case I have."

"You're willing to do that?"

"Sure. Can you make arrangements for Tito's body to get to the Tenderloin perimeter? If I give you the name of a business, an address?"

"Of course. Even if I have to rent a cart and haul him there myself. Then you can get him out of the Tenderloin?"

"Yes." Carlucci took one of his cards and wrote an address on the back. It was an import/export shop in one of the perimeter buildings, with ways both in and out of the Tenderloin. The police department had an arrangement with the owner, Nanos Spyrodakis. For a price, they could move almost anything or anyone into or out of the Tenderloin. A dead body? Carlucci sighed to himself. Getting Tito Moraleja's body out was going to be expensive.

He handed the card to Cage. "Can you have him there in two hours?"

"Yeah, no problem," Cage said, looking at the address. He turned the card over. "I guess I'll need this card if I want to get in touch with you."

"Yes. And be discreet over the phone."

"Sure thing, Lieutenant." He tucked the card into the back pocket of his jeans. "I'll let you know if I find out something."

Carlucci got up from the chair, finished off the warm Black Orbit. "Thanks for the beer." He set the empty bottle on the table.

The two men shook hands and Carlucci turned to go.

"Lieutenant?"

"Yeah?"

Cage was smiling, but it was a fearful smile. "Whoever does the autopsy on Tito? Tell them to be *damn* careful."

CHAPTER 12

The playground was enclosed by metal-sheet fencing topped by razor wire and rusted saw blades, the fencing broken only by two narrow gates. The gates were manned by street soldiers from the Polk Corridor in full battle colors: dark red ankle scarves wrapped tightly around black leather boots; khakis spattered with what appeared to be bloodstains; shining silver serpent belts loaded with hand ammo; arms wired with coils of jolt-tubing; shielded glasses and dark green bush hats.

Caroline slowed as she approached the east gate with Lily and Mink, the mother and daughter who were now living in Tito's old room in the death house, waiting for Mink to die. They had walked the several blocks from the DMZ, Caroline acting as escort and guide. In fact, she felt more like a bodyguard, watching out for Lily and Mink because they didn't have much street smarts yet, and they gave off an aura of being ripe for the street scavs.

A large sign in block letters hung beside the east gate: NO CHILDREN ALLOWED WITHOUT A SUPERVISING ADULT. Caroline, Lily, and Mink stepped one at a time through the two detectors, then were patted down by a woman street soldier who smiled and chattered aimlessly about the weather, Caroline's shirt, Mink's hair, and the stench of the garbage. Then the three of them stepped through the main entrance and into the playground.

When Caroline had been a child, her parents had brought her here to this playground several times over the years, when they'd been in the neighborhood visiting friends. Back then, the place had been overgrown with lush plants surrounding the swings and slides and jungle bars, stands of bamboo had lined the perimeter, and an island of trees, shrubs, blooming flowers, and thick grasses had stood in the middle of it all, the island surrounded by a shallow lake of water that the children waded through, splashed and played in. You could buy ice cream bars or Sno-Kones, hot dogs and soda pop and misty ices. You could have a picnic on the island.

Several years earlier, however, the playground had been the site of a major skirmish in the Summer Polk Riots. The place had been strafed with defoliants and cratered by mortars, the few remaining plants burned by kerosene fires. The playground had been rebuilt, the equipment repaired or replaced, a few benches installed, the metal-sheet fencing erected around the entire grounds, and the Polk Corridor street soldiers had taken it over. The playground existed, but it wasn't the same.

And yet, the dry, bleached-out prospect bothered the children a lot less than it did Caroline. The playground was full of running, shouting, jumping, swinging, and laughing children who were having a great time. Mink stayed close to her mom until they reached an empty bench facing the denuded island that had once been nearly overgrown. Now the island was covered in sand, with several swing sets, a couple of twisting slides, and a large, multilevel maze of wire-mesh cages; it was still surrounded by a shallow, water-filled moat. Lily and Caroline sat on the bench. Mink stood beside them for a minute or two, watching the kids on the island, and those walking barefoot through the moat; then she ventured away from the bench and walked toward the small footbridge that spanned the water. She crossed the bridge, and tentatively approached the swing sets.

"She won't play for too long," Lily said. "She gets tired pretty fast."

"What does she have?" Caroline asked. She'd avoided the topic before this because Mink had always been present.

"Leukemia."

Caroline was surprised. She'd expected something more exotic, one of the newly discovered or newly resurgent diseases, little understood and untreatable. She'd thought leukemia in children was fairly simple to treat these days, with a high rate of success. She said as much to Lily.

Lily shrugged. "She didn't respond well to chemotherapy. Two courses of treatment, and it came right back both times. Another round was out of the question, because the chemo itself was almost killing her. The doctor said her only real chance was a bone marrow transplant, or replacement with artificial marrow." She shook her head, traces of a sad smile tucking up the corners of her mouth. "Maybe if my own marrow was compatible . . . but it isn't. People don't donate marrow, they sell it. The artificial marrow's even more expensive. Not to mention the operation, the follow-ups, the drugs, all that stuff. No money, no insurance . . ." She turned to look at Caroline. "No transplant, no replacement. Mink's going to die."

Caroline didn't know what to say. She felt even more depressed. "Is there a father?" she asked.

Lily snorted. "Sure there's a father. *Had* to be, right? One way or another. But who knows where the hell he is, if he's even alive." She sighed heavily. "I haven't seen him or heard from him in six years."

Caroline looked back across the water at the island. One of the swings became available and Mink climbed onto the wide fabric strap, grabbing the thick chains. From a standstill, she pumped her legs and pulled back and forth on the chains, and quickly got herself going. The arcs got bigger and bigger, and she let go with one hand, waved at Lily and Caroline with a big smile. The women waved back.

"How long does she have?" Caroline asked.

"Two months. Maybe three." Lily shook her head again. "No one really knows."

It was all so unfair. But then there was nothing new about that, and nothing Caroline could do to change it. She put her hand over Lily's and squeezed. Lily squeezed back, and the two women remained there on the bench, holding hands, and watching Mink play.

• • •

Caroline met her father in the lobby of one of the city's holding morgues. He looked more tired than usual, drawn and distracted, but he smiled and hugged her when she walked in. The lobby was cooler and darker than outside, but she suspected it was going to get even colder.

"You sure you want to look at him?" her father said.

"You said you wanted to make sure it was Tito."

"Well, he was chipped. And I could show you pictures. He doesn't look good. He looks pretty bad."

She smiled to herself. He wasn't completely sure how to act around her in this situation; half father, half cop. A woman in uniform sat behind a desk in the back corner, watching them with a bored and sleepy expression; otherwise the room was empty of people and furniture. Even the walls were completely blank, a depressing industrial gray.

"I want to see him," Caroline finally said. It was one of those things that was partially true, and partially untrue.

Her father nodded to the woman at the desk, who fiddled with the console in front of her. The door beside her clicked, and she said, "Go ahead, Lieutenant."

He led the way through the door, along a narrow corridor, down a flight of steps, along another short corridor, then finally through a heavy, solid metal door and into a large room brightly lit by fluorescents. Two gurneys stood near the center of the room, one empty, the other with a covered body. There was an old metal utility sink attached to one wall, and two walls were racked with refrigerated lockers. Caroline wondered how many bodies were being stored here right now.

Her father went to the head of the occupied gurney and waited for her. He put on a pair of surgical gloves he'd taken from his jacket pocket, then took hold of the cloth covering by one corner, and looked at her. She nodded, and he carefully folded back the cloth, exposing the head.

She didn't look down at first. She kept her gaze on her father, the exposed face in the lower edges of her vision. A faint, unfamiliar smell rose, a chemical smell. Some kind of preservative, she imagined. Or would that have been used yet? Maybe something else. Maybe she was imagining the smell.

She tried to remember whether she had ever seen a dead person before, up close like this. There was her grandmother's funeral when she was quite young, seven or eight, but she could not remember if there had been an open casket; if there had been, would she have been allowed to see her dead grandmother? There were simply no images from that funeral in her mind. She'd been older, fifteen, when her grandfather had died, but the casket had been closed, she remembered that distinctly; her grandfather had lost so much weight in the course of his illness that, according to her father, he was almost unrecognizable. He and his sister had decided that no one should remember their father that way.

Caroline finally looked down. It was Tito. Yes, it was Tito, but he almost didn't look real. His lips were purple, his skin was strangely pale, like brown ash, covered with raw, red, purplish patches, and his open eyes looked like glass marbles. She felt a chill emanating from him, but she didn't know if that was real or imagined.

"Is it Tito?"

She looked up at her father, looked back at Tito, and nodded. So many times in the past few months he had been so sick that she'd thought he would be better off if he died soon, ended his suffering, but looking down at him now, now that he *was* dead, she was no longer so sure. She only knew that she was already beginning to miss him, and the pain of that was growing—slowly, but steadily.

Her father gently pulled the cover back over Tito's face, adjusted the cloth so it hung smoothly across the skin.

"I expected it to be colder in here," she said. Even as she spoke, it seemed to her a strange thing to say, but it just came out. "So the bodies won't decompose."

"He won't be out here long," her father replied. "He'll go back into one of the lockers as soon as we leave."

She nodded and reached out, laid her hand over Tito's chest. The cold seeped through the cloth and into her skin, even her bones, but she left her hand there, certain that it was important for her to feel that cold, to know what it was like. As though some crucial understanding would come from it. *She* would be that cold one day, and that day might not be that far in the future.

"What do I do to make funeral arrangements?" she asked.

"Nothing, for now."

She looked up at him. "What do you mean?"

"It could be a while."

"What are you talking about?"

"We need to have an autopsy done." He seemed ill at ease, which was so unlike him. "But it's a low priority, so it could be a while."

"Why an autopsy? He had AIDS."

Her father shook his head. "Yes, but that's not why he died." He was reluctant to go on. "Something else killed him."

"What?"

"No idea. That's why the autopsy."

"What the hell is going on here?"

Her father looked increasingly uncomfortable. "I really don't know, Caroline. It's complicated, especially because I really don't know much right now. But there might be a connection to another case I have right now."

"What kind of connection?"

This time her father hesitated a long time. But if he knew her at all, he would realize that she would not let this go. He would realize he had to tell her.

"Cancer Cell," he finally said.

"So Mouse was right."

"Maybe. And maybe about the Core, too. Tito died in a street clinic in the Tenderloin, half a block from the Core."

"What happened, Papa?"

Apparently he *did* know her well enough, because he eventually gave her the whole story. He started with putting out the department tracers, and getting a hit after the street clinic checked Tito's identity chip. He told her about going out to the RadioLand Street Clinic and finding that Tito had already died. And he told her about meeting Cage, and

Cage's concern about an infectious disease with some kind of connection to Cancer Cell.

"And there's a connection between that and another case you have?"

Her father nodded. "A murder case," he said. "Cancer Cell has come up in that case as well. But it could be a coincidence."

"You don't think so, though."

He sighed. "I really don't know, Caroline. I've got a lot of nothing on that case right now, so I'm following up every possibility. And in the meantime, Cage wants me to have Tito autopsied, see if we can't get some idea of what killed him. Maybe it won't be anything."

Caroline pulled her frigid hand back from the cloth over Tito, and stared at it.

"It's all right," her father said. "The cloth is impermeable."

But her hand was so cold, and she continued to stare at it, searching for some sign that no contagion had rubbed off onto it.

"Are you okay?" her father asked her.

She hurried over to the sink, turned on the tap with her elbows, and scrubbed her hands with large quantities of dispenser soap, the water as hot as she could stand it. Her father removed the surgical gloves and disposed of them in the wall bin beside the sink. Caroline continued scrubbing until her hands were red and painfully raw. She dried them with paper towels, tossed the towels into the bin, then turned to her father.

"I want to go now," she said.

CHAPTER **13**

Cage was dreaming of a giant anteater. The anteater, which appeared to be six or seven feet high at the shoulder and close to fifteen feet long, wandered slowly along the deserted streets of San Francisco, snuffling through tall, tropical ferns and dripping wet broad-leafed plants that grew everywhere.

Cage was standing alone at the second-floor window of an abandoned building, watching the anteater amble through the city. A phone began ringing somewhere. The anteater stopped, tilted its head, and looked at Cage. The phone kept ringing, the dream shook apart and darkened, and Cage shakily came awake.

The phone continued to ring, quietly chirping beside him. He hated that sound. The room was dark, almost quiet except for the phone. He glanced at the pulsing blue clock beside the bed: 4:43. He hadn't been asleep much more than an hour.

He finally reached for the phone, rolled onto his back, and put the receiver to his head. It rang once more, right in his ear. Cage pressed the answer button.

"Hello."

"Cage? Sorry to wake you." It was Paul's voice, which wasn't really a voice he wanted to hear right now. Actually, he didn't want to hear anyone's voice. "I've got a problem here."

Here had to be the clinic, which of course was only three

floors below him. Which was not always a good thing, being that close.

"You need me to come down there and help out?" He could hardly imagine getting out of bed right now, let alone treating patients. He was exhausted after working two double shifts at the clinic in the past three days while squeezing in a full day of image enhancements at the Pacific Heights Aesthetic Modeling Center.

"Yes," Paul answered. "But not what you think. You know a guy named Tiger?"

That helped get Cage alert and awake. He pushed himself up into a sitting position.

"Yeah, I know Tiger. Is he there?"

"He's here, all right. And he's hysterical, demanding to see you, demanding to be given some pills or a shot, says he's sick with some deadly disease. He's scared, Cage. Don't know what he's scared of, and he doesn't seem to actually be sick, but he said you would know."

Christ. He knew, all right. "Okay, I'll be right down. Try to calm him down. Tell him I said he's fine, and I'll be there in ten minutes."

"Calm him down," Paul said. "Sure thing. He wants a shot, I'll give him one. Sedate his ass."

"Just hang on, Paul, and I'll be right down."

"All right. But make it quick." Paul broke the connection.

Cage nodded to himself. Yeah, make it quick. He swung his legs out from under the sheet and over the side of the bed, and sat there for a few moments, trying to will himself awake. But his body and mind kept trying to shut down. If he lay back right now, he'd go out, he knew it.

He took a brief, cold shower and got dressed. He thought about making a quick cup of coffee, but decided he'd better get downstairs right away and see Tiger. Coffee probably wouldn't do him much good anyway; he was beyond the help of caffeine.

Outside it was still fairly dark, but already warm. The day was going to be hot, and he wondered if they were heading into their first big heat wave of the year. The first one was always a killer; people would be dropping in the streets.

The clinic entrance was just ten feet down from the apartment lobby. There were only three people in the waiting room—two older men sitting together, and a young pregnant woman. Mike Wilkerson looked up as Cage approached the desk and nodded toward the left hallway. "Cardenas is with someone in Exam Two," he said. "Your man Tiger is in Four."

"We got any fresh coffee?" Cage asked.

Mike nodded. "Just made a pot five minutes ago. Want me to get you some?"

Cage shook his head. "I'll get it myself. Exam Four, you said?"

"That's it."

He started back toward the staff room, but pulled up when someone began banging on one of the exam room doors and yelling. From the inside. He turned back to Mike.

"Is that my guy?"

Mike nodded, laughing. "Paul locked him in. He kept jumping out into the hall and shouting for help."

"Christ. I guess the coffee'll wait." He reversed direction, came around the counter, then headed up the left hallway and down toward Exam Four. Tiger was still pounding on the door when he reached it.

"Hey!" Cage shouted. "Jam it in there, will you?"

Silence for a moment. Then, "Dr. Cage?"

"Yeah." He took the chart and clipboard off the wall hook, glanced at it. Paul had started the chart, but hadn't written anything except: *Tiger. Diagnosis: MADMAN!* Cage unlocked the door and opened it. Tiger stepped back and let Cage inside.

Tiger immediately began pacing and talking at the same time. "Oh, man, you gotta help me. He's dead . . . goddamn, he's dead . . . and you gotta. . . ." Tiger was flushed and sweating, rubbing at his head with one hand while wiping the other hand up and down on his thigh. "I think I'm sick . . . I *must* be sick . . . he's fucking *dead*!"

"Tiger!" Cage barked it at him.

Tiger stopped pacing and blinked stupidly at Cage. "What?"

"Sit down, for Christ's sake. Just calm down a minute, and sit."

Tiger didn't move for a few moments, still staring at Cage as if he didn't know where the hell he was. Then he looked around and sat in the chair by the tiny window that opened out into the alley. Cage remained standing.

"Okay," Cage said. "Who's dead? Stinger?"

"Yeah, fucking Stinger. And he died a mess. He was vomiting blood everywhere and screaming and his skin was peeling off, and then he just died."

"You saw this?"

Tiger shook his head. "No, I told you. They were keeping him away from everyone, in some kind of isolation room, in some building somewhere, I don't know. But a woman I know, one of the people I was helping carry him that time, she's got better connections than I do. She knows someone who was there, who saw him die. She says everyone's really worried. She said Stinger's not the first one to die like that."

Great, Cage thought, that's fucking great. Just what he wanted to hear.

Tiger stood up, holding out his hands. "I got his blood all over me!" he wailed. "You gotta do something, I'm getting sick, and you have to give me a shot or some pills or something so I don't die like that. You *told* me to come here. You gotta *do* something you fucking boneman!"

"Okay, Tiger, okay. Sit back down, and I'll check you out. I'll give you a full workup, okay?"

Tiger sat down again and rubbed both hands through his short hair, face twisting into a grimace. He muttered to himself, eyes blinking spasmodically. Cage put on a pair of disposable gloves, and Tiger lost it again.

"I *am* sick!" he cried out, jumping to his feet and pointing at the gloves. "See? You don't even want to touch me!"

"Jesus, Tiger, calm down, will you? I put gloves on for everyone, for every exam I do. Standard precautions. It doesn't mean anything." Cage felt like he was trying to talk a potential suicide off a rooftop, except he didn't know what Tiger would do if he completely lost control. He didn't want to find out.

He spent the next fifteen minutes running Tiger through a general physical, talking to him all the while, trying to keep him settled. He talked about anything that came to his mind, as long as there was no connection to Stinger—random babble about the clinic, the possibility of a heat wave, the message streamers he'd seen the night before about some religious wack who was trying to recruit people for a pilgrimage to the North Pole. Tiger seemed to gradually loosen up a little. The tension eased out of his neck muscles, the flush left his skin, the sweating slowed, and the panicky jumping around of his gaze dwindled away.

Tiger seemed healthy enough. His heart rate was elevated, but Cage would have been surprised if it wasn't. Blood pressure, too, was elevated the first time he took it, but pretty much normal when he took it a second time as he was about to finish up. Temp was just over ninety-nine, but that wasn't much of a fever. Nothing else of much significance showed itself. All in all, Tiger seemed to be healthier than most of the people Cage saw at the clinic, and Cage told him as much.

"You sure?" Tiger asked. "I haven't been feeling any too good."

"Like what?"

"Feverish, for one thing. All hot, like I'm burning up."

"You don't have a fever, Tiger."

"I've been breaking out in rashes."

Cage's heart jumped a little at that, but he hadn't seen any during the exam. "I didn't find any signs of rash anywhere," he said to Tiger.

"They're gone now. But I've also been getting headaches, and I'm not sleeping so good, and sometimes I've been sweating a lot, and sometimes I feel like I can't catch my breath."

"Classic symptoms of anxiety attacks," Cage told him.

"What do you mean?"

"Stinger's dead, and you had that blood splashed on you, and you're so worried about getting the same thing that you're getting anxiety attacks about it."

"You mean I'm making myself sick?"

"Probably."

"*Probably*. But maybe not."

Cage sighed. "That's right, maybe not. I can't be sure. But I think you're fine."

"Can't you give me something to keep me from getting what Stinger had?"

Cage shook his head. "It's not that simple, Tiger. I don't know what Stinger had. Even if I did, I probably couldn't do anything. What he had might not even have been contagious." He was trying to convince himself as much as he was Tiger; he was still really worried about Nikki, and this sure as hell wasn't helping. The last time he'd talked to her she was still sick, maybe even feeling worse.

Tiger rolled his head from side to side, popping his neck. "Rashida's friends sure are worried that it's contagious. It's making them crazy."

Okay, Cage thought. Here was his chance to try to push things with Tiger. "Who's Rashida?" he asked.

Tiger continued rolling his head around, and the neck bones kept making loud popping sounds; it made Cage a little queasy. "She's a friend," Tiger said. "I told you. But she's got better connections to the big stoners."

"Tiger. Who do you work for?"

"I work for Stinger, and Rashida. And Birgitta." Tiger grinned. "You remember, the woman who wouldn't help us load up? That was Birgitta. She's a scary one, isn't she? Imagine what she'd do to a guy in bed."

"But who are they?" Cage pressed him. "Is there a name?"

Tiger shrugged. "I don't know, and I don't really give a shit. I just work for them. I do the work and they pay me. That's all that matters."

"Do you ever work in the Core?"

Tiger stopped rolling his neck and stared at Cage. "Are you out of your suffocating mind? We get close to the Core, sometimes, sure, but hell, look at where *this* place is. No, I don't work in that goddamn place. Shit, I'm not a genius, but I'm not a fucking moron, either. The Core." He shook his head and grinned at Cage.

Cage decided not to push it any farther. Tiger didn't know. It was quite possible he'd never even heard of Cancer Cell.

"So you really think I'm okay?" Tiger asked.

Cage nodded.

"And I can keep on working?"

"Sure. It wouldn't hurt to take a few days off, rest up a little. Tell them you *are* sick, even though you aren't."

"Shit, I don't know about that. I need the work. I need the money. And I take too much time off, they might give the job to someone else."

"Okay. Whatever you want. But before you go, you want to give me your number and address? So I can check in on you."

Tiger nodded. "Sure." He breathed in deeply once, then slowly let it out. "Maybe you're right, about the anxiety. I'm feeling a lot better now."

I'm glad *you* are, Cage thought.

An hour later he stood outside Nikki's door, hesitating. It was still way too early, only seven in the morning, and the chances of Nikki being awake were slim, but after his encounter with Tiger, Cage needed to see her. He needed reassurance. He'd been so busy he hadn't seen her in three days, just talked briefly with her a few times. He was afraid of what he would find.

He knocked softly. Nothing at first, and he was about to knock again when he thought he heard movement from inside. Then Nikki's muffled voice came through the door.

"Who's there?"

"It's me, Nikki."

"Who's 'me'?" she asked as she opened the door. She looked tired, but she was smiling. She was wearing green sweatpants and a gray T-shirt, and she was barefoot.

"Come on in. I was just going to make coffee. Want some?"

"I'd kill for some," Cage said. He followed her into the apartment.

The windows were open, letting in the warm, fresh early-morning air—as fresh as the city ever got, anyway. Nikki went to the stove, where water was heating, and added extra coffee to the filter cone set on her glass pot.

"How are you feeling?" he asked.

She turned to face him, smile broadening. "Wiped. But great. By great I mean the fever's broken, the headache's gone, no more sore throat, no more crunching bone aches. I'm bloody exhausted, but just great. On the mend."

Cage felt tremendous relief. He stepped toward her, put his hands on her shoulders, rose up on his toes, and kissed her forehead. "Believe me, I'm glad to hear it. I was starting to worry."

"Some bloody awful flu," Nikki said. "The worst I've ever had, I think. But . . . it . . . is . . . over."

The water began to boil, and she took the kettle off the burner and poured the steaming water into the cone. Cage crossed the room to one of the windows and looked outside. The air coming in was continuing to warm, and he realized that it was going to be a burner by midafternoon. Activity on the street below was still fairly sedate, though it was starting to pick up a bit. It would probably remain a slow day until things began to cool down as the sun dropped. No one would be quite used to the heat yet.

Nikki handed him a cup of coffee, and they sat together by the window. They spent a few minutes in silence, drinking their coffee.

"You've been busy," Nikki said. "You haven't been mother-henning me the past couple of days."

Cage nodded. "Double shifts at the clinic, and then I had to do a stint yesterday performing image enhancements."

"Oh, right, for that shipment we got. You must be as tired as I am."

"Probably." He shrugged. "You remember Tiger, the guy who met us with that shipment?"

"Sure."

"He showed up at the clinic today. A couple hours ago. Paul called me down."

"Was he sick?"

"No, just worried. He *thought* he was sick." He paused, almost wishing he hadn't brought it up. But she had a right to know. Besides, she was getting over the flu or whatever it was she'd had. She obviously hadn't picked up whatever it was that had killed Stinger. "Stinger's dead."

"Yeah?" It was all she said. But her gaze never left him.

"Yeah. He got pretty sick, and then he died."

"What from?"

Cage shook his head. "Tiger has no idea. He's not a part of the 'inner circle.' He wasn't around, he hadn't seen Stinger in days. He just heard from a friend of his that Stinger had died."

Nikki's expression didn't change. "So why did he go to the clinic?"

"He'd been working with Stinger. He's worried he's getting sick, that's he's got whatever Stinger had. But he seems okay."

She nodded slowly and gave him a rueful smile. "That's why you showed up here at this ungodly hour. Afraid you were going to find me on my deathbed?"

Cage smiled back. "Maybe a little."

"Sorry to disappoint you."

He laughed, shaking his head. "You never disappoint me, Nikki."

Nikki stopped smiling. "Except in love. I always disappoint you in love."

What could he say to that? Nothing. The two of them returned to silence, gazing out the window, drinking their coffee, and watching the day arrive.

CHAPTER 14

In a week and a half, no real progress had been made in the Naomi Katsuda case, and now the whole thing seemed to be going to shit on them. The strange thing was, Carlucci wasn't getting any extra pressure to solve the case, not from Vaughn, and not from Yoshi Katsuda, Naomi's father, and that bothered him. He would have expected pressure from both. Even Morgan seemed to have dropped out of the picture; Carlucci hadn't heard from him even once since the day Naomi Katsuda's body had been found in the Sutro Bath ruins. When Santos and Weathers asked for a meeting with him away from the office, he felt certain he wasn't going to get good news. And he was right.

The three of them met in China Basin at eight o'clock in the morning. When Carlucci arrived, Santos and Weathers were standing at a wooden railing, drinking coffee and watching a freighter being unloaded on the docks below them.

Ruben Santos and Toni Weathers had been partners for seven years. Ruben was Toni's first assignment when she transferred into Homicide, and most people in the department had predicted the partnership wouldn't last a year. Ruben was a small, wiry redheaded Latino, a short-tempered man whose emotions regularly got the better of him, while Toni was a tall, big-boned blonde, an even-mannered woman with a sharp, analytical mind. And they had fooled everyone. They complemented each other, were fiercely loyal to one another, and they had become one of the best Homicide teams in the entire city.

As Carlucci approached, he noticed there was an extra cup of coffee for him on the rail between them, steam rising through a tiny opening in its lid. They turned away from the ship and looked at him. Santos handed him the coffee and said, "I hate this fucking case."

Weathers gave Carlucci the faintest touch of a smile and one quick nod—her way of agreeing.

"You want to give it to Morgan?" Carlucci asked. "He's wanted it from the beginning." He knew what the answer would be.

"Hah," Santos replied. "Not a fucking chance. Besides, I'm not so sure Morgan would want it anymore." Santos had his coffee in his left hand, cigarette in his right; he took a long drink from the paper cup and a deep drag from the cigarette. "I'm going to kill myself with this shit," he said. Then, shaking his head, "That goddamn Katsuda. Yoshi, the father."

"What's the problem, Ruben?"

"What's *not* the problem?" He gave an exaggerated sigh. "The arrogant bastard won't talk to us, that's the biggest problem. More than a week since his daughter was killed, and he still won't talk to us. First, it's the grief thing, he's too upset over the death of his daughter. Then there was the funeral, more grieving, family members from out of town, family and friends down from New Hong Kong. Then he's too busy at the office, making up for time lost and trying to find a replacement for his daughter. We never get to talk to him directly, of course, it's always through one of his assistants. And we get messages from him, about how much he appreciates our efforts, and he'll talk with us as soon as he can, but he doesn't know anything about his daughter's death, or he would have talked to us sooner. Blah, blah, blah." He paused, hit on the coffee and cigarette again.

"We're trying to keep it chilled, right? I'm not out of control, Toni's doing a good job of keeping me smoothed out. We know we have to be careful. He's a fucking big shot, we can't just barge into Mishima and demand that either he talks to us or we'll arrest him. We haven't tried to get a subpoena. We know we've got a little political problem with this guy, so we've backed off. We're not a bunch of fucking gorillas, even if Morgan thinks we are. But this is bullshit, and we're going nowhere.''

''I thought Morgan was supposed to help us out, slick the way for interviews.''

Santos just shook his head in disgust, but didn't say anything. Weathers again gave Carlucci that faint smile. ''Oh, yeah,'' she said, ''Morgan's been a lot of help.'' But then she shrugged. ''To be fair, I think Morgan's been trying, in his own supposedly diplomatic and sophisticated way. And I think he's a little embarrassed about the stonewalling, embarrassed that he doesn't seem to have *any* influence at all with Katsuda. He *has* managed to get us in to interview other people at Mishima, people who worked with her.''

''But we can't get to Yoshi Katsuda himself.''

Santos made a kind of growling sound in his throat. ''Yeah, well, maybe we can. Now he wants to talk to you.''

''Morgan?''

''No. Katsuda. That's the latest message we got—he would be happy to speak with Lieutenant Frank Carlucci. He doesn't come out and *say* he won't talk to anyone else, but it's pretty fuckin' clear.''

''Why does he want to talk to *me*?''

Santos shook his head. ''No idea.''

Carlucci sighed. ''Christ, that's all we need.''

The three of them stood side by side, leaning against the railing and watching the ship below. Cranes were raising and swinging enormous crates from the ship to the dock; the crates were all marked with Japanese ideograms. A couple of U.S. Customs inspectors were wandering along the dock, glancing at the crates and talking to the dock workers, but neither of them seemed to be doing much actual inspecting.

''Will you talk to Katsuda?'' Santos asked.

''Of course. Not much choice, is there?''

''Sure there is,'' Santos said, grinning. ''We could just

haul his ass in. Do a full strip and body cavity search. The fucking works.''

Carlucci had to smile. ''You'd like that, wouldn't you?''

''I'd love it. I'd take pictures.''

Weathers, too, was smiling. ''Wouldn't mind it myself,'' she said.

''I thought you said we weren't gorillas,'' Carlucci said.

Santos wiggled one eyebrow. ''I lied.'' His grin vanished, became a grimace. ''I hate New Hong Kong,'' he said. ''I hate anyone who has any connection to that goddamn place.''

Carlucci nodded, understanding him completely. He glanced down at the coffee in his hands. He hadn't finished more than half of it, but he couldn't drink any more. His stomach was burning. He walked over to a trash can, dropped the coffee in, and walked back.

''All right, let's forget about Yoshi Katsuda for now. You've been able to talk to other people, right? Follow other lines of investigation? So what have we got so far? Since I haven't heard anything new from you, I assume it isn't much.''

''You assume right,'' Santos said. ''We've got shit.'' And with that he turned away and gazed down at the ship below; he didn't say any more.

Carlucci turned to Weathers, who shrugged and mouthed *He's okay*. She gestured with her head and walked toward the trash can. Carlucci followed her, and after she tossed away her empty coffee cup she lit a cigarette.

They remained by the trash can for a minute, but Santos made no move to join them. He continued to lean over the railing, staring down at the ship and docks. Carlucci and Weathers began walking away from him.

''So,'' Carlucci said. ''What do we have?''

''Ruben's right. We really don't have much of anything. We haven't been able to talk to the father, there is no mother, and there doesn't seem to be any other close family.''

''What do you mean, no mother?''

''No mother. Katsuda never married. There was a surrogate mother. Katsuda provided the sperm, and some unknown woman provided the ovum. Unknown to us. Apparently it's a big family secret. Maybe because the mother wasn't Japanese. Naomi was raised by her father and a household of servants, and she lived with her father until about two years ago.''

''Now *that's* interesting. How old was she, around forty?''

Weathers nodded. ''Forty-one. There's lots of 'interesting' stuff about the family, and the circumstances around her murder, but none of it leads anywhere, at least not yet.

''No one, naturally, has *any* idea why anyone would want to kill her. Everyone we talked to at Mishima who worked with her was very politely cooperative, but no one knew crap. And no one knew her very well. No one at Mishima would own up to actually being her friend, and no one knew of anyone who *was* her friend.''

''No boyfriend? Nobody she went out with on a regular basis? Or even irregular basis?''

Weathers gave him the slight smile again. ''Now there's another interesting bit that hasn't gone anywhere yet, but just might. Naomi lived in a very expensive condo on Telegraph Hill. Ruben and I have talked to her neighbors in the building. Most of them didn't know her very well, either, although everyone in the building seems to know everyone else on sight—so they recognize anyone who doesn't belong. But again, no friends. One guy, though, said he talked to Naomi a lot, though never about much that he'd consider personal or intimate. Actually he said he talked to her a fair amount about himself, but she never talked about her own private life. But he did say he'd seen her several times with a woman, leaving or coming in, and a couple of times sitting together on her balcony. Always the same woman. He said he couldn't be sure, of course, but he had the feeling they were lovers. Nothing very specific—he never saw them kissing or even holding hands. He said there was just something about the way they were together, he always assumed they were lovers.''

''Even if they weren't . . .'' Carlucci began.

"Right. We need to talk to her."

"No name?"

"No name. We've got his description, and I think the guy's got an appointment with one of the sketchers this afternoon. But if she hasn't come forward by now, it's not going to be easy to find her. We can't exactly take the sketcher's image and put it on the evening news, or stick it in the papers, or send it out over the nets."

Carlucci smiled. "Why not? We do it at the same time we haul Katsuda in for Ruben's body cavity search and photo session."

Weathers laughed. "Yeah, that'll keep this case low-profile." She took one last drag on her cigarette, dropped it to the ground, and crushed it. "Another funny thing about this woman, though. When we asked some of the Mishima people about the woman and who she might be, we got a lot of insistence that there was no way this woman could be Naomi's lover. They were quite certain that Naomi 'wasn't that way,' as most of them put it. The same people who said they didn't know her very well, who couldn't name any friends that she had or men that she went out with, these same people were absolutely certain about her sexuality." Weathers shook her head. "There's some kind of hang-up at Mishima about that. Probably doesn't mean anything, but it's one more interesting aspect of this damn case."

Carlucci stopped and leaned against the railing, rubbing his eyes. *This damn case* was right. "What about the Cancer Cell line?" he asked.

"Makes what we've learned about Naomi Katsuda look encyclopedic. We bring up the name, and we either get genuine confusion or what Ruben calls the 'dead fish-face' look followed by claims of ignorance. You *know* they know something about it, but they're not talking. No one's talking." She turned and smiled at him. "There you have it. Like Ruben said, we've got shit. But I've got a feeling, Lieutenant, that this isn't going to last. We'll find that woman, or something else will break, somewhere. Tran and Jefferson and Hong and LaPlace are all busting their asses

on this.'' She nodded once. ''We're going to find something and blow this wide open.''

''Great,'' Carlucci said. ''That'll make Yoshi Katsuda
happy.''

Her smile broadened into a grin. ''Fuck Yoshi Katsuda.''

He smiled back at her. ''Let's go get Ruben before he
decides to take a header onto the docks.''

CHAPTER 15

Caroline stopped and leaned against the back of a credit chip gazebo on the corner. The street barriers walling off the Core rose just a block away, warning lights blinking in the hot, damp Tenderloin night. She felt almost over-whelmed by the rush of light and movement all around her, the press of people, the constant noise and the constantly shifting smells, the dazzle of flashing electric color.

She had come in from the Chinatown side, through Li Peng's Imperial Imports. There was no way she could use any of the police "gates," but Louis Tanner, an old friend of her father's, had given her a way in. She'd made Louis promise not to tell her father about this excursion of hers. The cost of entrance was fifty dollars left in a charity jar on the counter of Li Peng's, a large and quiet Chinese herbal pharmacy. Then she'd walked through a back door and up seven flights of stairs, which had exhausted her. Then it was down seven more flights through clouds of smoke and lights, down through restaurants and gambling parlors, a public intimacy club, and finally out onto the street, inside the Tenderloin.

She had made her way through several blocks of heavy sidewalk and street traffic. Some of the alleys were less crowded, but she was afraid to venture into them; they tended to be darker, filled with steam and cooking fires, wild cyclists, and louder and sharper shouts and banging noises. Message streamers swam frantically through the air above the streets, bright green and red, shimmering with work advertisements, commercial come-ons, recruiting messages, and personal and political announcements.

And now here she was, a block from the Core, and half a block from the RadioLand Street Clinic; a block from the place Tito had disappeared into, and half a block from the place where he'd died. She could see the clinic sign across the street, simple blue phosphor letters glowing steadily in the night. Caroline continued to lean against the gazebo, gazing at the sign and resting. The night air was hot and heavy with humidity.

She pushed away from the gazebo wall, stepped toward the curb, then threw herself into a surge of foot traffic that swelled out into the street. She let herself be carried along until she got to the opposite sidewalk; once across, she broke away and moved close to the buildings, where she could walk along at her own pace. She passed a spice bar, a donut shop, a couple of unmarked doors, and a head juicer shop before she finally reached the clinic entrance.

Unsure of why she had come, she hesitated outside, wondering what she hoped to get out of meeting the doctor who had been with Tito when he'd died. Her father had said this doctor knew something about Cancer Cell, but so what? What was any of that going to change? Tito was dead. But she felt otherwise so directionless with her life right now, without much purpose, and this seemed like the only meaningful thing she could do. In some strange way, she felt she owed it to Tito.

The door swung outward and a woman emerged holding a baby in one arm, her other hand wrapped around the fingers of a four-year-old boy. The woman stared at Caroline a moment, eyes almost completely without expression, then turned and headed down the street with the children. Caroline caught the door before it closed, pulled it wider, and stepped inside.

The clinic waiting room was hotter than outside, but several fans blew the air around, which helped some, though it couldn't dispel the heavy odor of sweat. Ten or twelve people sat slumped around the room, and there wasn't much talking or movement. Behind the front counter stood a heavy redheaded woman with a pleasant face. Caroline approached her.

"Can I help you with something?" the woman asked. She smiled at Caroline, very friendly, but looked puzzled, as if Caroline didn't belong here.

"I called earlier today, and asked when Dr. Cage would be in. He's supposed to be here now, and I want to talk to him if he has some time."

"Yes, he's here. He's with a patient right now. If you want to sit down and wait, I'll let him know you're here when he's free."

Caroline nodded. "Thanks, I will."

"Do you want any coffee or tea or something to drink?" the woman asked her.

"No, thanks." She hadn't seen anyone else in the waiting room with coffee or tea. Did she stick out that much?

"I'm Franzee," the woman said. "And you?"

"Caroline." She and Franzee briefly shook hands.

She found an empty chair next to an old blind man who smiled at her as she sat down; he had only three or four teeth, and his face was quite wrinkled, but his dark, black hair had very little gray, and it was obvious that it wasn't dyed. She smiled back at him, remembered he couldn't see her, then said, "Hello." The old man's smile broadened, which did not reveal any more teeth, and he nodded a few times, but he didn't say anything.

She was exhausted. She didn't know if it was the heat, the trek through the Tenderloin, or the Gould's. Maybe all three.

A baby began to cry, and the boy holding it rocked it gently back and forth, cooing to it, patting and rubbing. Caroline closed her eyes and tried to block out the baby's cries.

She sensed someone standing in front of her and opened her eyes. A man stood just a couple of feet away, smiling at her. He was a good-looking man, even with the silly tattoo of a snake and staff on his neck, and his smile gave her a slight shiver.

"You wanted to see me?" the man asked.

"Are you Dr. Cage?"

"I am. And your name is Caroline?"

"Yes. Caroline Carlucci."

An eyebrow went up, and he said, "Oh. The lieutenant's daughter."

She smiled and nodded. "Sounds like the title of a romance novel—*The Lieutenant's Daughter.*"

He nodded, still smiling. "Yeah, it does. Wonder if it would be any good." When she didn't reply, he again said, "You want to see me?"

"I want to talk to you about Tito, Dr. Cage. And I want to ask you about Cancer Cell."

The smile vanished from his face, and he opened his mouth as if to say something, but then shut it. When he did finally speak, all he said was, "Forget the 'Doctor.' Just call me Cage."

"Do you have some time?" she asked.

He looked around the waiting room. "Yeah, probably. Let's go somewhere else, all right?"

"Fine." She got up from the chair.

Cage turned toward the front counter. "Franzee, I'll be across the street at Mika's. If you need me, buzz me over."

"Sure thing, Dr. Cage."

Mika's was an unusual spice and espresso bar across the street from the clinic—it ran up all six floors of the building, but only extended maybe thirty feet in from the street on each level, with half the tables out on tiny, individual balconies that jutted out from the building and over the sidewalk. Cage put some money in the hand of the man who greeted them just inside the door on street level. The man, dressed in a spotless white collarless shirt and black slacks, nodded at a woman dressed in exactly the same clothes, who in turn led them up a flight of stairs and out onto a balcony table on the second floor.

"It's too damn hot to be inside," Cage said as they took seats at the table.

The woman handed them menu cards and immediately left without a word.

"She's not our waitress," Cage explained. "They have a complex hierarchy here." He laughed. "I still haven't completely figured it out yet, and I've been coming here for two years."

Even outside on the balcony it was hot and muggy, but he was right, it would have been sweltering inside, since there was no air conditioning. Blues emerged from speakers mounted in the floor of the balcony above them, the vocals sung beautifully by a woman; the words sounded Russian. Although there were people seated and talking at balcony tables on either side of them, as well as above, the voices were all indistinct, camouflaged by the Russian blues and the sounds of people on the sidewalks just below, the street traffic and the shouts of hawkers, the blasting whistles of a pack of Rebounders wheeling along in the gutters. It was a good place to come and talk if you didn't want to be overheard.

"Better take a quick look at the menu," Cage said. "Someone'll be here for our order in a minute, and if you're not ready they don't come back."

"They don't come back at all?"

"Nope. Someone *else* will, eventually, a lower-level waiter or waitress, but it won't be for a while, and even when they do come and take your order it'll be a long time before you get it, even if it's only a cup of coffee. It's all part of the hierarchy I was telling you about."

"Okay," she said, laughing. She glanced at the menu card, which was spare. Coffee and tea drinks, spice concoctions, and a few imported beers. No food except for deep-fried onion rings and egg rolls.

A man wearing an old, ragged tuxedo and tennis shoes approached their table and looked expectantly at Caroline. "Green iced tea with lemon," she said without hesitation. "Sugar milk." He nodded quickly once and turned to Cage.

"Just coffee," Cage said. "Black, dark roast."

The waiter nodded again and left.

"Very good," Cage said, smiling at her.

Before she had a chance to ask him about Tito, a girl of about fourteen in a dark green ankle-length dress arrived with their drinks. She set them on the table and quickly left.

"I just realized something," Caroline said, reaching for her iced tea. "No one has said a word to us."

Cage nodded. "That's right. None of them will, until we're done and on our way out. Then Marko, the guy who met us at the front door, he'll talk to us, as much as we want. He and I have become pretty good friends over the past year."

"And you still have to bribe him to get a balcony table?"

Cage grinned. "That's why we're still friends." He sipped at his coffee, and the grin faded, but his gaze never left Caroline's face. "You want to talk to me about Tito and Cancer Cell."

Caroline nodded. She tried her iced tea, which tasted quite good, just sweet enough and refreshing.

"Why?"

"He was my friend."

"All right, he was your friend. I guess you've talked to your father about all this, then."

"Some. Enough to get me here. I know Tito died in your clinic, and not from AIDS. And I know that you and my father think Cancer Cell is involved somehow."

"So your father sent you to me?"

"No. He doesn't know I'm here. He probably wouldn't be thrilled. I think he'd just like me to drop it and go on with my life. Put it all behind me."

"But you can't do that," Cage said. Not a question, as if he understood her.

"No, I can't."

"So what is it you want to know?"

"I want to know what killed him. I want to know if Cancer Cell is somehow responsible. I have no idea why they did it, but apparently they were the ones who kidnapped him in the first place, and I guess I want to know why they did that, too."

Cage sighed. "I don't have any answers for you," he said. "I don't know what killed him. Probably never will. Your father was going to try to arrange for an autopsy, but the last time I talked to him he hadn't managed it yet." He shook his head. "I doubt it'll give us an answer anyway. And without knowing what killed him, it's pretty much impossible to know if Cancer Cell had anything to do with it. Hell, even if we did know what killed Tito, my guess is we still wouldn't know anything about Cancer Cell's involvement. They don't exactly advertise what they're doing." He frowned. "What *do* you know about Cancer Cell?"

"Nothing. As good as nothing, anyway." It occurred to her that he had been very careful and precise about answering her, and that he hadn't referred at all to one thing. "You didn't say anything about my last question," she said to him. "About why Cancer Cell would have kidnapped him in the first place."

He smiled. "You don't miss much." He leaned one elbow on the table, slowly turning his coffee cup in circles with his other hand. "Of course I don't really have an answer to that, either, but it's something I can make a guess at."

"So make a guess." He was being very cautious about Cancer Cell. Maybe there were good reasons for that.

"All right," he said. He drank more coffee and gave a sort of shrug. "Tito had AIDS. He was dying. Okay. The word on the street is that Cancer Cell will sometimes put together a 'contract' of sorts with terminally ill people. They agree to provide high-quality medications—antibiotics, painkillers, anti-virals, immune system boosters, whatever might help make them comfortable, or relatively symptom-free—in return for which the person agrees to allow Cancer Cell to use them for clinical trials of experimental drugs or procedures during the final stages of their disease."

"But Tito didn't have any high quality medications," she objected. "All he had was crap he got from free clinics."

"Like ours," Cage said, smiling.

She shrugged. "Whatever."

"Fair enough. But how do you know that's all he had?"

She didn't, actually. She'd always just assumed. "I don't, I guess. He complained about them, said nothing he had did much good."

"In the final stages, *nothing* does much good, high-quality or not."

"I suppose." She remembered sitting with Tito while he lay on the sofa watching TV, hardly aware of her presence, his hands and feet in pain, but his gaze way deep inside the television set, farther in than the flickering images, all the way through them. She would speak to him, and he wouldn't respond. Like he was already halfway into another world; finding his way into it, learning how to leave this one.

And she realized that right at this moment she was much the same way, staring into her iced tea, having forgotten for a minute where she was. She looked back up at Cage, who was gazing steadily at her. "So why would he have been abducted?" she asked.

"Because he didn't want to honor his part of the contract. I've heard of it happening. Cancer Cell will do whatever is necessary to enforce the contract."

Caroline shook her head, finding it all a little hard to believe. "He never said anything about Cancer Cell. Never even mentioned them."

"He probably wouldn't have, even if he'd known. And he may not have known who he was dealing with. Most of the time when you deal with Cancer Cell, the name never comes up. I know someone who works for them who doesn't even know."

"Mouse knew."

"Who?"

"Mouse. Strange creature. Person. When I went to Tito's and found him gone, Mouse was there, cleaning out the place. He's the one who said it might have something to do with Cancer Cell. He said the two men who came and took Tito away were taking him to the Core." And Mouse had known her father was a cop. Mouse seemed to have known quite a lot. What did that mean about the little bastard?

"That would fit," Cage said. "That's where Cancer Cell is, right in the Core of the Tenderloin."

"So they took him to the Core, experimented on him, gave him some god-awful disease, and he ended up dying a horrible death."

"As opposed to the peaceful and painless death he would have experienced with the AIDS."

Caroline glared at him. "That's not the point," she said.

"No, you're right," Cage admitted. "I'm sorry." He glanced away for a moment, then back at her. "But we don't know if that's what happened. We don't even know for sure that he was abducted by Cancer Cell. But even if we accept that as a given, what happened afterward . . ." He shook his head. "There's just no way to know."

"I want to find out," Caroline insisted, adamant.

He tipped his head to one side and gave her a faint smile. He had deep hazel eyes that glittered with the lights from the street. "How do you plan to do that?"

"I don't know." No, she didn't know yet, but an idea was beginning to form, vague at this point, but slowly coming into focus. She finished off her iced tea and leaned back in the chair, watching him. Yes, she had to admit to herself that she liked him, and was willing to forgive his insensitive remark about Tito. "You seem to know an awful lot about Cancer Cell," she finally said. "Nobody else seems to know anything about them."

Cage waved a hand in dismissal. "It's mostly guesses," he said. "I've been working here in this clinic, half a block from the Core, for two years. Street medicine. Cancer Cell seems to be their own kind of street medicine. You hear things, that's all."

"My father said someone else died from the same thing that killed Tito."

"No, that's not quite right. He *may* have. It's just a guess."

"Another one of your guesses," she said, smiling.

"Yes. Another guess. I didn't see this guy die. I just heard about it from someone else, and even that was secondhand. The symptoms were similar."

"But the man who died was a part of Cancer Cell."

"Probably. Yes."

"So *you'd* like to know what happened to Tito, too."

Cage nodded. "Yes, I would."

At that point, the girl who had brought them their drinks returned to the table and looked back and forth between them with a questioning expression.

"You want another?" Cage asked.

"Yes, if you have time."

"Sure. They'll buzz me if they really need me, and I don't think our conversation is quite finished, is it?"

She smiled at him and shook her head. "No, it isn't."

He turned to the girl and said, "Two more, the same. Thanks."

The girl nodded and backed away.

They didn't talk as they waited for their drinks. Caroline watched the sidewalk and the street below them, the steady, heavy traffic on both. She liked the feel of it all, the energy that rose from the streets and the people and seemed to flow into her, juicing her up a little. But she had to remind herself of something her father had once told her—that the Tenderloin out on the streets was quite different from what went on inside the buildings and up on the rooftops, behind locked doors and windows, in the hidden mazes of basements and subterranean passages, in the vast warrens of apartments and skin parlors and drug dens and flesh arcades. The streets were relatively safe, along with the visible shops and cafés and clubs, but beneath it all, like the submerged portions of icebergs, was the real Tenderloin, and you never knew when some of that would break out into the open, out of control. A dangerous place if you didn't know where you were or what you were doing.

The girl brought fresh iced tea and coffee and took away the old glasses. Caroline took a long drink, refreshed and cooled by it. She wiped the cold, condensed liquid on the outside of the glass and spread it across her forehead.

"I want you to put me in touch with Cancer Cell," she said to Cage.

He didn't react much, but she could tell it wasn't at all

what he had expected to hear from her. He sipped at his coffee, scratched at his ear; she could see that he wanted to smile, to dismiss what she had said as a joke, but he managed to keep the smile in check.

"Why?" he finally asked.

"I said. I want to find out what happened to Tito. I want to help *you* find out what happened to him and to this other guy. Find out if there *is* something to worry about."

He sighed, turning his coffee cup in circles again. "First, I'm not sure I would be able to put you in touch with them. Second, even if I could, you couldn't just straight out ask about Tito. You did that, you'd be lucky if they just cut everything off right there and told you to go away. You'd be lucky if they didn't haul you into the Core and make *you* one of their experimental subjects."

She smiled at him. "That's exactly what I want them to do."

"What the hell are you talking about?" Cage said, exasperated.

She breathed in deeply, and her smile faded. "I have Gould's Syndrome," she told him.

He was clearly taken aback, though whether it was from her admission that she had Gould's, or from the realization of what she was proposing, was unclear. He shifted in his chair, plainly uncomfortable, but he didn't say anything for a long time. When he finally did speak, all he said was, "I'm sorry."

"Thank you." Then, getting right back to it, she said, "I want you to put me in touch with Cancer Cell, and then I'll work out my own contract with them."

Cage shook his head. "That's crazy."

"What's crazy about it?" she asked him. Now that the idea was fully formed, now that she had given it substance by actually suggesting it aloud to him, it seemed perfectly reasonable to her. "I've got a condition that's terminal— just what they'd be looking for. I make them a deal. I'll offer myself up for any experimental treatments they might have for Gould's. Then I'll be inside, and I'll see what I can find out about what happened to Tito. I have nothing to lose.''

''I suspect you have a *lot* to lose,'' he said.

''What do you mean?''

''The Gould's hasn't gone active yet, has it? You don't look like you're suffering any of the effects from it.''

Caroline looked away from him, reminded of the incident at her apartment the night Tina had come over. ''It's just recently begun,'' she said, still not looking at him. Suddenly her sureness deserted her, and the dread threatened to return. She turned back to him. ''Most of the time I'm fine, but it *has* begun to go active, and I know what that means.''

''Then you know that you might have several good years ahead of you, several years where you are, in fact, fine most of the time, like now. That seems to me like a *lot* to lose.''

''I think I'm a better judge of that than you are.''

''Yes, I suppose you are.'' Something seemed to have gone out of him, and he appeared suddenly very tired. ''But I still think it's a lousy idea.''

''Why?''

Cage held up his hands, shaking his head. ''I don't really know anything about Cancer Cell, I don't have any idea what they would do to you. They give you some kind of experimental treatment, it could be extremely painful and debilitating. Maybe they'd just do some other kind of experimentation. Once you were in the Core, you wouldn't have much choice. If you were in the terminal stages, if you were really sick, I'd say sure, go ahead. But you're not sick.''

''But now's the time to find out about Tito and this other guy,'' she insisted. ''Two or three or four years from now, when I am really sick, it will either be too late, or it won't matter.'' She paused, tilting her head. ''You do have a way to put me in touch with them, don't you?''

''Maybe.''

''Will you do it?''

He leaned back, shaking his head and running his hand

through his hair. "I don't know," he said. "I don't like it."

Caroline didn't push it. She sensed that would be a mistake right now, that he'd dig in and flat-out refuse. Better to let him think about it for a while, get used to the idea. Let his worries about Cancer Cell and some disease breaking out of them nag at him.

His head jerked to the right, eyes widening, his attention caught by something in the street below. Caroline turned, scanned the street until she saw what it was. Half a block away, weaving back and forth in the street, was a pedalcart slowly moving toward them, bumping into parked vehicles and other traffic as it came. A woman was at the wheel, peddling weakly, slumped forward with beaded dreadlocks covering her face, barely in control of the cart. As it got closer it veered off the street through a gap between a minicab and a jit, then jounced up the curb and onto the sidewalk, scattering people before it crashed lightly against the clinic building, just a few feet away from the entrance and almost directly across from Mika's. The woman remained in the cart, almost upright now but apparently dazed.

Cage leaped to his feet, grabbed the balcony rail, and leaned out over the street.

"Nikki!" he cried.

Caroline looked up into his face, saw stark terror. She turned back to the street.

"Nikki!" he cried out again.

The woman looked up and across the street, searching. "Cage?" Then her gaze seemed to find him and she nodded once. She staggered out of the pedalcart, took a couple of steps forward, and stepped into the gutter, almost losing her balance. She held up one bare arm. Even from across the street there were two visible red patches on her dark brown skin. "Cage, I'm in trouble."

Then she sat down on the sidewalk, her feet still in the gutter, and dropped her head into her arms.

CHAPTER 16

Nikki.

Cage almost jumped to the street from the balcony, but held back. A broken ankle wouldn't do anyone any good. *Nikki.* Jesus. With one last look at her, he turned, pushed off the rail, and ran inside.

He bumped into a table, rattling glasses, grabbed someone's shoulder, barked out an apology, and bounced away narrowly avoiding the guy in the tuxedo, then shot toward the stairs. He took them two and three at a time, barely in control, and hit the ground floor running. There wasn't a clear path and he crashed into a woman, almost fell, spun around while somehow staying on his feet, then squeezed between two people and he was free. He flew past Marko, who shouted something after him, and went through the front door.

Out on the sidewalk he crashed into more people, but shoved his way through. At the edge of the street he hesitated and took a good look at the traffic; he didn't want to get himself killed. Breathing hard, he anxiously waited for a break. One lane at a time. An opening appeared and he took off, darting through the wake of a junker truck and just in front of a pair of scooters. Then there was a brief hesitation to let a public jit go by, and he was off again, shifting quickly left, hand on the roof of a delivery van, stutter-stepping behind another small truck, then between two parked cars and he was across, no more than twenty feet from Nikki.

She was still sitting on the curb, her feet planted solidly in the gutter, her head in her hands.

"Nikki," he said, barely more than a whisper, and he hurried toward her.

She looked up at him with alarm and held out her hand, warding him off. "Don't, Cage. For Christ's sake, don't get too close!"

He stopped, just a few feet away, then started forward again.

"Don't touch me, Cage. I mean it."

He stopped again, close enough now to reach out and take hold of her, but he refrained. Instead, he squatted, bringing his face level with hers. She didn't look good. Her eyes were red, her nose was running, and her breathing seemed labored. Even her dreadlocks appeared unkempt and limp.

"How are you doing?" he asked, feeling kind of stupid.

But she managed a tired smile. "Shitty. I'm sick, Cage. I'm in deep shit. I thought I was getting better, I really did, but was I ever wrong." Her smile faded and she slowly shook her head from side to side. "That fucking Stinger. I'd kill him if he wasn't already dead."

"Hang in there for a minute," he told her. "I'll get something set up for you in the clinic, and then we'll get you inside."

"You'd better get gloves and a mask on," she said firmly, "or I won't let you near me. You try to touch me with your bare hands, I'll kick your bleedin' balls in."

Cage had to smile. "All right. I'll be right back."

He stood and looked around, and immediately realized he wasn't going to have to ask people to stay back. They'd heard her yelling at him, and they were all giving her a wide berth, even as they stared.

Franzee met him at the clinic door as he came through. "What's going on out there?"

"It's Nikki. She's in bad shape. What's the status on the iso rooms?"

Franzee shook her head. "Both occupied." Then, still shaking her head, "Don't ask. You don't want to know."

"Exam rooms?"

"Three and Five are empty right now, I think. I'll check for sure."

Cage nodded. "All right. Keep one of them open."

He jogged down the hall to the staff room, grabbed a cot, a couple of blankets, and a pillow, then hurried back into the front room with them. He set them in front of the counter.

"Five?" he asked.

Franzee nodded. "It's open."

"Can you get that stuff set up in there? And I'll bring her in."

Franzee nodded again and dragged the cot down the hall. Cage put on a pair of gloves and pulled a medico-mask over his head, tugging it all the way down so it hung around his neck. He breathed deeply several times, trying to calm himself. Then he went out to get her.

Nikki hadn't moved, and though a crowd had gathered around her, they still kept back. There was a lot of mumbling and muttering, jockeying to get a better view. He wanted to strangle them all.

As he got close to her, she glared at him and pointed. "Put the damn mask on," she said.

"All right, all right." He pulled the mask up over his mouth and nose, then knelt beside her. "Think you can walk?" he asked, knowing damn well what her answer would be.

"I'm not a cripple, for Christ's sake. Of course I can walk."

He took her arm with his gloved hands and helped her to her feet. She took a couple of steps, then stopped and doubled over, her free hand on her knees.

"Nikki?"

She shook her head, her eyes clamped shut. "It's . . . it's okay," she got out, her voice croaking. Her hand was gripping his fingers so tightly his knuckles hurt. Then her grip eased, her eyes opened, she breathed in, and slowly straightened. "Okay," she said.

They made their way the last few feet to the clinic entrance. Just as they approached, the door swung open, held wide by Franzee. Cage led Nikki through the doorway, the waiting room, then along the hall to Exam Five, which was the last room at the end of the corridor. There he guided her to the cot and had her sit on it. Then he pulled up a chair, sat in front of her, and gave her a thorough workup. Focused on the task, on the details.

Her temperature was high, well over a hundred and two. Lymph nodes in her neck and under her arms and down around her groin were all swollen. Blood pressure was okay, though, and her pulse was still strong. The red patch on her arm looked like a severe rash. There was another small patch on the back of her other arm, and a third on the side of her neck.

When he was done, he helped her get dressed. She seemed so tired and weak, and she said her muscles and joints ached.

"I'm really thirsty," she said.

Cage filled a plastic cup with water and gave it to her. She drained it at once, and he gave her another, and finally a third.

"Have you taken anything for the fever?"

Nikki shook her head. "Not for a long time. I haven't been thinking any too clearly."

So he gave her some ibuprofen and a couple of acetaminophen, which she took with another cup of water. She dropped the cup onto the floor and slowly laid back and out on the cot, closing her eyes.

"I'm sorry," she said quietly. "I shouldn't have come here. You can't do anything. I just panicked."

"No," Cage said. "You did right. I'll figure out something for you."

Nikki rolled her head from side to side. "There's nothing. We both know that. I should just go home."

"No," he insisted. "Not nothing."

She smiled, her eyes still closed. "What, then?"

"I don't know yet. Something."

Neither of them spoke for a while. Cage sat almost motionless and watched her, a terrible pain slowly eating at his gut. It was terror, he realized. He was terrified of losing her.

But her breathing had eased, and she seemed calmer. The tension had left her face.

She opened her eyes and looked at him. "I'm going to die."

Cage shook his head. "We're *all* going to die, Nikki."

Her eyes flashed and she glowered at him. "Don't talk that kind of shit to me, Cage. I won't have it."

"I'm sorry," he said. Then, "But you're not going to die."

"Stinger and that other guy died."

"They didn't have any medical care."

Nikki gave a brief, harsh laugh. "And what the hell kind of medical care am I going to get? You guys are all good doctors, but this isn't a hospital, it's not even close."

"I'll get you into a hospital, Nikki."

She shook her head. "Yeah? Which one?"

"I don't know yet. I'll work out something."

Her expression softened as she watched him. "You will, won't you?"

Cage just nodded. He didn't know how he was going to arrange it, but he would figure out something. He was going to get her out of this goddamn place and into one of the top-flight hospitals where they would be able to keep her alive until they figured out what she had, or until it ran its course.

"I love you, Nikki."

"I know you do, Cage. And I love you, too. I'm sorry it couldn't ever be the way you wanted."

"You don't need to apologize."

"Sure I do," she said, smiling. Then she rolled onto her side and closed her eyes. "I'm going to sleep for a while now."

"Okay. I'll come back and check on you in a little bit."

Out in the hall, he disposed of the gloves and mask, then wandered into the waiting room. He was surprised to see Caroline Carlucci looking up at him from one of the chairs.

He'd completely forgotten about her. He crossed the room and sat next to her.

"Sorry about taking off like that."

Caroline shook her head in dismissal. "How is she? Is it Nikki?"

"Yes, Nikki. I don't know how she is. She's sleeping. I don't know." He rubbed at his eyes with his palms, forcing the flash of brightly colored lights across his vision. He wished he could go to sleep himself.

"Has she got the same thing Stinger and Tito had?"

Cage nodded. He didn't want to open his eyes, not for hours. But he finally did, and looked at her. "I can't be sure, but I think so." Then he explained what had happened with Stinger and the finger hooks.

"She got sick a couple of weeks later, but I thought it was just the flu, something like that. It had been a long time. I was a little worried, but then she started getting better. We both thought she was through the worst of it, we both thought . . ." He grimaced, grabbing the back of his neck with his hand and rubbing. "Christ, we both thought wrong."

"What can you do for her?"

"I don't know. Get her into a good hospital, somewhere. No one will want to take her, so I don't know how I'm going to manage that, but I've got to. She'll die if she stays here." Then he looked at her again, a thought occurring to him. "Wait . . . maybe." He dug around in his jeans until he found her father's card. "I'm going to call your father," he said. "We'll see what kind of pull he's got."

"Cage?"

"Yeah?"

"When you talk to him, don't tell him I'm here. Don't even tell him you've seen me."

For the first time since Nikki had appeared on the street, he remembered what he and Caroline had been talking about at Mika's. He gazed silently at her for a few moments, feeling like he completely understood her. "I won't."

It took him several minutes to get through to Carlucci as

a dispatcher tried tracking him down, but Cage finally heard his voice.

"I still haven't managed to get an autopsy for Tito, yet," Carlucci said.

"No, that's not why I called. I've got a big favor to ask for. A *huge* favor."

"Great," Carlucci said. "That sounds hopeful."

"I've got another one here. At the clinic."

"Another dead person?"

"No. Just sick. But with the same thing." He paused, trying to figure the best way to put it. Shit, just go straight with it. "Her name is Nikki, and she's my closest friend. She got it from Stinger, the other dead guy, and she means the world to me. Understand?"

There was just the slightest pause. "I understand," Carlucci eventually said. "What can I do?"

"I need to get her into a real hospital, or she's going to die. We can't do shit for her here."

There was a long silence at the other end of the line. Cage glanced at Caroline, who was watching him.

"You there?" he asked.

"Yeah, Cage, I'm here. I'm just thinking. All right, let me talk to some people. I'll call you back."

"Okay. Thanks, Lieutenant."

"Sure thing, 'Doctor.' "

Cage smiled and hung up.

"Anything?" Caroline asked.

"Maybe. He's going to talk to some people, then call back." He breathed deeply once, feeling some sense of relief. He had the feeling that Carlucci would come through. But he wasn't going to leave the phone until he heard something definite.

"Your closest friend," Caroline said.

"What?" He was only half paying attention to her.

"Nikki. What you said to my father. That she means the world to you."

"Yeah." Nodding, and thinking about her lying on the cot back in the exam room. "I know this is going to sound ridiculous, but . . . she saved my life. Not in a metaphorical or symbolic sense. The real thing. She pulled my ass out of some deep, deep shit years ago, down in L.A. Maybe I'll tell you about it sometime." He shook his head and looked back along the hallway, half expecting Nikki to walk out of Exam Five, smiling, arms out, saying she was just fine. "The least I can do now," he said, "is return the favor."

He wanted to go back and check on her, but he was afraid to leave the phone. It was irrational, he knew Franzee would answer it and come back to get him, but he just could not leave. He looked back at Caroline, trying to take his mind off Nikki.

"What happened over at Mika's?" he asked. "After I hurricaned out of there."

She smiled. "I took care of everything. A little bit of confusion. I tried to pay the wrong person, the girl. She was quite shocked."

The phone rang and Cage answered it before the first ring had quite finished.

"Cage," he said.

"An ambulance is on the way," Carlucci said. "We have a couple of street access points into the Tenderloin for emergencies. It'll pick her up and take her to St. Anthony's—that's the police and fire departments' hospital."

"Jesus. How did you manage that?"

"Sold my soul to the Devil."

"Shit, he can have mine, too," Cage said.

"It actually wasn't that difficult," Carlucci told him. "I just had to lie about a few things."

"I owe you, Carlucci."

"You sure do, Cage. I'll cash in someday. Anything else?"

"Not a thing."

"Then I'll let you go. It shouldn't be long, maybe fifteen, twenty minutes. And we'll talk about all of this later."

Cage said good-bye and hung up the receiver. He looked at Caroline. "Your father pulled it off. Ambulance is on the way. He's arranged to have her admitted to St. Anthony's."

"That's great."

He nodded. Now he could go back and check on Nikki.

"Cage," Caroline said. "One more thing."

"What's that?"

"*Now* will you help me get in touch with Cancer Cell?"

He didn't have think about it this time. He nodded slowly. "Oh, yeah. As soon as possible."

ISABEL

Things were getting strange in the Core. People were dying.

Isabel sensed the changes, she could smell them—the people in here now smelled like fear.

One day, in the shadowy light below street level, she saw a man die violently, shaking and screaming while several other people watched him, afraid to get close. And when the man had died, the people left him. Only later did someone come back, pour liquid over him, and set him on fire. Isabel smelled the stench for days whenever she got near that passage.

Another time, she saw the woman who had been cutting up Henry, saw her die in much the same way as the man, only she was alone in a room, surrounded by paper lanterns and multicolored rocks. Isabel felt a certain satisfaction when the woman stopped moving at last, dead.

Two other times in her travels she saw dead people, bodies twisted, eyes open, teeth bared, lots of blood. And she knew something bad was happening here.

She began searching for a way out.

She wasn't sure she actually wanted to leave the Core—she had the sense that outside the Core would be many more people, passages and rooms would be more crowded, there would be fewer places to hide, fewer places to be alone—but she felt a need to be prepared. If the Core continued to get stranger, crazier, and more out of control, she needed to have a way out.

She had a fairly good sense of the Core's boundaries,

and so she explored them, probing. Although she occasionally wandered up staircases into the building floors at street
level and higher, she really spent no time there looking for
a way out; there were many ways out onto the streets themselves, but she could see the high, brightly lit electrified
barriers blocking the streets, could see all the doorways and
windows of the buildings outside the Core itself completely
blocked by brick and metal or firmly secured wooden
planks. The only way out would be underground.

Isabel did see men and women leaving the Core through
below-ground passages, concrete tunnels, but there were always locked doors or other barriers she would not be able
to pass. She would have to find her own way out.

Dawn had arrived, gray and already hot. The Core was
quiet, her regular passageways empty. Isabel moved carefully along the outer perimeter, one hand on the corridor
wall, feeling her way, feeling for an opening. The wall was
cool, almost smooth, though there were cracks and chips in
it, and places where mosses grew. Colorful markings covered much of the concrete.

There was a break in the wall, a branching corridor, narrow, maybe three feet wide. Isabel entered it, took a few
steps forward, but it ended abruptly. Mortared brick
blocked the corridor, sealing it from floor to ceiling, wall
to wall. There was no way through.

Isabel crouched in front of the brick and examined the
walls on both sides. On her left, just above her head, was
a small, square opening covered by a deteriorating mesh
screen. She reached up, gripped the screen with both hands,
and tugged. The screen came free, scattering bits of dirt
and dust and broken bits of metal.

Isabel pulled herself up and into the opening. She
scraped her hips on the rough edges of the opening, but
worked herself all the way in. She was inside a metal duct
of some kind, the walls cool and smooth. She couldn't see
anything, but she smelled damp earth from somewhere.

For several moments she didn't move, listening, sniffing
the air. Then she crawled forward. Progress was slow; she

couldn't move her limbs much. But she inched her way along through the dark.

She came to a T, the duct widening as it branched in both directions. Isabel took the right branch, figuring the left headed back into the Core. In the larger duct, the going was easier. She hadn't gone far when the duct bent right, narrowing once again. After a slight hesitation, she squeezed into the narrow section and continue crawling forward.

The duct opened out into dark open space. Isabel remained at the opening for a minute or so, trying to make out the room. There was actually a little more light here, and eventually she could see a narrow corridor. To her right, just barely visible, was the same brick wall, she realized; the other side.

She worked her way out of the duct and dropped to the floor. At the other end of the corridor from the brick wall was a dim rectangle of light. Isabel padded along the passage, then up several steps to a door with a glass window covered by cobwebs. She brushed away the cobwebs, then pressed her face against the glass.

On the other side of the door was a large room filled with boxes and crates, drums and large glass bottles, and all kinds of other miscellaneous junk scattered everywhere. Two men were sitting on chairs, smoking cigarettes and drinking from green bottles.

Isabel turned from the window and headed back down the steps. She would go back into the Core for now, but this was just what she needed—a way out.

EPIDEMIOLOGY:
TRACKING THE SOURCE

CHAPTER 17

Sometimes Carlucci hated this goddamn job. He sat at his desk, sweating in the heat and staring at the sketch artist picture of the woman who *might* have been Naomi Katsuda's lover, the woman nobody could find. And after a week of negotiations with Yoshi Katsuda, who supposedly wanted to talk to him, an interview had finally been arranged, but it was still four days away. The case was going nowhere fast, and it pissed him off.

He tossed the picture onto his desk and leaned back in his chair. Santos and Weathers were doing everything they could, he knew that. But there had to be another way to go at this case. And the only other way he could think of was through Tito's abduction and death. So far, though, not much had happened there, either. Cage hadn't come up with anything; in fact, when they'd talked yesterday, Cage had said he now doubted he would ever be able to arrange for Carlucci to meet with anyone from Cancer Cell. Something about them being too wary of cops. Carlucci had the feeling Cage was being evasive, but he couldn't do a damn thing about that.

So what else? He leaned forward, dug around through the stacks of files and notes on his desk until he found his file on Tito Moraleja. Then he leaned back again, opened the file, and leafed through it. There wasn't much. Tran's official report of their visit to Tito's room. An addendum about the parrot, and several transcripts that had been made of the parrot's useless utterances. CID had given up on the parrot in disgust, but Kelly had taken a liking to it, named it Horus, and brought it home with him. And finally there were his notes on his talks with Caroline and Cage. He glanced through them.

Mouse. That familiar name again. He knew it from somewhere, someone's weasel, something like that. Wait a minute . . . wait . . . He looked back at the parrot transcripts and skimmed over them. Yes, there it was: "... *mouse . . . asshole . . . it's the mouse in the house.* . . ." Well, let's see what he could do with it. He cleared the piles away from his desktop, exposing the keyboard. The screen blinked to life and he ran a restricted search on Mouse's name.

He went down the hall and got a couple of cans of cold lemonade while he waited. The air wasn't much cooler out in the hall than it was in his office. Every time the air recycling system was renovated in the building, the promise was made that *this* time it would all work perfectly. It never did. What they needed to do was tear down the building and start from scratch. But that was never going to happen either.

When he got back to his office, the search was complete, and he had a large batch of records to sift through, most of which he knew weren't going to be at all relevant. He settled in, opened the first can of lemonade, and went to work.

An hour and two cans of lemonade later, he thought he'd found what he was looking for—notes about a guy named Mouse in two different reports made by Sandrine Binoche, an undercover narcotics cop. He didn't know her. He checked in with the duty logs, found out she was off-duty today; but he put out a priority call, and fifteen minutes later he had a callback from her.

"Lieutenant? Sandrine Binoche here."

"Sorry to bother you on your day off," he said.

"That's all right. I'm taking care of my sister's three kids while she and her husband take a bike ride—give them some time to themselves. And I can use any damn excuse to get a break from the little monsters for a few minutes. So what can I do for you, Lieutenant?"

"A case I'm working on. I'm trying to find out something about a guy named Mouse, and you mention someone with that name on a couple of your recent reports. You know the guy?"

"Oh, yeah, I know the guy. He's a nasty prick."

"What's he look like?"

"Short, skinny little bastard, maybe five feet at the most. He's got pink eyes, but he's not exactly an albino. Had all his teeth pulled a few years ago and replaced with a set of shiny metal choppers. Very attractive."

Carlucci nodded to himself as he listened to her while rereading Caroline's description of him. "That's the guy," he said. "That's the same guy, all right. What can you tell me about him?"

"He does a little of everything, none of it good. Sells a lot of crap drugs, which sometimes gets him shit-kicked by his customers, but he doesn't seem to mind it that much. Runs wireheads once in a while. Used to middleman for people trying to find body-bags. Acts as a courier for Fat Buddha on occasion. You know Fat Buddha?"

"Yeah." Fat Buddha was an empire builder in the DMZ, fancied himself a kind of crime lord. The cops had pretty much quit trying to get at the guy once they realized he kept to the DMZ and wasn't trying to expand out of it and into any other part of the city. Besides, he was a strange sort of stabilizing influence in the DMZ. "So where can I find Mouse? In the DMZ?"

"Sometimes. But he also spends a lot of time in the Polk Corridor, and that's the part of the DMZ you'd be more likely to find him in, where it butts up against the Polk. You sure you *want* to find him?"

"Yeah, I'm sure. Anything else I should know?"

"Just watch your ass, Lieutenant. You being a cop won't make one bit of difference to him. And watch his hands— he likes knives, and he always keeps a few stashed on him."

"All right, Binoche. Thanks."

An hour later, Carlucci was walking along the lower end of the Polk Corridor, just a couple of blocks from where it met the DMZ and then the Tenderloin. Two o'clock in the afternoon, the heat from the sun overhead was cut by a breeze blowing in from the west; but the relief came with a price—a terrible stench of rotting food that only let up whenever the breeze did.

This was the crappy end of the Polk. A few blocks north it began to slowly go upscale, blending into a somewhat prosperous retail core with bookstores, theaters, clothing boutiques. Here at this end was a different story. The bars were seedy, darker, and more numerous, the retail stores sold cheap junk and used merchandise, restaurants and coffee shops were risky to your health. Instead of hair salons, scarification parlors. Rather than a body-electronics store, a series of shock shops. And where you might find a day spa in the upper Polk, here you would only find hump rooms renting by the half hour.

Carlucci walked slowly along, searching the sidewalks and street for Mouse, glancing into stores and alleys. He hadn't gone two blocks when a boy who couldn't have been more than twelve or thirteen offered him a cheap blow job. Maybe it was better that he looked more like a pedophile than a cop, although it surprised and depressed him. Half a block farther on, he shook his head at another approaching boy before the kid could say anything.

He bought a cup of coffee and a sweet, sticky pastry of some kind from a man selling out of a basement window, then sat next to a couple on a nearby bench. As he worked on the pastry and coffee, he scanned the street and sidewalks, searching for Mouse. Some of the people moving past him were lethargic, dragged by the heat, but a lot more were moving fast, either speeded out or running on natural chemical imbalances—it was impossible to tell the difference between the two. Plenty of freaks, but no Mouse.

Just as Carlucci ate the last of the pastry, the guy next to him grabbed the wrapper out of his hand, wadded it into a ball, then popped it into his mouth and began chewing on it. The woman with him leaned forward, smiled, and said, "Thank you."

"You're welcome," Carlucci said. Then he got up, the man still chewing like mad, the woman still smiling, and walked off. There were too damn many people like that on the streets.

Carlucci walked slowly along Polk, looking into stores and doorways, glancing up at apartment windows, checking out people sitting or lying in parked cars. If he'd been a vice or narcotics cop, he could have made half a dozen different arrests right there on the street; of course, if he *had* been a vice or narcotics cop, he wouldn't have bothered with any of them. They were all too trivial.

He stopped on a corner and scanned the street in all directions, and decided it was pretty much a pointless waste spending any more time in the Polk. He couldn't put it off any longer, so he walked down to the end of the Polk and into the DMZ. The sidewalks became more crowded, and the walled boundaries of the Tenderloin seemed to radiate the heat from the sun, and there was no breeze here for some reason—the temperature seemed to jump five or ten degrees just like that.

He stood on a corner, blinking against the heat and the reflections of the sun coming at him from strange angles, and tried to adjust to the DMZ. Besides the greater heat, the feel of the air around him had changed. The lower end of the Polk was seedy and a little bit wacked, but the atmosphere here in the DMZ felt distinctly dangerous and deranged. He'd have gone a little bit crazy if he'd known Caroline had been coming here to visit her friend Tito, so it was probably better that he *hadn't* known. He certainly couldn't have stopped her.

Again he tried to keep an eye out for Mouse as he walked along, but now it was harder. There was more movement all around him, more noise, everything strangely colored and frantic and slightly out of sync from normal expectations, which gave him a constant jittery sensation at the edges of his attention, made it difficult to focus. Even the smells were different, everything with a slightly acrid tinge—cooking food, tobacco and pot and fireweed smoke, spilled booze, burning rubber, piss and vomit. Even the occasional strong scent of flowers from lush, overgrown plants hanging above the street had a bitter edge.

Carlucci stopped in front of an urban taxidermist and

looked into one of the windows. Several complete, small animal skeletons were mounted on pedestals with identification labels: CAT; PARROT; FERRET; CHIHUAHUA. A sign dangling above them claimed that all the skeletons were guaranteed to have been organically cleaned by maggots and that no chemicals were used. In the other window were several huge, stuffed rats. Over them was a sign that said: BIG FUCKIN' RATS!! YOUR CHOICE, $10.00.

A shouted curse and loud laughter caught his attention and he turned away from the display windows to see what was going on. Two people were struggling with a fat, bare-chested man, trying to load him into an organ scavenger van. But it was unclear if the man was actually dead; he seemed to be moving, breathing maybe, perhaps even struggling against the two scavengers. Carlucci started toward them, unsure if he would actually intervene—it might only get him killed here. But as he got closer, and they shifted their hold on the man, Carlucci saw that most of the back of the man's head was gone, bloody red and gray of brain tissue exposed to the heat and the sun.

The heat was starting to get to him, along with the stench and a crazy kind of sensory overload. Just ahead, past a rocket-bottle joint, was a bar with its front doors open wide and some kind of slash-and-burn music blaring out into the street.

Carlucci stepped into the bar, almost blinded by the change in light. Light from the street came in behind him, casting strange shadows that mixed with the interior gloom and a jittery kaleidoscope of colored lights coming from the tiny stage. There was no band on the stage, just a couple of tall speakers and silhouette cutouts of four musicians.

The front section of the bar was a thick maze of tables, most of them full, with hardly enough room to walk among them. Booths lined the front windows, the glass tinted so dark almost no light came through them from outside. In the back was a long bar, also full. The people were all shouting at each other over the music.

Carlucci wondered how badly he wanted a beer. Badly enough. He worked his way through the tables and managed to squeeze into a spot at the bar. He leaned sideways against the Formica counter and scanned the room as he waited for the bartender. No sign of Mouse, but then he hadn't expected to see him; he was just hoping for a shot of absurd luck.

The bartender, a big, fat, ugly guy close to six and a half feet tall with a ponytail, stopped in front of Carlucci and squinted at him.

"A beer," Carlucci said. "Whatever you've got on tap."

The bartender cocked his head, then leaned forward until his face was only inches from Carlucci's. "I don't want you in here," he whispered.

"Why not?"

The bartender didn't answer, just shook his head and pulled back.

"I just want a beer," Carlucci said.

"I know what you are," the bartender said. But he stepped to the tap and pulled a beer into a large pint glass, then came back and set it in front of Carlucci. "Let's make it on the house."

"Let's not."

The bartender shook his head again. "Five bucks," he said. He took the money from Carlucci, stuck it in his shirt pocket, and moved down the bar.

Carlucci took several deep swallows. The beer wasn't very cold, and it didn't have much flavor, but any liquid cooler than the stifling heat was welcome. He drank some more.

Instead of turning around, he tried to scan the crowd by looking into the mirror on the back wall. But there were too few open spots on the mirror, and the lighting was so inconsistent that it was impossible. So he shifted around, leaned his back against the bar, and he got his absurd bit of luck: Mouse.

Mouse was just coming out of the back corner hall by the bathrooms, moving to the rapid beat of the music. Around his neck was a neuro-collar blinking green, presumably in time to his heartbeat. He smiled at people as he moved through the crowd, metal teeth flashing, slapping hands and heads. Someone scowled and flipped him off, and Mouse just laughed. He stopped at a table not far from

Carlucci, leaned over, and slipped something into the front of a woman's blouse. The woman kissed Mouse on the cheek and bit his ear, and he moved on.

When it became clear that Mouse was headed for the front doors, Carlucci drained his beer, belched long and loud, then set his glass on the bar. He left another five on the counter, smiling to himself as he wondered if it would stay there long enough for the bartender to see it, then pushed off and headed casually toward the front entrance.

He was almost there when Mouse finally pushed through and out onto the street. Mouse glanced in both directions, then turned left. Carlucci squeezed past the last table, stepped out through the doors, and turned automatically left. And there was Mouse, just half a block away. Carlucci followed.

Although Mouse was as distinctive as they came, he was so short it was surprisingly difficult to keep him in sight. Carlucci would lose him for a minute or two at a time, then catch a glimpse, and not always where he expected. Mouse crossed the street once, so he was moving right along the boundary of the Tenderloin, but Carlucci stayed on this side. Mouse probably wasn't going into the Tenderloin, and if he did there would be no way to follow him. Mouse talked to someone in a beer kiosk, there was an exchange of money and packets, then Mouse came back across the street, now only twenty feet away.

Carlucci stayed with him to the end of the block, across the intersection, and along another half block. Then Mouse veered sharply to the left and disappeared from view. When Carlucci reached the spot where Mouse had disappeared, he was at the entrance to a narrow, filthy alley strewn with trash and shattered crates, lit as much by a couple of drum fires as by the light coming in from the street. Two men dressed in thrift store suits and ties stood in front of one drum fire, cooking large hunks of meat impaled on metal rods. The drum fire farther in was unattended, but burned brightly, casting flickering shadows up the alley walls.

Carlucci saw movement just past the second drum fire and caught a glimpse of Mouse's blinking neuro-collar.

Hesitating for a few moments, he stood gazing into the alley, then shook his head and entered it.

"Hey!" said one of the men at the drum fire. "Got any barbecue sauce?"

The other man wheezed out a laugh, and Carlucci didn't reply. He nodded at the two men as he passed them, and they both laughed. The stench of the cooking meat nauseated him.

The ground was covered with gravel and broken glass and potholes filled with water and oil. He had to pay as much attention to his footing as to the flickering lights and shadows in front of him.

When he reached the second drum fire, he stopped and searched the gloom ahead. The alley appeared to dead-end about fifty or sixty feet farther on, the brick wall of the building on his left angling across to meet the one on his right. There was one door on the left, some boarded windows, and then on the right, up near the dead end, a break in the wall—a doorway or alcove, or perhaps even a covered passage through to another alley or the street. There was no sign of Mouse.

No, he was not that stupid. This was as far as he went. He didn't need Mouse that badly.

Something slammed hard into his left shoulder, spinning him around and knocking him to the ground. He tried to push himself up to his knees, but his left arm collapsed under him, suddenly shot through with a hot, searing pain. Confused for a few moments, he rolled onto his back and scooted toward the alley wall, gaze darting around in search of his attacker. No one was anywhere near him, but as the pain in his shoulder increased, he finally realized what had happened: He'd been shot.

Shit.

How bad? He stopped for a moment and tried feeling around his left shoulder with his hand. More pain, and lots of wet. He pulled his hand back and looked at it. Shit again. Too goddamn much blood.

With his one good hand and arm he dragged himself to the alley wall, then worked his way up into a sitting position. He hadn't heard the shot. Silenced? What the hell did it matter?

Christ, he wasn't thinking straight. He grabbed for the com unit on his belt, pulled it free, and switched it on, pressing the emergency signal and beacon. There was a faint crackle, and only a few seconds' wait before a man's voice came on.

"Emergency response," he said.

"Officer down," Carlucci said. He didn't need to say any more, didn't need to identify himself—his signal would do that.

"Lieutenant Carlucci?"

"Yes. I'm in real trouble here."

"Can you give me your location?" The beacon would work as a homing device, but it would take time to lock on to it. The closer you could direct them, the faster they could get there.

"The DMZ," Carlucci said. His heart sank as he said those words. Christ, he didn't want to die here. "Near Polk . . ." Christ, what street had he been on? What had he last crossed? He couldn't remember, he could hardly think. "I'm in an alley," he managed to get out. "Off Larkin I think . . . ? Sutter . . . ?"

"Officers and aid cars rolling, Lieutenant. Stay with me now, all right?"

Carlucci got out a strangled laugh. "Sure. Where the hell am I going to go?"

He was almost directly across the alley from the drum fire, and he stared at the orange and yellow flames, watched the glow of embers inside the drum through small, jagged holes that had burned and rusted through the metal. The dispatcher was still talking to him, but he no longer paid any attention. He couldn't stay focused on anything but the flames.

Then he remembered the other drum fire, and he turned his head toward the mouth of the alley. He could see the two forms by the other drum fire, outlined by the light coming from the street, and he thought they were looking at him. But they were making no move to leave their cook-

ing and approach him, which was just as well. He didn't
need the kind of help they would offer.

"...still with me, Lieutenant? Lieutenant? Come *on*
Lieutenant, say something."

"I'm still here," he finally managed to say, and he tried
to focus back in on the dispatcher. He closed his eyes,
hoping that would help. For a moment it seemed to, but
with his eyes closed he felt an overpowering urge to drop
off to sleep.

Then he heard movement off to his left, sensed a shadow,
and he opened his eyes. Mouse was standing over him,
grinning down at him with flashing metal teeth.

"Hey, Mr. Cop Man. I don't think you'll be needing
this." His hand darted out and snatched the com unit from
Carlucci's grip. He stepped back, then swung his boot forward and kicked Carlucci hard in the ribs.

Jesus Christ. Carlucci closed his eyes against the pain,
against the sight of that nasty little prick standing over him.
Binoche was right. He opened his eyes, tried to lurch up
and grab for the com unit, but Mouse was too quick and
jerked it out of the way.

"This what happens you fuck around with the Mouse.
Hah!" Mouse snapped his teeth at him.

Carlucci heard sirens, but there was no way to know if
they were for him or not. Even if they were, they sounded
too far away, they would never get here in time. And if
Mouse walked away right now, even without doing anything else, if he took the com unit ... Carlucci didn't know
if anyone would be able to find him. He'd lie in this damn
alley and bleed to death. Here in the fucking DMZ, for
Christ's sake.

Suddenly Mouse jerked upright, eyes bulging. He took a
single staggering step, then seconds later his face and forehead exploded, blood and flesh and bone splattering everywhere. The neuro-collar went crazy, flashing all kinds of
colors as Mouse fell forward and collapsed across Carlucci,
the com unit still gripped in his hand. Blood poured from
what remained of Mouse's head, pooling on the ground
next to Carlucci and soaking into his pants and shirt.

He tried to roll Mouse off of him, but he didn't have the strength. He was fading in and out. Mouse's neuro-collar was dead now, no lights at all. Carlucci tried for the com unit in Mouse's hand, but he couldn't reach it. He tried again to move Mouse, but still couldn't manage it.

His shoulder was going cold, and he could no longer feel anything in his left arm, his left hand. Blood was everywhere, slick and slippery, and the stink of it filled his nostrils, mixing with the stench of the cooking meat.

Sirens were getting louder. Or were they? Suddenly he couldn't hear them at all, he couldn't hear anything.

Then the sirens returned, loud and piercing, only to fade away once again.

This fucking place, he did not want to die here. The flames of the barrel fire seemed to grow, leaping upward, then out at him, licking him with their heat.

He tried to turn his head toward the mouth of the alley to see if anyone was coming, but when he did a shower of silver glitter washed over his vision. He let his head fall back, the glitter faded, and the flames returned.

There was a voice from the com unit, but he couldn't make out the words.

Sirens again. But they were too late, and it was all for nothing.

He closed his eyes and tried to hang on.

CHAPTER 18

Caroline had imagined the meeting would take place in the dead of night, in some dark, hidden subterranean room reached by endless and confusing twists and turns through dimly lit passages and guarded doorways. Instead, they met Rashida at midday, in the open courtyard of a three-story building.

A warm and steady rain had been falling since early morning. Caroline and Cage were led across the courtyard by a short man wearing jeans and sandals and a serape. Rashida, slim and dark with long black hair and dark brown eyes, was sitting at a table protected from the rain by a second-floor balcony. In front of her was a package of cigarettes, a stone lighter, and a beautifully worked turquoise and copper ashtray. She was smoking a cigarette, and nodded in greeting, asked them to sit down, then asked them if they wanted anything to drink.

"I can offer you coffee or tea, or lemonade," Rashida said. Her voice carried just the trace of an accent that Caroline couldn't identify, but assumed was Middle Eastern of some sort. "There is no alcohol here, but if you want, I can send Adolfo to buy some beer for you."

"Lemonade will be fine for me," Caroline said.

"The same for me," Cage added.

Rashida nodded at Adolfo. "Bring a pitcher."

Caroline looked around the courtyard. Across the way, sheltered from the rain by a large palm, a man squatted in front of a small brazier, cooking something on a grill sus-

pended above the coals; from the smells that wafted across
the courtyard, she guessed it was fish. Occasionally someone would come into the courtyard from one of several
alcoves in the building, hurry through the rain, then enter
one of the other alcoves. Two old women sat out on a third-
floor balcony down in the far corner, a tarp stretched over
them from the roof to keep the rain off. The two women
were drinking something from a dark brown bottle, small
glasses in front of each of them. Every so often one of them
cackled. Except for the steady clatter of the rain, the courtyard was fairly quiet, much quieter than the streets outside.
Caroline was surprised that it could be so quiet anywhere
inside the Tenderloin.

Beside her, Cage seemed antsy, constantly shifting po-
sitions in his chair, gaze darting in all directions. She
wanted to put a hand on his shoulder or thigh, silently tell
him to relax, but she thought that might embarrass him.

Adolfo reappeared, now wearing a wide-brimmed straw
hat and carrying a tray with a large glass pitcher of lemonade and three ice-filled glasses. He set the tray on the
table, filled all three glasses, then left.

Rashida put out her cigarette, and glanced back and forth
between them. "I don't like this," she said. She sipped at
her lemonade, then fixed her gaze on Caroline. "Cage tells
me you want to meet with me. So tell me what you want."

"I need to get in touch with Cancer Cell," Caroline said.
"Cage says you're involved with them. That you are a part
of them, a member, whatever."

"Is that what Cage says?" Rashida shook her head. "I
have nothing to do with Cancer Cell. I don't know anything
about them, and I don't plan to learn anything about them.
If that's why we're here, then this is all a waste of everyone's time." She sipped at her lemonade again, still shaking her head.

Caroline didn't say anything. She didn't know how to
respond. She had nothing but Cage's word about Rashida,
nothing to back herself up with, and she felt as if she'd
been hung out to dry on this.

But Cage wasn't going to leave her there. He leaned

forward, staring hard at Rashida. "Don't give me that crap," he said. "I *know* you're Cancer Cell."

Rashida smiled. "And how do you know that?"

"Tiger."

"Tiger?" Now she laughed, shaking her head. "I doubt Tiger even knows what Cancer Cell is."

"I doubt it, too," Cage agreed. "He doesn't know who he works for. But he works for you and Stinger, and I know Stinger, and Stinger's Cancer Cell, too. Or he was until he died."

Rashida continued to smile, but Caroline could see her struggling with it, and her eyes had gone hard.

"Yeah, I know he died, and I know you watched him die," Cage said.

No one said anything for a long time. Caroline was afraid Cage was going to push it, push at the way Stinger died, raise the question of what had killed him, and she realized she was holding her breath, trying to will Cage to let it go. She felt almost certain that if he pursued Stinger's death, it would be the end of this meeting, the end of their only chance.

But Cage didn't say any more about it. He slowly leaned back in his chair and drank from his own glass, then looked away, his attention shifting to the man who was cooking the fish.

Rashida had stopped smiling, and she turned to Caroline. "Why do you want to get in touch with Cancer Cell?"

"I have Gould's Syndrome."

Rashida nodded once, hesitated a moment, then said, "Okay. I'll ask it again. Why do you want to get in touch with Cancer Cell?"

Caroline took a deep breath, then answered. "There's no cure for what I've got. No treatment except for some symptom relief, nothing that really changes anything. And it's terminal. I'll probably be dead by the time I'm thirty, and no one can do anything about it." She shrugged. "But maybe Cancer Cell can. I have heard that they are out on the cutting edge of medicine, flying with experimental treatments, drug therapies. I am willing to offer up myself as an experimental subject in return for whatever Gould's Syndrome treatments Cancer Cell wants to try.''

Rashida didn't reply at first, looking back and forth between them. She shook her head a couple of times, almost but not quite smiling, then she looked away. No one quite seemed to know what to say.

The rain had grown heavier and clattered loudly on metal canopies, plastic, the palm fronds, and the walkways. There was a cracking roll of thunder, and a few moments later the rain became a deluge, dumping out of the sky. But that lasted only a minute or so, and then it let up until it was little more than a drizzle.

"Cage."

He looked at Rashida and said, "Yeah."

"You will leave now."

"What are you talking about?"

"Just what I said. This is as far as you go. You have nothing to do with this anymore. I'll talk to Caroline alone.''

"And then what?"

She shook her head. "Good-bye, Cage."

"No, I'm not leaving now, I'm not leaving her alone here with you. I'm not leaving without knowing what's going to happen to her."

Caroline reached out for his arm, squeezed it. "Just go, Cage." She held his gaze, and nodded once. "Go on. You got me here. That's enough."

"It's *not* enough," he said, shaking his head.

"It has to be, Cage. It's *my* life, *my* disease. My risk. And I'll be fine."

He looked like he wanted to protest further, to argue some more with both of them, but he just shook his head again. He stood up from the chair, gripped Caroline's shoulder. "You take care of yourself."

"I will."

"And you . . .'' he said, turning to Rashida. But he didn't say any more, just sighed, turned away, and hurried across the courtyard the way they had entered.

When he was out of sight, Caroline turned back to Rashida. "All right," she said. "It's just the two of us."

"I should have sent you away, too," Rashida said.

"Why didn't you?"

Rashida shook her head. She looked across the courtyard at the man who was cooking his fish over the coals, waited until the man glanced toward her, then signaled to him, holding up two fingers. The man nodded, did some things with plates and bottles, took some fish off the grill, and put more on. Then he stood up and hurried through the rain with two plates in his hand, crouching over to shield them. He set one plate in front of Caroline, the other in front of Rashida, then added napkins and forks.

"Thanks, Hernando."

Hernando nodded, then hurried back to his fire.

"Please," Rashida said. "Dig in. Hernando makes a great grilled fish. It's the sauce he brushes on." She began eating.

With her fork, Caroline cut a piece of the fish, watched the steam rising from it, and blew on it before putting it in her mouth. It was whitefish of some kind, very flaky and tender, and coated with a dark, sweet sticky sauce. Rashida was right, it was delicious.

They ate without talking, Rashida refilling both of their glasses. The rain continued to fall, but the air grew even warmer. At first, Caroline tried to figure out what was going on, what Rashida was trying to accomplish by sending Cage away, and then having the fish brought over. But she decided it didn't really matter. It was actually quite pleasant sitting here in the damp heat, listening to the rain fall all around them. She relaxed and let herself enjoy it.

When they had finished eating, Rashida signaled to Hernando again, who came and took away the plates. She lit a fresh cigarette, took a couple of deep drags on it, then looked at Caroline.

"You don't look like you have Gould's," she said. "How can I know for certain that you do?"

"The same way it was diagnosed in the first place. I'll be glad to give you a blood sample."

"You'll do more than that. You'll submit to a complete

physical and we'll do the blood work and tox screens and whatever other testing we think is necessary."

"So you *are* with Cancer Cell," Caroline said.

"Better you just don't mention that name again," Rashida replied, and looked away. That was probably as close to an answer as Caroline would ever get.

Rashida finally turned back to her. "Has the Gould's even gone active yet? You look like you're doing fine."

"Yes, the Gould's has gone active. Just recently. Only one minor attack so far, but it was definite."

"But you might have years ahead of you of relatively good health. And you have no idea what's in store for you here, if we go ahead. *I* have no idea."

Caroline smiled. "You're making all the same arguments Cage made. He tried to talk me out of it, too." She paused. "I'm not sure I can explain it very well. But I know what the progression of this is like, and I don't look forward to it. Maybe if Can . . . if your people have something experimental they want to try, maybe the chances of it working will be better if I'm in the earlier stages. I'm just trying to give myself the best chance I can."

Rashida took a deep drag on her cigarette, then put it out even though it was only half gone. "I have to be honest with you. I've never dealt with anyone with Gould's Syndrome before. I don't know if anyone has been doing any research on it, or has any treatment ideas. It's possible no one has anything, and that we *can't* do anything for you."

That was something that hadn't occurred to Caroline. But there was no point worrying about that now. "I understand," she said.

"Fine then," Rashida said. "We've got an exam room set up in the building here. We'll take care of that today. And we'll want you to stay here until the test results are in and I've had a chance to talk to people. Then we'll go from there."

"Okay. Let's go do it."

Rashida shook her head. "Not quite yet, if you don't mind. There's no hurry." She smiled. "I don't get out much. I'd like to just sit here a while, drink lemonade, smoke cigarettes, watch the rain, maybe have some more of Hernando's fish. Join me?''

''Sure,'' Caroline said, smiling back. ''I'll skip the cigarettes.'' She leaned back in her chair, holding the glass of lemonade. She thought she should be apprehensive, maybe even frightened about what was to come. But she wasn't. She was very comfortable with Rashida, and she was, for the moment, quite content.

CHAPTER 19

The first time Carlucci fully came to, it was night. He was on his back, surrounded by darkness except for a rectangle of light off to his left. He had the vague recollection of coming around maybe two or three other times, but he'd never been fully conscious, never completely realized what he realized right now: He was alive.

He felt almost giddy, despite the growing awareness of pain in his left shoulder and arm. Alive. He was alive, and Mouse was dead.

Where was he?

The room was dark, but his eyes were slowly adjusting to the darkness, and objects were becoming visible. He turned his head to the left, toward the rectangle of light— a doorway. He saw white walls, linoleum floors; then, at the far edge of his vision, hanging above him and to the right of the bed—he turned his head back to bring it into focus—reflecting the light from the hall, was a clear fluid bag hanging from a metal hook, with clear tubing running down and looping into his right arm.

Of course. He was in the hospital. Where else would he have been? He'd been almost afraid to find out.

He closed his eyes for a minute, tired from just that tiny exertion of looking back and forth and trying to decided where he was. Sounds filtered into the room now, sounds he hadn't noticed before—quiet, indistinct conversation; a squeaking wheel; a regular tapping sound, from outside the room but nearby; a gentle hum.

He opened his eyes again, and turning back to the right once more he could see the broken amber rays from a street light slashing in through the window blinds. Then there was a rustling sound, also from the right. He raised his head, fighting the vertigo, and looked over the side of the bed.

Andrea was asleep on a futon beside him, wrapped in a light blanket, her face on the pillow illuminated by bands of amber light. Her mouth, as usual, was partially open, and her hair was slicked to her cheek.

She was beautiful.

Seeing her brought a strange pressure to his heart and the beginnings of tears to his eyes. He lay back, gazing up at the blank, dark ceiling, and blinked back the tears.

He was alive.

He woke again later that same night. Nothing had changed. The hospital remained relatively quiet, though he heard someone pacing up and down the hall. Andrea was still asleep. A persistent, dull ache throbbed in his shoulder, but somehow he didn't mind it that much; the pain helped keep his head clear, and right now, in this dark peace and quiet, he wanted to think.

He wanted to think about who had shot him. Not Mouse. At first, right after he'd been shot, as he was crawling across the ground, scraping and cutting himself on the gravel and broken glass, he *had* thought Mouse was responsible. But Mouse had been in front of him, and he was pretty sure he'd been shot from behind. That was something he'd have to ask the doctor about. And then, of course, Mouse had been shot himself—he'd had his whole head blown off.

Carlucci thought about that some more, replaying what he could remember of that whole grisly scene. Two shots to Mouse, he thought. The first one that seemed to catch Mouse by surprise, then a few seconds later, with Mouse still standing, teetering above him, the one to his head.

Something blocked the light coming in through the doorway. Without turning his head, keeping his eyes half closed, he shifted his gaze to the left. Mostly what he could see was silhouette, but he recognized the uniform. Someone had stationed a cop outside his door. Carlucci didn't move, and a few moments later the cop backed out and moved out of sight. Carlucci could hear the creaking of a chair.

He almost laughed. Protection. Whoever had shot him in the DMZ wasn't likely to come after him in the department hospital.

He returned his thoughts to the shooting and the circumstances surrounding it. It was possible, he supposed, that the real target of the shooting had been Mouse, and he just got in the way. Or that no one in particular was the target, that it was just a random shooting—someone who saw two people in an alley in the DMZ and decided to shoot them. It wasn't an outrageous notion, though he had a hard time giving it much credence. It went against his training and experience—whenever a cop was shot, the assumption was always that the officer was either the intended target or got in the way of the commission of another crime.

He closed his eyes, having a difficult time focusing on the problem. His instinct was to assume that he had himself been the target, but did that really make sense? Could someone really have followed him, waiting for the opportunity, and taken it when he'd gone into the alley after Mouse? Or had he been set up by Mouse? That didn't make any sense either, since Mouse ended up with his head blown off. Besides, no one knew he was going to be in the DMZ, no one knew he was looking for Mouse.

Carlucci sighed heavily. He was going nowhere with this, just like the rest of the Naomi Katsuda case. In his gut, with no hard evidence to back it up, he believed there was a connection between the case and this shooting. But he couldn't at all make out what that connection was, and he had to admit that the whole idea seemed absurd on the surface. He closed his eyes and drifted quickly into sleep.

And the third time he woke, the room was full of light. Morning, he thought. A quiet, steady *click-click . . . click-click . . . click-click* came from the right. When he turned that way, he saw that the futon had been folded up into a small sofa, and Andrea was sitting in it, knitting. Knitting was something she did to relax, to keep her hands occupied; she'd taken it up when the two of them had quit smoking years earlier.

"Knitting booties for someone's new baby?" he said.

She looked up at him, gave him a huge smile. "Just a sec," she said. She made a note on her pattern, set the needles and sweater beside her, then got up and came over to him. She gripped his hand, squeezed, then leaned forward and kissed him. When she pulled back from him, he could see the tears welling in her eyes. "Hey, stranger," she said. She squeezed his hand again. "How are you feeling?"

He smiled. "Like somebody shot me." Then he shook his head. "I feel okay, I guess. Thirsty."

She poured a cup of water, held it for him while he drank through a straw. He drank all of it, she refilled the cup, and he drank a little more. Then he let his head fall back on the pillow, feeling a bit woozy, the cold water settling hard in his gut. "Thanks," he said.

She found an open spot on the bed and scooted up onto it beside him, taking his hand in hers again. "Jesus, you had me worried for a while, Francesco."

"How close was it?"

She slowly shook her head from side to side. "Too damn close. You'd lost so much blood by the time they got to you . . ." She brushed a couple of tears from her cheek. "The first ten or fifteen years you were a policeman I used to worry, I used to think about it a lot. But after a while I stopped worrying, because nothing ever seemed to happen to you."

"Just as well," he said. "Worrying wouldn't have prevented this from happening."

"But it might have eased the shock. I was just stunned when I heard. It was so unexpected, Frank. I . . . I was paralyzed." Tears were starting up again.

A uniformed cop appeared in the doorway, a young, beefy guy, hardly more than a kid. He looked nervous, hesitant about actually entering the room.

"Lieutenant?" the cop said.

"Yes?"

"Are you feeling up to talking? I'm supposed to let the investigating officers know when you come around, so they can talk to you."

"Who are they?"

"Uh, Younger and Oko—— Okokr——"

Carlucci smiled at the young man's struggle. "Oko-ronkwo," he said.

The cop nodded. "Yes. Sorry, sir."

"That's all right. Go ahead and put the call in, but ask them to give me a couple of hours. But before you do that, I want you to put a call through to Detectives Santos and Weathers, tell them I need to talk to them. I want to talk to them *first*."

"You got it, sir." He backed away and walked down the hall.

"Toni and Ruben came in a couple of times to see how you were doing," Andrea said. "You're working on a case with them that has something to do with you being shot?"

He shrugged, and winced with the pain. "I don't know. It's possible."

"The Naomi Katsuda case?"

"Yes."

Andrea shook her head. "Then leave it to Ruben and Toni. Stay out of it. It's nearly gotten you killed."

He cocked his head, tried to look puzzled. "I'm sorry, did you say something?"

Andrea just shook her head again. She gave his hand another squeeze. "I better go call Christina. She's spent a lot of time here, but she's home right now. I promised I'd call her as soon as you came around."

"Yeah, I'd like to see her. What about Caroline?"

"I don't know," she said, frowning. She hesitated. "I haven't been able to get hold of her. No answer at her place. I've left messages, but haven't heard back from her."

"How long *has* it been?"

"A couple of days."

Carlucci didn't know what to say. He could feel the fear

and panic rising in his gut. He closed his eyes and tried to breathe slowly and deeply. Caroline. For years he had worried about her because of the Gould's. Every time anything out of the ordinary happened, he worried. He'd never been able to control it. It was something that drove everyone in the family crazy, *especially* Caroline. So maybe he was overreacting again now. But when he opened his eyes and looked into Andrea's face, he knew he wasn't.

"Call Bernie," he told her. Bernie Guilder was a captain in the department, and Carlucci had known him his entire career.

"I already did," Andrea said. "He's started working on it. I'd hoped something would have come up by the time you came around."

"All right, all right. I'm sure . . ." But he stopped, realizing how stupid it was. "Go call Christina."

She nodded, slid off the bed, and gave his hand one more squeeze. "I'll be right back."

Then she left, and Carlucci was alone with his fear.

CHAPTER 20

Cage hated hospitals. Strange thing for a doctor, but there it was. When he was actually working it wasn't so bad; he had too much to think about. But when he wasn't acting as a doctor, when he was visiting a friend or relative who was a patient, his skin itched all over, and he broke out in a sweat.

He felt that way now, standing at the top of the stairs and looking down the long, bright hallway toward Carlucci's room. What didn't help was not knowing why Carlucci had called him. There was also the desire to go down to the second floor immediately, where Nikki was—he desperately wanted to see her, talk to her doctor again, but he wanted to get this visit to the lieutenant out of the way first.

He took a deep breath and started walking. A third of the way along the hall a cop sat outside a door, and Cage headed directly for her, figuring that was Carlucci's room. Of course with all the security checks people had to go through every time they entered the hospital, that cop was probably unnecessary.

The cop stood as he approached. She was a tall, stunningly beautiful woman who looked like she could tear him apart without breaking a sweat, and he resisted the urge to salute. But he did check the room number on the wall beside her. Yes, it was Carlucci's room. The door was open a few inches, but he couldn't really see inside.

"I'm here to see Lieutenant Carlucci," he said.

"And you are?"

"Dr. Cage."

The cop smiled. "Am I supposed to believe that?"

"Believe it, Tretorn." It was Carlucci's voice from inside the room. "Has he got a stupid-looking tattoo of a snake on his neck?"

"Yes, sir." She continued smiling, not at all flustered by Carlucci's response.

"That's him, then. Let him in."

The cop raised an eyebrow, still amused, and gestured with her head toward the door. "You heard the lieutenant. Go right in."

"You aren't going to escort me into the room?" Cage asked.

She shook her head. "I don't think so."

She settled back in the chair, watching him and still smiling. He walked past her, then pushed open the door and entered the room. Carlucci was sitting up in the bed, his left arm in a sling, his shoulder heavily bandaged. Sitting in a chair was a woman about fifty, whom Cage assumed was Carlucci's wife, and standing on the other side of the bed was a young woman, probably about twenty, who looked a lot like a younger version of Caroline. Another daughter.

"Cage. This is my wife, Andrea, and my daughter Christina. And this is Cage. Dr. Cage."

He shook Andrea's hand and nodded to Christina. "How are you doing?" he asked Carlucci.

"I'm getting the hell out of here tomorrow," he said. "My doctor would like me to stay put for another two or three days, but I'm going crazy in this place."

"That's good. Better to get out and moving around as soon as you can."

"You going to see Nikki?"

Cage nodded. "Yeah. As soon as I'm done here."

"How is she?"

"The same, I guess. Not so good."

Carlucci looked back and forth at his wife and daughter. "Christina, Andrea, could you both go out in the hall for a few minutes? I need to talk to Cage privately."

They gave Carlucci kisses and good-byes, saying they'd be right back, then left. Andrea was careful to completely close the door behind her.

Carlucci adjusted his position on the bed, scooting himself up straighter. "I'm worried about my other daughter," he finally said.

"Sorry?"

"Caroline. The one who was Tito Moraleja's friend."

"Oh, right."

"She's missing."

"Missing?" Cage felt a terrible twinge of guilt.

Carlucci nodded. "For several days now. We haven't been able to get in touch with her at all. We've left messages she's never answered. Andrea's been by her apartment, and there's no sign of her being there recently. I've got some people in the department checking things out, but nothing's turned up."

"So why am *I* here?"

"I'm worried, Cage. I want you to keep your ear to the ground. She was pretty upset by Tito's death, and an old friend of mine who used to be a cop told me that Caroline had recently asked him about a way into the Tenderloin. I'm afraid she may have gone in there with the crazy idea of trying to figure out what happened to Tito."

He dug through a pile of stuff on the little table beside him, found a photograph, and held it out to Cage. Cage stepped forward and took it from him. It was a picture of Caroline sitting in the sun, smiling, eyes squinting against the light.

"That's her," Carlucci said. "You're on the streets inside. Keep a look out for her. I know it's a lot, but maybe ask around some." He paused. "You said you owed me, remember?"

Cage nodded, the guilt ratcheting up a bit. But he couldn't say anything to Carlucci. He had promised.

"I'll do what I can," Cage said.

"Thanks, I really appreciate it." He paused. "Let me ask again. Just the two of us. How *is* Nikki?"

"I don't know. In bad shape, I guess." Cage really didn't

want to talk about it. "Her chances aren't good."

"I'm sorry," Carlucci said.

Ten minutes later Cage stood outside Nikki's room, waiting for Dr. Verinder Sodhi to show, panic rising in his chest again. He could see her through the rectangular window cut into the large wooden door. Nothing had changed. She still appeared to be asleep, her eyes closed, bits of hair damp and slicked to her face.

"Doctor Cage?"

Cage stepped back from the door and turned toward the voice. A short, dark-skinned, dark-haired man approached him, hand out. Cage shook Dr. Sodhi's hand.

"How's she doing?"

Dr. Sodhi shrugged, then shook his head. "The same, I'm afraid. No improvement."

"And you still don't know what it is she's got?"

"No, I'm sorry, I am afraid not. We've been doing the testing right here in our labs, and so far we have not made a positive hit. I have taken the liberty of sending some blood samples to the CDC, with a rush notice, but I would not put much hope in that. We will be lucky if they do any testing within a month."

"She'll be dead by then."

Dr. Sodhi pursed his lips and tilted his head. "Or she will have survived. That, too, is a possibility. Besides, we are continuing our own testing. We may yet have some luck."

"Sure. Of course, even if you identify the disease or condition, you still may not be able to do a damn thing."

"That is true, Dr. Cage. But it may tell us *exactly* what to do. And even if not, it may help us focus the treatment."

Dr. Sodhi seemed so calm about the whole thing. But then it wasn't someone *he* loved dying in that room. Cage blew out a deep breath and shook his head to himself. He knew he wasn't being fair. "What *is* the current treatment?" he asked.

"We have been dosing her heavily with broad-spectrum antibiotics, but they do not seem to have had any benefit as of yet. If we had time, of course, we could try a number of courses of more specific antibiotics.''

''But we don't have that time.''

''Probably not. And of course, if it is a *virus,* which is my own inclination at this point, no antibiotic will be any good at all. We have also tried antifungals, but again without success.''

There was a sudden flurry of activity around them, several medical personnel hurrying past and into a room two doors down. Cage tried to ignore the commotion, which had not distracted Dr. Sodhi in the least.

''All right. Antibiotics aren't doing any good, and if it's a virus, well, the reality is most of the antivirals are shit, no matter what their makers claim. Do we agree on that?''

Dr. Sodhi nodded with a faint smile. ''I would sooner trust in prayer.''

''So what *is* being done for Nikki? Anything?''

''Yes. We are constantly chasing her electrolytes. Her body cannot seem to maintain the proper balance. Every three hours we recheck her chems, and we change her drips accordingly.''

''So what's the real problem?''

Dr. Sodhi pursed his lips again and frowned with his eyes. ''Most of her major organ function is deteriorating. Kidneys, liver, also the pancreas. Her heart seems to be holding up, but not much else. We have even been forced to resort to a round of dialysis.''

''What the hell is going on?''

''We've done MRIs. Her organs are . . . disintegrating.''

''Christ.'' He turned away from Dr. Sodhi and looked in through the window at Nikki. She didn't look as if she was dying, but he knew she was. ''What's the prognosis?'' he asked, still looking at her.

''She is hanging on, but I truly do not know how much longer she can go on this way.'' There was a long pause, then Dr. Sodhi said, ''She is not the only one dying like this.''

Cage froze for a moment, his heart suddenly banging away at the inside of his ribs. He kept his gaze on Nikki for a few moments longer, then slowly turned back to Dr. Sodhi.

"What do you mean?"

Dr. Sodhi looked distinctly unhappy. "It is difficult to know for sure, of course, since we do not know what this is, and so have no way to positively identify it. But I have been talking with some of my colleagues—sorry, *our* colleagues—and I have heard of several similar cases. Most have some direct connection to the Tenderloin."

"How the hell do you know that?"

"I asked. Ms. Hester got sick in the Tenderloin, and as far as we know contracted it there, yes? From a man who also lived there. So I just asked. But there are so few cases right now, and no one knows what it is. Still, the illness is bad enough that doctors are starting to ask questions."

Cage shook his head. "But no one's getting any answers."

Dr. Sodhi smiled. "No, no one is getting answers."

Cage turned back once more to the window. "I'd like to see her, if it would be all right. Talk to her, if I can."

"It's possible. Sometimes she is coherent, sometimes not. But please, wear a mask and gloves when you go in, and dispose of them properly when you leave. You must know how important that is." The small man suddenly looked quite sad.

Cage nodded. "Thanks, Dr. Sodhi."

He opened the door to Nikki's room and stepped inside, wearing gown, gloves, and mask as Dr. Sodhi had insisted. The panicky feeling returned, and he breathed very slowly and deeply, fighting it down. When he felt he was back in control, he took the last couple of steps to the bed, his knees brushing against the metal frame.

Nikki appeared flushed, her skin and hair damp. The head of the bed was packed with monitors blinking in various colors, and Cage had to concentrate to avoid checking each of them individually, to avoid running his own diagnostic exam on her. She was not his patient, and he did not really want to treat her as one. He was sure he could do no better than Dr. Sodhi, and he wanted to be with Nikki as a friend, not as her doctor.

"Cage." The voice was a whisper. Her eyelids fluttered, then opened slightly, and she managed a faint, barely discernible smile.

"Hey, Nikki."

"I'm still alive."

"Yes, you are."

"I feel like shit." She coughed, and the smile twisted into a grimace of pain. She closed her eyes; her entire face was tight with the pain.

He took her hand in his, and her fingers gave a weak squeeze. Several moments passed, then the pain seemed to ease, and her face muscles relaxed a bit. But she did not open her eyes.

"Nikki?"

She opened her eyes. "I'm still here."

There was a long silence. Cage did not know what to say, and Nikki probably didn't have the energy to speak much, even if she wanted to. There was a padded chair against the wall, and he let her hand go, then pulled the chair over next to the bed. He sat facing her and took her hand once again in his. He could feel the warmth of her skin through the thin glove.

With the door closed, the room was very quiet. There was pulsing light from the monitors, but mercifully the volume had been turned off. The temperature was surprisingly comfortable, cooler than outside, but not cold the way air-conditioned rooms and buildings so often felt. But the room felt terribly empty—there were no signs of visitors, family, or friends. No flowers, no cards, no books or magazines or bubble messages. As if Nikki had never been here, or had already gone.

"I told you that guy Stinger was an asshole," she said.

"You were right. But he's a dead asshole." And immediately regretting saying it.

"I will be, too," she replied. "Dead, not an asshole."

"No you won't."

"Cage, please, don't."

"I'm not, Nikki. You saved my life. It's my turn to save yours."

She smiled, but closed her eyes and slowly moved her head from side to side. "Not in this life," she said. "Maybe in the next."

"Nikki . . ." But he didn't know what else to say. She was right, and he couldn't stand it.

"I *do* think there's some other kind of life after this one," she said. Her voice was quiet, but strong. She opened her eyes, but she didn't look at him, just gazed up toward the ceiling. "Maybe reincarnation of some sort." She paused. "No, actually, that's an idea I kind of like, but not one that really *feels* right."

"What feels right?" he asked her.

"Survival of the spirit. Our consciousness. Not heaven, no angels or God or anything, but our spirits continuing on in some way, aware, and still connected a little to this world."

"Like ghosts?"

She smiled. "A little. Just there, just barely there so people sense our presence without knowing what it is they're feeling. Like a shiver of memory."

She didn't say anything else for a long time, and Cage realized that she very much believed what she had just said, and that it gave her a certain amount of comfort. She was having an easier time facing the idea of death, her own death, than he was.

"I'll come back and haunt you," she said, finally turning to look at him. "In a good way. When you feel something, that shiver of memory, don't be afraid of it. It'll be me."

Cage didn't know what to say. He wanted to tell her she wasn't a ghost yet, but she would say she would be soon, and then he'd say no, and then she'd get pissed at him again for trying to deny what they both knew was the truth—that she was dying, and there was nothing anyone could do. And he did not want to face that.

She squeezed his hand. "Let it go, Cage. Let *me* go."

He slowly shook his head. "I can't, Nikki. I just can't."

CHAPTER 21

Caroline stood at the open window of the room they had given her on the fourth floor, and looked out on the courtyard below. The sun was shining down through a hazy sky, baking the building and the courtyard; late morning, and already it was hot, though there was a slight breeze that came in through the window. Across the way, in the shade of a palm, Hernando crouched over his brazier of coals, just as he had two days earlier. This time he was cooking long, thin strips of dark meat. Hernando had spent much of the past two days there at his grill, cooking meat and fish and sometimes vegetables. Periodically he would fill a plate or two and disappear into the building. Other times people came to him with their own plates, which he loaded with food. He drank beer steadily as he cooked, one bottle after another. He seemed quite content.

Caroline, too, felt content, despite having been kept in this room for two days, effectively a prisoner. Two days with little to do, nowhere to go, and no responsibilities. Two days to read and doze and think. And she'd begun to rethink what she wanted out of all this.

The room was small, maybe ten feet square, with a bed, a stuffed chair, a very old dresser with empty drawers that smelled of cedar. Rashida had sent someone to Caroline's apartment to pick up a few changes of clothes, toiletries, and half a dozen books. Caroline wasn't locked in the room, and she had free access to the bathroom and shower down the hall one way, and the kitchen down the hall in the other direction. But there was always someone with her, watching her door, joining her in the kitchen, standing outside the bathroom waiting for her to emerge. She really didn't mind.

Rashida came several times to visit, and they talked about a lot of things, but never about Cancer Cell or experimental treatments or any of that. Sometimes she stayed for an hour or two, and they would go to the kitchen and have tea, or a bite to eat, and sit at the table, talking. Caroline had the feeling Rashida was lonely, that she didn't get out in the real world much. She liked Rashida, and she thought Rashida liked her.

She saw Rashida enter the courtyard from the street gate. Rashida glanced up at the window, then walked over to Hernando. She spoke to him for a few minutes, then crossed the courtyard and disappeared into one of the alcoves. A couple of minutes later there was a quiet knock, the door opened, and Rashida stepped into the room.

She stood just inside the door for a moment, watching Caroline, then walked over to the chair and sat in it, crossing her legs. "Testing's completed," she said.

"And?"

"You have Gould's."

Caroline smiled. "Did you expect anything else?"

"No. But we had to be certain."

"So do I start on some experimental treatment program?"

"It's not that simple," Rashida said. "There's a lot we have to talk about first."

Caroline nodded. She went over to the bed and sat on it, her back propped by the pillow against the wall. "Then let's talk."

"Your father's a cop."

"Yes, he is. Does that make a difference?"

"It makes some people suspicious."

"He doesn't know I'm here. He doesn't know I approached you, and he wouldn't approve if he did know."

Rashida smiled. "I'm sure that would be convincing to those who are suspicious."

"It doesn't sound like *you're* suspicious."

"I'm not. Not about that, anyway. I believe you. But I am suspicious about plenty of other things. And I'm suspicious about you."

"Why?"

Rashida shook her head, still smiling. "I'm not sure."

"Then where do we go from here?"

"That's up to you. I talked to people while we were waiting for the testing to wrap up. No one's done anything specifically with Gould's. But there is someone who has been doing research on other neurological disorders, working on possible treatment approaches, and he's quite interested in seeing you. Working with you." She grinned. "He'd love to get his hands on you."

Caroline nodded to herself, thinking. She'd planned to wait until farther along to present her proposal, but maybe this was the best time.

"How much would he love to get his hands on me?"

"I'm not sure what you mean."

"I'd like something in return for giving myself over to you and this man who wants to turn me into a lab animal."

Rashida frowned, sitting forward. "What is this? I thought what you were getting was a chance at a cure."

"That's not really very likely though, is it? Realistically, the best that can be hoped for is that maybe someone will learn a little something new about Gould's. Maybe a new direction to look in, maybe eliminate a few approaches. The reality is, I am almost certainly still going to die in a few years." She paused, and when Rashida didn't respond, she said, "Isn't that the most likely outcome of all this?"

Rashida eventually nodded. "Yes, that's most likely what will happen. So what is it you want?"

"I have a friend. Two friends, actually, a mother and daughter. The daughter, who's eleven years old, has leukemia. Two courses of chemotherapy have been ineffective. The leukemia has come back each time. Her only hope is a bone marrow transplant, either from a compatible donor, or with artificial marrow. They have no insurance, no money, so no one will do it. They're living in a death house in the DMZ, and the girl is going to die in a few months.''

''And you want us to give her a bone marrow transplant.''

''Yes.''

Rashida shook her head. ''That's a hell of a lot to ask for. It's expensive, time-consuming, with all the follow-up necessary. I doubt they'll go for it.''

''I'm giving a lot in return,'' Caroline argued. ''Several years of being a human guinea pig.''

''And how do we know that? How do we know that once we've done the bone marrow transplant you won't just pull out?''

''You won't let me. You people are very persistent about tracking down people who don't honor the contracts they've made with you, persistent about forcing them to honor those contracts.''

Rashida shook her head again, frowning. ''You know way too much about us. How is that?''

''From Cage. He never thought this was a good idea, and he wanted me to know as much as possible about what I might be getting into. That's all. He tried to convince me to drop this.''

Rashida sighed heavily. ''I'm still suspicious. I like you, Caroline, but I don't trust you.'' She paused. ''It doesn't matter for right now. I can't make that kind of decision. I'll need to talk to people, and there will be a lot of discussion, and frankly there's no way of knowing which way it will come down.''

''Can we proceed with the rest of it until then?'' Caroline asked.

''We'd better. Arrangements have been made, and if you back off now, there's a good chance this would be the end of it. You'd never hear from us again.''

''Then let's do it. I'm willing to take my chances.''

''And if we don't agree to do the bone marrow transplant for your friend?''

''I still have my own life at stake. And maybe there will be another favor I can ask.''

"I wouldn't ask too many, if I were you. We are not in the business of handing out favors."

Caroline nodded. This whole thing was getting a little absurd, she thought. She really had no fear, but she was seriously beginning to question the notion that she had much chance of learning anything about Tito's death. Even if she ended up in the Core, they weren't going to be giving her free access to their facilities, she wasn't going to have long conversations with these people during which they would reveal all the Cancer Cell secrets, including what had happened to Stinger and Tito. But she still believed there was at least a chance, and that was worth something.

"So what's next?" she asked.

"Are you ready? To make a commitment right now, with no promises made about your friend? There is no going back after this. As you said, we do whatever is necessary to enforce our contracts. And we don't have much sympathy for extenuating circumstances."

"I'm as certain as I will ever be. That'll have to be good enough."

"Okay." Rashida stood.

"I'd like to call my parents before we go, let them know I'm okay. They're probably worried, they probably think I've disappeared."

Rashida shook her head. "I can't let you do that."

Caroline wanted to ask her why not, but figured that was pointless. So she tried something else. "Can you at least get in touch with Cage, ask *him* to call my parents?"

"Maybe. I'll think about it. Ready?"

Caroline nodded and stood. "Ready."

"I hope you're not claustrophobic."

Two hours later, Caroline was being carefully packed into a long, wooden box that looked uncomfortably like a cross between a casket and a shipping crate for weapons. The sides were lightly padded with foam rubber, and it was a tight fit. Rashida assured her that there would be plenty of air—the box was not airtight—but they gave her a mask and a small oxygen cylinder, and showed her how to switch it on. Just in case.

Rashida waved good-bye to her, smiling, then they placed the top on and screwed it down.

Rashida was probably right. Caroline could see tiny cracks of light above and around her. The wood smell was strong, combined with the odor of oil and something musty. She wondered what this crate had last been used for. Transporting someone else like her? She closed her eyes and tried to sleep.

It was hopeless, of course. Nothing happened for a long time, then she felt herself being lifted, carried a short distance, then set down. Then she was moving again, on a wheeled cart of some kind. She felt every bump, every crack in the ground.

At first she thought she should try to keep track of her movements, her changes in direction, her trips up or down staircases. But she almost laughed aloud at the absurdity of it. That was even more hopeless than trying to sleep.

After a while, the wheeled cart stopped, and she was lifted again and carried a short distance before being raised and then lowered. Then all the cracks went dark as she heard a loud thud.

There was only silence and darkness for a long while. She lost track of time, almost dozed off. Then she felt a vibration, an engine, maybe, and she was moving again.

It went on for more than an hour, though it was difficult to judge the passage of time. Moving, stopping, rolling, lifted up and set down, bumping along, crashing into a wall. The padding helped a little at first, but as time went on she felt more sharply each bounce, each rattle, each accidental drop by her carriers.

Finally the movement stopped, and she could hear the squeal of the screws being undone above her. A few minutes later, the top came off. Rashida looked in.

"You okay?"

Caroline nodded. Rashida took her hand and helped pull her up out of the box. She was in a small, windowless room. The walls and ceiling were concrete block, the floor was concrete, and all of the surfaces were painted a bright, soft white. In one corner was a sink and a toilet, in another was a small mattress with blankets and pillows. A wooden rocking chair and an empty wooden bookcase leaning against the wall were the only other furnishings in the room.

"Where am I?" Caroline asked.

Rashida just laughed. She pointed at a brown duffel bag on the floor next to the crate. "Your books and clothes and things are in there," she said. "It's not much. And the door will be locked. So try and make yourself comfortable. This will be your home for a while."

CHAPTER 22

His left arm in a sling, his shoulder bandaged and taped, Carlucci entered the Mishima building just before midnight. He still felt weak, and he had only been out of the hospital for two days, but he wasn't going to let this interview with Yoshi Katsuda wait any longer.

One of the guards at the front security desk studied his ID card and badge while another ran portable detectors over his body. A third guard stood a few feet back, the blinking lights on his armor showing a full charge. The first guard ran the card and badge through a scanner, and the second made a thorough but gentle search of the sling and bandage. When they were satisfied, they gave him a special access card for the express elevator that ran to the top floor. The second guard escorted him to the far end of the elevator banks, then waited until Carlucci had used the access card and stepped inside. The guard was still standing there as the doors closed.

The ride to the top was smooth and fast, acceleration and deceleration only barely noticeable. Once the elevator had stopped, Carlucci had to use the access card once again to activate the doors. They opened in near silence, and he stepped out.

The reception area was large, with pale carpeting, the walls and ceiling the color and texture of beach sand. There were low couches and chairs, and several planters with bonsais. Sitting at the reception desk across the room was a woman with a silver metal face. One ear was flesh, but the other, like the rest of the woman's face, was metal. It had to be real, because Mishima would never allow *faux prosthetique,* which had been quite the fashion rage a few years earlier, on any of its employees. The shining metal contoured to her skull had to be the woman's real face.

He approached the desk in a hush of quiet.

"Lieutenant Carlucci." The woman's voice, emerging through segmented metal lips, was cool and smooth. "Mr. Katsuda is waiting for you." Her tongue and teeth appeared to be real, as did the eyes looking out at him.

To her left, the wall swung open. When he hesitated, the woman said, "You may enter now."

He walked through the opening, and the wall swung closed behind him. Katsuda's office was enormous, on the building corner, and the two exterior walls were floor-to-ceiling glass. Katsuda stood at one of the glass walls, looking out onto the city. Against the wall to Carlucci's right was a long, dark wooden desk, the top surface shining in the light from two small, shaded lamps on either end. They were the only lights on in the room.

Yoshi Katsuda turned to him. "Lieutenant, have you ever been in this office before?"

"No."

Katsuda nodded. "Come and see the view then," he said. "It is, I have to say, quite spectacular."

Carlucci joined him at the wall of glass. Katsuda was thin and almost as tall as Carlucci. He wore a tailored, dark silk suit, a white shirt, and a simple black tie. Since he was Naomi Katsuda's father, he had to be in his sixties, or even older, but his skin was so smooth, and there was very little silver in his dark hair; he looked easily ten or fifteen years younger.

Carlucci looked out through the window. Katsuda was right about the view. The lights of the city below them were bright and shiny, flickering silver and blue and amber, with other red and silver lights of vehicles swirling everywhere. The city looked brilliant and alive in the night, the filth and poverty and decay effectively camouflaged by the darkness and the gleam of the lights. Out across the water, in the bay, Alcatraz was a blaze of floodlights and swirling neon. The casinos out on the former island prison had reopened a few months earlier, and the island docks were aswarm with luxury boats. To the left was the Golden Gate Bridge, beautiful as always, unchanged over the decades, a stunning lattice of amber and crimson lights spanning the entrance to the bay.

As if noticing the sling and bandages for the first time, Katsuda said, "I see you've been injured."

"Someone tried to kill me," Carlucci said.

"But I see they did not succeed. Are you recovering well from it?"

"Oh, sure. I'm doing just fine."

"I am pleased to hear it."

"Thanks for asking." Carlucci took a deep breath. "Mr. Katsuda, I want to talk to you about a murder attempt that was more successful."

"My daughter."

"Yes, your daughter."

"You met with my daughter a few weeks ago."

Carlucci was taken by surprise, and didn't immediately reply, wondering how Katsuda had known. Had his daughter told him about the meeting? Unlikely. Naomi Katsuda had been so circumspect about everything.

"Yes, I did meet with her. How did you know?"

"I could say that she told me about the meeting," Katsuda said, "but that would not be the truth." He gestured with his hand toward the two chairs near the other glass wall. "I think we'll be more comfortable if we sit," he said. "We will still have the view."

They walked over to the chairs and sat. "Can I get you anything to drink?" Katsuda asked. "I am sure we can provide you with whatever you like."

Carlucci smiled. "Yeah, I'm sure you can. But I don't want anything."

Katsuda nodded. "I, too, will pass." Then, resuming their discussion, he said, "We are a very influential and powerful family, which makes us the targets for any number of people—radical groups, criminals, even business competitors. Our security personnel have a directive to know where any of us are at any time, so that protection can be provided if it becomes necessary.''

''I see.'' Carlucci paused, feeling a tiny rush of tension. ''Is the surveillance around the clock?''

Katsuda hesitated before answering. ''Yes,'' he finally said. ''Why do you ask?''

''Where were the security personnel when your daughter was killed?''

Katsuda closed his eyes for a moment, then opened them again. ''Trying to find her. Naomi didn't like being followed, even if it was for her own protection. That was the main reason she moved out of our home. And she became quite good at losing the surveillance. That night, she had again been successful. And it cost her her life.''

''I'm sorry for your loss,'' Carlucci said, trying very hard to sound sincere. He did not like Yoshi Katsuda, and he had trouble believing the man was grieving over the death of his daughter.

''Thank you, Lieutenant. Now, shall we proceed with the official interview?''

Carlucci shrugged. ''This is *all* a part of the interview,'' he said. ''But before we go any farther, I want to know something. Why have you refused to talk to the investigating officers?''

Katsuda waved his right hand, a gesture of dismissal. ''It was inconvenient. I did not want to talk to them.''

''But they were investigating the death of your daughter.''

''I could not help them. There was no point.''

''You can't know that, Mr. Katsuda.''

''Yes, Lieutenant Carlucci, I can know that. My security personnel had lost her that night, and I did not know where she was. I have no idea why anyone would want to kill her. There is no way I could help in the murder investigation of my daughter. And as I said earlier, it was inconvenient. I did not want to speak with them, and so I didn't.'' He paused. ''I will be frank with you, Lieutenant. I have no faith in this city's police department. I do not believe they will solve my daughter's murder. I do not believe they will even come close. I did not want to waste my time with them." He paused again. "Power and influence can be extremely useful, and I use both freely."

Well, at least there's no bullshit from Katsuda about that. But that didn't mean the man wasn't hiding something about the case.

"Why are you talking to me, then?" Carlucci asked.

"I have been advised that it was in my best interest to speak with someone about the case. I have been advised that unless I did, the constant and rather annoying requests for interviews would not cease. Eventually, I was told, I might even become the subject of a subpoena. You are the supervising officer of the case. You are a lieutenant, a superior officer in the department. I prefer to speak with you."

Too good to deal with the peons, Carlucci thought, wanting very much to come out and say it. But it wouldn't be helpful.

"Do you know why your daughter met with me?" he asked.

Katsuda shrugged. "You asked her to." Telling him that the Mishima phone lines, too, were under surveillance, although that didn't come as a surprise.

"Do you know what we talked about?"

"No, but I can guess. My daughter had an obsession with a group of medical terrorists called Cancer Cell. I can think of nothing else she was involved with that would be of any interest to the police."

"She was involved with Cancer Cell?"

Katsuda shook his head. "Poor choice of words. The earlier phrasing is more accurate. An obsession. She was fascinated by them, and did what she could to learn about them. I tried to discourage her in this, but she was quite stubborn."

"What do *you* know about Cancer Cell?"

Katsuda gave a sigh of exasperation. A warning, Carlucci guessed. "I don't know anything about them. They were my daughter's obsession, not mine. They seemed dangerous. I avoid danger whenever possible.''

Carlucci didn't push it. He didn't think he was going to come away from this interview with much, but he wanted every chance he had, and he wanted it to go as far as possible. He took a copy of the sketch artist image from his coat pocket, awkwardly unfolded it with his right hand, then leaned forward and held it out to Katsuda. Katsuda took the picture and studied it for a few moments, then looked up.

''Do you recognize her?''

Katsuda handed the picture back to Carlucci. ''She looks vaguely familiar. Who is she?''

''We think a friend of your daughter's. A close friend.''

Katsuda stared at him for a minute, his gaze unblinking. ''My daughter was not a lesbian.''

''I didn't say she was.'' Toni Weathers was right. There was something odd about this.

''You certainly implied it, Lieutenant.''

''It's a possibility, that's all.''

''No.'' Katsuda crisply shook his head, his eyebrows furrowed. ''It is not a possibility.''

He held up the picture again, moved it closer to Katsuda. ''You don't know her.''

''No. As I said, the picture is familiar. If she was a friend of my daughter's, I may have met her, or seen her at some time. But I do not know her.''

Carlucci refolded the picture and stuck it back in his jacket. ''So you don't think we can solve your daughter's murder?''

''No.''

''Is it just your daughter's murder, or do you think the police are generally incapable of solving crimes?''

''I believe they are generally ineffective.'' Katsuda smiled. ''I am just being frank, Lieutenant. If a major crime is committed on camera, or in front of numerous witness, or you have a confession, the police do an adequate job of following through. But when something is difficult and motives are obscure, as in my daughter's case, you are hopelessly lost. You simply do not have the resources, financial and otherwise, and the world has become much too complex."

"Are you undertaking your own investigation?" Carlucci asked. "With your own resources, 'financial and otherwise'?"

"That is my business, Lieutenant, not yours."

"It is very much my business, Mr. Katsuda."

Katsuda shook his head. "Not if I say it isn't. You are forgetting who has the power here, Lieutenant. It is not you."

"You might be surprised."

Katsuda smiled, amused. "I don't think so." He stood up. "I would say our interview is at an end."

Carlucci remained seated for a few moments, angry with himself for responding that way. Katsuda was right about the power, on a surface level. But there were other kinds of power, and Katsuda didn't know everything. He finally got up and shook Katsuda's hand.

"Thanks for talking to me," he said.

"I doubt if I was much help."

"That's all right. I guess neither of us expected much." He started walking toward the wall he had come through, though at the moment there was no opening. He stopped a few feet from it and waited.

"Lieutenant."

"Yes."

"Why did someone try to kill you?"

Carlucci turned back to look at him. "I don't know."

"Were you chasing rats?" Katsuda asked, smiling slightly.

Carlucci's breath caught for a moment. His heart beat hard against his chest, somehow noticeable right now. He was surprised—by *what* Katsuda had just revealed, and by the fact that he had revealed it at all. It told him something important about the man.

"Yes," Carlucci said. "I was."

"A dangerous occupation."

"So it seems," he agreed.

"Perhaps you should give it up."

"The rat is dead."

"No great loss for the world, I imagine. But no great gain, either. Nothing changed." Katsuda touched his hair with his fingertips. "Good night, Lieutenant."

Carlucci started to turn, then stopped. "The woman out front, at the desk."

"My assistant. Yes?"

"What happened to her?"

"What happened? To her face, you mean?"

"Yes."

"Nothing. She did not like the face she was born with, so she changed it. I'm certain I can arrange the same thing for you, if you wish."

Carlucci shook his head. "I'll pass."

This time when he turned around, the wall was opening, and he walked through.

CHAPTER 23

Cage wandered the streets of the Tenderloin in a kind of trance. Nikki was dying. He knew that, and he couldn't get away from it. He had been back to see her twice more, but each time she'd been worse; neither time had she been coherent enough to talk. Neither time had she known he was there. She was dying.

It was midafternoon and the heat was intense. The air was heavy and muggy, but he hardly noticed it. The heat kept the street and sidewalk traffic light, which was just fine with him.

He bought a beer from a young woman caged into a tiny kiosk out on the edge of the sidewalk. Money went into one slot, the beer emerged from another, cold and wet. Cage could barely make out her features behind the narrow, thin bars, back in the darkness. She must be baking in there.

He sat on the curb in the shadow of a delivery truck and drank his beer. There was a sense in the street of people waiting—waiting for darkness, waiting for the temperature to drop, waiting for energy to return. Waiting for Nikki to die.

Jesus. And how many other people were going to die? In the days since his talk with Dr. Sodhi, Cage had made a few calls to other doctors and street medicos both in and out of the Tenderloin. Nothing explosive was happening yet, but cases were cropping up everywhere, many of the people already dead. Most inside the Tenderloin, but a few *outside*. No one thought too much about it yet, because no one was seeing more than one or two, and some none at all. Just another mystery disease or toxin attack. But the symptoms were too damn close to what Tito, Stinger, and Nikki all had.

Cage knew. Something was happening out there. Something was about to break out.

And he had helped Caroline work her way into Cancer Cell and the Core, right into the middle of it.

The street got suddenly quiet. There was a long break in the traffic, and Cage stood, stepped out from behind the truck, and looked out into the street. Nothing at first, and then he heard the first cries and moans, and he knew what was coming—a Plague Parade.

Christ, that's just what he needed now. He almost walked away, almost hurried in the opposite direction where he could try to find a bar or a café, anyplace inside where he could avoid seeing it. But he remained where he was, and waited for it to reach him.

Once a month or so a Plague Parade would appear on the streets of the Tenderloin. The name wasn't really accurate; none of the people in the parades were dying of diseases that were truly plagues—unless you considered life in the twenty-first century a plague. But that didn't stop them from using the name; it sounded better. Or worse.

The street was completely clear now. Groups of plague hierodules would have gone ahead and set up human barricades on the planned route—men and women in hooded robes and carrying censures, legless men on motorized wheeled platforms, Screamers with their mouths surgically sealed, humming through metal nose tubes. And here, people were clearing out from the sidewalks without any help, ducking into buildings and alleys, shops and cafés; those who remained waited for the parade with exhausted acceptance or morbid interest.

An extremely tall woman led the parade. She wore a black and white body-stocking skeleton costume, a grinning skull mask over her head. Arms and legs movingly nimbly, the skeleton woman danced from side to side as she led the parade down the street. But her dancing and grinning mask were the last vestiges of gaiety in the Plague Parade.

Following the dancing skeleton came two rows of four-wheeled carts pulled by barefoot men naked except for tattered loincloths. Each row consisted of six carts, and sitting in each cart were two or three people. Hand-painted signs hung from the sides of the carts, announcing the diseases within: ANKYLOSING SPONDYLITIS; LUPUS; EPSTEIN-BARR; HEPATITIS G; MALARIA; MULTIPLE SCLEROSIS; and so on. Cage picked up the pattern right away: They were all chronic illnesses.

Next in the parade, on foot or wheeled platform, came the physical birth deformities section. People hobbled along on clubfeet, or with one leg noticeably shorter than the other, some walked by with short, flippered arms or deformed heads, and a small group of legless men pulled themselves along on wheeled platforms, digging spiked knuckles into the pavement with each swing of their arms. Two women led by children walked with clouded white eyes gazing up at the sky, wearing signs that said "Blind from Birth."

Then came the strangest part of the parade, something Cage had never seen before. Two lines of hooded figures moved slowly past, bodies swaying in unison to a subtly shifting, deep, and penetrating hum. He could not tell if the hum came from the marchers, or if it was being generated by some electrical device. Stranger still, even though it was midday and the sun was shining directly onto the street, the hooded figures were surrounded by a pulsing, dark blue glow that obscured the figures and the air around them; as they walked past, even people standing on the opposite side of the street became distorted and weirdly shadowed. And most disturbing of all, when Cage looked at the heads of the hooded figures, he could see nothing within the hoods, only a darker blue glow and darker shifting shadows, as if there were no heads or faces within. A terrible, cold shudder went through him, and he wanted to turn away, but he was transfixed, and could not tear his gaze from them until they were completely past him and nearly half a block away.

Dizzy and buzzing inside, he finally turned his head and stared down at the ground, trying to regain his equilibrium. He couldn't shake the feeling that he had just witnessed something terrifying. The rest of the Plague Parade moved past him, but he hardly noticed any more of it, hardly saw the caged wagon of half-naked and completely insane people leaping and shouting and shaking the bars, or the pedalcarts loaded with people in the late stages of terminal diseases. He was barely aware of where he was.

But by the time the tail end of the parade approached, he was feeling almost normal. He watched the last of the stragglers limp and drag past him—a young man with no hair, no left hand, and no left eye, and half a dozen surgical scars across his chest and abdomen; and a woman and child, both blond, apparently mother and daughter, walking hand in hand. Around the girl's neck hung a cardboard sign lettered in black marker:

LEUKEMIA
NO MONEY

The girl was listless, her feet dragging. The mother was angry and defiant.

Half a block farther on was the rear guard of the hierodules, walking backward, facing the vehicle traffic that inched along in their wake, filling the street once again. Cage remained where he was until all signs of the parade were gone, and the streets and sidewalks were back to normal.

Back to normal. And what good was that? A hopeless, deteriorating state of affairs.

He looked down at the empty beer bottle in his hand. He wanted to throw it through a window, or smash it over someone's head, smash it over his own head. Instead, he tossed it into a trash bin, crossed the street, walked down to the end of the block, and entered a phone bank. Time to try calling Eric Ralston again.

The bank was a narrow, dark aisle lined with small, cramped private booths. Signs above each booth declared, in all seriousness, that the phone lines within were guaranteed to be cleared and clean. No one believed the signs.

He ran his phone card through the reader, and punched in the number for the CDC in Atlanta, which he'd now memorized after half a dozen calls in the past two days. Half a dozen calls to Ralston, half a dozen messages left, and no calls returned.

Cage had gone to medical school in San Francisco with Eric Ralston, and they had become friends, despite being headed in different directions afterward—Cage had gone to Southern California to do image enhancements and make money, while Ralston had joined the CDC. Cage's life and career had changed drastically since then, but Ralston had remained at the CDC, where he was now some kind of research director. They had stayed in touch over the years, talking by phone every few months, seeing each other maybe once or twice a year.

The call went through, a woman answered, and Cage asked for Ralston's office. When he got Eric's voice-mail system again, he defaulted out of it and back to the woman.

"Yes, can I help you?" the woman said.

"My name is Dr. Ryland Cage, in San Francisco, and I've been trying to reach Dr. Eric Ralston for two days," he said. "I've left several messages, but he hasn't called back. It's urgent that I speak with him, so I need to know if he's actually been in his office, or is he away?"

"Just a minute, Dr. Cage, let me check."

He crouched on the floor of the cubicle while he waited, the phone cord barely long enough. Quiet strains of chamber music played over the phone; at least there were no commercials or promotional announcements.

A couple of minutes later the woman came back on. "Dr. Cage?"

"Yes."

"Dr. Ralston *is* out of the office. He's in the field, and he has been for several days. It's an open-ended assignment, so there's no way to know when he will be back in the office."

"Goddamnit." Cage closed his eyes for a moment; he wasn't going to give up. "As I said, it's urgent that I speak to him. There must be a number I can call to reach him, wherever he is.''

"I'm sorry, Dr. Cage, you should know that I can't give out that information.''

"I *have* to speak with him as soon as possible.''

"I'm sorry, Dr. Cage. If you want to leave a message, I will note that it's urgent, so if he calls in—''

"Goddamnit, I've already left messages, and—''

She hung up.

Cage remained in a crouch, holding the silent phone to his ear and staring stupidly at the cubicle door. He breathed deeply and slowly, stood, and then punched in the CDC number. The same woman answered.

"Please don't hang up on me,'' he said, working hard to keep his voice calm and reasoned, afraid of pissing her off again. "This is Dr. Cage, and I apologize for losing my temper with you.''

There was a long silence, and he was afraid she had hung up on him again. But then she spoke.

"Apology accepted,'' she said. "And I'm sorry I so easily lost patience with you. It's been a little hectic around here lately.''

"Why?'' Cage asked. "Something going on?''

"Oh, who knows? They don't tell the support staff anything. They have panic attacks around here all the time and most of them turn out to be for nothing. But we always pay for it with this insanity.''

"Yeah, that figures. All right. I know you can't tell me where he is, or how to reach him. But could you get a message to him, telling him that I've called several times, and that it's urgent I speak with him, give him my phone and pager numbers?''

The woman sighed. "It won't be easy. When they're out in the field, it's an 'emergency only' status for contacting them.''

"This *is* an emergency,'' Cage said. "It really is.''

"Okay,'' she said, relenting. "I'll see what I can do.''

"Thanks. I really appreciate it.''

"Yeah, yeah, yeah.''

He gave her the two numbers, added the clinic number; she read them back to him, and said she would get to it as soon as she could.

"Thanks again," he said. "Keep my numbers, and the next time you're in San Francisco give me a call. I'll buy you dinner."

"Call me when you're in Atlanta," she said. "You'll never see me on the West Coast."

"I will. What's your name?"

"Never mind. Just call here, and if you recognize my voice, we'll go from there.'

Cage laughed. They said their good-byes, and he hung up the receiver.

Back out on the street, in the oppressive heat and sun, Cage's foul, despairing mood returned in full force. He wasn't going to hear from Eric, and even if he did it wouldn't do any good. Afraid to commit resources to something without convincing evidence, afraid to look foolish as they had so many times in the past thirty years or so, no one at the CDC would do anything until it was way too late.

He stood in front of the phone bank, the sun baking him, his head swimming, and his vision bleaching. Where was he? Thinking, figuring, he worked out that he was only five or six blocks from Hanna's Hophead Hovel. Cage hadn't been there in months. Hanna's was a hip spice bar, decor from eighteenth-century China, pictures on the walls of people smoking opium, fake opium pipe candleholders on the table, dark shaded lamps. But in the basement rooms below was the real thing—an opium and hash den, with rooms rented out by the hour and servants who would bring you your drug of choice and watch over you.

He closed his eyes, wanting desperately to go there right now, rent out a room for a day or two, and slide into oblivion. But that was just as useless as the Plague Parades, just as futile. And he had made a promise to himself to put an end to that.

Nikki.

CHAPTER 24

Carlucci stood at an open fifth-floor window and looked down on the Tenderloin as dusk fell. Activity was increasing, the streets and sidewalks filling despite the heat. Sweat rolled down his cheeks, dripped down his sides from under his arms, and formed a sticky, itching band around his waist. The weather service had been predicting a break in the heat wave for three days now, and each day it just got hotter.

Carlucci didn't give a damn. Right now he didn't give a damn about much, not even his job. Two weeks since he'd been shot, and still there was no sign of Caroline, no hint of what had happened to her or where she was, or even if she was still alive. A few days earlier a letter had arrived at the house, mailed from the Sunset Post Office, saying that Caroline was all right, she was just away for a while, she was not being held anywhere against her will, and everything was fine, so they shouldn't worry. The letter was worthless; if it was meant to reassure him and Andrea, it failed completely. And as time went on, he had become more convinced that she was here somewhere, in the Tenderloin, and that it had something to do with Cancer Cell. So now, because he had nothing else to do, he was about to go into the Tenderloin himself and look for her, despite what he knew to be the futility of his task. If nothing else, maybe he'd stir something up. What was the worst that could happen? Someone would take a shot at him?

He knew he wasn't thinking clearly, and that later he

would probably regret this, but right now that didn't matter. So he stood at the window, looking down at the street lighting up as darkness fell, and waited to descend. He rotated his arm and shoulder, slowly but steadily to keep it from getting stiff. No more sling, and not much left in the way of bandages, but he had to be careful so he didn't rip the wound back open. The pain wasn't bad, just a constant, annoying reminder to him of what had happened.

"Lieutenant? You're cleared."

Carlucci turned around. The cop was young, hardly more than a rookie, and Carlucci wondered why he'd been assigned here, to one of the police department's "gates" into the Tenderloin. This was usually a post for more experienced officers, where strange things came up and there was often a need for improvising, where the rule book sometimes had to be distorted or ignored altogether. Either someone had a lot of faith in the young man and was already grooming him for quick advancement, or someone had it in for the guy and was setting him up for a shitcan. He seemed like a nice kid, and Carlucci silently wished him well.

"Thanks," he said to the kid. Then he walked past him, through the door, and into the stairwell, and started down the steps.

After three flights, the steps ended at a locked door. Carlucci waited, hearing a thumping bass through the walls. There was nowhere for him to go, except back up. He had to wait nearly five minutes until finally the door unlocked and swung quickly open. A short, skinny, old man grabbed his arm and pulled him through. "Chop chop!" the man said in a loud whisper. The man slammed the door shut, jammed home the locks, then pulled down a large tapestry that completely hid the door.

The music was louder here, a wild and swinging reggae. He was in a corridor now deserted except for himself and the old man, who pulled at his arm again, urging him down the corridor away from the music. "Go downstairs."

"I know," Carlucci said. "I've been through here before."

But the man just shook his head, pointing with one hand and now pushing with the other. "Go now, downstairs and out the back."

Carlucci gave up trying to convince the man he already knew where to go. "Okay," he said. "I'm going." He walked down to the end of the corridor, then through a screen door to the outside and zigzagging wooden steps that went down into an alley.

He hesitated at the top of the stairs, his heart suddenly beating hard and fast and his ears ringing, thinking about the last time he'd gone into an alley. This was different, he knew that, but he couldn't completely stop that clutching at his chest and gut. He scanned the alley, which was short, a dead end only ten feet to his left where metal and stone and wood barriers had been erected as a wall between buildings and forming a part of the Tenderloin perimeter—no way in or out. The rest of the alley, maybe fifty feet out to the street, was empty except for trash bins and the scattered remains of an old motorcycle.

What the hell was he doing here? He shook his head and went down the steps. Then he hurried along the alley, turned the corner of the building, and plunged into the Tenderloin crowds.

At ten o'clock he was in the back of a pachinko parlor in the Asian Quarter, massaging his temples, trying to ease the headache he had from the constant clatter of balls and ringing of bells, the flashing lights and the dense clouds of cigarette smoke. He was sitting on a stool with his back against the wall, and he'd been here for fifteen minutes, waiting for a woman called Amy Otani. Amy Otani was a weasel for one of the department's undercover narcotics officers. Carlucci had spent most of the day calling in favors and promising more of his own to get the names of weasels and leeches in the Tenderloin, anyone he could contact and ask about Caroline or Cancer Cell. So far he'd come up empty, and he didn't really expect to do any better the rest of the night.

A short, round woman in a black skirt and flowered

blouse came toward him, expression stern. She stopped only a couple of feet away, frowning.

"You Carlucci?"

"Yes. You're Amy Otani?"

She blew air between her lips and shook her head, frown deepening, then nodded quickly once. "Yes, yes. Come with me, quickly." She turned and walked away.

He scrambled off the stool and hurried after her. She barreled around a corner and down a dark narrow corridor, then up a flight of steps and into a small room on the second floor. There was a desk and a couple of chairs, and the rest of the room was filled with wooden and plastic crates. When he entered, she closed the door behind him, then pointed to a chair, her arm and finger stiff and demanding. He sat in the chair, then she moved around behind the desk and sat, still glowering at him.

"You're a crazy man," she said. "You don't even have to tell me why you're here. I already know, because the word is out. You're trying to find Cancer Cell."

"Yes."

She shook her head again. "Yes, you're a crazy man. Always dangerous to ask about Cancer Cell, even when you're being careful. And when you're not being careful . . ." She made a kind of growling sound in her throat. "And you're not being careful, Lieutenant. Not at all. You were almost killed once, now you're trying again, looks like. Trying to make a success this time, yes."

"No."

She snorted. "Yes. Same thing, what you're doing."

"Can *you* help me contact Cancer Cell?"

"You don't understand, do you? Anyone who tries to help you find Cancer Cell now is as crazy as you." Now she was almost smiling, as if she couldn't believe he was serious. "This is my help, to warn you. To tell you. You make things too difficult now. Cancer Cell knows, unless they are blind and deaf and stupid. And they are not blind and deaf and stupid. No, Lieutenant. No one will help you."

"I'm trying to find my daughter."

Her expression became sorrowful. "If she *is* with Cancer Cell, the best thing for you is to stop right now. Go home, forget it."

"I can't," he said.

"Then no one can help you." She pointed to the door. "Go, Lieutenant. Don't make problems for me."

He nodded, then got up and left.

Three o'clock in the morning, exhausted and depressed, Carlucci stopped by the RadioLand Street Clinic a third time, hoping Cage had showed up. The first two times, Cage hadn't been there, and the doctors and staff didn't know when he would be. Apparently he'd become unreliable the past few days, not following the schedule they had worked out for the week, showing up at odd times, not showing up when he was supposed to. Dr. Samione, the woman Carlucci had met the day he'd come by looking for Tito, remembered him. She didn't seem upset by Cage's behavior; she said they had adjusted. It was a stretch for all of them, but they just didn't count on him, so when he did show up it was a bonus. He was going through a very difficult time, she said; it would pass. Nikki? Carlucci had asked her. She had nodded, but didn't say anything else.

Now he was back, and surprisingly Cage was here. But he didn't seem to be working. He was sitting in one of the waiting-room chairs, drinking a bottle of Black Orbit beer. Haggard and drawn, he hadn't shaved in several days. As Carlucci approached him, Cage looked up and saluted him with the bottle.

"Good morning, Lieutenant. I am told you've been looking for me."

"Hello, Cage." He wondered if Cage was drunk. "Are you all right?"

"No. But I'm not drunk, if that's what you're really asking. *Are* you looking for me?"

"Indirectly. I'm looking for my daughter. Caroline."

Cage nodded. "She's still missing."

"Yes."

"I'm sorry." He sighed. "But why do you want *me*?"

Carlucci gave him a half smile. "I'm desperate."

Cage laughed. "You'd have to be. Look at me, I'm a fuckin' mess."

"Nikki?"

Cage nodded, then shook his head from side to side. He finished off his beer.

"No improvement?"

"She's dying, Lieutenant. Your daughter's still missing, and Nikki's still dying. I don't know how she's managed to stay alive as long as she has, but it won't be long now. A day or two, maybe." He ran his hand through his hair. "I don't know where your daughter is."

"I want you to help me find her."

Cage laughed again, then nodded. "Let's go talk somewhere. Get something cold to drink."

"Back in your 'staff lounge'?" Carlucci asked, smiling.

"Christ, no. Not unless you want your brains boiled. But let me go get a couple of beers."

"All right."

He waited while Cage went into the back room at the end of the hall. The waiting room was half full, and it was hard to tell whether the people waiting were sick or just wiped out by the heat. Everyone was listless and quiet, the loudest noise in the room coming from the fans.

Cage came out from the back with two bottles in each hand. "It's hot," he said, shrugging. He gave Carlucci two of the bottles.

They went outside, and Cage gestured toward a bench half a block away, unoccupied for the moment. They walked down to it and sat, the extra bottles between them. Carlucci twisted off the cap and drank deeply. A sharp pain from the cold drove up into his sinuses, but the beer tasted awfully good right now.

"How's the arm?" Cage asked.

"It's all right. It aches quite a bit right now, but that's because I've been wandering around in this godforsaken place since dusk."

"Looking for your daughter?"

"Yes."

"Christ, Carlucci. If she's been missing all this time, what the hell are the chances you're going to see her walking around in here?"

"Pretty much zero." He looked at Cage. "But what would you do? Stay at home and wait to hear something? I've done enough of that."

"I understand," Cage said. "But what the hell do you want from me? I haven't seen her."

Carlucci took a folded photo of Caroline from his pocket and handed it to Cage. "Just in case," he said. "Keep an eye out for her. Ask around."

"Here? In the Tenderloin? Walk around and show people this picture and ask them if they've seen her? Are you out of your mind?"

"No. I don't really expect you to do that. What I really want you to do is put me in touch with Cancer Cell."

"Jesus, you *are* out of your mind."

"No. The first time we talked, you said you might be able to do it."

"Yeah, I said *might,* and it turned out I didn't know what the hell I was talking about. Besides, that was then, this is now, and they're not the same." He cocked his head. "Do you have any idea what's going on in this city right now, with this goddamn disease, whatever it is? The one that killed Stinger and Tito, the one that's killing Nikki?" Without waiting for Carlucci to answer, he went on. "Of course you don't. No one does. But this thing is spreading. It's starting to pop up all over, but no one knows what it is, no one knows where it's come from. No one knows there are other cases out there. But this thing has probably come from the Core, somehow, and Cancer Cell has to know that. And the last thing they're going to want to do is talk to anyone. I think they've pulled in tight and closed the hatch over themselves."

Carlucci thought about that for a while. Then he said, "And if Caroline did try to contact them, what would they have done?"

"Who knows? But she probably didn't. How would she know how to do that?"

Carlucci just shook his head. None of it made much sense, but he didn't know where else she could be. "Are you *sure* you can't get in touch with them?"

Cage shook his head in exasperation. "Christ, Carlucci, I've been trying. I've got a bad feeling about this disease. I've been trying to get in touch with them for days now, and it's been a goddamn stone wall. They might as well not exist."

Carlucci didn't know what else to say. He had felt as if Cage was his last chance. "What the hell am I going to do?" he said.

But Cage didn't have an answer for him.

CHAPTER **25**

Caroline had been in this room for well over a week. She was surprisingly comfortable in it, despite the locked door and the lack of windows. Two or three times a day she was taken to some exam room or lab, where Dr. Mike asked her questions, examined her, and ran her through batteries of tests. Dr. Mike was tall and emaciated, with wire-rim glasses and short, unkempt hair. He probably wasn't much older than thirty, but he acted as if he'd been a doctor all his life. Other than the questions he asked, he didn't talk much; Caroline wasn't sure that he really thought of her as another person. He was in a world of his own.

Rashida confirmed her impressions of Dr. Mike. Caroline and Rashida had talked a lot in the past week, and Caroline thought they were becoming friends. Rashida came by at least once a day, and often twice. In the evenings she would sometimes stay for hours. They would drink tea, talk, and listen to music on Rashida's disc player.

She almost felt she could tell Rashida the real reason she was here. One way or another, though, she was going to have to do something soon. She was learning nothing, really, about Cancer Cell, about what they were doing, what their facilities were like, or anything else. She had to admit that she knew no more about Cancer Cell or the disease that had killed Tito than she had known before coming here.

One evening Caroline was sitting on her bed, reading an older novel by Alana Wysocki, when she heard the door being unlocked. She looked up to see Rashida walk into the room and close the door behind her, then lean back against the door, looking at Caroline with an almost dead expression.

"What is it?" Caroline said, setting down her book.

"I believed you," Rashida said, her tone even and neutral. "More than that, I thought we were becoming friends."

"We are," Caroline replied. What had happened? She thought she should be frightened, but she wasn't.

"I don't think so." She remained at the door, watching Caroline.

"What is it?" Caroline asked again.

"Why are you here?" Rashida shook her head, as if she didn't expect a truthful answer.

Caroline decided not to give her any answer at all. She wasn't afraid, but she felt she had to be careful. She had the distinct feeling she didn't quite know what this was about.

"You *do* have Gould's Syndrome, don't you? There's no way you could have faked that, is there?"

"Of course I have Gould's."

"But this sad story about your friend's daughter with the leukemia, all a crock to suck me in."

"No," Caroline said, shaking her head. "Mink really does have leukemia. She and Lily are living in a death house in the DMZ, and without a bone marrow transplant, Mink is going to die."

"If you're not lying, that's even worse. Using them like this, to get close to us."

"I just want to help them," Caroline insisted.

"I should have known when it turned out your father was a cop. But we thought, hell, a cop's daughter isn't immune to things like Gould's. And you *do* have Gould's. But that's not why you're here, is it?"

"I don't know what you're talking about."

Rashida leaned forward, getting angrier. "You're really starting to piss me off," she said. "We've found out."

"Found out what?"

Rashida shook her head, smiling unpleasantly. "The daughter of some New Hong Kong big shot has been murdered, and the murder is being blamed on us. Nothing official yet, but it's clear. Someone carved 'CC' into her forehead, and the cops have made the connection they're supposed to make. And guess what? Your father is in charge of the investigation. Not only that, but he's been digging around the Tenderloin, trying to get somebody to give us to him. I'm not sure why, though. He's got *you* in here. What more does he need?"

"I don't know anything about that," Caroline said.

Rashida stepped forward, fists clenched, eyes wide. "You expect me to believe that?"

"It's the truth."

"God almighty." Rashida turned away, then paced back and forth in front of the door, shaking her head and half laughing.

"It's the truth," Caroline repeated. But she knew it was futile.

"I'd search you for some kind of transmitter, but we already did that. What were you supposed to do, find out exactly where we were and how to get in and out of here, then escape and show the cops the way in?"

Caroline got up from the bed and walked halfway across the room, then stopped, gazing steadily at Rashida. "I don't know anything about my father's cases. That's not why I'm here."

"Why then?" Rashida said, sneering. "You think we're going to find you a cure?"

Caroline hesitated a moment, then slowly shook her head. "No."

"Okay. Charitable works, then, to get this poor little girl her bone marrow transplant." The sneer was still there in her voice.

"I would love to get Mink a transplant, give her a shot at living, but that would have just been an added benefit. No, that's not why I'm here."

For the first time, Rashida looked uncertain. She watched

Caroline closely, and finally said, "All right, then. Why are you here."

"Tito Moraleja was a good friend of mine."

Rashida's expression changed from uncertainty to confusion, but she didn't say anything right away.

"You know who Tito was, don't you?" Caroline asked.

Rashida slowly nodded. "Yes, I know who he was. But—"

"You abducted him," Caroline said.

"Yes," Rashida admitted. "We had a contract, and Tito was trying to renege. It was just business. But I still don't understand. Are you trying to take revenge because we abducted your friend?"

"No, nothing as simple as that. I'm trying to find out what killed him. And what killed Stinger."

Now Rashida looked surprised, and a little stunned. "Jesus," she said. Then, "This really has nothing to do with your father's investigation, nothing to do with the Katsudas and New Hong Kong?"

"Nothing," Caroline said. "I really don't know anything about that. My father has no idea I'm here, and believe me, he'd go nuts if he knew."

Rashida nodded. "This is starting to make a little more sense."

"Maybe to you."

She laughed. "Let me go make some tea for us, and I'll be right back. We've got a lot to talk about."

Ten minutes later, Rashida returned with two large mugs of green tea. Things were clearly better between them, but Rashida had still locked the door while she'd gone for the tea. Caroline was sitting on the bed again, Rashida on the chair.

"How did you know about Tito?" Rashida asked. She was tense again. Maybe not about the same thing, but something.

"Cage," Caroline answered.

"Cage? How the hell did *he* know?"

"Tito ended up at his street clinic, and died there. I guess

it was pretty obvious it wasn't the AIDS. I hear it was
pretty awful.''

"Yes, I imagine. He was your friend?''

"Yes.''

"I'm sorry. And what about Stinger? How did you know
about *him*?''

"Cage again. I'd gone to talk to him about Tito, and he
told me about Stinger.''

"And how did he know about Stinger?''

Caroline smiled. "Your friend Tiger.''

Rashida closed her eyes and sighed. "I should never
have said anything to him. Big mistake.''

"Why did you?''

Rashida opened her eyes, but frowned, almost closing
them again. "I panicked. I got scared, seeing Stinger die
that way. Tiger, well, he's a sweet kid, and he knew Stinger
was sick. He'd helped me bring Stinger into the Core when
Stinger went into crisis. He was afraid, too. He'd gotten
some of Stinger's blood on him, and he was afraid he
would get whatever Stinger had.'' She sighed again. "I had
to tell him that Stinger had died.'' After staring into her
cup for a minute, she looked back up at Caroline.

"So, what was it? You and Cage knew about two people
who had died the same way? It could have been anything.''

"It had Cage worried. Both people with a connection to
Cancer Cell, both dying pretty horribly.'' Caroline hesitated, wondering how much she should say. Everything, she
decided. "There was something else. A woman named
Nikki.''

Rashida nodded. "Yeah, Cage's partner.''

"She's got it, too. Apparently she got it from Stinger.''

"What a mess,'' Rashida said.

"Yes,'' Caroline said. "It's a mess. So tell me. What is
it?''

Rashida didn't say anything. She stared at Caroline for
a while, thinking, then got up from the chair.

"Aren't you going to tell me?'' Caroline asked.

"I don't know. I'll have to talk to my colleagues. It's
not that simple.''

"Nothing ever is."

Rashida smiled and shrugged. "Let me ask you something. Mike, he doesn't really have much to go on with you, for the Gould's. Anything he tries will be taking shots in the dark. And whatever he tries might make you sick, fuck you up but good. Now that all this is out, why you're really here, do you still want to put yourself at his mercy?"

"I'm willing to trade myself for a bone marrow transplant for Mink."

"Forget Mink. Forget the bone marrow transplant. It's not going to happen. Just you. No other deals. You get nothing else, just an extremely improbable chance at some kind of treatment or cure. Are you willing to submit yourself as an experimental subject?"

Caroline didn't have to think about it very long. It was never for herself, she'd never held out any hope for it. "No," she said.

Rashida nodded. "That's what I thought." She walked to the door and opened it. "We'll talk again." Then she went through, closed the door, and locked it.

Caroline didn't hear from Rashida until late the next day. She didn't even hear from Dr. Mike. A woman she'd never seen before brought breakfast and lunch to her, escorted her to the shower, but never said a word.

Sometime around what she guessed was midafternoon, the locks clicked, the door opened, and Rashida stepped in.

"Want to go on a tour?" she asked.

"Of what? The labs?"

Rashida shook her head. "The Core."

Rashida led the way down a short, narrow passage that ended at a security door with coded electronic locks. She popped open a wall cubicle, took out two flashlights and a couple of what appeared to be black handguns. She handed one of the flashlights to Caroline.

"You ever use a stunner?" Rashida asked.

Caroline shook her head.

"Better you don't carry one, then." She put one of the

stunners back, then keyed in codes for the door locks. Just before activating them, she checked a security screen. "All clear," she said. She activated the locks and the door hissed open. "Let's go."

Caroline followed her past the door, which automatically hissed closed behind them. They were in a concrete-walled corridor, dimly lit by irregularly spaced overhead lights.

"So we *are* in the Core," Caroline said.

"Oh, yeah. Nowhere but. How much do you know about it?"

"Nothing," Caroline admitted. "Stories you hear about crazy people living in here. Crazier stories about ghosts and strange creatures wandering the buildings."

"Well, some of the people in here are a lot weirder than ghosts, if you ask me. But most of them are also much less dangerous than you might imagine. You just need to know how to treat them, how to talk and relate to them, and you do that in ways that are unlike relating to normal people. Mostly you get into trouble if you say the wrong thing, or say something in the wrong way. If you just pay attention, and listen carefully, the clues are usually there. And when it's time to leave, you leave. That's all."

"You sure make it sound simple."

"In a way it is. Hopefully we won't run into too many of the locals, but if we do, just follow my lead. And when in doubt, just ignore them."

"But you've got a stunner with you," Caroline said.

Rashida smiled. "Of course. These *are* crazy people. Sometimes no matter what you do or say, no matter how careful you are, things go to shit. But we don't want to kill anyone, so we use stunners." She held up her weapon for a moment, then stuck it into her belt. "Follow me."

The passage angled slightly downward, and as they continued it became cooler and more damp, with an occasional puddle of muddy water on the floor and water dripping from the ceiling or down the walls. Then they took a side branch, unlit but strangely both hot and dry for a hundred yards until they emerged into another cool and damp main passage. This time they only went about fifty feet before

Rashida ducked into an alcove and cement steps leading upward.

They climbed three flights and came out in the hallway of what had once been an office building. A few rotting remnants of carpeting and padding remained on the concrete floor, and light came in through a tall window at the far end of the hall. There were doors on both sides.

Rashida stopped at the last office on the right. The glass window was painted over so they couldn't see inside. "The Fat Man lives here," she said, smiling.

"The Fat Man."

Rashida nodded. "The Fat Man himself." Still smiling.

Caroline wondered if she was supposed to know who the Fat Man was. She didn't have a clue.

"Who's the Fat Man?" she asked.

"A kind of low-rent slug. You'll see."

Rashida tapped on the painted glass. A few moments later, a high-pitched voice said, "Who's there?"

"Rashida. And a friend."

The door cracked open, and an eye appeared in the narrow opening. Rashida waved at the eye. The door opened wider, revealing a tiny, ancient black woman in a light brown robe and sandals. Rashida and Caroline stepped inside, and the old woman slammed the door shut. "Is all right," she said to a tall, beefy man in the corner behind the door; he was holding a pistol in each hand, the guns pointed at Rashida and Caroline. The man spun the pistols around like a cowboy in an old Western and planted them in the holsters on his belt. Then he squatted on the floor and closed his eyes.

"Hallo, Rashida." The old woman grinned and cackled. She had no teeth, or at least none that were visible.

"We're here to see the Fat Man."

"Yes, yes, yes, he's expecting you. And you," she said, staring at Caroline. Then she waved at them and led the way to the door on the other side of the room. She kicked the door three times, then opened it and flapped a hand at them. "Go in, go in."

The room on the other side of the door was large and lit

by dozens of candles, and oppressively hot. The stench of body odor hung in the air, biting at the nose. In the far corner, suspended in a hammocklike webbed chair that hung from the ceiling, was a fat, grossly bloated man wearing only shorts. His skin was drenched in sweat and from the chest up was dotted with a couple dozen dermal patches; he was sucking at a long flexible tube connected to a several-gallon tank mounted on the wall.

The door slammed shut behind them; the Fat Man stopped sucking on the tube and grinned. "Rashida, my darling one. You have something for me?"

"Yes, Fat Man. I do." She unbuttoned her shirt pocket and removed several packets of dermal patches. Then she stepped forward and held them out to him.

The Fat Man took the packets, opened them, and studied the patches for a minute. He sighed heavily and nodded. "Very good, my darling one." Then he turned to Caroline. "Tell me, new one. Why have you come to the Core?"

Caroline turned to Rashida, who nodded. "Tell him the truth."

She looked back at the Fat Man. "I had a friend who had been abducted by Cancer Cell—"

"To fulfill a contract, no doubt," he said.

"Yes, apparently. He got quite sick, somehow found his way out of the Core and into a street clinic, where he died. I came here to try to find out what it was that killed him."

"And what killed Stinger," the Fat Man said.

"Yes. And what is killing a friend of mine."

"And what has killed others here in the Core." He shook his head, which caused the webbing to shiver along with the rolls of fat on his body. "It's a terrible thing." When everything had stopped shaking, he said, "And you know nothing about your father's investigation of Naomi Katsuda's murder?"

She glanced at Rashida, starting to realize what was going on here.

"Answer me," the Fat Man said.

Caroline turned back to him. "No. I don't know anything about it."

"You have no intention of trying to discover the way in to Cancer Cell, then escaping so you can tell the police how to find them."

"No," she answered sharply, angry at the interrogation.

The Fat Man licked his lips, his tongue swollen and dark, then reached for the flexible tube and sucked at it again. He let the tube go and belched loudly, grinning. "She's telling the truth," he said to Rashida.

Caroline whipped around and glared at her. "You trust this . . . this *thing's* judgment more than you trust me?"

"I don't really know you, do I? I've known the Fat Man for years, and he's quite reliable." She sighed. "I'm sorry, Caroline, but we have to be sure. There's too much at stake. You must understand that."

Caroline closed her eyes for a moment and nodded. She understood. It was just so bizarre, being in this room with this gross, bloated thing judging her.

"Yes, I'm disgusting," the Fat Man said. "I'm fat and I'm ugly and I stink, but I'm smarter than anyone in the Core, smarter than most anyone in this entire city, and I know almost everything that's going on in here. That may not mean much to you, but it means everything to me."

Caroline watched him, morbidly fascinated by the way his bloated lips and tongue moved as he spoke, and when he was finished, she said, "Okay, Fat Man. Smart Man. What's the story with this disease?"

The Fat Man looked at Rashida, who shrugged, then nodded. "Tell her," she said. "Tell her everything."

"Everything? That would take my entire life, and I still would not be finished."

Rashida looked at Caroline and shook her head. "He's smart, but he's also one huge smart-ass." She turned back to the Fat Man. "Everything about the disease."

"I know, my darling one, I know." He sucked a few more swallows from the tube, knocked the tube away, then shifted his position in the web chair, farting several times as he grunted and moved about. Finally he seemed to be comfortable, and he turned his gaze and smile on Caroline.

"This disease started inside the Core," the Fat Man began. "Not inside Cancer Cell, but out here in the Core. Now, how the agent of the disease got inside the Core is a mystery even to me, but considering the nature of this place, not so surprising that something like this happened. A number of the Core residents came down with it, became quite ill, and after two or three had died, the others started going to Cancer Cell."

Caroline looked at Rashida for an explanation.

"We provide medical care to people in here. Compensation, if you will, for our expansion throughout the Core. We started out quite small, and we've added labs and production facilities over the years, snaking all through the buildings here as well as belowground, closing off quite a bit of the Core in the process. In return, to keep down the hassles and attacks from the crazier ones, we give them medical care. When sick people started showing up, we took them in and tried to help."

"We exchange information constantly," the Fat Man said, "and as the seriousness of this disease became apparent, we've been working together to try to learn as much as we can about it. They give me the hard data, and I do interpretation and analysis. I look at the trends, and the changes in the trends." His disconcerting smile was gone, and his expression had become quite serious and grave. "It started quite a while ago, months ago. And although it began here, not only has it made it out into the Tenderloin, it's gone out into the main city, though no one out there seems to know it yet. And it has changed. So much of this is guesswork, because reporting standards aren't exactly very high here in the Core." The Fat Man smiled and scratched at his crotch. Caroline tried to ignore it, and suppressed a touch of nausea. "But my best analysis indicates that initially the incubation period was rather long, perhaps as long as two or three weeks. Which is probably why, despite its high mortality rate, it has managed to spread out into the city."

"How high *is* the mortality rate?" Caroline asked.

"Close to one hundred percent."

Caroline's heart sank for Nikki, for Cage. "How close to one hundred percent?"

The Fat Man shook his head. "No known survivors. But I would never claim a full one hundred percent. There will be survivors somewhere, sometime. There will be people who are exposed to it who don't contract it. There always are. But those are going to be exceptions, *rare* exceptions." He paused, seemed to think for a few moments, then went on. "The incubation period, however, seems to be declining. From the reports I've been getting, from Cancer Cell as well as from my other sources in the Core, and my sources outside, in the Tenderloin and in the city, I would say the incubation period is down under a week. It might go down to just a few days. I would guess that over the next several weeks, there will be a small explosion of cases appearing. More inside the Tenderloin, but many outside as well. At this point, I would be very surprised if it hasn't been carried outside the city, into other states, perhaps even other countries." The Fat Man paused, then gave Caroline a tight, disturbing smile. "There's a plague in the making."

After leaving the Fat Man, Rashida brought Caroline to a small, roofless room at the top of the tallest building in the Core with an incredible view of the surrounding buildings of the Tenderloin.

It took them half an hour to make their way along a maze of passages, up and down staircases, encountering several clumps of odd people who let them pass with hardly a word, through two floors of rubble, and up one final rickety ladder to a locked hatchway. Rashida used a magnetic key to unlock the hatch, then they climbed through and into the room. She locked the hatch after them.

They sat together on a makeshift bench of boxes and cracked wooden planks, looking out through windows that had almost no glass remaining in their frames, and large holes that had been punched or blown into the walls. It was late afternoon, the brown-orange sun hanging low in the sky, but it was still hot. From here, the Core did not seem quite so awful, though it was still just four square blocks of rubble and ruins, and Caroline said as much to Rashida.

Rashida laughed. "You've had a very atypical tour through the Core, though. We avoided all the trouble spots, the places the real crazies tend to haunt, and we got lucky besides. So don't get romantic about this place. It's a hell-hole, believe me." She laughed again. "But it's home."

"You trust the Fat Man's assessment of this thing, this disease, whatever it is?"

"He's a monster, but I've never known him to be wrong about anything of importance."

"And a human lie detector."

Rashida shrugged. "If you can call him human. He's been a great help to us over the years. Not just for the information, but acting as a kind of emissary for us with various groups in the Core. We probably couldn't have made it in here without him."

Caroline finally decided to just ask the question she most wanted to ask. "What *is* the purpose of Cancer Cell?"

Rashida didn't answer at first. She gazed out the window and down at one of the street barriers blocking off the Core from the rest of the Tenderloin. "That's hard to say. There is no single purpose for everyone, and things have changed over the years. But if there's been anything like an over-riding philosophy, I'd say it would be to increase access to the best drugs and medical treatments available. Entities like New Hong Kong, governments, and corporations have essentially complete control over health care in this coun-try, and it's not even close to being fairly distributed." She turned to Caroline. "But I don't need to give you a lecture about that, do I?"

"No, you don't. I know what it's like. I've been lucky, because my father is a policeman. But people like Tito don't have anything."

"We try to manufacture high-grade pharmaceuticals and make them available on the street, at a much lower cost than the drug companies allow. And we try to do cutting-edge medical research that places like New Hong Kong or the major drug companies can't be bothered with because there might not be a profit in it. And we want people on the street to have access to new treatments and procedures at something like an affordable price.'' She paused. ''I guess we're just trying to equalize things a little. Bring a little fairness.'' She smiled and shook her head.

''But you experiment on people, sometimes without their consent.''

''We always get their consent to begin with,'' Rashida said. ''Sometimes they change their minds.''

''Like Tito?''

''Like Tito.''

''And then you abduct them and experiment on them by force.''

''We enforce the contracts they willingly signed. We always fulfill our part of the contract, and we expect them to fulfill theirs.'' Her expression hardened, and she waved at the view they had. ''This is the real world we're living in, and working in. Your friend Tito did quite well by us. You thought he suffered a great deal in the last months of his life, and he did. But his suffering would have been much greater without the drugs we provided for pain, to fight infections, to battle his depressions. In return, we wanted to be able to try experimental procedures, treatments, and drugs on him, so that if nothing else we might be able to help others in the future.'' She shook her head. ''I'm not going to apologize for what we do, or how we do it. We've made some decisions, and we've provided tremendous benefits to people who otherwise wouldn't have access to the kind of drugs and health care we give them.'' She looked away from Caroline. ''And *that's* the purpose of Cancer Cell. You can do what you like with it.''

Caroline didn't say anything. They remained in the room for a long time, not speaking, and watching the sun set on the city, and the light begin to fail.

CHAPTER 26

Cage was half drunk when the call came through from Eric Ralston. He had been half drunk pretty much all of his waking hours the past couple of days. It was a compromise. He stayed away from Hanna's, and he wouldn't let himself get completely smashed, in case something came up at the clinic, but he had also given up on getting through the days completely sober. Nikki was going to die any day now. She had become comatose, unresponsive, kept alive by artificial lungs and heart and blood. It was amazing that she had hung on this long, but it wasn't going to continue. She was going to die.

He wanted to be with her, sitting at her side, but the doctors wouldn't let him, not when they didn't know what was killing her. Standing outside her door and looking at her through a rectangle of glass was just impossible. So he'd given up, went by twice a day to stare at her for half an hour, and spent the rest of his time wandering around in a trance.

He was in his apartment, sitting at the window, dazed by the heat of the day and the alcohol, drinking one more beer and watching the street below him, hardly registering a thing. His skin was slick with sweat. He wasn't even sure what time it was—sometime in the afternoon, he thought, judging by the heat, but it could have been noon, or four. The shadows should have given him an idea, but he couldn't concentrate on them enough to work it out. He didn't give a shit.

The phone rang. He looked at it, thought about not answering. He would be useless at the clinic right now. But the phone kept on ringing, and finally he answered, just to stop it.

"Yeah?"

"Cage? Is that you?"

"Yeah, it's me, who else would it be? Who are you?" He didn't recognize the voice.

"Eric."

"Eric." Then it dawned on him who it was, and he sat up straighter in the chair, blinking crazily, as if it would help drive away the alcohol haze. "Eric, for Christ's sake."

"Cage, you son of a bitch. I just talked to Mandy, back in Atlanta, and she gave me your number. She said you've been calling for three or four days."

"Yeah, where the hell are you?"

There was a long hesitation, then Eric finally said, "Right here, pal. San Francisco."

Fear jumped inside his chest, and Cage got to his feet. He began pacing around the apartment, still trying to clear his head. "How long have you been here?"

Another slight hesitation. "Five days."

"And you didn't call me?"

This time there was the longest silence of all, and Cage knew he wasn't going to like where this conversation went. He picked up his beer from the windowsill, took it over to the sink, and poured the rest of it down the drain.

"I couldn't," Eric finally said.

"But you are now."

"Against my better judgment. I'd been wavering, and when Mandy called, hell, I just decided I'd better."

"Why are you here in San Francisco?"

"Cage, you've got to promise me everything I tell you is confidential. And I don't mean half-assed. This is the real goddamn thing, my man, and I'm hanging my ass out over the fire by talking to you."

"I promise," Cage said, the fear jerking up a notch. He had stopped his pacing, and stood at the window. There was no breeze, and the heat and stink of the street drifted in to him. "I've got a terrible feeling that the reason I was calling you is the reason you're here."

Eric didn't reply, and Cage didn't know what else to say. He sat down again in the chair and leaned his head against the window frame, closing his eyes. He wanted another beer. He wanted ten, one right after another, sinking him into oblivion.

"Okay," Eric said. "Let me run this by you. Something superficially a little like some of the hemorrhagic fevers. But different, really. Unique. Severe, red oozing skin rashes. Severe organ deterioration. Vomiting blood. Seizures. Death."

Cage didn't answer right away, wishing somehow that none of this was real. Maybe it wasn't as bad as he feared. He opened his eyes. "That's it," he said. "How come you guys know about it, but no one around here does?"

"Hell, Cage, it's what we're supposed to do. Be on top of this shit when it happens."

"How the hell do you guys know *anything*?"

"We're getting some help. We've got sources, the people who picked this up and first notified us."

"Who?"

"I can't tell you that."

"Have you got ideas for treatment? From your sources or whoever."

"No," Eric said. "Not a damn thing. Our sources are pretty sure it's a virus, but that's it. And near as we can tell, it's pretty close to a hundred percent fatal."

Cage nodded to himself. His flicker of hope was gone, just like that.

"Why?" Eric asked. "Have you got someone in your clinic with it?"

"No." He paused. "Do you remember Nikki?"

"With the cheeks of gold?"

"Yes."

"Beautiful woman. Of course I remember her." Then, "Not her."

"Yes."

"How long has she had it?"

"Four weeks, maybe longer."

"And she's still alive?"

"Barely."

"Where is she, Cage? Not in your damn clinic, I hope. No offense, but—"

"No, she's in St. Anthony's."

"Then maybe there's hope. We've been hearing two weeks maximum."

"No," Cage said. "She's dying. Another day or two at most."

"Don't give up yet. You're a doctor, you know as well as I do that strange things happen."

"Yeah, I'm a doctor. And I've seen her going steadily downhill, no matter what they've done. Her internal organs are shot. There's no recovering from where she is, Eric. None."

"I'm sorry," Eric said.

There was a long silence. Cage wanted to hang up, return to his grieving, his waiting. His drinking. But there was too much more to come, he knew that.

"Okay, Cage, now listen to me." Eric's tone had changed, become stronger. "You've got to get out of there. Now. Today, tonight, whatever. The sooner the better."

"Get out of where?"

"The Tenderloin."

"What the hell are you talking about?"

"Remember what I said earlier. You can't breathe a word of any of this, or I'll lose my job. In fact, they'll throw my sorry ass in jail."

"I promised you once, for Christ's sake. I promise again. What the hell is going on?"

"As of dawn tomorrow, we're putting the Tenderloin in quarantine."

Cage started to laugh, then choked it off. "You fucking can't be serious, Eric."

"I'm serious, Cage. This is bad shit, and that's the only way we're going to stop it from breaking out."

"That's a crock of shit. It's not confined to the Tenderloin, if it ever was."

"It started in there, we know that."

"Maybe. I'll grant that. But if it did, it's already broken out. I know of half a dozen probables outside the Tenderloin, which means there are probably a hell of a lot more than that."

"No," Eric insisted. "We're certain that as of right now it is completely confined to the Tenderloin. Any cases outside are just coincidentally similar."

"Jesus Christ, Eric, that's bullshit and you know it."

"That's the official position, Cage. The decision's been made."

"I can't believe I'm hearing this from you."

"Cage, do you know where this thing started?"

"How the hell would I know that?"

"You're an intelligent man. You're there on the streets. I figure you have a pretty good idea."

"Do *you*?"

"Oh, yeah. The goddamn Core, that's where." He paused, probably for effect. "Cancer Cell."

"It's a possibility."

"No, it's a certainty. And we're going to take care of them."

"What do you mean?"

"At the same time we establish the quarantine around the Tenderloin, we'll establish an interior quarantine around the Core. We'll bring everyone in the Core out, transfer them to an isolation clinic we're setting up out on Treasure Island, and then we'll go in and sterilize."

Cage started pacing again, all the effects of the alcohol apparently banished. "You people are all out of your fucking minds," he told Eric. "You can't quarantine the Tenderloin. You won't even be able to quarantine the Core. You have any idea what that place is like? How many ways there are into the Core? The kinds of passages and routes in and out?"

"The military is getting prime intelligence. They'll be able to set up the quarantine."

"They're kidding themselves, Eric. They'll never find all the ways into that place."

"They will." Eric was adamant.

"They won't. But even if they could, you know who's in there? You know *what's* in there?"

"Cancer Cell."

"Yeah, but they're only a small part. The Core is the weirdest fucking collection of social misfits and freaks in this hemisphere. They won't all come out and go into your nice isolation clinic. They'll fight you every step of the way."

"The military will be prepared for that."

"What are they going to do? Kill everyone who resists?"

Eric didn't answer. Cage stopped pacing a minute, trying to slow his breathing. He was getting worked up, and it wasn't helping anything.

"I can't believe I'm having this conversation with you," he said.

"I'm just . . . trying . . . to help you, Cage. I'm putting my ass on the line here. I called to give you a chance to get out before the quarantine goes into effect. I didn't call to argue CDC and military policy."

Cage stood by the window, slowly shaking his head and gazing out at the streets and buildings that were about to become a prison. Something was wrong with this whole thing. "You people are absolutely insane," he said. "*If* this disease started in the Core, it's already broken out of the Tenderloin. A quarantine is useless. And a quarantine of the Tenderloin won't hold together anyway. The whole thing is insane."

He waited a long time for Eric to respond. When he finally did, his voice sounded weary. "You have a better idea, St. Cage?"

Cage sat down, feeling weary himself. "Use your resources to help identify the virus, work on the development of a vaccine or treatments, public education to prevent its spread."

Eric laughed. "That's a joke, and you know it."

"Something's fishy about this whole thing, Eric."

"Don't push it, Cage."

"This is going to be a disaster."

Eric sighed heavily. "Get the hell out, Cage. Now."

"I can't do that, Eric."

"You're a crazy son of a bitch."

"So are you. So's the whole fucking CDC."

"Cage. Just remember your promise. Not a fucking word."

"Don't worry." His anger and frustration were almost gone, overtaken by exhaustion. There *was* going to be a disaster. "I guess I should thank you for calling me."

"Yeah, well." There was a long pause. "Cage?"

"Yeah?"

"I'm sorry about Nikki."

"Thanks."

What the hell else was there to say, for either of them?

"I'll call you," Eric said.

"Do that."

"Good-bye, Cage."

"Good-bye, Eric."

He hung up the receiver. Dawn. Less than twenty-four hours away.

Caroline. Jesus. She was in the Core. He had to try to get her out.

Another impossible task. There was no time. His only way to contact Cancer Cell was through Tiger, and Tiger didn't even know who they hell they were. He'd have to contact Tiger, who'd have to contact Rashida, if that was possible, and then . . . and then, nothing. Shit.

The phone rang. Eric again? He picked it up and answered.

It wasn't Eric. It was Dr. Sodhi.

Nikki was dead.

CHAPTER 27

Out of desperation, Carlucci requested a crash session with Monk, one of the department slugs. He was surprised when he got word that Monk agreed. That Monk wanted the session to begin at four o'clock in the morning was also a surprise, but a much smaller one. The slugs were strange creatures, to say the least.

He stood outside the slug's quarters on the top floor, waiting for the entrance to unlock. The entrance panel chimed, then the door slid aside. Carlucci was hit by a wave of stunningly dry heat. He had forgotten about the heat, so dry he could feel a scratching at his throat with each breath. He stepped inside, and the door slid closed behind him.

The last time he had been here, the *only* time, Monk's quarters had been a maze of constantly rotating panels casting bands of shifting light and shadow, obscuring the room. This time, however, the main room was completely open, though dimly lit. He could see the kitchen in the back corner, with a table and chairs, and huge picture windows that formed most of the wall to his right. Padded armchairs were set in front of the windows. Another spectacular view, probably, like the one from Yoshi Katsuda's office.

Monk came through a door and into the kitchen, half walking, half dragging himself with two arm-brace canes. His thick, bloated body was completely covered by a slick black material, like a thin, shiny wet suit, and his head was enclosed in a goggled, form-fitting flexible helmet studded with blinking lights. His lips were the only flesh visible.

"Come on back, Lieutenant." Monk's voice was deep, but normal. The other time Carlucci had been here, Monk had spoken to him much of the time through overhead speakers, his voice amplified and with a slight echo effect. "Have a seat." Monk dropped heavily into one of the overly wide armchairs at the kitchen table.

Carlucci walked through the main room, his footsteps nearly silent on the carpeting, then sounding quite loud on the vinyl floor of the kitchen. He pulled out a chair across the table from Monk and sat.

"Do you want something to drink?" Monk asked. "You'll have to get it yourself, my manservant doesn't come on until six. The refrigerator is well stocked."

Carlucci shook his head, remembering now—an aged, thin Asian man in a black suit who had served him coffee. "Why no *Wizard of Oz* effects this time?" he asked.

Monk made a hacking sound that Carlucci assumed was a laugh. "Not much point to it. It didn't impress you last time, did it?"

"No."

"No. I wasn't going to waste your time or mine." Monk laid his black-coated arms on the table, gloved fingers wriggling like short, fat snakes. "It's been a long time since that session."

Not long enough. He wondered what Monk's face looked like under that strange helmet, what his eyes looked like behind the tinted goggles.

"You're here about your daughter," Monk said. "Caroline."

Carlucci didn't reply, too stunned. He shouldn't have been. He tried to remind himself of what Brendan had said about the slugs, and Monk in particular, three years ago— that they would regularly surprise you with the intuitive leaps they made, that they processed so much information so quickly from so many different sources, and were always well prepared for their sessions. Monk would have spent the past several hours trying to figure out why Carlucci had called for this crash session. He would know that word had gone out throughout the department about Caroline, that she was missing, that people were searching for her.

"You're also here to ask me about what's going on in the Tenderloin, about the possibility of a disease outbreak. Or you should be."

Carlucci leaned back in the chair, a sharp headache beginning already. He should have known.

"Why don't I just sit back and listen, then?" he said. "I don't need to ask you any questions. I can just listen to your answers."

"This is not a sideshow," Monk said. "I'm not performing like some huckster, trying to impress the rubes. This is my job. This is what the city pays me for. This is why you're here."

"Of course it's a sideshow," Carlucci replied.

"Is this your way of trying to charm me so I'll help you find your daughter?"

Carlucci slowly shook his head, sighing. He was being stupid. But it was hard, trying to talk to this thing across the table from him that looked like some mutant freak from a bad late-night movie.

"I'm sorry," he said. "That was unfair. It's four-thirty in the morning, I haven't slept, and I'm worried about her."

Monk nodded. He adjusted his position, making a strange squishing and slithering sound.

"You know she's missing," Carlucci said.

"She's not missing," Monk replied. "I know where she is."

Carlucci could feel his heart start racing, but he tried to stay calm, tried not get excited, afraid this was some bizarre joke from Monk.

"Where?" he asked.

"In the Tenderloin. In the Core. With Cancer Cell."

Carlucci didn't know what to say. Too many questions rose, all at once.

"Are you sure?"

Monk made a gesture that might have been a shrug. "I'm fairly confident in my analysis, but of course I can't be sure."

"Why?"

Monk shook his head. "I don't know."

It was like the last time. Every time Monk had said "I don't know," Carlucci had been fairly certain that the slug *did* know, or at least could make a pretty good guess. He felt exactly that way right now, and the frustration ate at his stomach, because he knew there was nothing he could do to force Monk to come clean.

"How do you know?"

This time it was Monk who sighed. "You know I can't answer that kind of question."

"Can't, or won't?"

"Can't. I rarely know exactly what information leads me to what conclusions. I can only tell you with a fair degree of certainty that she has, somehow, contacted Cancer Cell, and that she is with them, in the Core."

"Alive?"

That shruglike gesture again. "Presumably. You will just have to wait to find out."

"Or go in and get her."

Monk threw his head back and laughed, a hacking bray that grated on Carlucci. He wanted to strangle the freaky bastard. It *was* an absurd notion, going into the Core, he knew that, but what did Monk know? It wasn't *his* daughter who was missing.

"What do you know about Cancer Cell?" Carlucci asked, keeping his anger in check.

Monk shook his head. "Nothing. I even requested a session with Kelly in CID, hoping he might know something, but he didn't."

"Why did you do that?"

"Information is my blood. I don't like not knowing about something that may one day become important."

There was something wrong about all this, too, Carlucci could smell it.

"You said I was here to ask about Caroline, which was right. And that I was here to ask about this disease thing, or should be. Why didn't you say anything about the Naomi Katsuda murder investigation? That, too, is going nowhere. Shouldn't I be asking you about that as well?"

"Yes, of course. That, it seemed to me, was a given. It didn't seem worth mentioning. Besides, I have nothing to offer concerning that case." He paused, glancing down at the table, then back up at Carlucci. "Her death is a complete mystery to me."

A lie. Carlucci was certain. There was something, he believed, to be learned from Monk's lies and omissions as well as from what he actually offered. The difficulty lay in deciphering them.

"How did you know I was interested in this 'disease thing'?"

"Tito Moraleja's body in the temporary morgue." Monk snorted with a twisted grin. "There's no connection between Moraleja's death and Naomi Katsuda's murder—your official rationale for holding the body with an autopsy request. So your interest had to lie elsewhere."

"And?"

Monk's expression, what little of it Carlucci could see, appeared to take on real gravity.

"You are right to be concerned. There is a very deadly disease that is preparing to break out of the Tenderloin. Caused by a virus, contagious, and with a mortality rate nearing one hundred percent. A disease with no preventative vaccine and no treatment. How's that for a fucking nightmare, Lieutenant?"

Once again, Carlucci didn't know how to respond. Monk seemed both so certain and so sincere. No fooling around, no deception, no showmanship. As if he *knew*.

He knew.

"What the hell is going on?" Carlucci finally asked.

"There's even a name for the disease, now," Monk said. "Core Fever."

"Monk—"

"Let's go over by the windows, and you'll be able to see firsthand."

"See what?"

Monk's only response was to struggle upright with his canes. Breathing heavily, he dragged himself out of the kitchen, then across the carpet toward the large picture win-

dows. Carlucci remained at the table, watching until he
reached one of the armchairs and dropped into it. He laid
the canes on the floor at his feet, then craned his neck
around to look at him. "Come on, Lieutenant. The answer
to your questions."

Carlucci got up and walked over to the windows, keeping
away from Monk. He remained standing, and looked out.

They had a fairly good view of the Tenderloin from here.
Lights were going crazy all around it, bright floods and
flares, spinning colored lights on emergency vehicles,
blinking barrier lights. Looking down between two buildings, to the perimeter of the Tenderloin itself, he could see
what appeared to be the beginning of a military cordon.

"What the hell is going on?" he asked again.

Suddenly a whole fleet of helicopters appeared, headed
into the heart of the Tenderloin. They moved in quickly,
and began landing on rooftops deep inside, and then he
realized they were landing on buildings that roughly enclosed the Core. Where Caroline was.

He turned to look at Monk, who was actually grinning.
He stared at the slug, waiting for an answer. Monk finally
gave it to him.

"Quarantine."

ISABEL

It had begun.

Isabel didn't know what was happening, but she knew it was time to go. Things were even crazier now, people running and screaming, loud bangs, the smell of smoke. There would be nothing for a time, almost dead silence, and then it would start up again, different, but somehow feeling all the same. It was too crazy, and she was afraid. Anything could happen.

She worked her way toward the opening she had found earlier, moving quickly and quietly along the passages, sinking back into shadows and alcoves whenever someone appeared.

A small fire burned within a circle of stones at one intersection of corridors. Isabel hung back, watching closely, waiting, but no one seemed to be near, and she quickly skirted the flames. A terrible smell came from within them. There was a body, a dead fat man lying belly up, his throat cut and his eyes open.

Farther on, a woman squatted in front of a small pit dug out of the dirt floor, rocking on her haunches and humming, flanked by burning candles. Water glistened in the pit, and there was movement in the water. There was no other way, so Isabel slowly crept past, on the side of the pit opposite the woman. As she passed, the woman looked up and gazed at Isabel; the woman smiled, but continued humming and rocking, and made no other move. Isabel pushed on.

Finally she reached the short dead-end passage and entered it. The grate was still on the ground, the opening clear. She checked the main corridor once more to make sure there was no one nearby, then returned to the opening and pulled herself up and into it.

She squirmed forward as quickly as she could manage, afraid of being exposed. Her way was a little easier this time, since she knew what to expect. When she entered the wider duct, she took the right branch again, then right once more at the next chance, and before long she was emerging into the dark passage on the other side.

Isabel dropped to the floor. She stood unmoving for a long time, listening. Faint sounds came to her through the opening, but nothing from the passage around her. She moved forward to the rectangle of light at the far end, the window in the door. At the bottom of the steps she hesitated for a moment, then climbed them and put her face to the glass.

The room on the other side was the same, except that this time there were no people inside. Careful as always, she remained at the window for quite a while, watching. No one entered the room. Feeling safe, she took hold of the doorknob and tried to turn it.

The doorknob wouldn't budge. She tightened her grip, and turned harder. Still nothing. The door was locked, or the knob rusted shut. Once more with both hands gripping the knob, but again it wouldn't turn.

She was trapped.

PART FOUR

QUARANTINE

Rashida came into Caroline's room, flushed and breathing hard. She was wearing a surgical mask and gloves, and carrying a flashlight and a small leather bag.

"Come on," she said. "We have to go. *You* have to go."

"Go where? What's going on?"

"Quarantine."

"Quarantine? Where?"

"The Tenderloin. The Core. There's not much time. Let's go." Then she shook her head. "Don't bring anything with you. I'll give you the only thing you'll take out of here."

"What are you talking about?"

"Later. Let's go."

She followed Rashida out of the room and down the corridor. Tension and a sense of urgency infected the air, extra bursts of it exploding whenever someone rushed by, or she saw frantic activity in one of the open rooms they passed. They stopped for a few moments when they ran into Dr. Mike, who passed a silent message to Rashida, his eyes saddened. Then Dr. Mike went one way, and they went another.

"What's happening?" Caroline asked again.

They turned into an empty, narrow corridor, which ended at one of the Core gates. Rashida checked the security panel, unlocked the door, and pushed Caroline through. She stumbled forward in the dim light, then Rashida came through after her and sealed the door, bringing complete darkness.

Caroline didn't move, waiting for Rashida. Rashida's hand gripped her arm; the gloved fingers felt cold on her skin.

"Don't lose me now," Rashida said, her voice just above a whisper.

"Don't lose *me*," Caroline answered.

Rashida quietly laughed. Then, before they went any farther, she said, "The CDC and the military have quarantined the Tenderloin. They've announced the impending outbreak of a fatal disease whose source is the experimental laboratories of a medical terrorist group called Cancer Cell."

"How can they say that?"

"Hell, they can say any damn thing they want to, can't they? They're calling it Core Fever. They've announced that Cancer Cell's labs are in the Core, and they've sent in special troops and equipment to establish a second quarantine around the Core itself."

"Is that possible?" Caroline asked.

"Not completely," Rashida answered. "But they've done extremely well, far better than I would ever have imagined they could do." She paused. "They have very good intelligence." There was something about the way she'd said that last thing that implied betrayal. "They're going to destroy us."

"What do you mean?"

"Just that. They've given us until noon to come out through one of their quarantine stations, and that means everyone in the Core. There are teams in isolation suits ready to process us, then they're going to transfer all of us to isolation wards somewhere until we either get sick or stay healthy long enough to convince them that we haven't been infected. And then after we're all out, they're going to come through and sterilize the entire Core. But of course we won't all come out, and it's going to be a fucking disaster."

"What do you mean by that?"

"Forget about Cancer Cell. All the other people here in

the Core, the social misfits, the psychopaths, you think they're all going to surrender themselves in a nice quiet and orderly manner? You think they're going to surrender themselves in *any* kind of manner? Shit. A few of them will, probably, but most of them won't. A lot of them will actively resist, with any means they have. Hell, even some of my colleagues will probably resist.'' She sighed heavily. ''There will be bloodshed. And there will be a lot of it.''

''And Cancer Cell will be destroyed,'' Caroline added. Her eyes had adjusted to the darkness, and she could faintly make out Rashida's features, enough to see her nod in reply.

''Wiped out. They'll destroy the labs, they'll burn and sterilize everything, they'll wipe out all records, they'll destroy whatever they can get their hands on.'' There was another pause. ''But they won't get their hands on everything. We're getting *you* out of here.''

''Through the quarantine?''

''Yes. There's a way they won't know about. A way that won't be blocked.''

''How can you be sure?'' Caroline asked. ''What about the source of all their good intelligence?''

''Only four of us know about it. The four remaining original founders.'' She shrugged. ''I can't be sure. If one of the four of us is a weasel, then none of it matters anyway.''

''Why me? Why not you, or one of the others?''

Rashida didn't answer right away. ''We trust you,'' she finally said. ''And one or all of us may *need* to go into isolation wards.''

So that's what the mask and gloves were all about. Caroline didn't know what to say. She wanted to ask for more details, but decided it was better to let it go.

''Here,'' Rashida said, handing her the small leather bag. ''You take these with you. That's our price for getting you out.''

''What is it?''

''Backup modules of all of our most important records, all of our research. We're trying to transmit the same data out of the Tenderloin, but the military's managed to cut off almost every single transmission cable. We've got one left, but we don't know if it's getting through. And they're flying jammers in the air above the Core, blocking all air transmissions. And you better believe they're not going to let any of us take a damn thing with us when we leave.''

Caroline looked down at the bag, feeling a strong sense of responsibility. She looked back up at Rashida. ''What do I do with it once I'm out?''

''Hang on to it. Someone will get in touch with you. I'm not sure who it will be. That depends on who survives all this crap without being blown. But, this is important. It will be a woman who gets in touch with you. If a man approaches you, claiming to be one of us and asks for these, don't turn them over. Claim ignorance, run, brain the bastard, whatever. Got that?''

''Got it.''

''Okay. Any other questions? No? Good; let's go.''

Rashida didn't use the flashlight. The light was dim, but got brighter in spots, and there was usually enough to see ten or fifteen feet ahead. She seemed to know exactly where she was going.

They made a lot of stops and starts, sometimes retreating whenever someone appeared. Several loud echoing cracks sounded together, gunshots perhaps. At one point a hand reached out from a hollow in the wall, grabbing at Caroline, but Rashida smashed the hand with her flashlight, bringing out a brief cry. A figure shot out of the hollow and scurried down the passage in the direction from which they had come.

More sounds came from overhead, sometimes muffled, sometimes sharp and clear if Caroline and Rashida were near one of the stairwells leading up to the buildings above—banging sounds, grunting, music, loud hisses, a steady *whap! whap! whap!,* whimpering and hushed conversations and cackling laughter.

At one point, Rashida led the way up a metal ladder, then into a small room at street level with a paneled window. They crouched in the darkness, then Rashida opened the panels, letting in light and sound from outside. An amplified voice was blaring through the streets.

". . . BY TWELVE NOON TODAY, AT ONE OF THE LIGHTED BARRIER GATES AT STREET LEVEL, OR ONE OF THE UNDERGROUND PROCESSING STATIONS. YOU WILL BE EXAMINED AND PROCESSED AND TRANSPORTED TO ISOLATION WARDS FOR YOUR OWN HEALTH AND SAFETY, AND FOR THE HEALTH AND SAFETY OF THE CITIZENS OF SAN FRANCISCO. . . ."

Rashida chuckled. "Right, that will be effective, appeal to their better instincts."

". . . WILL BE SHOT. AGAIN, ALL RESISTERS WILL BE SHOT. THE SITUATION IS TOO GRAVE . . ."

She closed up the panels, bringing back the darkness. They remained in the room for a minute to let their eyes adjust back to the dim light, then Rashida led the way back down.

It wasn't much farther. They passed two bodies in the corridor, one face up with its throat cut, the other face down across the first. A little farther on they passed a woman sitting in front of a small pool of water; candles bobbed in the water, and the air smelled of burned wax.

Finally Rashida directed her down a short, dead-end passage, and they stopped in front of the left wall. There was an opening around chest level, but it was impossible to see more than a few inches into it.

"The grate's gone," Rashida said. She was looking around on the floor. "There it is." She picked it up, studied it, then set it back down, leaning it against the wall. She turned to Caroline. "This is it. You crawl through that duct. It will be a very tight squeeze at first, but it opens out at a T-branch. When it does, you go right, then right again at your first opportunity. You'll come out on the other side of this brick wall." She pointed at the bricked-up barrier across the passage. "There's another short passage, then a few steps leading up to a door to a basement storage room. To the left of the door, there will be a tiny depression in

the concrete wall, and inside will be a key.'' She paused.
''You'll be out. You'll still be in the Tenderloin, still in
quarantine, but you won't be in the Core any longer.''

''And what about you?''

''What about me? Who knows where I'll be?''

''Will I see you again?''

''Doubtful.'' There was a long silence. ''Go, Caroline.''

She wanted to give Rashida a hug, but it wouldn't be a
smart thing to do. ''I hope I do see you again.''

''Just take care of that bag.''

Caroline nodded. She put the bag in the duct first, pushed
the bag forward, then crawled in after it. Rashida was right,
it was extremely tight. She squirmed more than crawled her
way along, her arms extended in front of her, pushing the
bag forward as she went. Even breathing was difficult. But
it wasn't long before she reached the T-branch, and the
ducting widened. From there it was almost easy.

Hanging on to the leather bag, she stuck her head out of
the duct and into the passage on the other side of the wall.
Dark here, too, with a rectangle of light off to her left—
the door. Caroline lowered the bag to the ground, then let
herself slide out, dropping and rolling. She got to her feet,
found the bag, and picked it up.

A scraping sound behind her.

Caroline froze. She listened hard, and thought she heard
breathing. Slowly, so slowly, she turned around.

In the shadows, crouched against the wall, eyes wide,
was a large monkey.

''It's all right,'' she said, keeping her voice soft. ''I
won't hurt you.'' It was hard to tell exactly how big the
monkey was, or what kind it was. ''It's all right,'' she said
again.

The monkey didn't move. Keeping every movement
slow and deliberate, Caroline walked along the passage toward the door. She periodically looked back at the monkey,
but it didn't follow her. When she reached the steps, she
climbed them, then felt around in the wall next to the door
until she found the key.

She looked through the window. As Rashida had said, it

was a basement storeroom, filled with crates and sacks and drums. There was no one inside. Caroline unlocked the door, and opened it.

She stood in the doorway and looked back at the monkey. She couldn't stand the idea of it being trapped in here. How had it got here to begin with? The same way she had, maybe. It could go back, she supposed, but that wasn't a good idea right now.

"Come on," she said. She gestured at the monkey to join her, and said, "Come on," again. "You can come out with me."

It was probably a stupid idea. What the hell would the monkey do out in the Tenderloin? But she still felt sick at the thought of trapping it in here.

"I'll leave the door open for you," she said. "You can leave if you want."

The monkey hadn't moved except to turn its head toward her. She could just see its eyes in the gloom.

"So long," she said.

And she left the door open behind her.

A half hour later she reached the RadioLand Street Clinic. Cage wasn't there, but Franzee said he had been hoping she would show up, and she told Caroline how to get up to his apartment. Soon she was standing outside his door, knocking.

"It's open," Cage called from within.

She opened the door and stepped inside. Cage was sitting at one of the windows, gazing down the street in the direction of the Core. She closed the door, took another couple of steps, and then he finally turned.

He stared at her for a minute, then a faint smile worked its way onto his face. "I can't believe you're here. I can't believe you got out."

She smiled back. It was good to see him. "Rashida got me out."

"Through the quarantine?"

She nodded. "Yeah. Have I got a story to tell you." But there was something strange about him, something sad and defeated, and then she realized what it had to be. "Nikki?" she asked.

"Dead," Cage answered, the smile disappearing. He breathed deeply once. "Dead."

CHAPTER 29

Carlucci rode in one of the department helicopters above
the city, swinging a wide arc around the quarantine perimeter. He wanted to get a sense of the whole picture, but
they couldn't get too close without risking being shot out
of the sky. Allegedly there was close cooperation between
the army and the San Francisco Police Department, but in
reality the army and the CDC were calling all the shots,
and they were not allowing any encroachment of the air-
space above the quarantine zone, police or otherwise.

The quarantine perimeter was irregular, but seemed to be
fairly solid and settled in, street barriers manned by squads
of armed soldiers, reinforced by trucks and jeeps and
mounted gun posts. But the quarantine perimeter was not
exactly synonymous with the Tenderloin perimeter—they
hadn't been able to manage that. In several sections of the
DMZ, meeting armed resistance, the army had eventually
given up and included those strips of the DMZ inside the
quarantine, like weird bubbles on the Tenderloin boundaries. Those would be sticky areas, too, in the long run; the
Tenderloin, being for all practical purposes a walled city,
was already self-contained, though maintaining a quarantine around it for very long would be difficult. But the DMZ
strips were zones of chaos. The quarantine around them
couldn't be very secure.

Farther inside the Tenderloin, the quarantine around the
Core was nearly impossible to make out, too far away and
obscured by the intervening buildings. But Carlucci tried to

see if anything was happening, thinking about Caroline. He assumed she would come out with the other people from the Core, be processed and transferred to the isolation wards out on Treasure Island, but until he knew she actually had, he would worry.

He asked the pilot to set down on the rooftop where an observation site had been set up for the police, on a building a block away from the Tenderloin but tall enough to give them a decent line of sight. The pilot nodded, banked around, and five minutes later dropped Carlucci off. He hurried away from the copter, and it took off, giving him one final blast of wind from the blades.

He didn't know most of the cops at the roof's edge, but he was surprised to see Vaughn, the Chief of Police, standing there with the others and watching him approach. Vaughn was a tall, thin man, handsome and graying with distinction, charming without being slick—the perfect political animal on the police force, which was why he was Chief. Even now in the growing heat of the day he looked cool and comfortable in a light sand-colored silk suit, dark brown shoes, and tie. Vaughn and Carlucci had been something like enemies for years.

"Hello, Frank," Vaughn said as Carlucci reached the group. "Good to see you."

"Andrew." They shook hands. "I'm surprised to see you out here."

"Dramatic moments for the city. The Chief should at least make an appearance out on the front lines, right?" Smiling, like they were sharing a joke. Then his look turned serious. "I'm sorry to hear about your daughter."

"You say that as if she was dead."

"Frank, come on, that's not what I meant. But she has been missing for a long time. I can imagine how I would feel if one of my children had gone missing like that." Vaughn had two sons, one a lieutenant in the navy, the other a rising corporate lawyer in one of the city's biggest law firms. "My sympathies were sincerely given."

Carlucci nodded. They probably were. "Sorry," he said.

"And thanks." He nodded toward the Tenderloin. "What's been happening?"

"Not much, yet." They walked to the edge of the roof, two cops moving aside to make room for them. Then, subtly but clearly, all of the cops moved away to give them a small zone of privacy. "It's not quite noon, yet," Vaughn said. "But I don't expect much to happen immediately. They'll wait an extra hour for stragglers before going in with force."

From the edge of the roof they had a pretty good view of about two blocks of Tenderloin perimeter and the quarantine line. As Vaughn had said, things looked pretty quiet at the moment. The real action, though, wasn't going to take place here, not yet anyway—it would occur at the Core, and they couldn't see any of that at all from here. Just as well.

"What do *you* know about Cancer Cell?" Carlucci asked.

Vaughn laughed and looked at him quizzically. "Who have *you* been talking to? Kelly?" He shook his head. "That man is obsessed with Cancer Cell. He's the only person in the department who seemed to give a rat's ass about them before today."

"I'm surprised you know about Kelly's interest." He didn't see any point in pretending he wasn't aware of it himself.

"You shouldn't be, Frank. I make a point of knowing things like that about the officers working for me."

"And what are my interests?" Carlucci asked.

Vaughn smiled again. "Your obsessions are more abstract than most. But they are what should be, in good police officers, the obvious ones. Truth. And a striving for *rightness*. But they aren't obvious anymore, and they aren't held by many. I admire you greatly for those obsessions, Frank."

"Do you?"

"Oh, yes. I know what you think of me—my corruptions. They are great, it's true. But I'm much more complex than you give me credit for. I will never let you get in my way, Frank, but I do admire you. Accept the compliment. It *is* sincere."

He studied Vaughn, wondering if he had underestimated the man all these years.

One of the other cops called out, and there was pointing toward the Core. Carlucci and Vaughn turned to look. Something was rising above the ruined buildings, a strange podlike structure propelled in a jerking flight upward by a ring of jets trailing white smoke, a bizarre arrangement of fins and wings around it presumably acting as a steering mechanism. Big enough to contain two or three people. The pod continued to rise until it was forty or fifty feet above the buildings, then it veered away from the center.

Tracers shot up from the ground, followed a few seconds later by the ratcheting cracks of gunfire; they quickly zeroed in on the pod, tiny flashes appeared beneath it. Then there were several crumping sounds, and suddenly the pod exploded.

Bits of flashing metal sprayed out and down, along with larger chunks of what might have been body or structural parts, some licked by flames. A small piece with one of the jets apparently still intact spun crazily through the air, sometimes rising, sometimes diving, white smoke spinning about until it suddenly arced away and down and disappeared behind a building. Then all that was left in the air above the Core was dissipating smoke.

"A valiant effort," Vaughn said. "Unfortunately, there will be others. On the ground or in the air, it won't matter, they will all end like that." His voice seemed to carry real regret. "It's going to be bad in there."

"They'll be able to do it," Carlucci said. "Clear out the Core."

"Oh, certainly. But they'll be dragging bodies out of there, and a lot of their own. They have no idea."

"You have a better grasp on the realities than I would have expected."

Vaughn laughed. "Maybe when this is all over you and I should sit down and have a long talk. We might learn a lot about each other. We might like each other more.''

''Yeah, maybe.'' His phone beeped. He took it off his belt, flipped it open. ''Carlucci.''

''Papa?''

''Caroline?'' He could hardly believe he was hearing her voice, and a shiver went through him.

''Yes, it's me, Papa.''

''Hold on a second.'' Vaughn was looking at him, eyebrow raised. Carlucci walked away from him and the others. ''Are you all right? Where are you?''

''I'm fine, Papa.''

He was standing out in the middle of the roof, far enough from the others for privacy, but he could see Vaughn still watching him.

''Are you in the Core?''

There was a slight hesitation, then Caroline said, ''How did you know I was there?''

''A long and ugly story,'' he said. ''Are you out?'' He'd caught the ''was.''

''Yes, I'm out. That's a long story, too. But I'm still in the Tenderloin. I guess I'm going to be here for a while.''

''Have you talked to your mom?''

''Yes, I called home first.''

''Where are you now? Where are you going to stay? Maybe I can get you out.'' But he knew even as he said it that it would be impossible. They would not be making any exceptions with the quarantine.

Caroline just laughed. ''Forget it, Papa, you can't get me out. But I'll be fine. I'm with Cage, and he said I can stay in Nikki's apartment. He said you knew who she was.''

Again that word. ''Yeah. Is she still alive?''

''No.''

He nodded to himself. ''Tell Cage I'm sorry.''

''I will, Papa.''

And then he didn't know what to say. She was out of the Core, she was temporarily safe, but she was still in the Tenderloin, stuck there for the duration of the quarantine.

''It's so good to hear your voice,'' he finally said. ''We were . . . well, you know.''

"I'm fine, Papa. It'll be strange for a while, but I'll be okay here. You know how to reach Cage, yes?"

"Yes. Is he there with you?"

A few moments later, Cage came on the line.

"I'm sorry about Nikki," Carlucci said.

"Thanks."

"Listen, Cage. The Tenderloin is your home. Caroline doesn't know it for shit. Take care of her, will you?"

It sounded as if Cage was laughing. Then he said, "You're her father, all right. She probably doesn't need it much, but I'll take care of her, Carlucci. Don't worry about her."

Yeah, right. "Thanks, Cage."

"You bet. Here she is again."

There was another short pause, then Caroline was back. "I'll be okay, Papa."

"I know. I love you, Caroline."

"I love you too, Papa. And I'll talk to you soon."

"Good-bye."

"Bye, Papa."

Carlucci clipped the phone back to his belt, then looked back at the other cops. Vaughn was still watching him. He didn't want to go back and answer Vaughn's questions. Besides, he'd seen enough here. He turned away, and walked toward the rooftop stairwell.

CHAPTER 30

Cage and Caroline stood at the edge of Nikki's apartment rooftop, crowded in on both sides, leaning over the metal pipe railing and gazing down into the Core. The roof edges of all the buildings facing the Core were lined with people, like spectators at a sporting event, except most everyone seemed to realize that only disaster was coming.

The heat was incredible, and the acrid smell of sweat was heavy in the air, almost cloying. Below them, on the outer streets of the Core, the soldiers must have been roasting. Cage was surprised at how many there were, armed and armored, masked and gloved, some patrolling the outer perimeter, others manning the checkpoint processing stations that had been set up at the street boundaries and in the ground floors of a few of the border buildings. In the streets just outside the barriers, military ambulances waited, surrounded by more soldiers. Periodically one would pull away, lights flashing, heading out of the Tenderloin. Medical personnel were nearly invisible. And it was impossible to know what was going on underground—probably just as much activity, if not more.

He wasn't sure why they were here, watching. No, that really wasn't true, he realized. He knew why Caroline was here—in the short time she'd been inside, she'd developed an affinity, or at least a concern, for Cancer Cell. Maybe even the other people inside the Core. She wanted to know what was going to happen to them; she wanted to *see* what was going to happen. And he just wanted to be with her.

Her presence helped ease the pain of Nikki's death. Being alone made everything worse.

It was twelve-thirty, but not much had happened yet. The repeating message blaring out over the speakers had changed, now announcing that the army was granting an extra hour before they went in to remove all remaining people by force.

Movement below them slowed, almost ceased completely, and the soldiers turned to one of the buildings across the street. One of them gestured, and the message broadcast was cut off. Everything got quiet.

"Hey!" It was a voice from inside the building. "Hey, don't shoot, I'm coming out. No one's going to shoot, are they?"

"No one's going to shoot you," an officer said. "Just come on out and proceed to the checkpoint."

A few moments later, a tall, skinny man wearing only a tiny racing swimsuit and sunglasses emerged from the building. He stepped gingerly, his bare feet treading lightly across the debris scattered all over the ground. He was a strange-looking man, his face deeply tanned while the rest of his body, from the neck down, was incredibly pale, glistening with an oily substance.

The man walked carefully out into the middle of the street, then stopped. He looked up at all the people on the rooftops, then raised both hands high above his head, grinning. Then he bowed, looked back at the soldiers, and said, "Take me to your leader!"

The soldiers approached, but didn't get closer than about five feet from the man. They used their rifles to point the way, and escorted him to an open doorway in the building next to the one Cage and Caroline were on. Cage leaned out over the railing, saw the man stop near the door until the arms of people in isolation suits took his arms and pulled him inside.

Cage turned to Caroline and smiled. "Too bad it couldn't all be like that."

She didn't smile back. "I'm worried about them. Rashida and Dr. Mike and the others. I don't think they're going to come out. I think they're going to stay in there as long as possible, and then they'll fight. And if they do that, they'll be killed."

"Probably. But it's their choice," he reminded her. "They could come out right now, leave everything behind."

"Everything is right," she said, her voice going hard. "Their work, their *lives* are in there." She shook her head. "Rashida seemed to think that wiping out Cancer Cell was one of the goals of this whole thing." She looked at Cage. "Do you think she was paranoid?"

He shrugged. "Maybe not. But it doesn't matter, does it? They *are* going to wipe them out."

"Thanks," Caroline said. "You're a real comfort."

One o'clock approached without further incident, at least not within their sight. They did hear a few scattered gunshots, but they couldn't tell if they were coming from another part of the Core, or somewhere else altogether.

Then Cage felt a slight tremor. Brief, but noticeable. He looked at Caroline. "Did you feel that?"

She had just started to nod when there came a string of muffled explosions, shaking the building. Then another string, and suddenly, just inside of the street barrier at the end of the block, the road opened up and caved in, sucking in half a dozen or more soldiers. Smoke poured out of the crater, and a third string of explosions went off, these much louder, and more pavement collapsed, catching several more soldiers.

Shouts and gunfire erupted, aimless and pointless as far as Cage could tell. The Core street barrier was right on the edge of the crater, and he could see it shifting, the tall structure of concrete and metal and wood tilting forward. Then the ground beneath it collapsed and it crumbled with crashing sounds and clouds of dust and smoke.

It was getting difficult to tell what was happening, with smoke and dust billowing everywhere, and chaos among the troops, but it looked as if troops from outside the Core were forming across the street just behind where the barrier had been, determined to prevent anyone from escaping through the breach. But it was probably pointless; it was difficult to imagine that anyone could actually climb up out of the crater to make an escape, and that would be the only way to get to the breached barrier without going through the Core troops, who were already pulling together. A group of them surrounded the crater, rifles aimed at the dark and smoking interior. Cage wondered how long it would be before they went in after their comrades.

Several objects came flying out of one of the buildings, hurtling toward one group of soldiers. When the objects hit the ground they burst into streaming sheets of flame. Gunfire followed quickly, which was immediately returned by the soldiers. Two explosions tore out huge chunks of the building. Someone screamed, then two more rockets or mortars struck the building, blowing a hole in the second floor. The gunfire seemed to intensify.

There was a cry on the roof a few feet away from them, and somebody staggered back, arm bleeding. There was another cry on the building next to them, and a woman pitched over the edge, falling five floors to the pavement.

Cage grabbed Caroline by the arm, pulled her back from the railing and down to the ground. "Stay put," he said. "Don't try to run yet."

She nodded, and they lay on the roof together while most everyone panicked around them. Cage watched people stumbling over each other, trampling anyone who fell. When the worst of it was well past them, they crawled a few feet farther back from the edge of the roof and sat up, watching the mad rush. Eight or nine people were lying on the roof, writhing in pain, moaning. Christ.

"You mind helping me?" he asked her. "I'd better start checking them out."

"Sure, whatever I can do."

They could still hear gunfire and explosions from the Core, more sporadic now, but not exactly fading away.

"Did I give you the key to Nikki's?"

She shook her head. He dug around in his pocket for his keys, unhooked Nikki's from the ring, and handed it to her.

"I want you to go down to Nikki's apartment. Inside the

closet by the front door, up on a shelf, are a couple of med-kits. Those will have to do for now.''

She nodded again. "I'll get back as quickly as I can.'' She got to her feet, staying in a crouch for the first few steps, then standing upright once she was about twenty feet from the edge of the roof. She hurried to the stairwell hatch, and Cage crawled across the roof to the closest victim.

By the time night fell, the worst of the fighting seemed to be over, but the Core was in flames. Cage and Caroline were back on the roof again, watching the buildings burn; gunfire was infrequent and sporadic. It seemed safer now.

The army had announced that everything was under control, the quarantine and the Core secure; there was only a bit of mopping up to do. The CDC, too, had made an announcement, that all residents of the Core, and all those who, in the skirmishes, had risk of exposure to them, were safely tucked away in isolation wards on Treasure Island. Everything was fine.

But there had been no official casualty reports on the broadcast media; all that was reported was that there had been some injuries. There was no mention of fatalities. The street newshawkers, however, *were* reporting numbers, though they were calling them guesses or approximations. The number of dead soldiers and medical personnel was being given in the thirties and forties, with the number of injured going over a hundred. Unknown numbers of civilian dead and injured in the Core, and small numbers of dead and injured outside the Core from stray gunfire and explosions. The newshawkers had raw footage of bodies being pulled out of the craters, or loaded into ambulances; there was lots of blood.

Now, though, things were quieter. There were few people on the rooftops now. And with the coming of darkness, the army seemed content to maintain the quarantine perimeter, and had ceased their forays into the Core buildings. It was too risky now, anyway, with nearly all of them on fire. It was completely unclear as to how the various fires had begun, or by whom. Fire department trucks and crews surrounded the Core, and though they periodically hosed down the perimeter buildings, they did not do a thing to even slow the fires in the Core buildings.

"They're going to burn it to the ground," Caroline said.

"They won't all burn to the ground," Cage replied. "We'll have some good hollow hulks left behind. Scarred and gutted, but with walls intact."

"But no people."

"No," he agreed. "No people."

"And no more Cancer Cell."

And no more Cancer Cell. Cage wondered if anyone knew what the real repercussions of that would be. Cancer Cell had been a good source of black market pharmaceuticals, a cleaner and cheaper source than most others.

"Yeah. And all this for nothing," Cage said.

"What do you mean?"

He shook his head. "This whole quarantine has been a fiasco from the beginning. This disease, whatever it is, isn't confined to the Tenderloin, and it sure as hell hasn't been confined to the Core for a long time, if it ever was."

"Who said it was?" Caroline asked.

"Oh, yeah, that's right, you were inside when all this came down. The CDC said it was. They claimed that most cases were confined to the Core, with possibly a few outside but definitely in the Tenderloin. *Maybe* it started, somehow, in the Core, but none of this," he said, gesturing at the flames licking up at the night sky, "will do much good."

"Then why do it?" Caroline asked.

"I don't know. Maybe they're ignorant or stupid, or so afraid of the reality that they deny what's going on. Or public relations, maybe, for when all hell breaks loose. They'll claim they did what they could as soon as they could." He gazed steadily into Caroline's eyes. "And maybe they had other purposes. That's why I said that maybe Rashida *wasn't* being paranoid." He shook his head. "The whole thing stinks. And they won't be able to hold it together once word gets out that more and more cases of the disease are showing up outside the quarantine."

"You're pretty sure about that, aren't you? That there are cases outside the Tenderloin."

He nodded.

"But maybe the quarantine will confine the worst of it, make it easier to deal with the cases outside, keep it from spreading."

"It's too late for that."

"How do you know?"

He shrugged. How could he explain it? A gut feeling that was almost a certainty. He turned back to watch the burning buildings. "I wonder how many people are still in there."

CHAPTER 31

The heat wave finally broke. Cool ocean air rolled into the city along with dark and heavy clouds, and it rained for two days. Temperatures plummeted, daytime highs finally dropping below eighty.

But the improved weather didn't improve Carlucci's disposition. The only thing he could do was his job. And for right now that meant Naomi Katsuda's murder. Besides, he still believed there were connections between her murder and Cancer Cell and this impending plague.

But the damn case was still a dead end. Santos and Weathers had pretty much stopped working on it, not because of disinterest or even despair, but by default. There was nowhere else to go. The only lead now unexplored was Naomi Katsuda's mysterious friend, who remained unfound. And that was something he could work on; there was one more way to go with it, and he was the only one who could. He hated to do it, but there was no other way.

And so, at eleven in the morning, with the temperature a pleasant seventy-four degrees, he walked to the stretch of Geary Street that ran between the Financial District and the Tenderloin. He stopped in front of a door inside a small alcove, narrow, carpeted stairs visible through the glass. On the glass, in gold leaf lettering, were two business names: LINDSEY TRAVEL SERVICES and ALICE BASSO, PHILATELIC CONSULTANT. On the right, mounted in the brick, were two intercom buttons, and Carlucci pressed one.

"Yes?" Alice's distinctive voice, recognizable even through the crackling of the intercom.

"Hi, Alice. It's Frank. Carlucci."

"Frankie, my darling boy. Come on in."

The door buzzed, and he pushed it open. He climbed the worn, dark green carpeted stairs to the second floor, then walked down the short hall to Alice's office. The door was open, and she had a customer inside with her.

The walls of Alice's shop were lined with bookcases, and the bookcases were crammed with stamp albums, stock books and binders, and small file drawers. One bookcase was filled with catalogs and other reference books. There were also two long glass display cases, two tables, and several chairs. Alice's customer, a man in his fifties wearing a business suit, sat at one of the tables, studying a stamp under an illuminated magnifier. Alice was sitting across from him.

She was closing in on eighty, and needed a cane to get around, but she was still a handsome woman. Tall and big-boned, with a beautiful smile and beautiful teeth, and thick silvery hair, she had a strong presence; her face was wrinkled and lined, but it suggested character rather than decay.

"Frankie." She was the only person he knew who called him that, the only person who had done so since he was fifteen, when he had insisted on being called Frank.

Her customer glanced at him, then returned his attention to the stamps in front of him. Carlucci approached the table, leaned over, and kissed Alice on the cheek. "Hello, Alice." He walked over to the one armchair in the room and sank into it, waiting for Alice's customer to finish.

The man stayed another hour, then wrote out a check and left with a small envelope he tucked into a locking leather briefcase. Alice got up with the help of her cane, walked behind the glass cases, and put the check in her safe. Then she limped over to the padded wooden chair beside Carlucci and dropped into it. She never sat in the armchair because it was too hard for her to get up from it.

"I want you to tell me that this is a social visit," she said to him. "That you're taking me to lunch and a couple of stiff drinks.'' She shook her head, smiling. ''But I can tell from your face that this is just business.''

''I need to talk to Istvan,'' he said.

''Oh, Frankie,'' she said, sighing heavily. ''Istvan doesn't want to talk to you. You know that.''

''I need him, Alice.''

''Not this time, Frankie. He made me promise not to tell you.''

Carlucci hated all of this, but he felt like he had no choice. He got up from the chair, walked behind the glass cases, and opened her address and com number file drawer.

''Don't do it, you bastard!'' Her voice was anguished, but she knew she couldn't stop him. Nothing would stop him now, not even guilt.

He thumbed through the cards with Alice's fine and delicate handwriting, all in green ink. They weren't in alphabetical order, which made things difficult; he had never figured out what her system was. Then he found it: Istvan Darnyi. He copied down the address. There was no other number; Istvan had done without a phone for years. Then he closed up the file drawer.

''I'm sorry,'' he said, turning back to her. But she wouldn't look at him. There were tears on her cheeks, working their way down through the wrinkles. He felt awful.

He walked over to her and tried to kiss her cheek again, but she pulled away, holding up her hand.

''I'm sorry,'' he said again. ''Good-bye, Alice.''

But she still would not look at him, and did not answer.

Istvan's address was an apartment in North Beach. Carlucci stood outside the building, looking up at the third floor. He thought about walking away without talking to Istvan, leaving the man in peace, but he couldn't do it.

Istvan Darnyi had been a policeman for twenty years, a detective first in Vice, then Narcotics, and finally Homicide as his talents became apparent. What Istvan Darnyi was great at was finding people. He didn't need much to work with, and in fact the less there was, the better he seemed to work. A name without any other information, or a photograph without a name, or no name, no picture, just some other miscellaneous bits of information, that was all he needed. Just something to start with.

Istvan never forgot anything, never forgot a picture or chart or table he had seen, and had an uncanny knack for putting disparate pieces of information together. But that memory was also his burden. The longer his career went on, the worse each job was. Because as he would start working on finding someone, working with little information, his digging inevitably led to associations with past cases, and once that began, he could not put aside any of the memories or images of those cases, which included crime scene photographs, autopsy photos, firsthand viewings of mutilated corpses, or the anguish of friends and relatives of the dead, all of it swirling around in his head, filling his dreams and turning them into nightmares, disturbing his sleep so badly that eventually he would hardly be able to sleep at all until the investigation was over. And even then it would take days for him to put everything out of his memory, since even the slightest reminder would trigger it all back full force.

It got to be too much. Divorce had been the first price he'd paid, but not the last. It was killing him. He applied for full disability, which was granted, and he resigned. He had always been a stamp collector, more a hobby than anything too serious, but when he retired he retreated completely into the philatelic world, trying to keep the rest of the real world out and away.

But Istvan and Carlucci had once been close friends, and twice before Carlucci had asked him for his help. He had known what it cost Istvan, but each time the case had seemed important enough. And after both times he had promised never to ask for Istvan's help again. The last time, not quite believing Carlucci, Istvan had told Carlucci he never wanted to see him again, and he had disappeared. Until now, Carlucci had never tried to find him.

But here he was, feeling guilty, and feeling sorrow for his old friend. He truly had never intended to bother him

again. So he made a promise to himself, that this time
would be the last.

Apartment 3C. The name on the security system was
Stephen Darnell. Carlucci pressed the button. A minute
passed, then a harsh crackling voice answered.

"Yes."

"Istvan. It's Frank Carlucci."

There was a long silence, no response at all. But the
intercom sounded as if it was still open. The silence continued, Carlucci waited. Finally the door buzzed, and he
pushed it open.

Istvan met him at his apartment door, holding it open.

"Hello, Istvan."

Istvan just nodded, and closed the door as Carlucci entered.

Istvan led the way among tables and shelves, through
two small rooms filled with boxes and albums of stamps,
to the kitchen in the back. The kitchen was tiny, but bright,
full of windows that looked out onto the street.

"Sit down," he said. There was a square, wooden table
with two chairs. In the middle of the table was a crystal
vase with blue and yellow flowers. "I'll make coffee." He
seemed sad and resigned, as though giving in to the inevitable.

When the coffee was done, they began. Carlucci told
Istvan everything he thought might have any relevance,
from the day Caroline asked him to help find Tito, to the
quarantines imposed by the CDC. Istvan listened, asking an
occasional question. They drank strong black coffee, and
Istvan, after closing the kitchen door so the smoke would
not get to the stamps, smoked one cigarette after another.
For the first time in a year or two, Carlucci felt that strong
craving again.

When he was finished, he handed the sketch artist picture
to Istvan, who took it from him and studied it. They sat in
silence for several minutes, Istvan continuing to smoke as
he thought and studied the picture.

He nodded once, then looked at Carlucci, his expression
still sad. "I'll find her for you," he said.

"Thank you, Istvan." He paused, wondering if he could be convincing. "This will be the last time. I mean it. The next time I come to see you, it will be just for a visit. Just two old friends, talking."

"Don't bother," Istvan replied. "We are not friends anymore." He shook another cigarette from his pack and lit it. "I'll call you."

CHAPTER 32

It was raining again, and the sound of it spattering against the windows was soothing. Caroline lay on top of the sleeping bag spread across the old wood and canvas cot, eyes closed, listening to the rain. She was sick, and she was afraid to tell Cage.

Fever made her head swim, and she felt sick to her stomach. Swallowing was difficult, and there was a sharp and throbbing pain at her temples. It had come on so quickly, she hadn't been prepared for it. All this time, struggling with her fear of the Gould's, and now she may have contracted a disease that would kill her in a matter of days, not years. Crazy.

She opened her eyes and sat up slowly, leaning back against the wall for support. Where was the telephone? She couldn't remember. Her eyes ached. Maybe it was just a bad flu. Yeah, and maybe she was going to live to be ninety years old.

She looked around the room, and finally saw the phone on top of the small bookcase near the window. She had to call Cage, if only to tell him to stay away. She had volunteered to help out at the street clinic, and when she didn't show up, he would come looking for her.

After resting for a minute or two, she got to her feet and walked over to the phone. She picked up the receiver, then sat in the chair by the window. She raised the window and stuck her empty hand out into the rain. Yes, it was cool. She cupped her hand, let it fill with rainwater, then brought it back in and splashed it across her face. It felt great. She did it twice more, then sat back in the chair and punched in the clinic number.

Cage came anyway, as she'd known he would.

"Don't touch me," she told him when he came into the apartment. "Stay away." And she was reminded of Nikki sitting at the curb outside the clinic after crashing the pedalcart, yelling at Cage to stay away from her.

But he didn't stay away. "You know how many times I've been exposed to this disease?" he said. "Between Nikki and Tito and the other people I've seen at the clinic in the past few weeks? Way too many times. I must have some kind of natural resistance or immunity to it."

"Lucky you."

"Besides, we don't know that that's what you have."

She glared at him. "Yes we do."

He shook his head. "The incubation period's too short. Even if you were exposed to it the very first day you were in the Core, it hasn't been nearly as long as the time between Nikki's exposure and when she came down with it."

"We don't know when I was exposed. Besides . . ." She frowned, thinking about Rashida. "The incubation period has been getting shorter."

"How the hell do you know that?"

She told him what Rashida and the Fat Man had said about the changes they'd noticed, their thoughts and speculations about the disease.

He didn't say anything after that, but he made her take something for the fever, then put her back to bed. After making some tea for both of them, he sat in a chair that he pulled up near the bed.

"You should go," she tried again. "You should just leave me alone."

Cage just shook his head. She lay back on the cot and closed her eyes. She was glad he was here.

CHAPTER 33

Cage felt as if his life were coming apart on him. He thought maybe the whole world was coming apart.

He sat in a chair by the open window of what had once been Nikki's apartment, listening to the night sounds of the Tenderloin and watching the lights and people on the street below. Caroline was sleeping on the cot just behind him, and he listened to her breathing, which at the moment was calm and even.

Core Fever. There wasn't much doubt now. She had it, and she had it bad.

He couldn't believe he was going to go through this all over again. He'd never had much of a chance to recover from Nikki, and he felt completely unprepared to watch Caroline die. But, like so much else these days, he didn't have a choice. Not one he could live with, anyway.

It had been just two days since she'd called him. He had brought one of the clinic cots and moved into the apartment; he'd also brought extra sheets and blankets for Caroline to sleep in instead of the sleeping bag, hoping to make her more comfortable. He still worked his shifts at the clinic—he *had* to; things were falling apart there, too—but he slept and ate here, and nursed Caroline, feeding her when she could eat, making broth and tea for her, providing her with a steady stream of cold damp cloths for her face. He helped her make her way to the bathroom, and helped her shower once or twice a day to stay clean and cool. She tried to get him to wear gloves whenever he touched her, but she had given up on that after the first day.

They were seeing probable new cases of Core Fever every day at the clinic, and there was nothing they could do for those people. They had no facilities to care for them, no rooms or beds or staff. All they could do was send them home, where they were more likely to expose family members and friends and neighbors.

As far as Cage was concerned, the quarantine around the Tenderloin had become completely unconscionable. Clearly a majority of cases were inside the Tenderloin, but more cases of Core Fever were appearing *outside* the Tenderloin every day. In fact, cases were being reported outside of San Francisco, even as far away as New York City—not in the traditional media, which was being uncharacteristically reticent about those cases, but among doctors and other health professionals.

But the CDC was still claiming that the cases outside the Tenderloin were *not* Core Fever, and so maintained the need to continue with the quarantine. With no real hospital facilities in the Tenderloin, and no effective ways to isolate those who came down with Core Fever, the quarantine was turning a bad situation in the Tenderloin into a nightmare— leaving people who were dying without even the benefits of comfort care, and severely exacerbating the transmission of the disease.

Eric Ralston had become unreachable. The number he'd given Cage had been disconnected, and calls to the CDC in Atlanta went nowhere. If nothing else, he wanted to try to shame or guilt Eric into arguing with his colleagues for a dismantling of the quarantine, but he couldn't do that if he couldn't even talk to him.

The only positive thing Cage had heard in recent days were a couple of unconfirmed reports of people surviving Core Fever. But with no way yet to make a certain diagnosis, no antibody test or anything like it, it was impossible to know for sure if the survivors had actually contracted Core Fever rather than some other serious illness.

Yes, he decided, the whole world *was* coming apart.

"Cage?" Caroline's voice was quiet.

He turned around and looked at her. She was lying on her side, eyes barely open.

"How are you feeling?"

"Terrible."

"Do you think you can eat anything?"

"No. But I'm thirsty."

The water pitcher beside the cot was nearly empty, and the water was tepid, so he fixed a fresh batch of ice water, filled a glass, and held it for her, putting the straw in her mouth so she could drink without raising her head.

When she finished, she turned onto her back and closed her eyes. "Thanks," she said.

"Sure. Anything else?"

"Not right now."

There was a long silence, and he thought she had gone back to sleep. He sat and watched her steady breathing, feeling an ache in his chest. He hadn't known her very long, but he'd come to like her quite a lot, and he couldn't believe he was going to lose her before he'd even had a chance to really know her.

"Cage?"

"Yes."

"Have you told my parents yet?"

"No." He hesitated. "I wanted to be sure. I was going to call them tomorrow."

"Don't." She opened her eyes and looked at him. "Don't tell them."

"Why not?"

"What's the point? So they can worry themselves sick, waiting to hear that I've died? They can't come here to see me, I can't get out, so what's the point?" She closed her eyes again, breathing hard for a few moments.

"They're your parents. They'd want to know. They'd want to talk to you. You might want to talk to them."

"No," she said one final time, opening her eyes to look at him. "Wait until I'm dead."

CHAPTER 34

Carlucci was driving himself and Andrea crazy, wandering around the house, unable to sit still, until Andrea told him to stay put somewhere or get the hell out of the house. So he finally retreated to the basement and his trumpet, hoping that music would relax him.

It didn't help.

He was waiting for too much, unable to do anything *except* wait—for the quarantine to end so Caroline wouldn't be trapped inside the Tenderloin; for Istvan to get back to him about the missing woman; for some other break to materialize from Ruben and Toni or one of the other teams; for some resolution to the Core Fever situation. It was all making him nuts, and he felt like he was on speed, frazzled and jittery and wanting to rip off his skin.

The basement door opened, and Andrea came down a couple of steps. Miles Davis was on the stereo, the sound track from *Siesta*, haunting and beautiful.

"Turn that off, please." Andrea had to raise her voice above the music, but her tone was strangely uneven, her expression fixed and lifeless.

Something was wrong.

He grabbed the remote and cut off the music. The sudden silence was disquieting. He set his trumpet beside him on the couch and sat forward.

"What is it?"

Andrea took another couple of steps down, then sat on the stairs.

"Cage called."

"Caroline?" He wanted to stand up, but he felt suddenly immobile.

She nodded. "She's got it. Core Fever. She's got it." She gazed helplessly at him. "She asked him not to call us. But he thought we would want to know." She slowly shook her head from side to side. "But I don't," she said, her voice getting quieter, harsher. "This is something I don't want to know at all." And then she put her face in her hands, elbows on knees, and began to cry.

Carlucci felt dizzy, a terrible ache in his chest. He struggled to his feet, knees weak. When he was sure he wouldn't lose his balance, he walked to the stairs, grabbed on to the railing, and pulled himself up, one difficult step at a time until he reached her. He sat beside his wife, put his arm around her, her shaking driving through him, and then he, too, began to cry.

Incredibly, the day got even worse. He would not have thought it possible.

Andrea was sitting out in the backyard, staring at the garden, or perhaps at nothing at all. She hadn't moved for more than an hour after asking to be left alone. He stood at the kitchen window, looking out at her, wishing he could do something to comfort her, wishing he could do something to comfort himself, and wishing more than anything else that there was something he could do for Caroline. But he had been wishing that for years, and he could no more do anything for her now than he ever could.

The phone rang, and when he answered it there was someone babbling hysterically at him.

"Wait a minute, wait . . . just a second and calm down. Who is this?"

The babbling finally broke, there was some sniffling and wheezing, then, "Mr. Carlucci?"

"Yes. Who is this?"

"Paula. Paula Ng." Christina's roommate.

"Paula, what is it?"

"Oh, Jesus, Mr. Carlucci. It's Tina, I think she's got it."

He thought his heart stopped. Certainly his breathing did, and a strange, very quiet rushing sound filled his ears, and something funny happened to his vision, as if it had become pocked with bits of glitter.

"You think she's got what?" he finally managed to say, wondering if his voice was loud enough for her to hear. He could imagine only one answer to his question, but he had to ask it anyway.

"Core Fever. Oh, God, Mr. Carlucci, I don't know, maybe it's not, but she's so sick, and she was getting those rashes across her chest, and we didn't know what else it could be, but no one out here's supposed to be able to get it, but what else, I don't know, Tina got so scared and I got scared and—"

"Where is she, Paula?"

"On her way to St. Anthony's. I called an ambulance, I gave them Tina's insurance chip, and they took her to St. Anthony's, and they left me here, and I don't know what to do, I wonder was I too close to her or did we drink out of the same glass or what, am I going to get it too—?"

He hung up on her. He knew it was rude, he knew it was an awful thing to do, but he couldn't take it anymore, he couldn't listen to one more word of it.

There was a deep, thrumming ache driving through him, and he was barely aware of anything else. He felt as if his heart had collapsed, and could hardly beat anymore. He didn't move for a long time, several minutes, maybe longer. When he did finally move, it was only to return to the kitchen window and look out at Andrea, wondering how the hell he was going to tell her.

They sat together in the tiny visitors' lounge at the end of the corridor, gratefully alone. Christina was in an isolation room, in a drugged sleep. When Carlucci and Andrea had arrived, Christina had been scared, and became hysterical when they had come into the room with gowns and gloves and masks on; the doctors would not let them enter the room otherwise. She would not calm down, and eventually Dr. Sodhi had sedated her.

Technically Christina was diagnosed as ill from an unidentified agent, probably viral or bacterial, but they all knew. Dr. Sodhi pointed out that the CDC was not currently recognizing any cases of Core Fever outside of the Tenderloin, though they were asking that all presumptive cases be reported to them. This was Dr. Sodhi's second patient with Core Fever. The other had been Cage's friend Nikki. Nikki had lived for two or three weeks. Christina probably wouldn't.

Carlucci held Andrea's hand, the two linked hands resting on his thigh. Neither of them had spoken for a long time.

"Both of them," she said. "We're going to lose both of them." She began to slowly shake her head from side to side, making a faint, high keening sound. Then everything stopped, she dropped her hands to her side and opened her eyes, and turned to look at him. "I feel a little bit insane. And I want to become hysterical." Something like a smile appeared. "I can't quite believe this is happening, because I don't see how I can actually stand it if it really is, I don't see how I can stand it *without* going insane." Then the strange smile disappeared. "You know that feeling of relief you get when you wake up from a particularly disturbing dream, that almost rushlike sensation when you realize that it was a dream, and that you won't actually have to face whatever it was that was happening?"

Carlucci nodded, knowing exactly what she meant.

"I want that feeling, Frank, I want it so badly I could scream, and I know, I *know* I am not going to get that feeling. And that makes me want to scream even more." She paused, staring hard at him.

He continued his silence, helpless and paralyzed by grief.

"For Christ's sake, Frank, talk to me!" She pulled her hand back, balled it into a fist, and swung, punching his arm. "Talk to me!"

She struck him twice more, but he still could not say anything. Then she stopped, threw her arms around him, and buried her face in his shoulder.

CHAPTER **35**

She awakened, and opened her eyes. But the light hurt, and she closed them again. She felt awful.

Was she alone? She listened, heard sounds from the street coming in through open windows, but nothing from the apartment.

"Cage?"

"Yes."

"Are you here?"

"Yes, I'm here."

She heard floorboards creaking, the sounds of Cage settling into the chair beside the cot, then felt his hand take hers. She tried opening her eyes again, just a crack this time, wanting to see his face. Yes, he was there, looking down at her. She hadn't been sure.

She thought about raising her head to look around, look down at her arms, see if the rashes were there yet, but she didn't even try. It was impossible.

"Can I get something for you?" he asked.

She closed her eyes once more. "What time is it?"

"Uh, three-thirty, four, something like that."

"In the afternoon?"

"Yes."

"Tell me how Nikki saved your life," she said.

"Now?"

"Now." And she tried smiling, though she wasn't sure she managed it.

There was nothing for a while, and she wondered if he

was gone. But she couldn't open her eyes to look for him.

"I was living in L.A.," Cage began. "Young hotshot doctor doing image enhancements for the rich and famous. Well, mostly just rich. A few who were on their way up and later became moderately famous. And I made a lot of money. Lived in a high-security beachfront condo, drove around in an armored convertible, zoned myself out in nightlife."

"You?" Caroline said.

"Yeah, me. Then I was kidnapped, by a group called El Espíritu de la Gente—Spirit of the People. They took me into a housing project in East L.A., one of the newer ones built just after the turn of the century, where . . ."

The image of Cage driving along a coastal highway in a convertible filled her vision, pulsing as it repeatedly flashed from left to right, her eyes flickering as she followed it. His hair blew behind him, longer than she'd ever seen it on him, arm resting on the door, a cigarette between the fingers of his right hand, miniature, shiny sunglasses covering his eyes. She almost laughed.

". . . the clinic had no intention of paying any kind of ransom, either in cash or medicine, but these people didn't care that much, they figured to force me to provide medical care for the people in the project. . . ."

Was that Cage talking? Yes, but what the hell was he talking about? Kidnappers? Oh, that's right, she'd asked him to tell her about Nikki saving his life . . . she had to pay closer attention.

". . . so they gave me this nice tattoo on my neck. They thought it was funny, and I guess it was. I didn't think so at the time, but I can see the humor in it now. I've never had any desire to remove it. It's a good reminder to me of what . . ."

Tito had a tattoo on his arm, a diamond necklace wrapping around his elbow. She should have looked for the tattoo in the morgue when she'd gone with her father to identify the body, then she would have known for sure . . . but that was crazy, that had been Tito, there was no doubt . . . and so cold . . . but she was so hot right now, and she couldn't imagine that she would ever be as cold as Tito was that day.

"... no longer useful to them. In fact, I was becoming a problem. I knew, deep down in my gut, that they were going to kill me—it was the easiest way to take care of the problem. And that's when Nikki made her . . ."

Cage. She wiggled her fingers. Yes, he was still holding her hand, and it felt good, keeping her from completely coming apart and dissipating into the air, and she didn't want him to ever let it go.

"... Nikki half dragging me down the hall . . ."

Nikki? Was she here? No, Nikki was dead, dead from Core Fever, the same thing raging through her right now.

"Cage? Are you here?"

He squeezed her hand. "Yes, Caroline, I'm here."

"Cage. Tell me how Nikki saved your life. That day at Mika's, you said you would tell me someday."

There was a long pause, and she wondered if he was still there, but he squeezed her hand again.

"Sure," he said. "I'll tell you." And he began. "I was living down in L.A., hotshot young doctor, doing image enhancements, and making a lot of money. . . ."

It was dark and she was alone. She lay on the cot with her eyes open, flashing colored lights from outside providing a strange illumination, casting a few shadows on the ceiling above her.

"Cage?"

No answer.

"Cage?" Louder this time.

Still no answer. She *was* alone.

Suddenly she was afraid. She was sick and she was dying and she didn't want to be alone, she wanted Cage here with her, holding her hand or placing cold wet cloths on her forehead, talking to her, bringing her tea or water, just *being* here.

It was hot, and she could hardly breathe. Her arms itched and burned and her joints ached and she thought her head was going to burst, and she almost wished it would, to

release all the pressure building inside. Then she realized
there were other pressures, too, farther down. Her bladder.
Oh, God, she didn't think she could get up, but she didn't
want to wet the bed, not now, not when she was alone and
she would have to lie in it. . . . She remembered the bedpan
Cage had brought, it was under the cot, but she didn't want
to use that, either. Besides, if she could manage that, she
could manage getting herself to the bathroom, it wasn't that
far away.

What was happening to her?

She closed her eyes for a few moments, breathing slowly
and deeply, gearing herself up for it. Then she opened her
eyes, pushed back the sheet, and turned onto her side. She
reached over the side of the cot, stretching until she touched
the floor, then half rolled, half fell out of the cot and onto
the floor, hitting her side and going over until she was on
her back and staring up at the ceiling again, her nightshirt
twisted underneath her. A giggle squeaked out of her as she
imagined herself rolling her way into the bathroom, over
and over. But she breathed in deeply again, then rolled
halfway over once more and pushed herself up to her hands
and knees.

It seemed to take her a long time to get to the bathroom,
and yet, strangely, as she began to crawl across the old pink
tiles of the bathroom floor, she was surprised that she was
already there. She lifted the toilet seat lid, then pulled herself up onto the seat, leaning back against the tank with
great relief. After resting for a few moments, she pulled up
her nightshirt, and peed.

As she sat there peeing, amazed at how full her bladder
had been, she struggled to keep her head upright, but finally
she just leaned forward, elbows on thighs, and held her
head with her hands. The room was spinning around her,
but closing her eyes only made it worse, so she kept them
half open and tried focusing on a piece of cracked tile between her feet.

When she was done, she wiped herself, reached back
with her right hand, and flushed the toilet. Then she discovered she couldn't move. She wanted to stand up and

walk back to the cot, or at least get back on her hands and knees and crawl, but she could not move.

She thought it should be possible, but somehow she just couldn't. She had no energy, and no will to call up any energy.

I'm dying, she thought. She couldn't move, and she was going to die here, and Cage was going to come in and find her sitting on the toilet, dead.

I'm dying, she said to herself again, and this time it drove deep into her, and she knew, for the first time she really knew it was true.

She lifted her head from her hands and looked around the bathroom, through the door and into the apartment, half expecting something to look different. Nothing did. She knew she was dying, and nothing was different, and somehow it was all okay.

She could move again. She slid off the toilet and onto the floor, then stretched out on the cool, pink tiles, facing the door so she could see the rest of the apartment. The tiles felt soothing on her skin.

It *was* all right. She only wished she could think more clearly about it all, keep focused on what was happening to her, focused on this new knowledge, this final realization. But it was there, she knew it was there, and finally everything was all right, even dying.

CHAPTER 36

Cracks had begun to appear everywhere: in the Tenderloin quarantine; in the CDC's insistence that Core Fever was confined to the Tenderloin; and in Christina's few remaining immune system defenses. She was going downhill fairly quickly. She was dying. Caroline, too, was dying, if she wasn't already dead. Carlucci hadn't been able to get through to Cage for almost two days, now, and had no idea what was happening with his older daughter.

Carlucci had tried taking time off work, but it was far worse for him with nothing to do. Andrea's disposition was different, and she took leave from the law firm, spending most of her time at the hospital with Christina. But Carlucci couldn't do it, and so he went back to work during the days, returning to the hospital in the evenings.

It wasn't much better at work, and he felt numb and helpless, wandering zombielike around the department. The Katsuda case was still completely stalled, and he couldn't bring any interest to any of the others. He heard nothing from Istvan Darnyi. He canceled the autopsy request for Tito Moraleja—they knew now what he had died from, and it didn't matter anymore—and released the body for cremation. Everything was dead-ended, including Carlucci.

Word running through the department was that the quarantine was about ready to give. Desperate for something to do, Carlucci went out to the rooftop observation post set up closest to the Tenderloin. The young cop who had been working at the Tenderloin entrance a few weeks earlier was stationed at the edge of the roof, sitting on a stool and looking through binoculars mounted on a tripod, and Carlucci joined him.

"Hello, Lieutenant. Good to see you again."

They shook hands. "I didn't catch your name that day," Carlucci said.

"Prosser, sir. Adam Prosser."

"Anything happening yet?" he asked.

Prosser shrugged. "Lots of activity on both sides of the quarantine perimeter, but no real moves yet. It's only a matter of time, though. You should see the soldiers. Nervous as hell. They know. The whole thing is stupid."

Carlucci agreed. He couldn't understand why the CDC and the military were trying to maintain the quarantine anymore. Rumors had been ramping around for weeks now of Core Fever cases outside the Tenderloin, but in the past couple of days the mainstream broadcast media were finally starting to report the same thing.

"You want to take a look, sir?" Prosser got up from the stool and backed away from the mounted binoculars.

Carlucci sat on the stool and looked through the binoculars. They were clear and powerful lenses, directed at a section of the quarantine perimeter surrounding one of the DMZ bubbles, soldiers and barricades stretched across a street just a block from the Tenderloin. But pressing up against the barriers from the inside was a mob of hundreds, swelling and shifting around. Lots of fists were raised, but he could also see knives and shock sticks and clubs and guns and stun-pumpers.

Prosser was right about the soldiers. They *were* nervous, and rightfully so. The mob threatened to burst through the barriers and overwhelm them, and the only thing that might stop them was mass slaughter by the army. Carlucci suspected that prospect terrified most of the soldiers.

He adjusted the binoculars, then moved them from side to side, checking out the surrounding area. Something caught his eye, and he stopped. Gone. He moved them, and found it again. Emerging from an alley half a block from the quarantine perimeter was a group of figures wearing hooded robes. They swayed in unison as they slid along, maybe twelve or fourteen of them in pairs. For a moment Carlucci thought he heard them chanting or humming, until he realized he was actually too far away from them, and whatever he heard had to be coming from something else, machinery nearby, something like that. But who were these people? They were slightly blurry, so he tried adjusting the focus, but he couldn't sharpen the image. A pale blue glow seemed to surround them, like an electric mist. He followed them as they swayed across the street and then entered another alley, disappearing slowly by twos until they all were gone.

He cut the binoculars over to the next street, hoping to see them emerge, but though he waited for several minutes, they didn't appear. He looked back at the previous street, then along other streets in the area, but didn't see any sign of them.

And then, about a block from the barriers where the mob threatened, Carlucci saw Istvan Darnyi. He was standing in the doorway of a Middle Eastern deli, talking to a heavyset man with dark hair and wearing a white apron. Carlucci swung the binoculars back to the barriers, where the tension continued to build, then back again to Darnyi, who was still talking to the man.

"Shit."

"What is it, Lieutenant?"

Carlucci just shook his head. He straightened, stood, and stepped away from the binoculars, searching the streets on his own. There, Darnyi, about two blocks away. He turned and headed for the stairs.

By the time he reached the deli, Darnyi was gone, and the doors were locked up. Carlucci put his face to the glass door, but there was no one inside, and all the lights were off except a cool white glow in the counter display cases, illuminating sliced meats and cheeses.

"You looking for someone, Lieutenant?"

Carlucci stepped back from the deli, looked around the

street. There was no one around, though he was sure he recognized Istvan's voice.

"I'm right here," Istvan said, stepping out of a deep alcove no more than thirty feet away.

"Yes, goddamn it, I'm looking for you." He walked toward Darnyi, shaking his head.

"Why?"

"I saw you from an observation post. All hell's about to break loose at the quarantine perimeter"—he pointed down the street—"and we're no more than a block away. I don't want you killed before you find that woman."

Darnyi smiled. "Then we better get out of here."

But they'd hardly turned away when an explosion rocked the air, rattling windows, and gunfire erupted. Shouts ripped through the afternoon, and the noise of more explosions. But it wasn't coming from behind them, it was coming from the right, maybe another block or two away.

"That way," Darnyi said, pointing to the left.

They crossed the street, and then the gunfire and screams exploded down at the barriers, as if in response to the other shots and screams. Just before they went around the corner, Carlucci glanced down the street and saw the barriers begin to collapse, and the soldiers beginning to panic.

"Let's get the hell out of here," Istvan said. They broke into a run.

They'd run along one short block, and had started down a second when a convoy of military vehicles came around the corner and filled the street in front of them. Some went past them as they pressed against the buildings, but others stopped and blocked off the street and sidewalks.

Carlucci and Darnyi backed off, then headed around to the left, away from the Tenderloin. But they could see more military barriers being set up two blocks away.

"This is insane," Darnyi said. "They're going to try to hold the quarantine, contain the breakout with a new perimeter." They stopped, taking stock. "What's the matter with these people?"

Behind them, they could see a frenzied mob spilling out

of the barriers amid gunfire and crumpling bodies, soldiers
going down, a troop carrier already on fire.

"Inside," Carlucci said.

Darnyi nodded. They searched both sides of the street.
The block was mostly abandoned and condemned buildings, which was just as well. A door was open across the
street, and they ran for it. There was barely enough room
to push through, and they managed to get it shut behind
them. Searching in the dim light through dust and dirt and
rubble, they found some two-by-fours and wedged the door
shut.

They were in an entryway with no exits except for a
stairwell leading up through darkness. They climbed up a
flight, but the door on that level was locked, and they
couldn't budge it. So they went up one more. The door
here was unlocked, and they went through, emerging into
a room filled with broken furniture and empty crates and
piles of loose paper everywhere.

They approached the windows, safe for the moment two
floors above the street, and watched the chaos below. People swarmed the street and sidewalks, mostly men, but
some young women too, a few of them armed. Gunfire was
blasting away all around them, punctuated by deep, loud
explosions and scattered screams.

"The quarantine's a goner," Istvan said. "This will go
on for two days at least. Then it will run itself out of steam,
finally." He shook his head. "This is a bad one."

Carlucci nodded, thinking about Caroline. Would he be
able to get into the Tenderloin now and get her out, or
would he have to wait until all this settled down? He shook
his head to himself. Get her out for what? So she could die
in a hospital instead of where she was?

His phone rang. He unclipped and answered it.

"Frank." It was Andrea.

"What is it?"

"You'd better get to the hospital as soon as you can."
There was a slight pause. "I don't think Tina's going to
last much longer."

He looked out the window. The street was still full of

people, waves surging from side to side. There was a burst of gunfire, and someone screamed.

"Frank, is that gunfire?" Andrea asked.

"Yeah. I'm in the middle of a goddamn riot. The quarantine's coming apart. Shit. All right, I'll get there as soon as I can."

He hung up. "I've got to go," he told Istvan.

"It's not so good out there right now."

"I don't have any choice."

Istvan nodded, but didn't ask anything.

"Call me as soon as you find her."

"Of course."

"I've got to go," Carlucci said again. He breathed in deeply, and prepared himself to plunge into the chaos below.

ISABEL

The Core was dead.

Silence everywhere, and strange smells. Sometimes the air burned her nose, or something wet burned her feet or hands when she touched them. No people alive or dead. All the bodies had been cleared away. And through it all, the smell of old fires and something terrible, sickening, she could not get it out of her nose; and black soot everywhere, on walls and ceilings and floors.

There were new passages now, and some old ways were gone. Walls had disappeared, collapsed timbers and stone had formed new ones; new openings to the outside had become plentiful, letting in the light of the sun or the moon.

Isabel explored the new Core, the buildings above the street where she had rarely dared to go before. No people, no bodies anywhere, in any of the rooms, and no animals except for dead rats already stinking or being eaten by other rats.

She had spent two weeks living in the dead-end passage just outside the Core and in the storage room on the other side of the door. There had been some food in the room, and she occasionally had emerged from it into the city to scrounge for more food and water, but there were so many people, so much light and noise and color and madness everywhere that she had stayed below as much as possible. She would have spent all her time in the dead end passage, but during the first few days after she escaped the Core, terrible burning smells drifted through the air vent, and she'd been forced to move into the storage room to avoid them. But she had broken the lights in the room, making it dark and easier for her to hide if someone came. Only once did someone come into the room, but when they could not make the lights work they left, and didn't come back until yesterday. Then finally someone had returned, fixed the lights, and people began to work in the room again. Isabel decided it was time to return.

She found laboratories like the ones she had been raised in, but everything in them was burned or smashed or broken, all destroyed. She wandered through them, hoping to find food, but there wasn't any.

Isabel liked the new silence in the Core, the new echoes of her movements. She felt safe. Food would be a problem, but she could always go back through the storage room if she needed to. And she had a feeling that it would not be long before strange people moved back.

PART FIVE

PLAGUE

Carlucci watched Christina while Andrea slept. Christina had not been conscious for two days now, and the doctors didn't think she ever would be again. So it was a great shock when she opened her eyes and looked at him. Her face was flushed, her arms and neck covered with rashes. There was terror in her eyes.

"Who . . . who are you?" she whispered.

"Your father, Tina."

But her eyes widened, and her head jerked spasmodically from side to side. "No. No. You're . . . who *are* you?" Terror in her voice as well as her eyes.

The doctors would be pissed if they knew, but he couldn't let his daughter die like this, and so he reached up and pulled down his mask, revealing his face.

"It's me, Tina. Your father." He pulled the chair up closer to the bed. She reached out tentatively toward him, lightly touched his cheek with one finger.

"Daddy?"

"Yes, Tina, sweetie, it's me." He gently took her hand. "I'm here."

The terror left her eyes for a few moments, then seemed to return.

"It was the shot that gave it to me," she said. "The special shot. I know it." She was trying to raise her head up from the pillow.

"What shot, Tina?"

"Don't let them give you the special shot, Daddy." Then

she let her head fall back and her eyes closed. "Daddy."

"I'm here, Tina."

"I'm so hot, Daddy."

"I know, sweetie. I know."

He continued holding her hand, but she didn't say any more, and soon her breathing deepened.

"Tina? Tina, baby, are you awake?"

There was no answer.

When Andrea came in an hour later, Carlucci disposed of the suit and gloves and mask, then called Paula.

"Paula, this is Frank Carlucci."

"Hi, Mr. Carlucci. How's Tina?"

"The same. Listen, Paula, I've got to ask you something. Maybe she was just feverish, but Tina said something about getting a shot, a special shot. Does that make any sense to you?"

There was a short pause, then Paula said, "Yeah, actually. About three weeks ago, someone from St. Anthony's came to the apartment for Tina. He said they were out giving booster vaccinations, and he gave her one."

Carlucci felt sick, one more terrible thing crashing down on him, but he tried to hold himself together.

"What about you?" he asked.

"No, it was only people with police health coverage, through St. Anthony's."

"A guy, you said?"

"Yeah, a guy."

"What did he look like?"

"You know, white outfit and funny white shoes. A medico. I don't really remember, I wasn't paying that much attention."

"Okay, Paula. Thanks."

"What is it, Mr. Carlucci? Did the shot make her sick or something?"

"No, I was just checking. Thanks again, Paula, and I'll talk to you later."

"Say hi to Tina for me, will you? And tell her they won't let me see her, or I would."

"I will."

He broke the connection and stood there in the hospital corridor, afraid to move, afraid that if he did move, he would completely fall apart.

The checking was a formality, but he needed to have it confirmed, and it was. There had been no special booster vaccinations given, and even if there had been, St. Anthony's would never have sent anyone out to do it, they would have notified everyone in the program and asked them to come into the clinic itself.

Carlucci stood outside his daughter's room, looking in through the glass window in the door. Andrea was sitting next to the bed; Christina lay unmoving, eyes closed. She hadn't opened her eyes again.

He didn't know what to do with the information he now had. Someone had shot her up with Core Fever virus. Why? Something to do with him, it had to be, there was no reason for anyone to want to harm her, to kill her this way. But what? No threats had been made, before or after.

Or was that true?

He remembered Yoshi Katsuda hinting that being shot had been a message of sorts, a warning. But what the hell was this? No one had ever said to him, hey, stop investigating or your daughter will die. Nothing like that had ever been implied, by anyone.

Dr. Sodhi came down the hall and waved a greeting. As he approached he said, "Lieutenant, I'm glad you are here. I wanted to talk to you."

"About Tina?"

Dr. Sodhi shook his head. "No, not exactly. The CDC has made an announcement."

Carlucci snorted. "What, that they're canceling the quarantine?"

Dr. Sodhi smiled. "No. They recognize that the quarantine is over. I believe they would be too embarrassed to actually announce the official end of it. Better to ignore it, is their philosophy, I would imagine. No, they have announced that with the help of the medical facilities of New

Hong Kong, the virus that causes Core Fever has been identified, and an antibody test developed. More than that, because the virus is very similar to one that New Hong Kong
has recently been studying, they have a preventative vaccine ready to put into production.''

Carlucci tipped his head. ''That sounds like a crock,'' he
said. ''Like one huge pile of horseshit.''

Dr. Sodhi shrugged. ''Perhaps. But that is the announcement that the CDC has made. With the breakdown of the
quarantine, they will go into production of the vaccine immediately, and begin distribution of it as soon as possible
here in the city.''

Carlucci wanted to laugh. It was all becoming so absurd.
''Preventative,'' he said. ''Not a treatment, not a cure.''

''No.''

''Then what good is it?'' He turned away from Dr. Sodhi
and returned to Christina's room.

And then, less than an hour later, she died. Quickly, and
far more easily than they had ever expected. He and Andrea
were both in the room trying to decide what to do for the
night, when Christina went into a brief convulsion, and her
heart stopped.

Doctors and nurses came rushing in, but Carlucci and
Andrea had already discussed this. They stood at Christina's side and told the doctors ''No.'' No attempted re-
suscitation, no trying to jolt her heart back into beating.
They wanted to let her die in peace.

There were no arguments. All of the medical staff except
for Dr. Sodhi left. Dr. Sodhi stayed only long enough to
confirm that her heart had, in fact, stopped beating. Then
he, too, left, and they were alone with her.

They left the hospital together. It was nearly midnight, but
the sounds of the rioting were still loud. Istvan had been
right, it would take at least a couple of days to die down.

Two uniforms were waiting in front of the hospital with
a squad car to take them home. Carlucci recognized them,

but he couldn't remember their names. Springer, he thought, was one of them. He couldn't bring himself to ask.

They got into the backseat of the squad car. The two cops didn't say anything, just got into the front seat and pulled away from the hospital. No one said a word the entire trip out to their house.

When they arrived, the two cops remained in the car. Carlucci thanked them for the ride, then he and Andrea got out and walked slowly up the walkway, climbed the steps to the front porch, then stopped at the door.

"I don't want to go in, Frank."

"I know."

The house seemed different. Caroline and Christina had both been out of the house for some time, but now neither of them would ever enter it again, even for a visit. It *was* a different house now.

Andrea turned away from the front door, walked back across the porch, and sat down on the top step. Carlucci sat beside her, waved at the cops, and watched the squad car pull away.

The neighborhood was quiet. They were far enough away from the Tenderloin and the downtown area, and the rioting hadn't reached them. Probably never would; too much a residential neighborhood, and the quarantine had been miles away.

The night air was warm, the skies almost clear except for the normal haze. The moon was nearly full, and well past its zenith. A cat yowled from somewhere nearby. If he listened carefully, he could hear the faint popping sounds of gunfire, the muted sounds of breaking glass or screeching metal.

"What are we going to do?" Andrea said. "About Caroline, I mean. I want to see her again before she dies."

He didn't want to have to answer her; he felt he didn't have the strength to speak. But he swallowed, his mouth dry, and he said, "Maybe tomorrow it will be better. If we can get an escort—"

"I don't care about an escort. Just get us in there, Frank."

He nodded. "All right, I will."

They remained there, watching the moon and the blurred stars, and neither of them said another word.

CHAPTER 38

Something changed during the night.

Cage noticed it in her breathing first. For days it had been labored, but during the night it became deep and easy. Then her fever broke, and by dawn her temperature had dropped to just under a hundred and one.

He was afraid to hope. Nikki, too, had rebounded before getting worse. But that had happened before the Core Fever had really taken hold of her; that was not the case with Caroline. Still, he was afraid. He wasn't sure how much he could take; if he let himself hope, he didn't know if he could handle it when she worsened and died.

The day was coming, bright gray light flowing in through the glass. Cage raised a window, letting in the morning air. The streets of the Tenderloin were relatively quiet. Although the rioting had begun in the Tenderloin and the DMZ, it had spread outward from the Tenderloin perimeter, through the quarantine barriers, and out into the city. Frustration and rage had been directed outward, leaving the Tenderloin itself relatively undamaged and unharmed. The announcement of the test and vaccine for Core Fever had done little to calm people—there was too much suspicion, all of it probably justified—and the rioting had continued out in the city, but the Tenderloin's own natural barriers kept it outside.

The cot creaked, and Cage turned around. Caroline had rolled onto her side, facing him. Her eyes remained closed, but she looked as if she might open them at any moment.

He was still afraid to hope, but she looked so much better.

Several hours later, her temperature finally dropped below a hundred. Even her color looked better. Cage sat beside her, waiting. Now he was beginning to hope in earnest; it was impossible not to.

In the late afternoon, he discovered her bladder had let go. He took off her nightshirt, moved her onto the sleeping bag on the floor and washed her, then took her nightshirt and the sheets down to the laundry room in the building basement. Back in the apartment, he washed the plastic sheeting in the tub, replaced it on the cot along with clean sheets, then moved Caroline back to the bed. She half awakened as he moved her, her eyes fluttered open, and she mumbled a few words, but she was soon asleep again, and he was sure she would never remember being awake.

He called in to the clinic, told them he wouldn't be able to make it in at all for a day or two. He couldn't tell Franzee why he wasn't coming in; he was afraid to say it aloud, to put his hopes into words. He had not realized he could be so superstitious.

As evening wore on, and her temperature didn't climb, his hope grew, though he could hardly believe what was happening. He sat in a chair beside her through the night, dozing, periodically checking on her. As dawn approached, her temperature was down to ninety-nine, and he knew.

Around six or seven, there was a knock at the door. When he got up and opened the door, Carlucci and his wife were standing out in the hall. They looked exhausted.

"I was going to call you in a while," Cage said. "I can't believe you're here."

"We wanted to see her one last time," Andrea said. "Be with her."

Cage smiled. "I think you may have wasted a trip."

"What the hell are you talking about?" Carlucci asked. "Is she already—"

Cage shook his head, cutting him off. "No. I think she's going to live."

•   •   •

She woke, unsure of where she was, or what had happened to her. Her eyes were still closed, and they started to open automatically, but she kept them shut.

How long had she been asleep? It seemed like days. Maybe it was. She'd been sick. Yes, that's what . . . Core Fever. No, impossible. Was she still alive? Yes, and not so hot anymore. What was happening?

Caroline opened her eyes. No, that couldn't be right. She was seeing her parents sitting beside her, and they were looking at her.

"Caroline?" Her mother's mouth moving, and it was her voice, but that was impossible, wasn't it?

Caroline closed her eyes again. She still ached a bit, but she felt better. On the other hand, she was still hallucinating. She was in Nikki's place, and if anyone would have been here with her it would have been Cage. Maybe she should just sleep a while more.

"Caroline?" Her father's voice this time, quiet and tentative.

She tried opening her eyes again, and they were both still there.

"Caroline, are you awake?" Her mother.

"Is it you?" she asked. Still thinking it couldn't be. "Where am I?" She moved her hand to the side, feeling the canvas. Yes, she was on the cot.

"You're in the Tenderloin," her mother said.

"Nikki's?"

"Yes," her father answered. "Nikki's apartment."

"Cage."

"He's here."

"How . . . ? You're here," she said. "How? I told Cage not to tell you. I made him promise."

Her mother reached out and took her hand, a sad smile on her face. "He broke his promise," she said. "Thankfully."

Caroline tried to pull her hand away, but she was too weak. "Don't touch me," she said. "Please, don't, you'll catch it."

Her mother shook her head. "There's a vaccine," she

said. "Besides, Cage doesn't think we could catch it now. He thinks you're almost certainly not contagious anymore."

"Not . . . ? How can that be?"

"He thinks you're going to live."

No, it was too much. She had to be hallucinating. She closed her eyes once more, but she could still feel her mother holding her hand. And then, somehow, she knew. Her parents *were* really there, her mother was holding her hand. And, most of all, she was going to live.

She was going to live.

She slept for a while, and when she woke again, her parents were still in the room—her mother in a chair beside the cot, her father doing something at the stove or sink. She worked herself up with her elbows and looked around the apartment, but she didn't see Cage anywhere.

"Where is he?"

"Cage?" her mother asked.

Caroline nodded, then dropped back onto the cot.

"He'll be back in a while," her mother said. "He said you were going to be fine, and he thought we could use some time alone together."

Caroline wanted to see him. He had stayed with her through it all, taken care of her, done everything for her. Risking himself, he had kept her alive, and she wanted to see him. Cage.

"How did you get here?" she asked. "Through the quarantine?"

"The quarantine's gone," her mother said.

"Why? Is the disease gone? Core Fever?"

Her mother shook her head. "No. It's a long story. The quarantine collapsed. Core Fever is everywhere. People knew. The quarantine was a joke."

"Then why . . . ?" Then she shook her own head in reply. "Never mind," she said.

Her father approached, holding a steaming mug. "Chicken broth," he said. "Cage said it would be good for you. You want some?"

She nodded. When was the last time she'd eaten?

They helped her sit up, propping her against the wall with pillows. She was still incredibly weak, and she could barely hold the cup. But the broth tasted good, and she slowly sipped at it, relishing both the taste and the heat going down her throat and into her belly.

When she'd finished the broth, her father brought the cup to the sink, then returned to the cot and sat down beside her mother. The way they were looking at her gave her a sinking feeling in her gut.

"What is it?" she asked.

"It's Tina," her mother said. "She got it, too."

"What?" Unbelieving. "Core Fever?"

Her mother nodded, but didn't say anything more.

"How sick is she?"

But her mother just shook her head, unable to speak, the tears beginning, dripping down her left cheek.

"No," Caroline said, shaking her head from side to side. "No."

But another voice inside her answered *Yes,* and she knew her sister was dead.

CHAPTER 39

Eric Ralston finally got in touch again. Now that the quarantine was gone, and all the announcements had been made by the CDC about tests and a vaccine, Eric called.

"I've been trying to reach you for days," Cage said, hardly bothering to hide his anger. He was in the clinic, between patients. The waiting room was full. "You bastards with your fucking quarantines."

"We did what we thought was best," Eric replied.

"Best my ass."

"Cage, give me a fuckin' break here."

"Why the hell should I?"

"Look, you want me to just hang up? I don't have to put up with this crap."

"All right, all right. Hold on a second, will you? Let me get this on another phone." He transferred the call from the clinic line to his own phone, then walked down the hall to the staff room, closed the door, and sat at the table. "Why *did* you call, anyway?"

"I'm calling to help you out, you ungrateful son of a bitch."

"Yeah?" Cage said. "And how are you going to do that?"

"You want some Core Fever vaccine for that shitty little clinic of yours?"

Jesus. "Of course I want some vaccine. How soon can I get it?"

"A few days. Shipments are already starting to come

down from New Hong Kong, and it shouldn't be too long before their people get production going in labs here on the ground.''

''New Hong Kong, those fuckers. You've been in bed with them from the very beginning of this, haven't you?''

''Cage, come on.''

''They were your source, weren't they, for all the info on Core Fever? The source you said you couldn't reveal.''

There was a long pause, and then Eric finally spoke again. ''Let's just say they helped us quite a bit. Look, what's the point in slamming them? They were the ones who identified the virus and made the antibody tests possible. They're the ones with the goddamn vaccine, for Christ's sake! You should be grateful.''

''I am *not* grateful,'' Cage said. ''What I am is suspicious as hell. Aren't you? I mean really, Eric, the odds that the Core Fever virus is so close to some virus that they're studying that they've got a bloody vaccine all ready to go for it? What the hell is really going on?''

Another long silence. When Eric spoke again, his tone was cold. ''Look, Cage. You want some vaccine or not? I told you before I don't have to listen to this crap. I'm trying to do you a favor. You think the vaccine is going to be readily available? Not for a long time, not until production really gets up and running.''

''But aren't they going to make it available here in the Tenderloin first? This is the source of the damn disease, remember? The highest concentration?''

Eric laughed. ''Get real, Cage. Do you think anyone here or in New Hong Kong gives a shit about the Tenderloin? Over the next couple of weeks or so, the only people getting the vaccine will be those with pull or money, preferably both.''

''You bastards,'' Cage said, shaking his head to himself. ''You quarantine the Tenderloin and bottle up the worst of Core Fever inside it, and then you don't give us the vaccine.''

''I'm *trying* to give *you* some of it, Cage.''

Neither of them said anything for a while. Cage tried to

calm himself down, not lose his temper. Any vaccine he could get would be a godsend; he couldn't afford to lose that.

"I'm sorry," he said. "I know you're trying to help me out here. Probably risking your job, right?"

"Maybe not this time. They *know* the first batches should go into the Tenderloin. But listen to me, Cage. I'm doing the best I can. Yeah, it's all a mess, and it's not fair, but I am trying to do right by you, by some of those poor people inside with you."

"Have you been vaccinated yet?" Cage asked.

This time there was only the slightest hesitation, then Eric said, "Yes. Am I supposed to be ashamed of that?"

"No," Cage replied grudgingly.

"Thank you." Then he said, "Okay, I'll call you as soon as I can get a batch of the vaccine to you."

"Thanks, Eric."

"You're welcome, you son of a bitch."

"Later, when the worst is over, maybe we can have a normal conversation again, yes?"

"Yeah, maybe. I'll call you."

Cage broke the connection and went back out front to take the next patient.

CHAPTER 40

Carlucci felt like they were bringing Caroline home from the hospital. In a way, that's what they were doing. She was still weak, though walking around a bit now, and she'd agreed to stay at their house for several days rather than go back to her apartment. Andrea had extended her leave from the law firm, and even Carlucci was taking time off from work.

They were all four walking around in a dead woman's apartment—he could not forget that, though he had never actually met Nikki—and it felt awkward. Andrea was fussing over Caroline, trying to make sure they had everything together. Cage had arranged for a car to take them to one of the police gates; there, outside the Tenderloin, would be a police car to take them home.

Cage came up to him, glanced at the two women. "I'd like to talk to you in private for a minute."

Carlucci nodded. They went out into the hall, which was deserted, and Cage closed the apartment door.

"About this vaccine," Cage said. "I don't know whether the cops are going to get an early crack at it or not, but I'm going to be getting some in the next day or two. So, if it looks like it'll be a while, you and Andrea can come by the clinic and I can take care of it for you."

"How the hell are *you* getting vaccine?" he asked Cage.

Cage smiled. "Like everything else, it's who you know."

Carlucci shook his head. "I don't know what's going on. I'm sure I'll find out when I get back."

"Think about it, though," Cage said. "I'll even go out to your place if you want. Caroline was lucky. Your other daughter wasn't. Most people won't be."

Carlucci nodded. "I'll find out what's happening through the department, and then I'll talk to Andrea about it. Thanks. I appreciate the offer."

Cage shrugged and smiled. "I told you before, when you got Nikki into St. Anthony's, that I owed you."

"Not anymore," Carlucci told him. "You've more than paid back with Caroline."

"I didn't do anything. There wasn't anything I *could* do. It was her own immune system that did the work."

"No," Carlucci insisted. "It was more than that. You stayed with her, you took care of her. You kept her alive. If you hadn't been there, she would have died."

"Maybe."

Carlucci knew there was no "maybe" to it. Cage had saved his daughter's life. He stepped forward, put out his arms, and hugged him. Cage didn't seem completely comfortable with it, but he didn't pull away. Carlucci released him and stepped back, grinning.

"I'm Italian," he said.

Cage smiled, maybe a little sheepishly. Then his expression got serious again. "There's something else I wanted to talk to you about. Some things that have gotten lost in the past few weeks."

Carlucci nodded. "Go ahead."

"The first time we met, you were trying to find out about Cancer Cell, and I was trying to figure out if there was some disease about to break out. Well, we know about the disease, and Cancer Cell doesn't exist anymore. But there's still a lot of weird shit around, a lot of things that just plain stink. I don't know whether you're digging into anything anymore, but—"

"I'm not done with Cancer Cell," Carlucci told him. "What do you mean, they don't exist anymore?"

"Everything they had was in the Core. Everything got destroyed when the army went in. I'm not sure how many of them even survived. They didn't all come out voluntarily."

"How do you know all this?"

"Caroline. When she feels up to it, ask her about what happened when she was in there with them. Food for thought."

"I will."

"But there's more. I don't know if there's a connection, but all this crap about New Hong Kong identifying Core Fever and having a vaccine for it, Christ, that stinks too. It's too damn much of a coincidence. I thought at first that maybe they were just trying to capitalize on Core Fever, and this would be some cooked-up vaccine that they'd sell to the government but wouldn't do any good. But that can't be. If it turned out to be useless, there'd be hell to pay, and even New Hong Kong can't afford that much bad publicity. So it's got to be a real vaccine for Core Fever."

"Well, I'm not done with New Hong Kong, either. I've still got a murder case that's tied in somehow to all this." He paused, wondering how much he should tell Cage. But he felt as if he had to tell *someone,* and he couldn't tell Andrea or Caroline. Not yet. "And another murder case," he finally said. "My daughter Tina."

"Your daughter?" Cage said, confused.

Carlucci nodded. "A few days before she came down with Core Fever, someone showed up at her apartment claiming to be with St. Anthony's and claiming that there was some kind of supplemental vaccination booster program going on. And this guy gave her an injection of something."

"Jesus Christ." Cage looked stunned. "There was no 'booster' program, was there?"

Carlucci shook his head.

"Why?"

"I don't know, yet. I'm going to do everything I can to find out." He felt suddenly very tired, and he sighed heavily. "But first I'm going to get Caroline back home, and then I've got a funeral to arrange."

"I'm sorry," Cage said.

Carlucci nodded. Cage understood; he'd lost someone, too.

CHAPTER 41

"I've found her."

It was Istvan. Carlucci was in his office, his second day back at work, four days after Tina's funeral. "Where is she?"

"No," Istvan said. "Not on the receiver." He paused for a moment. "You remember the place, the last time we talked?"

In the middle of the rioting, the room on the third floor of the vacant building near the DMZ. "Yes," Carlucci said. "I remember."

"Meet me there. Tonight, ten o'clock."

"All right."

Then Istvan hung up. Carlucci put the receiver down, staring at it. Istvan was probably right to be cautious. Ten o'clock. It was going to be a long wait.

By nine Carlucci was so alone in a dark, secluded section of Golden Gate Park, near the Panhandle, that he couldn't see how anyone could be tailing him. From the cover of a small stand of bushes at the edge of the park he watched Fulton Street, looking west. When one of the electric buses appeared a few blocks away, he stepped out onto the sidewalk and walked to the bus stop just before the bus arrived. He boarded alone, then got off under the multilevel freeway ramps near Van Ness.

From there he made his way on foot along streets that had been torn up and half burned by the riots. Few street lights were working, so the streets were lit by lights from apartment and restaurant windows and dozens of barrel fires fueled by wood from buildings that had been abandoned long ago or damaged in the recent disturbances. He wasn't exactly comfortable walking the streets, but everyone was wary, so they all tended to avoid each other. Finally he reached the border of the Tenderloin, worked his way past the ruins of the old quarantine perimeter, then up a few blocks to the vacant building.

The entire block was deserted and dark, lit only by a couple of amber street lights. Carlucci remained outside the building for a few minutes, listening, watching. Then he ducked into the entrance and crawled through the opening he and Istvan had found before. Once inside, he felt his way to the stairs, then up to the third floor. Faint light came in through the windows, casting the vaguest of shadows, showing the ruined furniture. But there was no movement.

"I'm here," Istvan said, stepping out from the back corner. He was alone.

"I was hoping she would be with you."

Istvan shook his head. "She's scared, Lieutenant. She won't tell me why."

If she was scared, then she was probably the person he needed to talk to.

"What's her name?"

Istvan shook his head again. "I promised her I wouldn't say. I promised I wouldn't bring you to her."

"Then what the hell am I doing here?"

"You're going to talk to me."

"Talk to you."

"Yes. You're going to tell me how to convince her that it's safe for her to meet with you."

"And how am I going to do that?"

"You're going to tell me exactly why you're looking for her, and what you'll expect from her, what you'll *do* to her. The truth. Then I'll talk to her again, and she'll decide. If she decides yes, I'll make arrangements for a meeting. If she decides no, our business is ended."

"I told you," Carlucci said. "I'm investigating the murder of her friend. She's the only lead we've got left."

We just want to know if she knows anything about Naomi's murder. If she's so scared that she's gone to ground, I'd guess she does." He shrugged. "That's it. I just want to talk to her about it."

"And if she *does* know something? What will you expect of her? Testimony in court?"

"I don't know. You know that, Istvan. It depends on what she knows."

"And if she does know something crucial, and you want her to testify, and she doesn't want to, will you take her in with force?"

"No. I'll try to convince her, but I won't try to force her to do anything she doesn't agree to. You know my word is good."

"Is it? How many times have you promised not to ask for my help again?" Istvan looked out the window at the deserted street below, and then he shook his head. "Go," he said. "I'll call you when I know."

CHAPTER **42**

They were sitting on several hundred doses of Core Fever vaccine, and they didn't know what to do with it. Cage, Paul, and Madelaine were at the table in the staff room, surrounded by beer and soda bottles and melting ice they'd removed from the refrigerators to make room for the vaccine. The fans were blowing, but they had the door closed and locked, and the room was hot. If word got out on the street that they had Core Fever vaccine, they'd be overrun.

"Okay," Madelaine said. "Here's an idea. We don't tell anyone about it. But every patient who comes in, we vaccinate. Whatever they come in for, whatever we do for them, we also give them a shot of the vaccine. If they're sick with something, it's easy, we tell them it's an antibiotic. Same thing if we're treating a wound of some kind. A broken arm, ah, let me see, I don't know . . . okay, we tell them it's a shot of some special hormone that promotes bone healing or something like that. We improvise. We have Franzee keep a running list up front so we don't vaccinate anyone twice. We get enough people coming through here we'll go through the vaccine pretty damn quickly anyway."

It actually sounded like a pretty good idea to Cage, and he said so. He looked at Paul. "What do you think?"

Paul sighed. "I suppose. If someone already has Core Fever, the vaccine isn't going to do them any more harm. It's a wasted dose for us, but that's a lot better than what would happen if we made an announcement. But this is all bullshit. The feds should be starting here, vaccinating as many people as they can as quickly as they can. They'd be able to provide the security to keep things under control."

"Of course it's bullshit," Cage said. "But we do what we can with what we've got. We should be glad we've got *anything* the way those bastards are."

Paul gave a twisted smile. "Friends in high places."

"Better than nothing."

Paul shrugged. "All right, let's do it that way."

"Good," Cage said. "And we'll start right now with the two of you, and then you can send Franzee and Buck back here and I'll vaccinate them. When Mike and the others come in on their next shifts, we'll take care of them, too."

"What about you?" Madelaine asked.

"I'm going to pass," Cage said. "If I haven't gotten it by now, with my exposure, I never will."

Madelaine shook her head. "That's stupid, Cage."

"No it's not. I really believe I don't need it. Someone else does."

After vaccinating all four of the others, Cage stayed for a while in the staff room, sitting alone at the table with another beer, one of the fans blowing on the back of his head.

He missed Caroline. He missed her a lot.

He missed Nikki, too, so much sometimes that he wanted to smash his head against a wall. But Nikki was dead, and he knew he would never see her again. Caroline was still alive, he knew she was out there, but he had not seen or talked to her since her parents had taken her back to their house.

He was confused about his feelings for her. They had not known each other that long, and most of the time they had spent together had been while she was deathly ill. So how well could he know her? There was guilt along with the confusion. Irrational, he knew that, but he felt it nonetheless. Guilt over Nikki, who had died not that long ago. They had been friends, deep and close friends, and he had loved her.

He shook his head and finished off the beer. There was

too much going on even to think about getting involved
with someone, especially someone who might not return
the feelings. He didn't know what, if anything, Caroline
thought about him. He had been her doctor, though he had
never really thought of her as a patient. So, better *not* to
call her, better not to pursue anything.

Christ. It was all excuses. He was hopeless. Cage thought
about having another beer, then decided against it. He
would work for a while in the clinic instead. Vaccinate
some people against Core Fever. Save some lives. That
was, after all, why he was a doctor, wasn't it?

CHAPTER 43

The DMZ was a mess. The disintegration of the quarantine and the rioting that followed had left chunks of brick and stone and shattered concrete littering the sidewalks and alleys, some of it swept into piles, some not. Most of the broken glass had been cleared away, and plywood was nailed over half the windows on the street level. Building walls were pocked with bullet holes, and rust-colored patches of dried blood were everywhere.

Caroline worked her way through the ruins, feeling safer than she ever had before. The DMZ residents were too busy trying to pull things back together and get their businesses going again to make trouble, and there was a rather strange sense of community on the street.

She stopped in at Mama Chan's. Incredibly, all but one of the main street windows were intact. Inside, about half the tables were occupied. The usual Chinese music played on the tiny speakers scattered throughout the restaurant. Standing behind the counter near the back was Mama, a short, thin woman about a hundred and seventy years old—at least that's what Tito used to say.

Mama Chan waved at Caroline and called her over to the counter. "Have some soup," Mama said. "War wonton or egg flower. I make you some Chow Fun noodles."

Caroline shook her head. "Maybe later. I'm in a hurry, I'm trying to find someone. I just wanted to see how you were doing."

Mama shrugged. "I'm alive, and I can cook. Everything's a mess. You need some soup."

Caroline gave in without more fight. She didn't have the energy to argue, and if Lily and Mink were still in the death house, they weren't going anywhere. "Okay," she said. "War wonton soup, a *small* bowl. No noodles."

Mama Chan nodded, then of course dished up a large bowl of soup and set it in front of Caroline. She brought over a pot of tea, then walked down the counter to harass one of the waitresses.

The soup was good, and Caroline discovered she was actually hungry. She ate every bit of it, and almost wished she hadn't said no to the noodles. When she was finished, she left money on the counter, called out a thanks to Mama, and left.

Two blocks away, the death house seemed unnaturally quiet. The front door was propped open, and the lobby stank of rotting fruit. Would rioters have pillaged a death house? It seemed unlikely.

She climbed the stairs to the third floor, then walked down the hall to Tito's old room. She was tired and hot, and was a little bit afraid of what she would find inside. She knocked, but got no answer. When she tried the door, it was unlocked; she pushed it open and stepped inside.

Lily was sitting in a chair by one of the windows, staring out into the airwell, an elbow propped on the windowsill, chin resting in her hand.

"Lily?" Caroline said.

"Go away." Lily didn't turn around.

No one else was in the room. A suitcase was open on the sofa, and in it were a few piles of clothes. The bedsheets were thrown onto the floor. Dirty dishes and glasses were scattered across the countertop and piled in the sink.

"Where's Mink?" Caroline asked.

"Where do you think?" Lily still didn't look at her. "Hanging out at the Luxury Arcade with all her friends, playing electric Ten Pins and SuperSkeet. Having a great time."

She took a few more steps toward Lily, but stopped while

she was still several feet away. "She died?"

Lily finally turned to look at her. Her face seemed almost dead, her eyes dulled, her skin slack. But she didn't say anything.

"When?" Caroline asked.

"A week ago." She closed her eyes. "I don't know." She kept her eyes closed and her head swayed gently from side to side. "I. Don't. Know."

Caroline wanted to walk up to Lily and put her arm around her, try to comfort her, but she had the feeling it was exactly the wrong thing to do.

"Is there anything I can do to help?" she asked.

"Yes. You can go away. You can leave me alone. Or, if you have a gun, you could put it to my head and put me out of my misery. That would be all right, too." She opened her eyes and stared lifelessly at Caroline. "One or the other."

"I'm sorry," Caroline said.

But Lily didn't respond at all, except to turn back to the window and stare outside. Caroline turned around and left.

She returned to the Tenderloin. Physically the Tenderloin seemed much less changed than did the rest of the city—there was less evidence of rioting or looting, and there were very few people wearing masks or gloves—but the feel of the place wasn't much better. There was less fear in the air than in the city outside, but there was more despair and resignation. Too many people were dying, too many people had died. Life went on, but it wasn't the same.

No, it wasn't the same at all. Tina was dead, Mink was dead, Tito was dead, Nikki was dead. Probably Rashida and Dr. Mike were both dead.

And she was alive. She'd contracted Core Fever, but she was alive.

She had entered the Tenderloin the only way she knew, through Li Peng's Imperial Imports again, and now she wandered aimlessly through the Asian Quarter. Dusk was falling, but it was still warm and humid; another heat wave

had begun. Why couldn't it just cook Core Fever right out
of the city?

Lights were coming on, flashing bright colors all around
her, but the miasma in the air made the lights seem oddly
lifeless. Streethawkers were listless, calling out products
and prices without enthusiasm; even the message streamers
swimming through the air above her seemed languid and
less than enticing. Only the smell of cooking food, strong
and seductive, was unaffected, though she noticed that people eating at outdoor cafés sat in odd arrangements, putting
as much space as possible between themselves and other
customers.

After nearly an hour of wandering through the Asian
Quarter, she finally headed for her real destination: the
RadioLand Street Clinic. She went from the Asian Quarter
to the Euro, and then to the edges of the Euro and the clinic.
Down at the end of the street, the old barrier to the Core
was in ruins, and anyone could easily go in or out. But
there was no reason to anymore. The Core was sterile and
lifeless now; even the old inhabitants were gone, taken
away and put into isolation, or killed. And Cancer Cell was
no more.

She walked into the clinic. The waiting room was full,
the air hot and stifling. She didn't see Cage or any of the
other doctors, so she went to the front desk, where Franzee
was talking to an old woman. When Franzee was done, she
looked at Caroline.

"You're looking for Cage," she said, smiling. It wasn't
a question.

"Yes."

"He's with a patient. Can it wait?"

"Of course. There's no hurry."

"I'd ask you to take a seat, but there aren't any."

"That's all right. I'll be fine."

She stood with her back against the wall, looking at all
the people waiting to get in to see a doctor, and thought
about Cage. She had tried not to think about him ever since
her parents had taken her home from Nikki's apartment,

and for the most part she had succeeded. But he was always there, in the back of her thoughts, waiting.

One of the doors down the hall opened, and two men came out. One was Paul. They went to the front counter, where they talked for a while, then the other man left, and Paul came over to her.

"You waiting for Cage, or is there something I can do?"

"Cage," she said.

Paul was grinning, staring at her.

"What?" she said.

"It's just so amazing to see someone who survived. It gives us all a little hope. So I'm happy as hell to see you."

She smiled. "Thanks, Paul."

"I'll talk to you later." He nodded at the waiting room. "Got some work to do here."

"Yeah, I noticed. What's going on, is it the Core Fever?"

"Some. But we've also had a cholera outbreak building all spring, and there was some kind of toxic gas release yesterday, which we're still seeing the effects of. One goddamn thing after another." He shrugged. "I'll see you."

She nodded, and he left to go take another patient. Sometimes she forgot that even before Core Fever had appeared this had been a busy place.

Paul took a young girl into one of the exam rooms, and a couple minutes later another door opened. This time it was Cage who came out. He saw her and stopped in the hall, staring at her. Then he finally came forward.

"Hey," he said.

"Hey yourself."

"What brings you to this bit of paradise?"

"You," she said, feeling her chest tighten.

Cage didn't respond right away. She couldn't tell what he was thinking, whether it was good or bad. So she waited.

"Hang on a minute, can you?" he said. "I've got a patient waiting, and I've got an injection to give him."

"Sure, go ahead." She gestured at all the people waiting. "You look like you're going to be pretty busy for a while."

He nodded. "Yeah, we're a little bit swamped, but my

shift is about over. I've been here twelve hours straight, and Madelaine's coming in soon.''

''Why don't I just meet you later? When you're done.''

''All right. Where?''

''Nikki's. I thought maybe I'd stay there again, for a few days, if that's okay.''

''Nikki's.'' He nodded. ''All right. I don't know when, for sure. Maybe an hour or two.''

''Whenever. I'll be there.''

''It's good to see you, Caroline.''

''It's good to see you, Cage.''

Nothing had been touched in the place since her parents had taken her away. There was a notice that had been slipped under the door saying rent was late, and had to be paid in two days or Nikki would be evicted. She would talk to Cage about that, see if he knew where she could pay the rent.

She spent the next two hours cleaning the apartment—washing dishes, throwing out old, rotting food, sweeping and mopping the floors. She hung the sleeping bag out of the window to air it out, and tossed the sheets and pillowcase into a pile in a corner of the room, sheets she'd sweated in while she'd been sick. Tomorrow she would go back to her apartment, get some clothes, a few books, and other things.

She had just finished moving Nikki's tapestries against one wall when there was a knock at the door.

''Come in,'' she called.

Cage opened the door and stepped inside, carrying a couple of brown paper bags. ''Dinner,'' he said, holding up the bags. ''Thai food from a little place around the corner. You hungry?''

She nodded, smiling. ''Very. And there isn't much here.''

He closed the door and looked around the place. ''You've been cleaning up. You really going to stay here?''

''For a while, yes.''

''Why?''

She shrugged. "I'm not really sure. It seems like the right thing to do at the moment." She wanted to tell him that he was one of those reasons, but she could not yet bring herself to do it. Later, perhaps. Instead, she smiled and said, "Let's eat."

CHAPTER 44

Her name was Amira Choukri, and she looked very much like the picture that the sketch artist had made. She was dark, her hair black with only a dusting of gray, and quite beautiful. Early forties, Carlucci guessed, maybe five-foot-five, or -six. She was wearing boots and jeans and a blue work shirt. If she was scared, she didn't show it.

It was close to midnight, and they were in what appeared to be an abandoned machine shop in an industrial area south of Market. Orange-tinged moonlight beamed in through dozens of cracked and broken windowpanes, casting a riot of shadows into the far reaches of the room. Carlucci, Istvan, and Amira sat on crates around a large electrical cable spool turned on its side. Istvan, with a sense of ritual, had brought cups and a large container of hot tea, and had just finished pouring cups for all of them.

"There will be no recording of this conversation," Istvan said.

"I know," Carlucci replied, holding up a hand. "You told me, and I didn't bring anything to do that."

"I am just confirming the ground rules," he said. "You may take notes, but this is not a formal statement. She will not sign anything."

Carlucci nodded. They had been through all this before. Maybe it was for Amira's benefit.

Istvan set a pack of cigarettes in the center of the cable spool, took one and lit it, then waved at Carlucci to go ahead.

"Why are you hiding?" Carlucci asked.

Amira glanced at Istvan, then took one of his cigarettes. She lit it and took a deep drag, staring at Carlucci. "If you don't know, I'm sure as hell not going to tell you." She cocked her head. "If you don't know, why are we here?"

Was this going to be one of those interviews where the person he talked to constantly played games with their answers? He hoped she was just being cautious.

"You knew Naomi Katsuda," he said. "If you're hiding, I'd guess you know something about her murder. That's why we're here. That's why I've been searching for you."

She gazed at him for a minute, then nodded once. "Yes, I knew her. We were friends."

"Just friends?" he asked.

She smiled and shook her head. "Friends isn't enough?" She sighed deeply. "Yes, we were more than friends. Yes, we were . . . lovers. We had to be discreet. Her father knew, but he couldn't stand the idea that his daughter wasn't straight. Wasn't 'normal,' as he used to say all the time. So he knew, but as long as we weren't open and public about it, he tolerated it."

"What would he have done if you hadn't been discreet?"

"We didn't want to find out. And as it turned out, we were right to be afraid."

Clouds were passing across the moon, and the light faded in and out. There was some illumination from a street lamp nearby, but it was dimmer than the moonlight, and Amira's features threatened to wash away in the darkness.

"What happened to Naomi?"

She smoked silently for a minute or two, looking away from him. She closed her eyes, and the clouds cleared away from the moon long enough to light the moisture at their corners, moisture that wasn't quite tears. Then she opened her eyes again and looked at him.

"Her father killed her, and carved up her forehead. That's what happened to her."

Jesus. Carlucci was stunned, completely unprepared for what he'd just heard. She hadn't said Naomi's father had arranged for his daughter's murder. No, her meaning was clear. Yoshi Katsuda had done it himself.

"How do you know he did it?" he asked.

"I *saw* him do it."

Jesus, he said to himself again. "All right. Tell me what happened."

Her cigarette was almost gone, and she dropped it to the concrete floor and lit another. She smoked in silence for a while, and Istvan, too, smoked steadily; Carlucci had to fight the urge to reach out and take one for himself.

"I was at Naomi's condo all day," she began. "I had the day off work, and I'd spent most of the day cleaning up around the place and getting things ready for dinner whenever Naomi got home. She'd said she'd probably be working late." She paused. "You've been in the condo, right?"

Carlucci shook his head.

"What the hell kind of investigation *is* this?"

"I'm not one of the investigating officers," he explained. "They've been through the condo, but I haven't."

"Then what the hell is your involvement in all this?"

"I'm the supervising officer on the case. And I'm doing everything I can to solve this damn thing."

She appeared to accept his explanation, though grudgingly, and she went on. "It's on two floors. The second floor is more like a huge loft, open, just a bedroom, and a bathroom. I was up there, taking a shower, when Naomi came home. It was late, close to eight o'clock. She stuck her head into the bathroom, told me she was home, and then went downstairs to have a drink and start on dinner." She stopped, looking outside through the cracked and shattered windowpanes. "I was out of the shower, and I was getting dressed when I heard the front door open. At first I thought she was just going out for a minute, something, but then I heard voices. Naomi's first, sounding pissed, and then someone else's. I listened hard, and recognized her father's voice. Knowing the way he felt about me, I decided I should stay out of sight, but I was curious. I got down on my hands and knees and crawled across the loft, as close as I could to the edge of the stairs, where I could hear them.''

She stopped again, and Carlucci could see a tightening in her face. ''But I couldn't really make out anything he was saying, and so I crept forward a little and looked over the edge. Her father was there, in the front room, with two of his security jackals, all of them facing Naomi. Then he finally said something I could make out. He said, 'You will never tell anyone. But you are my daughter, and so I will do this myself.' And then he moved so quickly I could hardly believe it. Suddenly there was a long thin knife in his hand and he shot forward and drove it into her chest.'' Amira was having a hard time breathing now, blinking frequently, still not looking at him. ''She cried out, but it was so brief, hardly a sound. And then she fell back, and he released the knife, letting it go with her. There was some jerking . . . and then nothing . . . and I knew she was dead.'' She was shaking her head now. ''So fast, so fast, and she was gone.''

She looked at her cigarette, took one final deep drag on it, then tossed it onto the floor near the others. But this time she did not light another.

''I couldn't move. I watched him kneel beside her, pull the knife from her heart, then carve something into her forehead. I couldn't do anything to help her. Nothing. She was dead. And if they found out I was there, I'd be dead, too. So I crawled backward, slowly, so slowly, praying no floorboards would creak, until I was at the bed, and then I crawled under it, and waited. But no one came upstairs, no one even looked. I heard more sounds, doors opening and closing, and then after a while just silence. But I was scared. I didn't move from under the bed for hours. When I finally did, and went downstairs, there were no signs of anything. Naomi was gone. There was no blood anywhere. Nothing out of place, nothing odd except a half-filled wineglass on the kitchen counter. Nothing.''

''If they didn't know you were there,'' Carlucci said, ''why have you been hiding?''

She finally looked at him, and there was a bitter smile

on her face. "I would have been next. He didn't know I had seen him kill her, but he also didn't know whether she'd told me whatever it was he had killed her for. He would assume she had. He wouldn't take any chances. If it was important enough to kill his own daughter for, he wouldn't hesitate to kill me just in case."

There was a loud scraping sound outside the machine shop, and a shadow shifted across the windows. He looked at Istvan, who returned his look, nodded, then got to his feet. He moved quickly and almost silently across the machine shop's concrete floor, to the side entrance and into the shadows. Carlucci and Amira waited in silence, neither moving.

There was strength in her, he decided, watching her, watching how she waited. She wouldn't scare easily, or without reason. He liked her.

A few minutes later Istvan returned. "It was nothing," he said quietly. "A kid scrounging through trash." He lit a fresh cigarette for himself, and Amira joined him.

"Why did Yoshi Katsuda kill his daughter?" Carlucci asked.

Amira shrugged. "That's the question, but I don't have the answer. Naomi wouldn't tell me what she knew." Again that bitter smile. "She thought it would be safer for me if I *didn't* know."

"But you must have some idea," Carlucci said.

"Sure. Some idea. But it doesn't mean anything. It had something to do with Cancer Cell. No big surprise there, they were Naomi's obsession."

"Why was she so interested in them?"

"Because they seemed to be trying to subvert New Hong Kong's overwhelming dominance of medical research. That, indirectly, worked to subvert Mishima, and in turn her father."

"Did she consider that good or bad?" he asked. "She *did* work for her father. For Mishima and New Hong Kong."

Her smile changed, became more amused. "It intrigued her." Then the smile left. "But I think she found out something about what New Hong Kong or her father was doing in relation to Cancer Cell. That's what had been bothering her, and it had been bothering her for months. I think it took her a long time to piece it together, to be sure. And I think she was just about there when her father killed her."

"Why are you still here in the city?" Carlucci asked. "Why not get the hell out?"

"I've lived here all my life. I don't really know anyone anywhere else. I don't see how I could have gone anywhere without leaving a trace somewhere, credit or ID. But here in San Francisco, I have resources, people I can count on, ways to go on *without* leaving any traces."

He smiled wryly. "Except for someone like Istvan."

Amira nodded, but didn't smile.

"Where are you staying now?" he asked.

Amira shook her head. "No. Because Istvan says I can, I trust you enough to come here and talk to you. But I don't trust you that much."

"Why do you trust Istvan?"

"Because he found me, and I'm still alive."

Simple enough. But this wasn't quite over yet. "I want to arrest the bastard," he said. "I want to lock him up, and I want to have him tried and convicted for the murder of his daughter."

"And I want to have Naomi restored to life."

"I can't arrange that, but I *can* take care of Yoshi Katsuda, if you testify. Eyewitness testimony is worth a lot to a jury."

But she just shook her head. "You think I'd live long enough to testify?"

"We'd make sure you would."

"Yeah. I'm reassured."

"If you don't testify, he remains a free man."

"If I don't testify, I remain alive."

"But will you ever be able to come out of hiding?"

Amira nodded. "That's a point. Someday, though. Something will change. Events. Maybe he gets Core Fever and dies, or goes to New Hong Kong, or moves to some other city. Or all of this blows over. Someday."

She didn't sound very convinced, and he pushed it. "But that could be years from now. Or he could find you, if he looks long enough."

"I'll take that chance."

Carlucci couldn't give up, he couldn't just let this go. Knowing what had happened was not enough. "Here's another option," he offered. "Sign a full statement, detailing what happened. That will be plenty for a probable cause hearing. With murder and a serious threat of flight, there's a good chance we can get him held without bail. Maybe we'll be able to plea-bargain, it won't go to trial, and you won't have to testify."

"Fat . . . fucking . . . chance. He'll have the best and sleaziest lawyers money can buy. He'll fight every bit of the way. It'll go to trial."

He shrugged. "Maybe. Probably. But you can decide *then.* You can stay where you are, not with police protection, but with your own. But Christ, give us a chance to bring . . ." He was about to say, "bring him to justice," but he didn't think that was right. "To bring the bastard down. He killed his own daughter. I do *not* want to let this go."

"I don't either," she replied. "But it won't bring Naomi back to life, and I don't want to die. And if I do make a statement, and you arrest the son of a bitch . . . he'll really come after me, then."

Carlucci nodded. "Yes, he will."

Amira shook her head. "I don't know."

I don't know, she'd said. Not *no.* There was a chance. But he knew he shouldn't push it. He would have to wait, give her time to think about it, time to think about what she could live with and what she couldn't.

He nodded, and stood. "Thanks for talking to me," he said.

"Sure thing."

"Think about it. And let me know. Or let Istvan know."

She nodded. "I will."

CHAPTER 45

Once again, when things started to go to shit, Eric Ralston became unreachable. He was still in San Francisco, still at the Hyatt Regency, but for two days Cage put calls in, and for two days there was no answer. He left ten or more messages, but never got a call back. It had become a pattern, and it confirmed to him that his new fears were well founded.

It was the first time he had brought Caroline up to his apartment above the clinic. As he walked in with her, he was conscious of how empty it looked and felt, like no one lived here, as if it were more cheap hotel room than someone's apartment. The bare minimum for furnishings; a handful of books, a few dishes on the counter. No paintings, no decorations of any kind. Nothing that made it look like a man named Ryland Cage lived here.

"It's not much," he said, feeling defensive.

"I remember," she said. "I was here for a few minutes once before, the day I got out of the Core."

That was right. He'd forgotten. "Can I fix you some tea or coffee or something?"

"Sure. Hot tea would be good." She wandered around the room, looking at the few pieces of furniture, the nearly empty shelves.

"Searching for signs of intelligent life?" he asked.

She just laughed. He went over to the kitchen, filled the teakettle, and put it on the stove.

"The rest of this floor is all prostitutes?" she asked. When he nodded, she said, "And you trade medical care for this apartment."

"Yes."

"I think they're getting the better deal."

He shrugged. "Maybe so. It's fine with me."

"Maybe some of the ladies have offered their services to help make up for it, hmmm?"

Cage could feel himself flushing, and he didn't respond. Some of them *had* offered their services free of charge. He'd even taken a couple of them up on their offers over the past two years, but he wasn't going to tell Caroline that.

"Are you blushing?" she asked.

He kept his face to the stove, but he could feel the heat in his ears, and they felt exposed.

"I'm only teasing you," she said. "I'm trying to get a laugh out of you. The past couple of days you've seemed real worried about something."

He wondered if he should tell her about what they'd been doing at the clinic. But why not? He could trust her. And she'd been through plenty already.

"I know someone with the CDC," he said. "You probably know the supply of Core Fever vaccine has been pretty limited up to now, there hasn't been much available on the streets."

"Not much? How about none? Same old crap, people with money are getting first crack at it."

"Yeah. Well, my friend at the CDC, he's gotten me a couple of large batches of the vaccine for the clinic."

"But that's great, Cage! Why does that worry you?"

The water started to boil, making a sick whistling sound in the kettle. He filled a small teapot with steaming water, and added a couple of tea bags. "I hope green tea is okay," he said. "That's all I've got."

He brought the teapot and two large ceramic mugs over to the small table by the window. They sat across from each other, and he looked inside the pot. "It needs to steep some more," he said.

"Cage. What is it?"

He looked at her, a sense of dread filling him. He had really come to care for her, but it seemed an impossible time for anything like a real relationship to develop.

He smiled. "I'm sorry, I'm just a mess." He pointed at his own head. "Inside. Bear with me." Then he stopped smiling. "We've had the vaccine for two weeks now."

"Two weeks? I haven't heard a thing about it."

"Paul, Madelaine, Franzee, and I are the only ones who know."

"You've been sitting on Core Fever vaccine for two weeks, and you're not giving it to anyone? There are people dying every day from it!"

Cage shook his head. "We're not sitting on it. We've been vaccinating just about every patient who's come in."

"I don't understand. I haven't heard a word at the clinic, or anywhere else for that matter. I would think the clinic would be swamped if people knew you had the vaccine."

Cage nodded. "Exactly. The clinic would be torn apart. We've been vaccinating people without their knowledge. Whatever they come in with, we've been giving them a vaccination, calling it an antibiotic, or immune system booster, cholera treatment, whatever it takes."

"Then why so upset? There isn't something wrong with the vaccine, is there?"

"Depends on what you mean by something wrong. It could be worse, I suppose, it could be contaminated and be killing people. No, what's happening is, some people who have been vaccinated are coming down with Core Fever."

Caroline didn't say anything at first, thinking. Cage poured tea for them both.

"Maybe they were exposed to Core Fever before they got the vaccine."

Cage nodded. "We thought that at first. And that could be it for a few of them. But if your friend Rashida and the CDC people are right, the incubation period is down to two or three days. In the past few days we've had five or six people come in with Core Fever more than a week after they were vaccinated here. *They* don't know that, of course, but we do."

"What does that mean?"

"Three possibilities. One, that everyone's wrong about the incubation period, but that's the least likely possibility. Two, that the vaccine isn't completely effective. Or three, that the vaccine itself is giving some people Core Fever."

"That's possible? That the vaccine could actually cause the disease it's supposed to prevent?"

"It's possible. It's happened before. It happened in the last century with an early version of polio vaccine. Depends on the nature of the vaccine. I've been trying to get hold of my friend in the CDC for two days now, see if I can't find out something. But either way is a serious problem. And either way, there's nothing we can do about it, because there isn't much of an alternative." He shrugged and gave her a kind of sick smile. "And that's what's been worrying me lately."

Caroline didn't say anything. She sipped at her tea, and gazed absently out the window.

Cage watched her, feeling depressed about everything—Core Fever, Nikki, his life, and Caroline. I *am* a mess, he thought. And, worst of all, he had no idea what to do about it.

Two hours later, he was still at the table by his window, looking down at the half-empty street below. Caroline was gone, back to Nikki's old place. The telephone rang. He got up, went over to the bed and sat, then picked up the receiver and answered.

"Cage."

"Cage, it's Eric."

He laughed. "About fuckin' time."

"I know, I know. But I'm pretty sure I know why you've been calling, and I've been trying to get some hard information so I'd have something to tell you. We've *all* been trying to get some hard information around here."

"Okay," he said. "Tell me why I've been calling you."

"The vaccine."

"The vaccine," Cage repeated.

"You've had people come down with Core Fever who have been vaccinated."

"Brilliant, Eric. First shot, bull's-eye."

"It's nobody's fault. The vaccine just isn't working out as well as we'd hoped."

"No shit." Cage closed his eyes and lay back on the bed. "What is it?" he asked. "Is the vaccine making them sick?"

"We don't think so. We're pretty certain that it's safe. It's killed virus, and the screening is damn good. We've been testing hundreds of samples the past few days, and not one of them has contained any live virus particles." Eric sighed. "We think the vaccine just isn't a hundred percent effective."

"You want to give me an idea of *what* percent effective, if it isn't a hundred?"

"We're only guessing right now, of course. It's been too soon, and we don't know what exposure rates have been—"

"Just get to it, Eric."

"Maybe fifty or sixty percent effective."

Jesus Christ. And that was probably high, because they'd want to put the best face on it they could.

"It'll get better, though. We've got people working on modifications right now. There's been more mutation of the virus than anyone expected. And we're stepping up production, going into full gear—"

"Stepping up production for a vaccine that's only fifty percent effective that you're still trying to change."

"It's *something,* for Christ's sake! And once we've made changes, and have a new vaccine, we'll give people who have had the first one the new one as well. Look, Cage, this is a logistical nightmare, can't you realize that? We're talking about trying to set up a vaccination program for three hundred and fifty million people. We're doing the best we can. . . ."

He had heard that too many times from Eric. Cage hung

up on him, got up from the bed, and sat down by the window again, looking outside. The people down there in the street had no idea what was happening to them right now, or what was very likely to come.

CHAPTER 46

It was raining, so there was no moonlight, and the light from the street lamps was dim, two distant amber glows obscured by sheets of warm rain. Carlucci approached the abandoned machine shop, pulling his slick-coat tighter—a wasted gesture; he was already soaked. He hurried around the corner of the building, into the alley, then ducked into the side doorway.

Sheltered from the rain, he stood there a minute before going in. He was afraid to hope, but he could think of no other reason Amira would want to meet him tonight—she was going to go through with it. She wouldn't need to meet him just to tell him she wouldn't do it.

He opened the door, stepped inside, and closed it. Darkness and silence. Without the moonlight he could hardly see a thing inside the machine shop, only vague shadows against darker shadows. He waited, listening. Nothing. Maybe they were late. After a couple of minutes, his eyes adjusted enough to make out the crates and cable spool where they'd sat before, but there was no one there.

He took a flashlight from the slick-coat pocket and thumbed it on, sending a narrow beam of white light across the concrete floor.

"Shut that damn thing off!" Istvan's voice, a harsh whisper from somewhere above him.

Carlucci complied. He remained where he was, unmoving. Several minutes passed. If Istvan and Amira were anywhere around him, he couldn't hear them.

Finally the narrow white beam of a flashlight appeared on the other side of the machine shop, up at the top of the stairs leading to an open, second-story work area. The light beam bobbed as someone carried it down the steps, and soon he could make out two forms behind it, moving toward the crates and spool. He joined them.

Istvan and Amira sat on the crates, and Amira set a plastic folder on the spool. Inside were several sheets of paper. "Let's do this right," she said. "Istvan told me. No question of authenticity. I've written it out myself, and I'll sign each page here in your presence." She took the sheets out of the folder and handed them to Carlucci. "Maybe you want to read it first, see if there's something I left out."

He sat on one of the other crates, used his own flashlight for light, and read through the statement. Everything was there, just as she'd told it to him when they'd been here ten days ago. Everything.

"It's fine," he said. He handed the pages back to her, and she signed and dated each one, then put them back in the folder and handed the folder to him.

"Will you testify?" he asked.

"Tell them I will," she said.

"But *will* you?"

"I don't know. Just do everything you can to avoid a trial, and we won't have to worry about it."

He had to be careful now. One move at a time, no missteps, cover his ass. And so, before he told Santos and Weathers, he went to the DA; he had to make sure he was going to get the support to go all the way.

Angela Del Carlo had been the district attorney for three years. She'd had to be hard and brash and tough to get the job in the first place, and she'd had to be tough to keep it. And she called all the shots on any high-profile case. There was no point in going to any of the deputy DA's with this; nothing would go forward without Del Carlo's approval. So Carlucci insisted on meeting with *her*.

It was late afternoon by the time he got in to see her, and she was in a foul mood. She was sitting behind her large, mahogany desk, which was covered with piles of papers and disks and a couple of different computer screens. She was wearing a dark brown suit, her hair tied back, and she was looking through a folder, turning the pages one after another.

"Have a seat, Frank." She looked up at him. "What the hell ever happened to the paperless office? We've been waiting for it since the beginning of this century, and I'd guess we'll still be waiting for it at the end of the century." She smiled. "That'll be fine with me, actually. If I ever have to read very much off a screen, that'll be the day I quit."

"Maybe something else will make you quit," he said. He sat in one of the two chairs on the other side of her desk.

Del Carlo frowned. "I don't like the sound of that, Frank. Especially with all this mystery, you won't tell me over the phone why you want to see me. Okay. Let's have it."

He held out the plastic folder with Amira's statement. Del Carlo took it from him, then sat back in her chair to read it. As he expected, she read it slowly and carefully, not glancing at him, not asking a question. When she was finished, she set it down on the desk and looked at him.

"Holy shit, Frank. You trying to shorten my career?"

"Not intentionally."

"That makes me feel much better." She shook her head, glanced at the folder again, then back up at him. "This is the real thing? I see your signatures, but . . . you talked to her? This is really her statement?"

He just nodded.

"You believe her."

"Yes."

"And she'll testify to this in court."

"She'd rather not have to," he said carefully.

"Yeah, no shit. But she will if necessary?"

"If necessary, yes."

"I hope to shit you've got her under police protection."

Carlucci shrugged. "Not exactly."

"What the hell does that mean?"

"I don't think she has much faith in police protection. She's in hiding, and she won't tell me where. That's probably best."

Del Carlo nodded. "But you have a way to get in touch with her when you need to?"

"Yes."

She sighed and slowly shook her head. "Yoshi Katsuda. Shit."

"I need to know," he told her. "If we go ahead and get an arrest warrant, will you prosecute? Will you put everything we've got into it and not roll over and drop the charges at the first hint of pressure from Katsuda and his attorneys?"

Del Carlo laughed. "Jesus, you're a bastard, Frank."

"I'm sorry I have to ask, Angela, but I need to know. This will be a monster if we go through with it. We'll take some vicious heat, you know that. I'm not going to stick my ass out over the fire, and *hers*," he said, pointing at the folder, "if I can't be sure of every bit of support you can bring."

She nodded. "You're right to ask, Frank. Has Vaughn seen this? I assume not, or I would have had him screaming at me already."

"No one's seen it except you."

"So if I told you to forget this statement, and just drop the whole matter . . . ?"

Carlucci shrugged. "No one else knows. You wouldn't have to worry about anyone making a stink about it."

"And this woman, Amira?"

"I don't think it would break her heart if we dropped the whole thing."

"But she came forward with her story. A little late, maybe, but she came forward."

"Not exactly."

"That phrase again," Del Carlo said. "What do you mean by it this time?"

"She didn't come forward. We've been searching for her for two months."

"Who is 'we'?"

"Santos and Weathers and I. Santos and Weathers are the investigating officers on the case."

She cocked her head. "But they don't know about her statement?"

"No. I found her, and I didn't tell them. We didn't know what, if anything, she'd be able to tell us if we found her."

Del Carlo didn't say anything more for a while. He knew she was trying to decide what to do. But he also knew she wouldn't take long, she wouldn't sit on it for days like some people. She would probably make the decision right now, in the next few minutes, and once she'd made the decision, she would never look back.

He was prepared for any decision she made. Certainly he wanted to go forward, he wanted to nail Yoshi Katsuda's ass to the floor, he wanted the man to pay, and not just for what he had done to his own daughter. Carlucci was beginning to suspect that Katsuda was responsible for a lot more—more pain and grief, and probably more deaths. Maybe his own wounds from that day he was following Mouse. Maybe even Christina's death.

But he was also ready to accept Angela Del Carlo's decision if she wanted to bury it right here and now. If they went forward, they would all be digging through shit and heat for weeks or months. He wouldn't miss that.

Del Carlo breathed in deeply once, then slowly let it out as she nodded. "All right, Frank. Let's do it."

That night he drank several shots of whiskey during the evening, knowing he wouldn't be able to sleep without it. Andrea didn't say a word—probably she assumed he was drinking because of Christina. There was that, too, but he tried not to think about her too much right now.

And then Cage called.

"I didn't wake you up, did I?"

Carlucci shook his head, then realized Cage couldn't see it. Christ, he was about half smashed. "No," he said. Then, "How's Caroline?"

"Caroline's fine. She's not why I'm calling."

"What is it then?" He wanted to just hang up and crawl into bed. He didn't want to have to think about anything else right now except Yoshi Katsuda.

"It's about the Core Fever vaccine. I thought you might want to hear this."

"Go ahead."

"I've talked to someone in the CDC. They haven't announced it publicly yet, and I'm not sure they ever will. But the vaccine is only about fifty percent effective."

That gave him a bit of a jolt, waking him up. "Fifty percent? What does that mean, exactly?"

"About half of all people who have been vaccinated, if they are exposed to Core Fever, will come down with it despite the vaccination."

"Christ. That's not good."

"No."

"So one hell of a lot of people who think they're safe from Core Fever are going to get it anyway, and die."

"That's right."

"Well, that's depressing news. But why are you telling me? I can't do anything about it."

"I just thought you would want to know. It's one more thing in all this mess, and it stinks of New Hong Kong. It *all* stinks of New Hong Kong, and I thought you had some case with those fuckers involved."

"I do," Carlucci said. "You think New Hong Kong deliberately came up with a half-assed vaccine?"

"No, it's not that. I can't explain it, it's just a gut feeling, but there's responsibility, somehow. They've been involved in this shit from the beginning, every step of the way, and I think there's something there that we don't know about. We may never know what it is. But I thought you'd want to know."

Carlucci nodded to himself, thinking. "Yeah," he said absently. "I *do* want to know. I think I know what you mean." He paused, trying to hang on to the thoughts that were jumping around in his head. "Thanks for letting me know." And then, before Cage could reply, Carlucci hung up.

There was something. Too many connections, but no real explanations yet. He punched up the department, then asked to be transferred over to Info Services. Marx answered the phone, which was perfect.

"Marx, this is Carlucci."

"Hey, Lieutenant. What can I do for you?"

"Put a trigger into the system for me," he said. "For Monk."

"The slug?"

"Yeah, the slug. I want to be notified immediately of anything that he does, any calls he makes or visitors or interview sessions, any calls that come in, *anything* to do with him. Can you do that?"

"Sure."

"Can you do it in such a way that he won't know about it?"

"Trickier," Marx said, and Carlucci could almost see him grinning. "But yeah, I can do it."

"Thanks."

"You got it, Lieutenant."

Carlucci hung up. He was tired. But tomorrow promised to be an interesting day.

When Santos and Weathers came into his office the next morning, he handed them each a copy of the arrest warrant. The two of them sat down and started reading, but Santos almost immediately leaped up from the chair. He kissed the warrant and held it high above his head.

"God bless the Virgin Mary!" he cried out. "We're going to nail the bastard!"

"Take it easy, Ruben," Carlucci said. "Sit down. It's not going to be that easy. We're going to have hell ahead of us over the next few weeks."

Santos sat down, grinning, holding tightly to the warrant. "Yeah, but we're going to arrest that arrogant prick. And if we do it late at night, he won't be able to get a bail hearing, and he'll have to spend at least one day in the clink."

"Just hold on there, Ruben. That's exactly why I don't

want you to get out of control. We're going to have to be
very careful with all this. We have to think out every move.
And arresting him at night is *not* what we want to do."

"Why not?"

"Because with the powerful attorneys he'll have, they'll
find a judge who will hold a bail hearing even at two
o'clock in the morning. And a judge who would do that
for him is not a judge we want to have—he'll be out. And
we're going to try like hell to have him held without bail.
We don't want him to take off to New Hong Kong. We'd
never see him again."

"You sound like you've talked with someone already
about this," Weathers said.

Carlucci looked at her and nodded. "I have. Angela Del
Carlo. Before I applied for the warrant, I wanted to make
sure we'd have the DA's office behind us."

"And if they hadn't been?"

He only hesitated a moment. They had to know. "I
would have buried it. You'd never have seen a warrant.
You'd never have heard a damn thing about it."

Weathers nodded. She understood. Santos understood as
well, but he didn't like it, and he scowled at Carlucci.

"How the hell . . . ?" Santos began. "How did you find
out it was Katsuda? What the hell have we got for a case?"

"The sketch artist image you two got from that guy in
Naomi Katsuda's condo."

"You found the woman?"

"I found the woman."

"How?"

Carlucci shook his head. "Sorry, Ruben. I can't tell
you." But he did tell them about Amira's story, and the
statement she'd made.

"Jesus Christ," Santos said, and he got up from the chair
again, pacing back and forth in the corner of the room. He
couldn't sit still. "But we're going to arrest the bastard."

"Yes," Carlucci said.

"When? Who?"

"The three of us," he answered. He stood. "Now."

•   •   •

Yoshi Katsuda was expecting them—there was no way to get up to his office without letting him know—but Carlucci didn't think he knew why they were coming. Carlucci had said there were some aspects to Naomi Katsuda's murder that urgently needed to be discussed, and, after some back and forth, Katsuda had agreed to see him.

There had been some confusion at the security post on the ground floor of the Mishima building. Carlucci had neglected to tell Katsuda that he wouldn't be alone, that two other police officers would be with him. There had been a call up to Katsuda's office, more discussion and negotiation; Carlucci had been insistent, stressing that Santos and Weathers were the investigating officers, and suggesting that they would not leave without seeing him. Finally Katsuda had cleared all three of them, and they had taken the elevator together up to the top floor.

Now they stood in the reception area, waiting. Santos kept staring at the woman with the metal face until Weathers elbowed him a couple of times.

"You should have warned me about her," Santos whispered to Carlucci. Weathers elbowed him again, and he grinned.

"Mr. Katsuda will see you now," the woman said.

"Ask him to come out here," Carlucci said.

The woman hesitated, then said, "Sorry?"

"I said, ask him to come out here."

She hesitated again, then picked up the intercom and spoke. A few moments later, the wall opened up and Katsuda came through it. He was dressed much as he had been the last time Carlucci had been here, in a dark suit and tie. He glanced at Santos and Weathers, then turned his gaze to Carlucci.

"There's something odd about this visit," he said. "I suspect you haven't been completely forthcoming with me."

Carlucci shrugged.

"You are under arrest for the murder of Naomi Katsuda," Santos said. He paused, waiting for a response. But Katsuda didn't say anything, he didn't even glance at Santos; he kept his gaze on Carlucci. Santos went on. "I will be reading you a list of your rights," he said. He took a card from his pocket to read from. There weren't going to be any mistakes. "If you have any question about any of them, feel free to ask. First . . ."

Katsuda waved at Santos, a gesture of dismissal, though he continued to look at Carlucci. "I waive the reading of those rights," he said. "I know what my rights are."

"I'm sorry," Santos replied. "I can't do that. We must read them to you. First, you have the right to remain silent. Second . . ."

Carlucci and Katsuda stared at each other as Santos went through the Miranda/Washington procedure. Katsuda's face betrayed no emotion, no expression at all other than bored indifference. Was he that confident? Or just that much in control?

When Santos was finished, he asked, "Do you understand these rights as I have read them to you?"

Katsuda nodded. "Yes, I understand them all quite clearly." And then a faint smile appeared on his face. "I understand a lot more now than I did before. And I will be calling my attorney before we leave here." He paused for a moment. "I'm impressed, Lieutenant."

"Don't be," Carlucci said.

"But I am. This will be futile for you in the end, but I am quite impressed that you are here with a warrant for my arrest."

"Is that an admission to the charges?" Santos asked. Weathers, a step or two behind him, was just shaking her head.

Katsuda finally turned to Santos, and gave him a disparaging look. "Of course not, *Officer*. Lieutenant Carlucci knows what I mean."

"So what does he mean, Frank?"

Carlucci shook his head. "Nothing, Ruben. Nothing that will ever be admissible in court." Then, to Katsuda, "You might be surprised, Mr. Katsuda. About the futility."

The smile broadened. "I don't think so, but that would be interesting, anyway."

"I hope you find a jail cell interesting, too."

"I don't believe I will be in one long enough to find it anything at all."

Carlucci finally allowed himself a brief, small smile. "You might be surprised about that as well."

Late that afternoon, Carlucci left the courthouse in good spirits. Because of the serious nature of the crime, and the perceived flight risk, and in no small part because of the passionate and persuasive arguments of Angela Del Carlo, Yoshi Katsuda was being held without bail.

CHAPTER 47

Night had fallen. The air was warm, but it was raining, too, and the sound of it reminded Caroline of the day she had realized she had Core Fever, the day she'd thought she would soon be dead. She and Cage had found a table at a junk store, so she'd retired the plastic crates and plywood Nikki had used, and put the table next to the largest window looking out on the street. She sat there now with the lights off, drinking tea and watching the colored lights flashing below her. The nights, though still the busiest time in the Tenderloin, still noisy and active, no longer had quite the same frenetic quality as the first time she'd come here. People seemed halfhearted as well as wary and resigned.

But she was beginning to like it here in the Tenderloin, in this apartment. It had been Nikki's, but she was finally beginning to feel like it was her own. Another week or two, when she felt more sure about it, she would move everything from her apartment in Noe Valley, make it permanent here. She smiled to herself, thinking of how her father would feel about that. Mom, oddly enough, would probably understand.

There was a knock on the door, and she called out, "Come in." Cage had said he would stop by after his shift at the clinic, so she was expecting him. The door opened, then closed.

"What if it hadn't been me?" Cage asked. "I could have been some maniac."

She turned away from the window and looked at his

dark, shadowy form coming toward her. "You *are* some kind of maniac," she said, smiling.

"Ha, ha." He sat across from her. "And why no lights?"

"So I can see better outside. I like this, watching the signs, the message streamers, the lights of the cars. That woman there, in the kiosk." She pointed toward the end of the block, where an old woman sat inside a tiny kiosk, selling cold beer. The old woman was smiling, talking to customers, drinking a beer herself. "I've been watching her every night," Caroline said. "She isn't letting all this get her down, the people dying, Core Fever, everything else."

Cage sighed. "Is that an admonition?"

"It's an observation. And here's another one. I don't think I've seen you smile in days."

He shook his head. "What's to smile about? Maybe that old woman manages to enjoy her life down there because she stays half drunk and she doesn't know what's really happening around her. Do *you* realize what's happening here? In this city, in this country?"

"Yes," Caroline said. "I do."

"I wonder. We have a full-blown epidemic going that very soon will become a pandemic. It's already breaking out in other countries. The damn disease is almost one hundred percent fatal, and the only vaccine we've got for it, which isn't even being widely distributed yet, is only fifty percent effective. People are getting sick in droves, and they are dying in droves, and there is not a whole hell of a lot we can do about it. Unless something changes very quickly, and the odds are not good for that, this thing is going to kill off a good chunk of the population in this country, maybe even the world. And it's going to kill off a bigger chunk here in San Francisco. This city is going to be unrecognizable a year from now. Probably the entire country is going to be unrecognizable."

"I know all that, Cage. My sister died from Core Fever, and I almost died from it. But I'm not dead, and neither are you. We don't just stop living because the world is going to shit around us. I'm not suggesting we try to ignore it, or pretend it's not happening, but we also don't curl up in a ball somewhere and stop living, and that's what you're doing. You might just as well put a gun to your head and blow your brains out."

"I've thought about it," he said.

"No you haven't. I know you, Cage."

He nodded. "You're right, I haven't. But sometimes I wish I *could* give it serious consideration."

"Look at that woman down there," she said. "There's something important to be learned from her."

He gave her a half smile. "Unless you've managed to romanticize the shit out of her, and she's really just a drunken psychotic who *doesn't* have a clue to what's going on."

"That's better," she said. "Not much of a smile, but it's something." She stood. "You want some tea or coffee?"

"Yeah," he said, nodding. "Coffee."

"I'll put the water on."

When she returned to the table, his back was to her and he was gazing out the window. She came up behind him and put her hands on his shoulders. He stiffened a bit, briefly, then relaxed. It wasn't much of a response. She wanted him to put his own hands over hers, but he didn't.

Her heart was beating a little faster and harder now, and her breathing was a little funny. Could she be wrong about his feelings for her? She didn't think so. He'd never said anything, but she was sure she could feel it from him every time they spent any time together.

"I'm going to have to take the initiative with this, aren't I?" she finally said.

"With what?" he asked, still not looking at her.

"You know what I mean."

He breathed in deeply once, then slowly let it out and nodded. He turned around then and looked up at her, and she leaned over, bringing her mouth to his. She kissed him, and this time he did respond, and her stomach and chest twisted around in a half-sick, half-ecstatic sensation she hadn't felt in a long, long time.

· · · ·

At midnight it was still raining. They lay naked on the open sleeping bag, which they had laid out on the floor. The room was dark, but there was the flashing and blinking of lights from the street, and she could see the reflection of sweat on his skin.

"You're smiling," Cage said.

"Shouldn't I be?"

"Well, I don't imagine that was the most exhilarating and profound sexual experience you've ever had."

Caroline laughed softly. "It was the first time you and I have ever made love. Of *course* it was a little awkward. We *both* were awkward. I imagine that's pretty normal with two people who don't know each other that way." She laid her arm across his chest and kissed his shoulder. "It certainly wasn't unpleasant, and it'll get better." She sensed his insecurity, and thought how absurd it was.

They lay for a while without talking. She really did feel quite wonderful, being beside him, feeling his skin against hers, feeling his heartbeat against her hand. It helped to remind her that she was still alive, and that despite everything happening around them, being alive was a wonderful thing.

"I know this is just crazy," he said, "but I feel a little guilty." He was staring up at the ceiling.

"Nikki?"

"Nikki."

"Why? Because this was her place?"

"Partly. And because I loved her, and she hasn't been dead for very long."

"Oh, Cage," she said.

"I *know* it's irrational, but it's there." He turned his head toward her, and managed a smile. "But I promise not to let it get in the way."

"I wonder if there's something wrong with you," she said, smiling back at him.

"What do you mean?"

"First, you fall in love with someone who doesn't love you in return."

"Nikki loved me," Cage said.

"Yes, but not in the same way."

"No, not in the same way. She never loved anyone that way. I didn't know that at first. I didn't understand that for a long time."

"Then she died. You lost her. Twice in a way. And now you're beginning to care for someone who's also going to die soon, in a few years at most."

Cage didn't say anything for a long time. He was facing her, but his gaze was unfocused, or focused on something far away that wasn't even in the room with them.

"Yes," he finally said. "Maybe there is something wrong with me. But I don't notice you objecting."

"No, I'm not objecting. A few months ago, I would have. I even kept putting off a stray cat that tried to adopt me, because I didn't want it to become dependent on me. I was afraid of what would happen to it after I died."

"So why the change?"

"Almost dying." She turned onto her back and gazed up at the ceiling herself. "I've come to terms with the Gould's in some real ways. Not completely, of course. I don't think that's possible. I suspect I'll have an occasional 'lapse,' wake up in the middle of the night absolutely terrified of dying, terrified and furious that I survived this disease that so many other people are dying from, only to have to die from something else in a few years while I'm still so young."

"Sounds to me like you've already had one or two nights like that."

"Maybe," she said, smiling again. She turned to him. "But I promise not to let *that* get in the way, either."

He reached across her, took hold of her hand. Then he pulled her on top of him, and soon their slick bodies were moving together once again.

CHAPTER 48

Carlucci was asleep and dreaming about Istvan Darnyi's apartment. He was sitting inside piles of stamp albums and stock books, open shoe boxes overflowing with loose stamps. He was trying to find stamps from the Italian states—Modena, Sardinia, Tuscany—but he was certain he wouldn't recognize them even if he saw them, and he wasn't all that clear why he was searching for them in the first place. So when the phone started ringing, bringing him out of the dream, he felt a great sense of relief.

His sense of relief faded quickly, however, as he came fully awake. The bedroom was still dark, only the faintest touches of gray to indicate morning was coming. A phone call this time of day was almost never good news. He grabbed the receiver to stop the ringing, trying to focus on the clock at the same time: 5:52. Jesus.

"Carlucci," he said.

"Lieutenant, this is Marx. Sorry to wake you up, but I've got something for you."

"Hold on a second."

He scrambled out of bed, glancing over at Andrea, who still seemed to be deep asleep, then stumbled out of the bedroom, down the hall, and into the kitchen, where he half collapsed into one of the chairs.

"All right," he said. "Go ahead."

"I was just getting ready to go off shift when it came through," Marx said. "The Monk trigger."

"Monk. What is it?"

"He's leaving."

"What?"

"He's leaving his quarters. He's arranged to have an ambulance van come pick him up at department headquarters, then take him to Hunter's Point."

The spaceport. "He's going to New Hong Kong," Carlucci said.

"That's what I would guess."

"What time?"

"The ambulance is scheduled to arrive at nine o'clock. I checked with Hunter's Point Security, and they have a special flight taking off at noon."

"Goddamn, Marx, you've done a hell of a job."

"Thanks, Lieutenant. But there's more."

"What?"

"It's not related, but I figure you want to hear about this."

"What is it?"

"Word is that Katsuda's managed to get a new bail hearing for this morning."

Carlucci closed his eyes. He wanted to crawl back into bed and go back to dreaming about missing stamps. "I didn't really want to hear that," he said.

"Sorry, sir."

"That's okay."

"He'll get out on bail, won't he, Lieutenant?"

"It doesn't look good." He opened his eyes and twisted his head from side to side. He must have slept wrong; there was a terrible, biting kink in his neck. "Thanks for calling."

"Do you want me to monitor Monk for you, keep track of what he's doing until he gets to Hunter's Point?"

"I thought you were getting ready to go off shift."

"I am, but I can stick around."

"You don't mind?"

"No. Never seen one of the slugs leave before. They just seem to stay inside their caves until they die. It could be interesting."

"Sure. I'd appreciate it. Give me a call if anything un-usual comes up."

"Will do, Lieutenant."

Carlucci hung up. He sat at the kitchen table, trying to decide what to do. He wasn't going to let Monk leave with-out talking to him first, that much he knew. But he felt there was something more he needed to do. He got up and made some coffee, hoping it would help him think things through.

An hour later he was showered and dressed, and he was still trying to put his thoughts together. There were things out there he thought he was close to understanding, those odd connections, but he wasn't there yet. And he had the feeling that if he didn't get the rest of the way today, he never would.

He sat at the kitchen table again, drinking one more cup of coffee, and picked up the phone to call Angela Del Carlo. He finally got through on the third number he tried.

"This is Del Carlo." There was traffic noise in the back-ground, and the faint sound of jazz.

"Carlucci here," he said.

"Shit." A horn blared and brakes squealed in the back-ground. "Goddamn it. All right, Frank. I know why you're calling, and it's true. I'm on my way to the courthouse right now."

"What's it look like?"

"Shit, that's what. McAdamas is the judge."

"That's not good," he said.

"She'd let her own killer go free if the money was right."

He blinked and shook his head, trying to figure out the logistics of that. "All right. Let me know what happens."

"Sure thing." The connection clicked off.

One more phone call, this time to Cage. Carlucci had one final big favor to ask.

It was a little after eight by the time he approached the RadioLand Street Clinic. The streets and sidewalks of the

Tenderloin were half empty; it was early in the morning, the dead time of day in here, but even so he figured it was probably worse than usual. Just like everywhere else in the city.

Cage met him as he walked in through the clinic entrance, then led him back to the staff room at the end of the corridor. The fans were going, keeping the room tolerable, just as they had been the first time they'd met. A lot had happened since they'd talked that day.

Cage picked up a small, narrow case, not much bigger than a paperback, and handed it to him. It might just fit inside his jacket pocket. "That's it," Cage said. "Two." He looked at Carlucci. "What are you going to do with them?"

"I don't know."

"Am I really supposed to believe that?"

Carlucci just shrugged.

"What is it?" Cage asked. "Revenge?"

"No. Some kind of justice, maybe."

"Sounds like a euphemism for revenge to me."

"Maybe so," Carlucci said.

"One last bit of news," Cage said. "I talked to my friend in the CDC late last night. Later today, they're going to make the announcement."

"That the vaccine isn't as effective as they've claimed?"

Cage nodded. "Too many news reports of people getting Core Fever after being vaccinated. They can't keep it quiet anymore."

"Then what?"

He shook his head. "I don't know. No one does."

Carlucci wasn't surprised. It kind of fit with some of the things he was putting together. Made sense of the timing.

"All right," he said. "Show me what to do."

As he neared Hunter's Point, traffic jammed up, slowed by crowds of people in the streets. He thought about putting up his flasher and punching the siren, but decided it might make things worse. Marx had said he was ahead of Monk anyway, and Monk wasn't going to get through this any faster than he was.

The crowds were headed toward Hunter's Point, something he should have expected. But there was no organization, just a chaotic milling that slopped over into the roadway. Carlucci moved forward in stops and starts, never reaching more than five miles an hour. The people moved back and forth in front of the car, sometimes turning to look at him, faces shiny with sweat. Night hadn't brought much relief from the heat, and the day was already beginning to warm up.

The crowds thickened and slowed as he got within sight of the main Hunter's Point gate. Security forces lined the fences, with a large contingent at the gates holding the crowd back. The main parking lot was nearly empty; the guards weren't letting any vehicles through. Several guards were directing vehicles away before they even reached the gate.

He thought he could talk his way into the parking lot, but decided it wasn't worth it. Hell, he might never get out. He swung the car away from the gates, drove a block, then turned a corner and pulled over to the curb. He locked up the car, then pushed into the crowd, forcing his way toward the main gate.

It took him nearly ten minutes to go the one block and the extra hundred yards to the gate itself. People shouted all around him, mostly things he couldn't make out. There were signs, though, held up above the crowd that let him know what this was all about: VACCINE NOW!! CORE FEVER KILLERS. NO MORE PHONY VACCINE! FREE VACCINE FOR EVERYONE!! The smell of the crowd, too, was bad—sweat and anger and fear. When he finally reached one of the guards, still twenty feet from the gate, he showed his badge and ID plates.

"Sorry, Lieutenant," the guard said. "The launch grounds are closed to everyone except authorized parties, and those going up on the next ship."

"I don't want to go onto the launch grounds," Carlucci said, almost shouting to be heard above the crowd noise.

"I just want onto the parking lot. I've got official business with one of the people you *will* be letting through."

The guard opened his mouth, closed it, and frowned. He seemed unsure. "You don't have jurisdiction in Hunter's Point," he finally said.

"I know," Carlucci replied. "Let's call this cooperation between agencies. I'm not going to cause you any problems. I just need to talk to someone for a few minutes before he goes." The guard still seemed unsure, so Carlucci went on. "I need to talk to Monk. Monk *is* approved access, isn't he?"

The guard nodded. "All right," he said. "Come on through. But check in with Captain Reynoso at the Security building, all right?"

Carlucci nodded. The guard gestured toward one of his colleagues, and the two men walked Carlucci to the gate, clearing a path through the crowd. After a brief talk to the gatekeepers, several guards formed a shield of sorts against the crowd, the gate opened, and Carlucci squeezed through, the gate and shield closing behind him.

He stood in the nearly empty lot and gazed out through the second line of chain-link fence to the tarmac and the lighted gantry and ship in the distance. The gantry lights sparkled, isolated out on the black tarmac, like they had no connection to the noise and smell of the crowd behind him. He glanced back at the crowd, then walked to the Security building by the gates leading onto the launch grounds.

Captain Reynoso was big, an inch or two taller than Carlucci, and she looked to be in a lot better shape. He showed her his ID and explained why he was here.

"Lieutenant, do I have your word that you won't be causing any trouble? That you won't be trying to arrest anyone, or prevent anyone with authorization from boarding?"

"You have my word," he said. "I just want to talk to Monk."

Reynoso seemed satisfied. She offered him coffee. He'd already had too much, but he accepted anyway. Reynoso went into another room and came back with two cups, handed one to him. The coffee was better than what he'd made at home.

They stood by the main window, looking out at the parking lot, the outer gates, and the growing crowds.

"It could get ugly out there," Carlucci said.

Reynoso nodded, but didn't seem concerned. "They've been out there for days."

"Can you handle it all right?" he asked. "I can call in help from the city."

She shook her head. "We'll be fine. Once we get our parties through, we can pull everyone inside, lock up the gates, and activate the fences. Fry anyone who tries to force their way inside." She turned to look at him. "My job is security, nothing else. I plan to keep my job."

He nodded. "I understand."

He stayed by the window and watched, waiting for Monk to arrive.

CHAPTER 49

Fifteen minutes later he saw a large van working its way through the crowd. The van's emergency lights flashed steadily, and the horn blared, barely audible over the noise of the crowd surrounding it.

"This will be what we're waiting for," Reynoso said.

The van finally reached the main gate. People pounded on it and rocked it from side to side, though they could have no idea who was inside, or what they were doing here. Then the gate swung open and the van drove through. The crowd surged forward behind it and the Security guards pushed in on them, forcing them slowly back, struggling for a couple of minutes before they were able to get the gate shut again. By then, the van had pulled up next to the Security building and stopped.

"Normally we'd bring them all inside," Reynoso said. "But we've got unusual circumstances."

"You've got a slug," Carlucci said.

Reynoso sighed. "Yes, we've got a slug. Let's go." She signaled to the processing crew at the other end of the building, then walked out the door and toward the van. Carlucci followed.

The driver got out of the van and handed Reynoso a packet of documents. She glanced at them, then looked at the driver. "You and the attendants will have to wait here," she said. "My people will drive the van, take the passenger out to the ship, then bring the van back."

The driver nodded. "That's what we were told."

"You can wait inside." She nodded toward the building. "There are chairs. Coffee, other things to drink."

Reynoso approached the open side door, leaned inside. "Mr. Monk?"

"It's just Monk," said a voice from inside the darkness of the van.

"Okay. Monk. There's someone here who wants to talk to you. Now, you are on Hunter's Point grounds, under our jurisdiction, so you don't have to talk to him. It's up to you."

"Who the hell is it?"

"Lieutenant Frank Carlucci of the San Francisco Police Department."

A deep rolling laugh sounded from inside the van. "Of course I'll talk to him. I was more than half expecting him. Send him in. There's plenty of room."

Reynoso stepped back. "Go ahead," she said to Carlucci. "But don't take too long. We've got to get him processed and loaded up. We've got a launch time to meet."

Carlucci nodded. He approached the van, ducked his head, and stepped up, standing bent over just inside the panel door. There wasn't much light inside the van. Monk was ensconced in something like a wheelchair surrounded by displays, fluid containers, and medical equipment. He looked just the same: a bloated, deformed body enveloped by shiny black rubber, head encased in a helmet, eyes hidden by goggles.

Monk smiled at him, the thick, distorted lips shiny with moisture. Carlucci stared at the slug, his mind blank, unable to remember what he'd wanted to ask.

"Well, Lieutenant?"

"You lied to me," Carlucci finally said.

"Of course," Monk replied. "Many times." He licked his lips, the tongue as thick and bloated as the rest of him. "Three years ago, at our first session, I offered you a chance at New Hong Kong. A chance at a very long life. Real life extension. A hundred and fifty years or more."

"You were so subtle about it, I didn't even know it was an offer at the time. I didn't figure it out until later."

"Yes, that was a problem. But you wouldn't have accepted the offer anyway."

"No."

"See, that's when so many of your difficulties began." He shook his head. "You were never very cooperative, and you've paid a high price for that."

"Tell me now, Monk. What is going on? What has been happening all this time?"

Monk laughed. "I *will* tell you, Lieutenant Francesco Carlucci, and you'll be sorry when I'm done."

Maybe so, Carlucci thought. He could feel the weight of the case against his ribs. But they would both be sorry. He looked around for a place to sit, his back already sore from standing bent over, and finally settled on a metal crate behind the driver's seat. He could just sit upright without hitting his head on the van ceiling.

"All right," he said to Monk. "Tell it."

Monk made a sound that might have been a chuckle. He made an adjustment to one of the control panels attached to the seat, and a panel began blinking green. Monk finally turned his goggled eyes directly toward him.

"Just confirming that you are not employing any recording devices," he said.

Carlucci just shook his head.

"Okay," Monk said, shifting his position. "I'll start with the main thing." He stared at Carlucci. "You ready for this?" And he paused again for effect. "New Hong Kong is responsible for Core Fever. Not Cancer Cell. Not *nature*. But New Hong Kong."

He paused, as though waiting to let it sink in, or waiting from some response from Carlucci, but Carlucci didn't say a thing. It was one of those statements that you immediately realize isn't at all surprising, that you half knew already because it fit with so many other things. New questions started swirling around in his mind, but for now he said nothing, just waited for Monk to go on.

And Monk did. "It all flows out of that," he said. "Once they were certain that it had fully taken hold in the Core and had begun to spread outward from it, presenting an undeniable health threat, they stepped forward to help. They were able to identify it as a virus—not difficult, since they had provided it—and they advised the CDC on containment measures.''

''The quarantines.''

''Yes, the quarantines. Particularly the quarantine of the Core. That was the real goal from the beginning. Sterilization of the Core. The Tenderloin quarantine was camouflage.'' He waved a hand toward Carlucci. ''Once that was accomplished, and enough time had passed to lend things a certain credibility, New Hong Kong announced the development of a vaccine for Core Fever.''

''A vaccine they'd had all along.''

Monk shrugged his bloated shoulders and nodded. ''Yes, a vaccine they'd had all along. They would never have released a virus like that one unless they had a vaccine for it.''

''That's real fucking humane of them,'' Carlucci said, barely able to keep his anger in check, along with all of the other questions that still waited to be asked and answered. ''But the vaccine is only fifty percent effective.''

''Probably closer to forty,'' Monk said. He might have winced; with so little of his face exposed, it was difficult to tell. ''That was a slight complication. It should have been close to one hundred percent effective. But somehow, probably through the use of the vector that introduced it into the Core, mutations occurred in the virus. There seem to be three major strains of Core Fever now, and the vaccine is only effective against one of them. Fortunately it is the dominant strain.''

''You call forty percent dominant?''

''It's a little over forty percent of all cases, the other two each are responsible for less than thirty percent. And they're working on developing a combination vaccine. The numbers should get better.''

''That's just terrific. It's insane, is what it is.'' Carlucci could hardly sit still; he wanted to stand up and pace, or just get up and smash something. He could hardly believe he was having this conversation.

"Why?" he finally asked. It was the question he had been dying to ask, the most important question of all, and it seemed unbelievable to him right now that Monk could give him anything resembling a reasonable answer.

"Several reasons, actually. It began with the need to eliminate Cancer Cell, and they came up with a way to do it that accomplished other desirable results as well."

"Cancer Cell?"

"Yes. It wasn't really sterilization of the Core that was the ultimate goal. It was the sterilization of Cancer Cell."

"Why?" Carlucci asked again.

"Business." Monk left it like that for a while, as if that answer explained everything.

"Business," Carlucci said.

Monk laughed. "Yes, of course. Cancer Cell was competition. It's that simple. Well, maybe it's not that simple, but that's the core of the matter." He laughed again.

"Competition," Carlucci said, prodding, trying to understand.

"Oh, yes, competition. One of New Hong Kong's most profitable businesses is the manufacture of high-grade, specialized, very expensive pharmaceuticals. They've got the patents all locked up here on Earth, in pretty much any country that could produce them."

"I know all about that," Carlucci said. "They ignore laws they don't like, and exploit those laws that are useful to them."

"They *are* a practical bunch," Monk said. "But Cancer Cell paid no attention to patent laws. Not only were they manufacturing many of these high-grade pharmaceuticals—not quite to the standard of New Hong Kong, of course, but close enough—they were selling them on the street at drastically reduced prices. Now, that didn't have *too* much effect on the legitimate sales, but New Hong Kong's profits on the black market, on the streets, are actually greater than those on the legitimate end. And Cancer Cell was cutting way into those. They were trying to make these otherwise expensive and difficult-to-obtain drugs moderately priced and readily accessible. And the people in Cancer Cell didn't have very high standards of living. That made it easy to keep prices artificially low." Monk shrugged. "A noble ambition, certainly, but one quite at odds with New Hong Kong's own philosophy, and one increasingly at odds with their business plans."

He paused and licked his lips several times. He reached up for a piece of flexible tubing hooked up to a fluid bag, put it in his mouth, twisted a valve, and sucked on it. He offered some to Carlucci, but he refused.

"There was one more thing, which clinched the deal for New Hong Kong. It appeared that Cancer Cell's researchers were making significant progress in the life extension area. New Hong Kong simply could not abide that. New Hong Kong is going to have absolute and complete control of any life extension treatments that are ultimately developed. In the coming years, control of that will be control of just about everything in life."

"All of this, Core Fever, the quarantines, all these people dead and dying, all this was to eliminate a business competitor?" Even as he said it, it sounded incredible.

"Essentially, yes," Monk answered. "As I said, it also was to have other positive benefits."

"Like what?"

"The people in New Hong Kong thought the population could do with a bit of culling, if properly directed. A fatal disease epidemic that began in the Core and spread to the Tenderloin would pretty much target the kinds of people New Hong Kong wanted. Especially when a vaccine soon became available, in limited quantities, to the right people. You probably noticed the vaccine still hasn't become widely available, although that will change fairly soon."

"I noticed," Carlucci replied. He shook his head, still having trouble believing what he was hearing. "Except the vaccine isn't as effective as it's supposed to be, so a lot of the 'right people' will end up getting Core Fever and dying."

Monk nodded. "I'm afraid so. As I said, that was a complication."

"That's not a complication," Carlucci said. "It's a major fuckup."

"That, too," Monk agreed, smiling. "One of the other benefits was *supposed* to be good public relations from a successful vaccine. New Hong Kong seen as the world's savior. Well, not now."

Carlucci continued to shake his head. He turned away from Monk and looked out the open door of the van. From this vantage point he could see part of the mob pressing against the outer perimeter fencing, and he could just hear a generalized noise from them. "This is incredible. And how many people are going to die before this is all over?"

"Over the next five years," Monk said, "about seventy million people in this country alone."

Carlucci swung back around and stared at him. He hadn't expected an answer, and he was stunned into silence.

"That's a worst-case scenario," Monk continued. "If the vaccine never gets any better. Approximately twenty percent of the population. There will be similar numbers in other countries, though it will vary greatly. In undeveloped countries, the percentages will end up much higher. In industrialized countries, probably lower, because they are already starting to take preventative measures." He paused. "But if they improve the vaccine, especially if they can get it close to one hundred percent effective, those numbers will greatly drop. Not soon enough for San Francisco, of course, or most of California. Or, to be honest, for a lot of the country."

"And they may not be able to improve the vaccine at all."

"That's a possibility, yes. But the researchers up in New Hong Kong are very good at what they do."

Carlucci hung his head in his hands and stared at the floor. He felt sick, and dizzy. And then, one final thing fell into place. He raised his head to look at Monk.

"What was Yoshi Katsuda's part in all this?"

"He was a liaison of sorts. All plans were made in New Hong Kong, and Katsuda's task was implementation of those plans here on Earth. He was to make sure everything went smoothly, make sure everything was done.''

"But his daughter found out about it.''

"Apparently. That was another complication, and he made it worse by killing her himself. He should have kept himself completely apart from that. He should not have spent the past two weeks in jail. He should not have caused New Hong Kong to expend so much in the way of resources to get him out." Monk cocked his head. "You know he's out, don't you?''

Carlucci nodded. "So he took care of everything here in San Francisco," he said.

"Yes.''

"Did that include my daughter?'' he asked. "Christina.''

Monk hesitated. "What about her?''

"She didn't catch Core Fever from anyone. Someone came by, took advantage of her innocence, and pumped her full of Core Fever virus.''

Again Monk hesitated, then he nodded once. "I'm impressed, Lieutenant.''

"*Fuck* impressed. They killed my daughter, didn't they? And you knew about it.''

"I said earlier. You've paid a high price for causing New Hong Kong so much trouble. You were one more side benefit to all of this. Both of your daughters would get Core Fever and die. You were to lose both of your daughters, and eventually they would have let you know they were responsible. They sent someone for Christina. They didn't have to for Caroline. She took care of that herself, going into the Core and contracting it there. Unexpectedly, of course, she survived. If it is any consolation, the decision has been made to leave her alone. They believe her survival has earned her the right to a continued life. Of course, with the Gould's she has a damn short life expectancy anyway." He paused. "Whether they will leave *you* alone is another matter. I have no idea what they will decide for you.''

"They may not have to decide. After all, I've been vaccinated for Core Fever. If I become exposed to it, I've only got a forty percent chance of being protected.''

"Limit your chance of exposure," Monk said. "That's my advice."

"Is that what you're doing? By going to New Hong Kong? Limiting your exposure?"

"Not really," Monk said. "If I had stayed in my quarters in the department, I could easily have eliminated any chance of exposure."

"But you have been vaccinated?" Carlucci asked.

Monk laughed. "Sure. Before it even broke out. And before we knew it wasn't all that effective."

Okay, that made it easier. "Then why are you leaving?"

"It's time. This country is going to be greatly changed over the next few years. No way to know how, exactly, but it's probably going to be a nightmare. Way too risky to stick around. No, it's time."

"Yes," Carlucci said. "It's time."

He took the case out of his coat pocket, opened it, and took out one of the syringes.

"Lieutenant . . . what is that?"

He didn't answer. He closed the case and tucked it away, then popped off the plastic cap over the tip of the needle.

"What . . . ? Don't come near me!" Monk cried. "HELP!" he shouted, pressing back in his chair. "HELP!"

Carlucci moved forward, grabbed hold of Monk with his left arm and his body, holding him fairly still. Monk squirmed and struggled, and he kept shouting for help, but he didn't have much strength, and the chair helped keep him pinned down.

Carlucci managed to keep him still, exposing Monk's left shoulder. Then he took the syringe and drove the needle through the black rubber and deep into Monk's upper arm. Monk cried out again, and Carlucci slowly squeezed the plunger until it would go no farther.

He pulled out the syringe, and released Monk, staggering backward. He managed to keep his balance, sat down heavily on the metal crate. Then he picked up the case, put the empty syringe inside, closed it up, and tucked it back into his coat.

"What did you do to me?" Monk's voice was hoarse with fear.

"You've got a forty percent chance," Carlucci said.

"What?"

"You're a slug," he said. "You're intelligent. You figure it out."

Captain Reynoso leaned in through the open side door and looked around the inside of the van.

"I thought I heard shouting," she said. "Is there a problem?"

"I don't think so," Carlucci replied.

"He—" Monk began.

But Carlucci cut him off. "You want to tell Captain Reynoso what I did, and why?"

Monk kept quiet. Reynoso stared at him a while, then turned to Carlucci. "I need to start getting him processed," she said. "With all his special equipment, it will take longer to get him aboard."

"I'm done here," Carlucci said.

Reynoso nodded and backed away from the van. Carlucci turned toward the door.

"Wait," Monk said.

Carlucci turned back. He was surprised to see Monk smiling, though it was a strange and twisted smile. "I'm waiting," he said.

"I didn't know you had the balls to do something like this," Monk said. "I would have bet against it."

Carlucci just shook his head. "It has nothing to do with balls."

He turned back to the door and pulled himself out of the van and onto the tarmac. He half expected Monk to call him back again, but the slug didn't speak. Reynoso was waiting about ten yards away.

The chopping sound of a helicopter came from the north, growing louder, and Carlucci looked up to see a dark blue private helicopter approaching Hunter's Point. He watched the copter come in, pass overhead, then slowly descend in the middle of the empty parking lot. No one emerged from the cabin until the blades had come to a complete stop and the helicopter was silent. Carlucci was not surprised to see Yoshi Katsuda step out onto the pavement.

Katsuda was accompanied by two large men who flanked him close on either side. Carlucci wondered if those were the same two men who had been with him when he had killed his daughter. Katsuda and the two men walked steadily toward him and the van, but stopped when they were still twenty or thirty feet away. Carlucci had the sinking feeling he was not going to be able to get close enough to him.

"Good morning, Lieutenant," Katsuda said, smiling. He was wearing one of his business suits, which meant they hadn't come directly from the courthouse.

"I see you took the time to change out of your prison clothes."

"They were not my style."

"What were the conditions of your release on bail?" Carlucci asked.

Katsuda shrugged, but didn't answer.

"Even McAdamas would not have released you without any conditions. You were certainly ordered not to leave the court's jurisdiction."

"That's true," Katsuda said, "but *you* have no jurisdiction here whatsoever."

"You're attempting to leave San Francisco illegally."

"I already have." He smiled again. "I am a fugitive from justice. But it doesn't matter. You can't do anything about it. My two assistants will not allow it, nor will Security here. I'm surprised they allowed you onto the grounds."

"It was a favor," Carlucci said. "Cooperation between security agencies. And I promised not to cause trouble." As he spoke, he tried to take a couple of casual steps closer, but he saw the two men tense. It was going to be impossible to get within reach of Katsuda.

"Then I assume you will honor your promise."

"The way you honor yours?"

"I am not an honorable man, Lieutenant. You are." And

with that he started walking toward the Security building, the two other men sticking close and watching Carlucci.

"Will you be returning for your trial?" Carlucci asked.

Katsuda chuckled, and Carlucci watched as he walked the rest of the way to the building and then went inside.

"Lieutenant!" It was Monk's voice from inside the van.

"What?"

"Come here. I have a proposition for you."

He turned wearily toward the van, walked up to it, and put his head in through the side doorway. "What, Monk?"

"You've got another syringe in that case, yes? Loaded with active Core Fever virus? Meant for Yoshi Katsuda?"

"Yes," he answered. He saw no point in lying about it.

"You will never get close enough to him."

"I know that."

"But I will." Monk was grinning that twisted grin of his again.

"What are you saying?"

"Leave it with me. I can get it aboard with all the rest of my medical stuff. And I'll make sure Katsuda gets it. Maybe not right away, but sometime in the next few days, I'll have the opportunity. I will *make* the opportunity."

"Why would you do that?"

"I don't like the man," Monk said. "I never have." His face took on something like a grim expression. "I've never had a daughter," he went on. "And it is now physically impossible for me to have one. But I know this. A father does not kill his own daughter, not for any reason. You are a good father, Lieutenant, and you are one hell of a good cop. You've earned it." He paused. "I may be a dead man, and it may be at your hands, but you've earned it. That's why I would do it."

He didn't have to think about it long. As had happened every time they'd met, Monk once again surprised him. He took the case out of his coat pocket, crawled into the van and toward the back, and handed it to Monk. They looked at each other for a few moments, then Carlucci worked his way back to the side door and got out.

He stood by the side of the van for a minute, watching Katsuda inside the Security building, then started walking toward the gate and the mob pressing against the fence. Right now, he wanted nothing more than to go home.

CHAPTER 50

He stood with Caroline and Cage at the edge of the roof, six stories above the street, and looked out on the deserted ruins of the Core. It had been three days since his encounters with Monk and Katsuda out at Hunter's Point. Not much had changed in the city. It was close to midnight, and a full moon shone brightly on the broken stone and concrete, flashing reflections from shattered glass and twisted metal. Nothing moved inside the Core.

"Whole neighborhoods of this city will look like this within a couple of years," Cage said. "Whole neighborhoods of other cities, too."

Carlucci shook his head. "You mean new ones. We've got a few areas like this right now, and L.A. already has entire neighborhoods that aren't any better. Not to mention New York, Chicago, Detroit, East St. Louis—"

"All right, all right," Cage said. "I take your point. New ones, more of them. Neighborhoods that right now seem alive and normal."

Normal. Carlucci wasn't sure that anything constituted a normal life anymore.

"Maybe they'll be able to improve the vaccine," Caroline said. There seemed to be real hope in her voice.

"It might take years," Cage replied. "It's foolish to hope too much."

"But sometimes that's all we've got," she said.

Carlucci looked at his daughter and smiled. He wasn't sure he could have held himself together if she had not lived through all this. He didn't know what he and Andrea would have done, how they would ever have managed to go on. They *would* have gone on, somehow, but he suspected it would have been awful, and that it would never have become any better over the years. As it was, they were still going to have some rough times ahead.

The city was unusually quiet. They could hear music playing somewhere nearby, Greek cantina, accompanied by drunken shouting and singing; a cat yowled, and a dog barked; a siren wailed in the distance, and then two cracking sounds—probably gunfire. Generalized traffic noise provided an almost soothing background to it all.

"Did anyone ever come to you for the disks the Cancer Cell woman gave you?" he asked.

Caroline shook her head. "No." Her disappointment was obvious. "But it hasn't been that long. Probably they're just being cautious after what happened. *I* would be." This time there wasn't much hope in her voice.

"Are you really going to move here, into the Tenderloin?"

"Yes," she said, nodding.

"Why?"

"That's not so easy to answer. Lots of reasons."

"Is Cage one of them?" he asked. He looked back and forth between them. "No one's said anything, but are you two . . . ?" He didn't know what words to use, what words wouldn't sound ridiculous.

Cage didn't say anything, but Carlucci thought the man was actually blushing. Caroline shrugged, half smiling. "Yes," she said. "Something."

He let it go. They obviously felt awkward talking to him about it, though he wished they wouldn't. He very much hoped they could find some love and happiness with each other. There wasn't going to be a lot of either around this city for a long while.

"Look!" Caroline pointed at one of the buildings inside the Core. "Did you see that?"

"What?"

"Something moved. An animal, maybe. Or a person. Could somebody still be in there?"

"Not *still*," Cage said. "Nothing was left alive in there after the military sterilizers went through, not even the rats. Only the cockroaches and ants. But I wouldn't be surprised to see people moving back in already. When you think about it, it's not much worse now than it was before, and all kinds of people lived there then." He paused. "It's what we do, I guess. We just go on. The story of so-called civilization."

Carlucci thought about what Cage had said, and decided there was some truth to it. But he wasn't sure if it was good or bad.

"I feel tired and old." He wasn't sure why he said it; it just came out.

"You're not old, Papa."

"Maybe not, but I sure feel like it." He shook his head. "I've aged a lot these past few months."

"You just need a break from things," Cage said. "We could all use a break. Take a vacation, get out of this goddamn city for a few weeks. I'd bet you've got all kinds of vacation leave coming to you."

He nodded. "Maybe I'll take a permanent vacation."

"Retire, Papa?"

He nodded again. "I've been thinking about it."

"Mom says you'll never retire until they force you out."

"Maybe I'll surprise your mother." He smiled. "Surprise myself."

No one spoke for a long time. He scanned the ruined buildings, the empty rooms and broken walls. For the first time, he thought he understood a little why someone would want to go live inside the Core.

"Papa?"

"Yes?"

"Papa . . ." She couldn't finish.

He looked at her. She seemed upset. "What is it, Caroline?"

"Papa, do you wish it had been Tina who had lived instead of me?"

Carlucci felt his heart collapsing inside him. "How can you ask that?"

"Because I have Gould's, and I'm going to die in a few years anyway. If Tina had lived instead of me, she would have had a long life ahead of her."

"Oh, Caroline." He turned and took her into his arms and pulled her tight, so tight against him. "We're so grateful you lived through it, you just can't understand what it's meant to us. We wish you both had lived, but never, never would we even think about the two of you that way." He held her even more tightly, trying to hold himself together. "Never."

He could feel her squeezing him in return, and he hoped desperately that it was okay, that he'd managed to say the right things—the true things. He looked at Cage, who was watching them uncomfortably.

"Take care of her," he said to Cage. He finally eased his hold of Caroline, and looked into her face, the tears smeared down her cheek. "And you," he said to Caroline. "You take care of Cage."

She nodded, trying to smile. "I will, Papa."

Then he pulled her to him and hugged her tightly again, afraid to let her go.

ISABEL

Isabel watched the three figures on the rooftop. She had come out into a patch of moonlight, had seen them outlined against the night sky, then had ducked back into the shadows, afraid she had been seen. Now she watched from darkness, through broken glass.

She was lonely. She had come to be very afraid of people, but now that they all were gone, and there were none of her own kind here, she missed them. Many had treated her badly, but a few had been kind.

The one called Donya, in her first home. Donya had taken such good care of them, would let them out of their cages when they weren't allowed, gave them special treats. And Donya had cried when Lisa got sick and was taken away and never returned.

And then, the one who had found her in the passage in the middle of all the craziness. She, too, had seemed kind, and had left the door open for her so she hadn't been trapped.

The rats weren't much company.

Isabel pulled back from the window and worked her way deeper into the building, staying in the shadows. Yes, she would welcome people back into the Core, and she was certain they would come.

But she would still be very, very careful.